A Queen from the North

Erin McRae and Racheline Maltese

AVIAN30
NEW YORK, NEW YORK
2017

Avian30
New York, New York
A Queen from the North by Erin McRae and Racheline Maltese
Copyright 2017
ISBN: 978-1-946192-07-3

www.Avian30.com

First Avian30 Printing: November 2017
Printed in the USA

TABLE OF CONTENTS

A Queen from the North is in many ways a very different book than we first set out to write. Some of that is because of what the story demanded; some of that is the world we live in.

Racheline and I were already tinkering with a number of ideas related to royal romance when I took a trip to England with my father in the fall of 2015. While we began our tour in London, our main goal was York, an ancient walled city set amidst a stunning countryside.

I fell in love with York and with Yorkshire. The huddled half-timbered buildings of the Shambles; the surrounding walls where one can easily see medieval piled on Viking piled on Roman construction; the soaring Minster Abbey; the breathtaking natural beauty of the Dales. But what struck me most — being a history geek with a fascination for how cultures manifest and endure strife — was York's history. York's history is not just the history of the United Kingdom. It's also the history of ancient Rome and the Vikings, and looming large over all of it was the five-hundred-year old struggle between York and Lancaster.

I was in a gift shop one afternoon when I overheard another patron ask the shop attendant about the jewelry on display. Necklaces bore the white rose of York, the red rose of Lancaster, or the blended red-and-white Tudor rose, as anyone's allegiances or aesthetics might prefer.

"Oh, yes." the attendant said of the Tudor rose. "We only sell *that* because we have to. We're much more about the white rose here. And definitely not about the red."

When we returned to our guest lodgings that night, I wrote Racheline: *I know what our royals book should be about.*

For all that this book was inspired by the past, it is not a reflection of real history. It contains a number of significant and deliberate departures from our world.

Some parts of the world will look familiar. Others will very much not. Prince Arthur's father, King Henry XII, is descended in direct line from Henry VIII and Anne Boleyn — though our Anne still lost her head.

There are no Stuarts or Hanovers or Windsors here. Scotland and Wales are joined with England to form the Unified Kingdom, but Ireland — from which my own family came to the U.S. — never suffered the depredations of English rule and has always been free and independent. They are ruled by their own High King who is eleven years old, but that story is for a later book in this series.

The Commonwealth still exists in our alternate universe, but the feelings of some of those countries — namely Canada — toward the monarchy are not necessarily what they are in our world.

Most critically, however, in this world the Wars of the Roses never truly ended. The Tudor unification attempted by Henry VIII fell apart after his death, and battles and political struggles between York and Lancaster persisted for centuries. The north — centered around York — and the south — centered around London — are locked in an eternal conflict that's left York very much the loser.

This is also a world without Brexit. Several drafts of this book had already been completed when the UK voted to leave the European Union in June 2016. For all that this book contains the political machinations of the alternate universe we created, none of what we have written here is intended to be an allegory for the actual United Kingdom's current political circumstances.

While I brought the strife between York and Lancaster to this book, Racheline brought witchcraft, insisting that the universe next door to us must always contain magic as we only fear it exists in ours.

A Queen from the North is, on some level, a story about alchemy — both on the page and in our process of writing it. We hope you enjoy your sojourn in the Unified Kingdom. We suggest you mind the birds.

Erin McRae (& Racheline Maltese)
May 2017

One for sorrow,
Two for joy,
Three for a girl,
Four for a boy,
Five for silver,
Six for gold,
Seven for a secret,
Never to be told.
Eight for a wish,
Nine for a kiss,
Ten for a bird,
You must not miss.

— 16th Century British Traditional

Chapter 1

ON TENTH ANNIVERSARY OF IMOGENE'S DEATH, ENGLAND MOURNS ITS PRINCESS

15 September
Year 20 of the Reign of King Henry XII

Arthur stared out the window of the car and watched the countryside pass in a blur of autumn colors. Visiting his late wife's grave was always sad, but the ritual unsettled him far more now than when she had first passed. Then, he had been too mired in his own sorrow to notice what else went on around him. Now, ten years on, he resented the public intrusion into his life and the requirement that he perform a grief that, while yet deeply personal, had been dulled by time. But the public still desperately cared. Perhaps because he had never remarried; perhaps because his people, who had loved Imogene and adored their relationship, hoped he never would.

"Your Highness, may I address something to you?" Georgina, his sixteen-year-old niece, asked from beside him.

He snorted softly. "Since when do you talk to me like that?" Certainly, she had not been so formal an hour ago when

1

she declared she would return from the burial site in his car and not the one shared by her sister, Princess Hyacinth, and her mother, Princess Violet.

"I am trying to get you to take me seriously," the girl, milk-pale and prim blond with a witch's green eyes, declared. She took after Violet, Arthur's sister. Arthur himself was taller and broader, with brown eyes and dark brown hair already going gray at the temples. In part because of conversations like this one.

"I always take you seriously, George. You know that."

"You have to get remarried."

Arthur turned his head to look out the window again. One of the prerogatives of being first in line to the throne was that he didn't have to acknowledge things people said if he didn't want to.

"I am serious."

"Yes, you've just said."

"Look, Arthur, the way I see it —"

He turned his head and raised an eyebrow to her. He hardly expected her to use titles or call him *sir* in private, but at least an *uncle* would do; some indication that at nearly forty he deserved a bare modicum of respect. But Georgina, who had demanded to be called George since she was eight, was bold, brash, and a teenager — a combination which God had ordained would always skirt the edge of terrible.

Arthur's gaze was enough to make her falter for a moment, but she continued. "The way I see it, you have three choices."

"And those would be?"

"You get over yourself, get married, produce an heir—"

"Yes, I am familiar with the concept."

"Never remarry and become a tragic, mythological figure —"

"Well on my way already, don't you think?"

George soldiered on. "Or embrace full-on loserdom, change your name, move to America, and have lots of sex with women who will sell the story to the papers."

Arthur was glad the privacy partition between them and the driver was closed. "That's startlingly specific."

George had the poor grace to look pleased with herself.

"Well," Arthur said, as if he was indulging a child much younger than this princess, "what do you suggest I do?"

"You need to get married. Urgently."

"Why is that?" Arthur was willing to listen to her. At least for now.

"Because, *as you know*, when I turn eighteen and you don't have an heir, my mother is going to announce that she's taking herself out of the line of succession. Which makes me next in line after you."

"And?"

"And I don't want it." George sat up straighter, as if to indicate her distaste for the weight of the crown.

"You're the only young woman in the kingdom who would say that."

"I'm not suited to be queen, and you know it. Find a woman who is, and the country will be happier. I'll be happier. And so will you be. You want a companion, not the friendship of your strange niece who plays hostess for you."

"And?" Arthur prompted once more. The look on George's face said she wasn't done.

She leant toward him and dropped her voice to little more than a whisper. "I had a dream."

"Again?"

"Yes."

"It's been a while," he said amiably, as if George were an ordinary child with run-of-the-mill nightmares.

"Yes."

"Which one was it?" he asked as the car accelerated past rolling hills and old stone fences back to the congestion of London.

"The one where all the ravens were dead."

Chapter 2

IS ARTHUR, PRINCE OF HEARTBREAK, FINALLY OUT OF MOURNING?

25 December
Year 20 of the Reign of King Henry XII

What I expected to happen over the holiday:

1) Get my acceptance letter from MIT.
2) Gary to propose.
3) Be welcomed into the loving arms of my family for Christmas.

What actually happened over the holiday:

1) Got rejected from MIT <u>and</u> got waitlisted at UC Santa Barbara.
2) Gary dumped me.
3) Mother declared me the problem child of the family at a formal Christmas dinner for forty of our closest friends and neighbors.

If that isn't in the running for worst Christmas ever I'm not sure what would be, but I'm definitely all right with not finding out.

Charlie says I can go to Kempton with him tomorrow for the races. Jo keeps telling us which parts of her body she's not interested in freezing off in order to socialize with any number of people she doesn't actually like. Mainly, though, Jo is allergic to horses. She says they make her sneeze, and everyone always forgets.

So, I'm going instead. Because being my brother's date at one of the biggest jumps races of the year is not the height of pathetic.

❁

Amelia sat and stared out the window of the train as it rumbled smoothly from York through the northern countryside toward London. She and her brother Charlie had left at an ungodly hour, and the landscape sweeping by outside was still dark.

Tired as she was, the quiet murmur of the other passengers was soothing. As the train moved further south and more people got on, the ambient accents shifted from Scottish and Yorkshire to the sharper — to Amelia's ear, at least — accents of the midlands and south.

England, Scotland, and Wales comprised the Unified Kingdom, a political entity that had existed since the eighteenth century. To the west, Ireland was a separate country whose ruling family occasionally intermarried with English royalty and otherwise watched the political turmoil of their cousins across the Irish Sea with amused and benign judgment.

Amelia couldn't help but feel a mix of envy and resentment toward them. And toward the Scots. They were part of the Unified Kingdom, but they had not only their own distinct voices but their own country. Even Wales was its own country, and Wales was nearly as poor as Yorkshire.

The Yorkish people, her people, were as distinct as the Scots or the Welsh. But rather than be recognized as a country within the Unified Kingdom in its own right, Yorkshire and the entire north — all the counties between the Midlands and the Scottish border — were seen as a backwater. Not worth government money or even a kind word in the myths and legends that drove the nation's tourism-based economy. Even the worst off of the south always fared better.

It wasn't a new issue, and it wasn't one Amelia had any power to solve, even if she was an earl's daughter. Her parents had never been disloyal to the Crown and had never advocated separation from the south, unlike some of their neighbors. This was, she knew, probably wise. Without acquiescence, she suspected Yorkshire would have even less than it already did. Still, Amelia wished it were possible for her, or them, to do more. She stewed on that as the train made its way southwards. Doing so was better than stewing on the mess of her own life.

"How are you holding up?" Charlie interrupted her brooding. He set his book on the table between them and gave Amelia his concerned big-brother look.

Amelia sighed in lieu of answering.

"That bad?"

"On the brightest of bright sides, I think Father's relieved his only daughter isn't going to be marrying a commoner."

"You know he doesn't care about things like that."

"Oh yes. Because Gary was from perfectly respectable new money. And marrying into perfectly respectable new money is all I'm expected to achieve. Hurrah for me, youngest daughter of a minor earl."

"Mother's favorite oops." Charlie teased her.

Amelia made a face. With two older brothers, she was the youngest of the family and the only girl. Charlie, her eldest brother, was forty, a solicitor happily married with two children, the eight-year-old twins Meg and Freddie. As Viscount Brockett and heir to the earldom, he'd been absolutely supposed to marry someone with a title. Probably a distant cousin. Preferably a duchess or a countess, but at least someone with *Lady* before their name. Instead he'd married Jo, a black woman from a Yorkish family that could trace its roots to the city's Roman founding.

Nick, Amelia's second brother, was thirty-five and resolutely single, despite Jo and their mother's attempts to set him up with any remotely eligible young man. At least his career in the City working for whichever investment bank didn't have the most scandals that week was going well.

Which left Amelia, the youngest child and, as of today, the failure of the family.

"So," Amelia said to Charlie. "I got rejected from my first choice school. My boyfriend of two years dumped me without warning or explanation. My mother announced both of these facts to the entire neighborhood. I'm twenty-two, and I will be starting my last term with no boyfriend and no career prospects. Happy New Year to me."

"You might still get into Santa Barbara." Charlie was ever eager to be encouraging.

"Charlie?" Amelia did not want to talk about backup schools right now.

"Yes?"

"Shut up."

"Yes, dear sister."

They exchanged sleepy smiles over the table. Charlie had always been her favorite. He often played a more substantial role in her life than their father, and he always took Amelia seriously. Even if she was the youngest. And even now that her life had gone completely to pieces.

❁

Snow had fallen the day before, and by the time the sun came up Amelia could see the white drifts still left in the hollows of the fields from the train window. Everything seemed picturesque and peaceful, even if the sky was overcast. It was England, after all.

When they alighted from the train onto the crowded platform at the racecourse station, Amelia shivered. Charlie stopped and solemnly adjusted the fur hat on her head so that it covered her ears better. Amelia didn't try to restrain herself from huffing as she brushed a strand of chestnut-colored hair out of her eyes.

"While I am a miserable failure of a human being, I am not a child."

"Whatever you say," he said.

Amelia couldn't resist punching him in the arm. Gently, because a lady did not brawl with her brother in public.

As they walked into the park, Amelia took a deep breath of air and felt herself relax. Jo may have been right to worry that bits of her anatomy would freeze off, but, despite the chill, the atmosphere was a holiday one. The crowd was loud and bustling, and the air smelled crisply of snow. After two weeks trapped in Kirkham House, the Brockett's estate, being an anonymous part of a large, happy crowd was bliss.

"Where are we sitting?" Amelia asked as Charlie shouldered a way through the throngs.

"You have your ticket. Did you not look at your ticket?"

"I was distracted by my misery."

"Of course." Charlie said with a smile. "Royal Box."

Some people might have found that prospect exciting. Amelia, though, knew better. "Which of your hideously dull work colleagues do I get to ignore in favor of watching the races?"

"No work people today. Just some people from Oxford. And Prince Arthur."

Amelia stopped in the middle of the crowd, unaware she was being jostled about. "Oh, you're kidding me."

"What's wrong with the Prince?" Charlie asked, wrapping an arm around her shoulder and leading her forward.

"Nothing is wrong with the Prince. There's a little bit wrong with the fact that you and Arthur, Prince of Wales, are school chums and that you didn't think it worth mentioning that royalty would be at the race today. Everything is wrong with the fact that the box is going to be crammed full of incredibly annoying people fawning over His Royal Highness."

"Look on the bright side, Meels," Charlie said, as they reached the door to the Royal Box. "You're short enough that you can just hide behind a potted plant."

❁

The room was overheated, and so overfilled with polite and exceptionally boring chatter, that Amelia actually considered taking the plant route. She knew most of the people in attendance but not well. There were no other northern nobility about. Possibly because they hadn't been invited, but also possibly because they'd all retired to their estates for the holiday season and were enjoying the snow, the superior tea, and the distance from London. Charlie's friendship with Prince Arthur gave their family a certain status other northern houses lacked, but at the same time, that friendship and status had drawbacks. Like being obliged to spend time in a room full of people who, if they cared about Amelia and her family at all, viewed them as dutiful pets.

Amelia's mother, however, would surely have something to say to her about expectations, obligations, and — considering recent setbacks — opportunities at an event like this. So, Amelia grit her teeth and made small talk.

Lady Margaret Evelyn, Baroness of Godstone, remembered speaking with Amelia at the garden party they'd been at together the previous autumn and asked how her graduate school applications had fared. Lady Golding of Colston Bassett asked in her reedy voice why Amelia hadn't brought her handsome young man with her. And Lady James of Langley Hall, who had three daughters of her own, all near Amelia's age, spoke so glowingly of their marriage prospects that Amelia finally had to excuse herself. Otherwise, she was going to start hollering that, despite everyone else's obsession with weddings, they weren't actually living in a Jane Austen novel.

Chatting with Lady Anne Beale and Lady Catherine Beale of Maidstone, two elderly sisters who lived together on their family's ancient and somewhat decrepit estate, was entertaining until they tried to draw Amelia into speculation as to which of the well-titled women here the Prince of Wales might currently be dallying with. The gossip pages were always full of speculation about Prince Arthur's lovers. A handsome royal widower and heir to the throne was simply the most brilliant catch available. Especially considering that the High King of Ireland, the nearest monarch geographically speaking, was eleven.

Eventually Amelia saw Helen Lawrence, Duchess of Water Eaton, an attractive if reserved-looking woman near the Prince's age, come inside from the balcony, which seemed the perfect place to avoid other people. Amelia decided she had been polite enough to mollify her mother. Even if she hadn't, escape was definitely preferable to losing her sanity — and her composure.

She retrieved her coat and was in the process of pulling her gloves on when she shouldered her way out the door and straight into someone. She hoped she would recognize whoever it was well enough to offer appropriate apologies without being met with condescension about her age, ill-developed manners, and general failure at being a successful young woman.

However, when she looked up, it was the Prince of Wales she had jostled. For some inexplicable reason he looked briefly delighted with her interruption before he turned his head to look out at the course with his binoculars again.

Amelia was horrorstruck. She considered apologizing. Certainly, it was warranted. One didn't just ignore having crashed into the future king of, well, everything. At least his security didn't seem to care. Which was also strange. Maybe they thought she was important. Or that she was so unimportant she didn't really exist at all.

"Your Royal Highness," she said eventually, because she had to say something.

Prince Arthur hummed under his breath.

Amelia had no choice but to keep going. "It's a really grim thing when no one teaches you how to apologize to a prince since it shouldn't be possible to crash into one." She was so thrown she couldn't continue to breathe without continuing to speak. "You shouldn't stand so close to the door," she added against all judgment and sense. "Also you're friends with my brother."

That got him to turn and look at her.

His Royal Highness Arthur Gregory James Edward, Prince of Wales, Duke of Lancaster, Lord of the Northern Isles, Prince and Great Steward of Scotland, was tall. To be sure, everyone was tall compared to Amelia, but he'd be tall compared to most people. In the cold grey morning light his features were strong and handsome. He had broad shoulders and a military bearing Amelia knew from photos and a touch of grey at his temples, which she didn't. His eyes were light brown, warm, and trained on her with an expression that was a mixture of vague excitement and curiosity.

"And you are?"

"Charlie Brockett's sister, sir. The Viscount of Kirkham," she clarified.

"Do you come with your own name?" The question was pointed, and she wasn't sure the answer was yes.

"Lady Amelia Brockett, sir." Belatedly, she dropped into a curtsy, which was less graceful than she would have liked it to be. Her glove was still crumpled in her hand. Once she straightened again, she tugged it on as quickly as she could.

"How is your brother?" the Prince asked, turning back to look at the course, this time without the binoculars.

"He's well. He's inside." She jerked her chin over her shoulder. "He's looking forward to seeing you."

"And the Viscountess Josephine?" He sounded as desperate for conversation topics as Amelia felt. Still, he was talking to her rather than dismissing her or having his security escort her back inside.

"Allergic to horses. Still. Sir. So, I came instead. Because horses." Amelia had never been less socially adept in her life. Although, she had also never talked to a prince before, at least not as something possibly approaching equals in conversational awkwardness.

"Well, it's nice someone is as eager to watch the sport as me. Unless you were running out here for some other reason."

She blinked at him in confusion. "Other reason?"

"People keep coming out here to smoke. And to flirt."

"Oh. Er. No. No, I don't smoke." Although this horrible interaction might drive her to it. She could find nothing to say to the mention of flirting. "The horses are very nice," she added. Then wanted to throw herself off the balcony at her own inanity.

"Which is your favorite?" he asked a little wildly, clearly still grasping for topics. Why didn't he just dismiss her and end the misery for both of them?

"Do you know anyone racing today?" It seemed best that her favorite should be whichever was his.

"No, not today." He didn't look at her, but the corners of his mouth twitched up.

"Well in that case," Amelia said. "I'm quite fond of Lady Molecular."

"The bay?" Arthur asked, with apparent surprise.

"Yes."

"She's not favored to win," Arthur pointed out.

"No. But I know her owner, we went to school together. She's getting her PhD in biochem. Hence the name."

"Ah," Arthur looked vaguely interested in that, but didn't follow up with any question or statement of his own.

Amelia knew the wise move at this point was to say her farewells and vanish back inside and away from this incredibly awkward encounter. Except, being out here seemed preferable to being stuck back in that room.

"I'm home for the holidays, and I needed to get out of the house. Is that why you're here too? Did you need to get out of the house?" The words tumbled out of her mouth, heedless of any sense she had ever possessed. She clamped her mouth shut, horrified at herself. Prince Arthur didn't live in a house, but a palace. Several of them.

But Prince Arthur tipped his head back and laughed, a true, delighted, laugh. "Something like that, yes." Then he actually looked at her. "The horses are coming around — the view is better from here." He patted the balcony railing.

Amelia took the invitation. One did not say no to a prince. She stepped up beside him and closed her gloved hands around the railing to keep them from trembling from the nerves and the cold.

"Do you ride?" he asked.

She nodded, relieved they weren't going to stand here in awkward silence forever. "Sometimes."

"Do you jump?"

"Of course I jump." She was a little indignant. She was a good rider and also clever enough to know when someone was trying to dismiss her abilities. "You?" she asked.

15

She already knew the answer, but it seemed rude to mention facts about Prince Arthur and his horses she knew only from articles on the internet. Priya, Amelia's flatmate back in London, had a picture of him riding at his estate at Gatcombe stuck on their refrigerator amidst a half-dozen photos of Bollywood movie stars.

"Yes," he said. "I used to have more time for it. Now, I'm limited to supporting our national team as best I can and taking over the Royal Box and causing a fuss every time I want to see a show. Everyone worries I'll break my neck whenever I get on a horse."

"Who's everyone?"

Prince Arthur waved a hand vaguely. "Whoever's paying attention enough to care about things like ravens and princes."

"Ravens?" Amelia wasn't sure their conversational drift from awkward to peculiar was an improvement.

"The ones at the Tower." Arthur's voice was curt.

Amelia was uncertain whether his irritation was for her or the birds. "If they leave the Tower, your kingdom will fall. Those ravens?" Amelia had no idea why they were talking about ravens of any sort.

"Yes, those ravens. Though it's your kingdom, too." Prince Arthur sounded amused.

"Yes and no. I'm from York. We'll survive most raven crises, I expect." It was a bold thing to say, and Amelia found herself holding her breath lest the Prince take offense.

But all he did was smile wanly. He looked melancholy. And thoughtful. No wonder the tabloids, when they weren't painting him as a playboy, framed him as sad. He was sad. And poetic. In an embarrassing sort of way.

"So, you are hiding out here from other people," Amelia said, trying to steer the conversation back to something like normal — or at least away from superstitions and major political rifts.

"Don't tell the papers," he said, with a conspiratorial look. Which was probably practiced, but that didn't make it any the less charming. Or effective. If Amelia's heart gave a slight flutter, that was her own business.

She grinned at him. "I won't. Promise."

"Tell me about your jumping, Lady Amelia."

Surprised that he cared about what she was saying enough to prolong this still slightly painful encounter, Amelia obliged. Soon, they were chatting about horses and riding. The Prince, once he finally settled into a topic, proved to be an engaging conversationalist. That, too, must have been practiced, but Amelia didn't mind. He was expending an effort, and that was what mattered. For the heir to the throne perhaps that was all that mattered.

Even more gratifyingly, he was the first person of the day — including Charlie — not to condescend to her at all. Strange, perhaps, to be treated like a competent human by the one person here who had the least reason to grant her time, courtesy, or anything else.

More people filtered out onto the balcony with the excuse that they wanted a better view of the horses and to get some fresh air. Based on the filthy looks Amelia was getting from some of the women, she had her doubts they had any intentions other than directing the Prince's attention away from her.

Amelia was not proud of it, but she had to admit to a small amount of satisfaction when it didn't seem to work. The Prince chose to continue with their conversation rather than speak with anyone else. Until Charlie banged out onto the balcony and insinuated himself into their conversation.

The Prince's face brightened at the sight of her brother. He shook Charlie's hand firmly and exchanged a manly, back-slapping hug.

"Charlie. It's good to see you."

"Likewise, Your Highness. How have you been?"

Charlie glanced sideways at Amelia as he asked, and Amelia knew that was her cue to leave. The one time she was enjoying herself at an event like this, and Charlie just had to come and rescue her.

❁

Amelia and Charlie grabbed a quick dinner at a Wagamama near Paddington Station in London before taking a late train back to York. Why the entire family needed to spend two weeks at Kirkham when her brothers had perfectly reasonable homes in London was beyond Amelia, but tradition was tradition. Besides, her mother liked having the whole family there when people came to take tours of the public part of the house and gawk at the Tower Crown that had belonged to King Edward V before Richard III had imprisoned him and his brother in the Tower of London. While a perfectly natural part of living in a Grade II Listed building, Amelia thought her mother had never entirely acclimated to the sense of intrusion upon her home.

It was bitterly cold but clear when they finally got back to York. As they waited in front of the station for their brother Nick to pick them up, Amelia blew out her breath to watch the steam curl away up toward the black sky and the stars that shone above the ancient walls of the city. On the side of the station, a poster celebrating three hundred years of British unification had been defaced with spray paint tracing out the White Rose of York.

When Nick arrived, Amelia and Charlie bundled themselves gratefully into the warm interior of his car.

"Somebody had an interesting race," Nick said by way of greeting.

"What?" Amelia asked absently from the backseat. She wondered whether it was worthwhile to nap on the forty-five minute drive to Kirkham House. Charlie made a curious noise as he buckled himself in.

Nick smirked over his shoulder. "Just wait 'til we get home. Mum will fill you in."

Sure enough, despite the late hour, their mother met them in the private dining room, which tour visitors never saw. The public dining room was decorated with heavy oak furniture and tapestries that illustrated the family's ancient ties to the northern line of nobility. This dining room, thankfully, was smaller and had more modern furnishings. But with Rebecca Brockett, Countess of Kirkham, sitting at her accustomed place at the foot of the table, the space was no less imposing. Despite the late hour she was impeccably attired and sat with the posture of a former dressage champion.

"Welcome home," she said warmly, although she did not stand. Lady Kirkham, with grey hair that was cut short and curled elegantly, had always looked slightly like a relic of an older time that no longer quite existed. Except that time most certainly did exist, in this house and this town and in the existence of Amelia's entire family. That her mother was absently scrolling through a tablet resting on the table did nothing to dispel that truth.

"Mum," Amelia said warily. She exchanged a glance with Charlie, who shrugged, looking as confused as Amelia felt. Nick, having received his greeting, stood by the fireplace, tracing a pattern on the stonework of the hearth with the tip of his shoe.

Lady Kirkham pushed back her chair and stood. She clasped her hands in front of her, as if about to make some momentous proclamation. "You met the Prince," she said to Amelia. She looked archly amused.

"Yes? Wait. How did you know that?" Amelia felt as though she were being accused of something but had no idea what.

"You were noticed." Still, that note of amusement; whatever Amelia had done she wasn't in real trouble. She just had no idea what she'd done.

"The *Daily Observer.*" Her mother took her tablet off the table and handed it to her. Amelia took it warily.

There was a picture, a bit blurry from the degree of zoom but distinct nonetheless. It looked as though someone had taken a mobile phone picture in the Royal Box at Kempton and caught a glimpse of the scene out on the balcony by accident. Amelia was clearly visible in profile, smiling; Prince Arthur had been captured with his head thrown back laughing.

Romance at the races? The article underneath read. *Lady Amelia Brockett, daughter of the Earl of Kirkham, corners His Royal Highness for conversation at Kempton Park. Could a post-Christmas fling be in the air?*

"Oh." Amelia shoved the tablet back at her mother.

"How did that come about?" her mother asked.

"Someone with terrible manners and no discretion sent an accidental candid to the papers?" Amelia suggested.

Her mother looked unconvinced. "Do be sure no one gets the wrong impression. And my goodness, you shouldn't be so familiar."

Amelia made a despairing noise.

"Also," her mother said thoughtfully, glancing at the picture again as she set the tablet down. "He's twice your age."

"Mum!" Amelia protested. One innocent conversation was being blown entirely out of proportion, and apparently she was going to reach new depths of embarrassment before the holiday was over. "It wasn't a big deal. I met Prince Arthur. Who Charlie is friends with. We were in the Royal Box. We talked for fifteen minutes about horses and then I escaped. I'm not trying to get with the Prince. I'm just trying to get into graduate school and flee everything wrong with my life!"

Chapter 3

PARADE OF MARRIAGEABLE WOMEN VISIT BUCKINGHAM

10 January
Year 21 of the Reign of King Henry XII

Back at school. Upside: Mum no longer asks concerned questions about my prospects and what my plans are for the future. Downside: I have nothing to do but homework and worry about my prospects and my future. I've started applying to jobs, too — research assistantships, mostly — because I desperately need a backup plan in case I don't get into any schools. For my sanity. Sure, I could live with Mum and Dad and Charlie would find me a job doing filing somewhere, but I don't want any of that. On the upside again: At least I'll be able to spend the summer working, or preparing for school if I do get in, instead of doing all that while also trying to manage the headache of wedding planning.

"Oi, mail!" Priya, Amelia's flatmate, hollered as she strode into their apartment with a cardboard box clutched to her chest. The curtain of her sleek black hair swung forward into her face as she dropped the letters on their all-purpose kitchen table/study area/mail repository. "I think you got invited to one of those royal garden parties or something," she said.

"What's in the box?" Amelia asked as Priya set it down in the kitchen. Their apartment comprised five tiny rooms: their bedrooms, the sitting room, the miniscule kitchen, and the bathroom. With London real estate being what it was, they'd been lucky to find this space even with their families' means. After the sprawling under-heated splendor of Kirkham House, Amelia was grateful for the cozy rooms and radiators that actually performed their office.

She was less grateful for the collection of pictures Priya had stuck on the fridge. The Bollywood stars and various Indian models, Amelia didn't mind. In fact, she strenuously approved of the shirtless photo of Sidarth Malhotra. What she did mind was the picture of Arthur, sitting tall astride a horse on his estate. She wanted to ask Priya to take it down, but doing so would only invite questions.

"Stuff I've left at Raveesh's house and half his liquor cabinet," Priya answered Amelia's question, rifling through the box.

Amelia picked the cream-colored envelope off the table. "Are you breaking up with him?" she asked as she slit it open. She had no idea what it was, but its appearance was at least interesting.

"We'd have to call it dating first, but seems like."

"His idea or your idea?"

"Mine, thank you."

"Then why'd you take his booze?" Amelia asked.

"Because I could?"

"Fair." Amelia looked down at the card in her hands.

The Lord Chamberlain is commanded by
The Prince of Wales to invite
Lady Amelia Brockett of Kirkham
to a private Tea
at Buckingham Palace
on Monday, 16 January, Year 21 of the Reign of King Henry XII
at 2 pm

Not a garden party. Not, in fact, something that made the slightest bit of sense.

❀

Amelia waited until the next day, when Priya was at a lecture, to call the phone number on the card. Not to RSVP; her pleasure at accepting the honor of such an invitation was something that had to be registered on paper. But because she still didn't entirely understand what she was looking at. And while Priya had shown no interest in the invitation, Amelia didn't want to encourage curiosity or create a need for explanations. Not until she knew herself what was going on.

The phone rang exactly twice before it was answered by someone young, officious, and Welsh.

"Um, yes, hello." She had no idea where to start and had clearly forgotten all of her phone training. "I've received an invitation to a tea, a private tea, and mostly I am confused and also concerned it's been misdirected."

"May I ask who I'm speaking with?"

"Oh, yes, right, sorry, hi. Amelia Brockett."

She listened to the sound of typing and felt faintly cheered the Palace seemed to have a database of these things. Databases got things wrong all the time.

"Lady Amelia Brockett?" the voice asked after a moment.

"Yes, I'm afraid so. I'm not the Lady Amelia you're looking for, am I?" She tried to ignore her own faint sense of disappointment, which was inappropriate and useless. Speaking with Prince Arthur at the races had been enjoyable until Charlie had interrupted. Another opportunity to do so would have been somewhat pleasant.

"Actually," the voice said, "You are. And I can assure you, since I suspect you're about to inquire further, the accuracy of our record keeping is very good. Now," he said, clearing his throat with some drama. "You should consider me your royalty customer service representative. Is there anything else I can help you with regarding the occasion?"

Amelia laughed, relieved at the offer and at finding someone with a sense of humor about whatever strangeness was afoot. Mr. Jones, as it turned out her royalty customer service representative was named, did his utmost to help. But most of the matters she was curious about were not things he was privy to. He could not, for example, tell her the reason for or subject matter of the tea. He could only advise her on what to wear, which they agreed she probably already knew how to handle, being an earl's daughter and suchlike.

Eventually, not wanting to ask if the royalty customer service representative joke was even something he was allowed to say, she gave into her own terror and whispered down the phone, "Is this about the thing at the races?"

Amelia could practically hear him smile. "I'm sorry ma'am, I wouldn't know which thing, or which races, or what His Royal Highness's considerations regarding you are."

Amelia barely stopped herself from blurting *Don't you read the* Daily Observer?

❁

Given the word *tea* on the card, Amelia expected to see at least a few other guests at the gate. But when the guard checked her invitation and waved her through, there was no one else in sight. At least no one who looked like they were there for a tea. With a sudden terror that she was late, Amelia glanced at the time on the card and then at her watch. No — she was a few minutes early. Where, then, was everyone else?

She was escorted by a liveried footman from the gate to a reception room, where she was handed over to another footman who led her, not toward the ballroom that she'd been to on occasion before with her parents, but around a corner, up a flight of stairs, and down several more hallways.

They finally stopped at a heavy oak door. Her escort knocked, then opened it at a sound from within.

"Your Highness," the escort said. "The Lady Amelia Brockett." Amelia glanced at him, hoping for a hint of what to do. He tipped his head, ever so slightly, toward the room. There was nothing else for it. She stepped through the door.

In terms of the scale of the rest of the palace it was a small room, which meant it was about the size of the private dining room at Kirkham House. The walls were painted a mossy green, there was intricately carved molding around the high ceiling, and large windows hung with heavy velvet drapes looked down on the brown lawn and the sweep of the Thames, steely dark under a heavy winter sky beyond.

Instead of the gaggle of people in afternoon dress milling about drinking tea and eating tiny sandwiches, there was only one person in the room. Prince Arthur himself sat at a small table facing the window, his profile turned toward the door. His long legs were stretched out under the table, and a fireplace crackled merrily in the gloomy January afternoon.

He glanced up when Amelia walked in and for a moment looked as startled as he had when Amelia had banged into him out on the balcony at Kempton Park.

"Your Highness." She curtsied gracefully this time, thank goodness.

He stared at her for another moment and then fumbled to his feet. He banged his knee on the table in the process and had to put a hand on the back of the chair to keep it from tipping over.

"What are you doing here?" he demanded.

"I was hoping you could tell me. Especially since you're the one who invited me," Amelia said, showing the invitation she still had clutched in her hand. She glanced over her shoulder at the door, but her escort had already closed it again. It was just her and the Prince, on opposite sides of the room, staring at each other in mutual confusion and something that, as it went on, began to feel like a challenge.

Prince Arthur opened his mouth as though he were going to say something else, stopped himself, closed his eyes, and took a breath. When he opened his eyes again he said, "Forgive me, Lady Amelia. I must have gotten my appointment schedule confused. How are you today?"

"More confused than I was five minutes ago, which is saying something."

Prince Arthur waved at the chair across from the one he'd been sitting in. "Please, have a seat. And hopefully I can explain."

Amelia sat down carefully, crossing her legs at the ankle and tucking them under her chair as ladies should. The Prince returned to his own seat and flipped open an ornate leather folio, putting on a pair of reading glasses as he did so. They gave him a bookish air, and Amelia scolded herself for finding the professorial look appealing. But the Prince was handsome, and now that Amelia wasn't dying of embarrassment and awkwardness, she could indulge herself in looking at the strong lines of his jaw and the richness of his brown eyes behind his glasses. She noticed the faint nick of a razor under his ear and wondered if he'd done that himself or if he had a barber who shaved him.

"As you're probably aware, my father the King is in ill health," the Prince said as he turned the pages over, not even looking at her. Amelia tried to read them upside down until he raised his gaze to her face.

She snapped her eyes back up to his. "Yes, I'm aware. I do live in Britain." Headlines like that were impossible to escape.

"Which puts me closer to the throne than the royal genealogists tend to prefer a childless widower to be."

"You take what the royal genealogists say seriously?" Amelia asked blankly. Breeding horses was one thing. The unsavory implications of the work tasked to the genealogists was quite another.

"Lady Amelia," Prince Arthur said. "I need a wife and an heir. My sister is next in line after me but she will recuse herself once Princess Georgina turns eighteen —"

"Why on earth would she do that?" Amelia asked before she could think the better of it.

The Prince fixed her with a stern gaze and continued. "The country needs youthful optimism and a clean line of succession. But thrusting an unmarried teenager into the role of heir apparent isn't ideal either, especially when she only has her younger sister, the Princess Hyacinth, and then rather distant cousins to succeed her."

"Sir —" Amelia tried to break in again. What the Prince was telling her was tantamount to state secrets. He should absolutely not be admitting to — or even discussing — potential weaknesses in the line of succession, especially not with a daughter of the northern nobility who could still be accused of plotting against the Crown just for breathing.

Amelia did her best to push down her fear. With a dawning sense of disbelief and horror, she could almost see where this conversation might go. Except that such a thing would make absolutely no sense.

The Prince kept speaking. "The monarchy may be a symbol of the dying world to some, yet this family of mine still very much exists. We kings and queens have ruled near a thousand years. It must not come to an end on my watch." He sighed and slumped his shoulders, clearly finished with his script. "I know it sounds ridiculous; I only wish it were."

"What does this have to do with me?" Amelia was almost afraid to ask, but she was more afraid not to.

"The genealogists put together a list," the Prince said. "All unmarried women of the peerage, in a certain age demographic, who do not have children and have not been divorced. As you might imagine, it's not particularly extensive."

"Why not include commoners?" Amelia asked faintly.

"By what criteria? There's a nation of those. If someone is going to be subjected to this life, they may as well go in as prepared as possible."

"Wouldn't it have been easier to hold a ball?"

Prince Arthur laughed. His whole face brightened, almost like it had at the races. "The treasury's already girding its loins for the inevitable royal wedding. Best not to run up an even bigger bill in the process of finding a bride."

"Are you...proposing to me?" She asked hesitantly. And then, more hysterically, "After five minutes? After talking about *genealogy*?"

"Hardly." Arthur sounded offended. "This is me asking if you'd agree to meet with me again to discuss the matter of marriage further."

Amelia stared at him. This couldn't possibly be happening.

"Your genealogy, though, is hardly irrelevant." Prince Arthur removed a piece of paper from the folio, spun it around on the table and pushed it at her.

"This is my family tree."

"Yes. We do our homework here," Prince Arthur flipped through his folio again. "You're attractive, well-born, and intelligent. Pursuing a graduate degree in the earth sciences, I believe."

"I graduate in the spring. I'm applying to PhD programs. I want to study climate change," Amelia managed to say, as if any of those words could be a defense against what was happening.

"All of which is excellent. You also happen to be the only eligible daughter of one of the oldest families of York. Both the city and the ancient house."

"How is that a plus?" Amelia was wary. Little good ever came of the rare times London mentioned York.

"Political marriages — at least of this form — are rather out of style these days. But the rift between the north and the rest of the country only grows."

"That's the Prime Minister's fault. And Parliament's." It was Amelia's turn to be offended now. "The most recent jobs bill—"

The Prince sighed. "Yes. I know. I agree with you. Yet as a member of the royal house I can hardly engage in politics. At least not on a parliamentarian's terms. But symbolism is mine. And what I can do is unite York and London — York and *Lancaster* — in a way they haven't been in centuries. I know this proposition is awkward, but we could make history, you and I."

"Awkward?!" Amelia exclaimed. "This conversation is *insane.*"

Prince Arthur blinked mildly at her. "I'm merely trying to apply the available resources to a set of problems. Before you judge, I suggest you consider the resources that could be applied to your problems were you to choose to help me with mine."

"You don't even know what my problems are!"

"I don't have to, to know we could help each other."

Amelia wanted to turn away from the intensity of his stare, but she couldn't. He was magnetic, and there was a sharpness, even a shrewdness, to him that hadn't been present at the races. His eyes may have been brown, but he was no prey animal. She couldn't help but lean in ever so slightly. In her mind she cursed both the table between them and this proposed conspiracy.

"Lady Amelia," Prince Arthur said, "do you want to be Queen Consort of England, Scotland, and Wales, Her Royal Majesty of Britain?"

"No!" Amelia pressed her feet firmly against the floor as the word came out of her mouth unbidden. The Prince was fascinating, but the question so baldly put was terrifying. Not to mention treasonous for her to answer in anything but the negative. She wondered, fleetingly, if this were a trap.

"Shall I call to have you shown out then?" His words were without rancor, but there was a coldness to them she did not prefer.

She shook her head. "No," she repeated more softly.

He smiled, and his whole face softened. Amelia had to force herself to make eye contact rather than stare at the sensuousness of his lips. "Tell me about that then, if you would," he said.

She glanced up at the ceiling for a moment, wanting a small respite from the danger of the situation. Just a few weeks ago she had sat on the train and listened to the shifting accents of the countryside and wished for a better fate for her people. The very same day she had met Prince Arthur for the first time. Now she was faced with an opportunity both completely unexpected and entirely surreal.

Amelia realized she was staring at the ceiling of Buckingham Palace, which didn't help in the least. She returned her gaze to the Prince. "I'm from York."

"As we've just discussed."

Amelia took a deep breath. If Arthur wanted to talk about the burdens of destiny and history, they would do so. On her terms as one of the people England had for centuries so brutally tried to exclude from its narrative.

"York was founded by the Romans," she said. "Emperor Constantine was crowned there. You think your monarchy has been around forever? That it rests heavily on your shoulders in all the terrible things it's done? People have lived in York for two thousand years. We had our own kings — and queens. So, I can't pretend to be overly invested in the fate of your house. Sir. The lineage of the north predates your throne and will outlast it, all attempts at otherwise aside. I have known this since it was drilled into me with bedtime stories and children's rhymes told to me by my parents and nurses."

"Which means?" Arthur prompted.

"You've just offered me a way for York to have a place at the table for the first time in a thousand years," Amelia said. "A seat which we should never have been without." Her heart pounded. "One of us is surely mad."

Arthur leaned forward. "And what say you to mad men?"

"Well, I can't say *no.*"

Chapter 4

A NEW PARAMOUR FOR THE PRINCE?

19 January
Year 21 of the Reign of King Henry XII

It's been four days since the Prince of Wales offered me a nearly Shakespearean bargain, and I've not heard a word from him since. Four days and suddenly he seems just like any other man. So, when, dear diary, is it reasonable to expect to hear from one's prince about destiny and dynasty?

I can't tell Priya. I can't tell anyone. He didn't forbid me to talk, but I know better. Who would even believe me if I did tell?

I may be uncertain and confused right now, but I saw how he looked at me. I have worked in laboratories long enough to recognize when a man believes he's just laid eyes on a long-sought solution. A scientist with a breakthrough after years of hard work. It's not quite how Gary used to look at me, like I was a prize he had won. I'm not sure how it's different yet, but it is.

On the fifth day, during which she spent six hours in the lab cursing over an experiment that simply would not cooperate, another cream-colored envelope arrived in the mail. Amelia opened it as soon as she got home, still smelling of chemicals and in desperate need of a bath.

This time, it actually *was* to a garden party. Amelia stuck the invitation on the fridge below the picture of Prince Arthur that was still there.

Amelia and the Prince were likely to have very little opportunity to interact at a garden party. If the matter of marriage were still on the table — and surely the garden party was not just some odd consolation prize — she wanted to discuss this situation with him more. Much more. In great and lingering detail. But she didn't know how or when.

Her mobile rang, and she fumbled through her coat pockets to find it. It was her mother, calling to inform Amelia that she and Amelia's father, as well as Charlie and Jo and even Nick, had received an invitation to the palace for a garden party a few weeks from now. Would Amelia like to go to dinner with them all afterward?

Amelia said yes and then took a deep breath. "Actually, Mum, I've an invitation to the party as well."

"Have you now? Does this have anything to do with that photo of you and the Prince at the races?"

Amelia bit her lip and wondered if her mother's tone — curious, amused, and definitely judgmental — was a reason to confess or a reason to wait. Somehow, her situation didn't seem the sort of thing to share over the phone. "I don't know." She did her best to sound normal.

"That's lovely. Do you want me to send down some clothes for you?"

It was on the tip of Amelia's tongue to say no, she had a good outfit at school, she was fine. But then she remembered that Prince Arthur had already seen her in that. She should probably wear something different. Even if she'd be wearing a coat over it. She resisted the urge to bang her head on her desk. "Yes. Thank you."

❀

At the palace, guests mingled in overcoats and gloves. People tried to hover near heat lamps set up around the garden without looking like they were cold. In the summer, the gardens of Buckingham Palace were lush and green, the flowers vibrant and beautiful. Amelia remembered coming to these events as a child and being admonished to stay out of the fountains.

Now, in the depths of winter, there was a stark beauty to the grounds. The texture of the stones and the bare branches of trees stood out clearly against the snow and the grey sky. The mingled breath of the assembled formed the faintest mist, as though they all existed on the edge of faerieland.

Surely, Amelia thought as she navigated her way through the crowd, she could find her family more easily if she weren't quite so short. Not that she particularly wanted to find her family. Once she did, she'd have to talk to them, and she still hadn't decided whether or not to tell them about the offer Prince Arthur had made her. Although, in public at a palace was probably not the place to break that news to her mother.

Jo found Amelia first and walked slowly with her over to the rest of the family — Nick, Charlie, and Earl and Countess Brockett.

"I thought you didn't like this kind of thing," Amelia said, grateful at the prospect of having Jo as a buffer between herself and her mother.

"Oh, I don't. Charlie just asked me very, very nicely." On her lapel, an enameled pin of York's white rose reflected the day's weak sunlight in daring protest.

Charlie turned at the sound of his name. When he caught Jo looking at him his face broke out in an unselfconscious grin. Jo smiled back, and Amelia had to look away. Happiness of the sort her brother and sister-in-law shared had always seemed the point of marriage. Could giving that up possibly be worth what Prince Arthur offered?

Amelia gradually became aware that people were staring at her. She wished she'd worn a different coat than the one she'd had on at the races or that her hat hid her face better. When she'd dressed that morning it had never occurred to her that people would recognize her. God damn the *Daily Observer* and whoever had sent in that picture of her and the Prince.

"Come on." Jo looped her arm through Amelia's. "Let's take a walk, so when people stare we won't have to know which of us they're being awful about." They made a loop of the garden, stopped at the food tents to grab tea and tiny sandwiches served on very fine china, and then cycled back to the rest of the family just as there was a susurration in the crowd.

Amelia was suddenly aware that Prince Arthur was there, mingling his way through the throng. His niece, Princess Georgina, was at his side. She was oval-faced, with deep-set eyes, and dressed in somber navy with her blond hair pulled back into a tight chignon. Georgina seemed to Amelia an odd mix of preternatural poise and the coltishness all teen girls possessed.

"They're coming over here," Jo hissed at her. Her voice, and the elbow in Amelia's side, were gently teasing.

When he reached them, Prince Arthur only glanced briefly at Amelia before he greeted her parents and shook Charlie's hand, though this time without the manly back-slapping hug. Princess Georgina said her hellos as well, and Amelia found herself deeply unsettled when the Princess's sharp green eyes fixed on her. Once Prince Arthur had worked through the proper order of precedence, he turned to Amelia.

"Lady Amelia." He took her hand with both of his, which was very much not protocol. Both of them were wearing gloves against the cold, but gloves could not conceal how big his hands were or the warmth Amelia could feel through the layers of fabric. His palms dwarfed her much smaller hands, and his grip was firm and sure.

"Your Highness," she said with the same curtsy she had used in a room at this palace just a week before. Except that had been in private. Now Amelia's entire family, not to mention scores of strangers, were watching.

"I trust school is going well?" he asked.

"Very, sir."

"I'm glad to hear it," he said with just the faintest hint of a smile before moving on to the next little gaggle.

Every member of Amelia's family present turned to stare at her, but she took no notice of them. She was looking at Prince Arthur as he strolled away from her, at the proud line of his shoulders that tapered down to his narrow waist. Suddenly, Princess Georgina turned her head over her shoulder to stare at Amelia. Amelia ducked her head and pretended to study the ground. How could the Prince think it wise she take the throne from this fox-faced witch girl?

❁

Presently came the announcement that the King and Queen Consort were arriving. The guests were chivvied by Gentlemen at Arms into two long lines while King Henry XII and Queen Cecile walked down the aisle between, greeting a few select attendees. One of the Gentlemen at Arms, who was roaming a few feet ahead of the royal couple, stopped in front of Amelia and informed her that Their Majesties would be speaking with her.

Amelia had never, ever been singled out for attention like this. No one else in her family had been either, to her knowledge. Her parents may have been important and docile enough to get invited to these parties with some regularity, but they were still from the northern peerage.

She stammered her way through her acknowledgement of the protocols. This had to have been Prince Arthur's doing. She wondered if the King and Queen knew what their son had offered her, or what they thought of it if they did.

Amelia felt her mother's eyes boring into the back of her head and could sense everyone else holding their breath. With a silent and heavy grace, her father shifted to the side so Amelia could step into the front row.

When King Henry, Queen Cecile at his side, reached where Amelia and her family were standing he did not greet her parents first or, in fact, at all. Instead, as they all made the proper bows and curtsies, the King turned his eyes — so very like Princess Georgina's — to Amelia. He was not a tall man, and his frailty was apparent. Even so, he shone with a delighted vibrancy.

"Lady Amelia," he said in a voice Amelia had heard on the radio and on TV every year at Christmas. His gaze was kind but remote, distant and assessing. A king sizing up a subject and deciding if she were worthy.

"Your Majesty." She ducked her head away from his gaze as Queen Cecile looked from one member of the family to the next, taking in their reactions and those of the people around them. Whispers had broken out, but they fell silent as the Queen's eyes fell on the crowd.

The Queen murmured something warm and polite, Amelia greeted her as well, and the pair moved on down the line.

Charlie put a steadying hand on Amelia's back, but Amelia didn't let herself lean into it. Now that the eyes of the King were gone from her, the eyes of everyone else in a ten-meter radius were trained on her instead. No daughter of York should be seen to collapse in the face of a Lancastrian king.

❁

Two hours later, night had fallen on London. Amelia trailed after her family as they made their way to a Chinese restaurant for dinner. Before they walked inside Charlie fell back, took her by the elbow, and steered her to a little lamp lit spot of pavement beside the door.

"What?" Amelia asked, blinking. "Whatever this is, can't we do it inside where it's warm?"

"We could," Charlie acknowledged. "But I thought you'd prefer not to have Mum overhear. Or anyone else."

Amelia folded her arms over her chest and said nothing.

"Arthur called me three days ago," her brother said.

"He did?" Charlie was the only person Amelia had ever known who talked about the Prince with such familiar terms. But then, he and Prince Arthur were friends, and he was allowed. Amelia was not, even though the Prince had asked her if she, hypothetically, wanted to marry him.

"He did. And he told me to watch out for you. And that's all he told me."

Amelia tipped her face up to look Charlie in the eye. "Do you have a question then?"

Charlie shook his head. "No. I just wanted you to know that whatever's going on, I know a bit more about it than anyone else except you two —"

"I assure you, I have no idea what's going on."

"— and you can talk to me. If you need to."

Amelia scoffed. "That would be like talking to you about subduction zones."

"Just, look, Meels." Charlie's voice was low and urgent. "He's twice your age, his life is stranger than we can fathom, and his first wife *died.*"

"Ten years ago; I'm not dating him; Princess Imogene died in a skiing accident; and that's not catching. Can we go inside now?" Amelia spoke brusquely to mask her rising anxiety. Charlie wasn't wrong. There was no way she could fathom what she was getting into.

Charlie wrung his hands. "I'm just saying, if he's taken an interest in you —"

"Do you think we're having an affair?"

"I think you're my only sister, and one of my dearest friends who happens to be the Prince of Wales can be a womanizer who doesn't always make the best choices."

"I promise you that's not what's going on." Amelia remembered pictures in the tabloids, photos from holidays Arthur had taken with one or another of his mistresses. There had been white sand and blue water, and the press had been blamed each time said mistress did not become a princess. Whatever was going on now certainly was not that.

"Then what is?" Charlie asked.

Amelia said nothing and met his gaze steadily. Her determination was rising. If she did want this — and she wasn't yet sure that was the case — it wasn't something she could pursue half-heartedly. She could panic and run, or she could carry on. And if she carried on, the stakes were far too high for her to do so casually. She owed her brother a better explanation. She owed herself a better choice. But this was neither the time nor the place to speak the words. She wasn't sure yet. And neither was the Prince.

Charlie's eyes moved over her face, looking for something. "I won't tell Mum and Dad," he said softly. "But you can't keep whatever this is a secret. Not for long anyway. I don't think you're made for it."

Amelia considered every bizarre thing that had happened to her since Christmas and found herself at once furious at his doubt and desperate to, somehow, someday, prove him wrong.

"Come on," she said, taking his elbow like she had no secrets and he was the one in need of familial support. "Let's go inside."

❁

Amelia woke the next day to half a dozen emails, sent by her brothers, her lab mates, and even Priya. They all contained the same thing: A link to an article about her appearance at the garden party at Buckingham Palace.

The Palace had released official pictures of the event, which included photos of Amelia and Arthur during their brief conversation — complete with inset zoomed-in shots of Arthur holding her hand — as well as ones of King Henry and Queen Cecile talking to Amelia.

Seeing herself in multiple photos with royalty was peculiar enough. The text that accompanied the shots was even stranger. Someone, very much not the Palace, had done their research and what appeared was a lengthy profile of Amelia including her family background, where she'd gone to school, what she was studying in university, and what her parents and brothers did.

Amelia deleted all the emails and cleared the website from her browser history. It felt like having a live grenade in her bag, carrying that around.

Lectures that day were full of turned heads and whispers that followed her wherever she went. Doing homework with other people staring at her was far more than she wanted to cope with, so instead of going to the library after her last lecture, Amelia went to the gym. An hour on the treadmill didn't exactly clear her head, but endorphins were wonderful things. By the time she was finished she was too worn out to worry about her classmates, her parents, Prince Arthur, or anyone else.

She had just left the gym and was trying to stuff her water bottle back in her bag when someone on the street shouted her name. She looked up, startled, and was caught completely off-guard as a flash went off in her face.

By the time she had blinked the spots out of her eyes, the photographer was gone. Amelia stood on the sidewalk, gritty London snow from a week ago in slushy piles around her, feeling far, far colder than the winter afternoon.

For the rest of her walk home, she jumped whenever anyone stood too close to her at intersections. Which, given that it was London and the streets were always busy, was frequently. Amelia was annoyed at herself, but she was more angry at the intrusion into her life that had made her so. What gave anyone the right to just *do* that to someone?

Back at the flat, Amelia made herself a cuppa with hands that were still shaking, then collapsed on the couch with her laptop. She didn't bother to shower or even change out of her workout clothes.

Priya found her hours later, half a cup of cold undrunk tea on the floor beside her and a half-completed lab report open on her stomach.

"What happened to you?" she asked as she took in the scene.

"I don't want to talk about it," Amelia said dully.

"Nuh-uh. House rule. If you're making the sofa gross you have to tell me how it got that way." Priya folded her arms and gave Amelia a judgmental look.

"That house rule is so you won't shag guys in the living room," Amelia pointed out.

"Yeah, like that's stopped me."

"Priya!"

"Relax, you weren't here. And it was just the one time — my life isn't as exciting as you think. Regardless the rule is still applicable. Even though the premise of it is flawed because it assumes I have shame. Which I do not. But you, apparently, do."

Amelia sighed. She could deflect Priya, but not forever. Eventually she was going to need to talk to someone about what was going on. "You saw the article about me," she said.

"*The* article? There are dozens now!"

Amelia let her head fall back against the arm of the couch. "Shit."

"What did you expect? You're dating the Prince of Wales! Which, by the way, *when* were you going to tell me?"

"We're not dating," Amelia said automatically.

"Really? Is that why he was making eyes at you at a royal garden party and *introducing you to the King and Queen?*" Priya shoved Amelia's ankles off the couch to make room for herself.

"He didn't introduce us."

"No? His and Her Majesty just decided to stop and say hi to you for no reason?" Priya folded herself onto the couch and grabbed a pillow to hug to her chest.

Amelia put her hands over her face and moaned. "Nothing I am about to say is going to make this less weird."

"So? Spill!"

"Prince Arthur is looking to marry again," she said, her hands still over her face. "Because of the monarchy. The Commonwealth. The continuation of the kingdom. The Prince of Wales is looking for a wife, and I'm the best candidate he could find." Amelia finally peeked at her friend from between her fingers.

"*What?!*"

"Apparently, the peerage isn't exactly teeming with eligible ladies. It seems I'm the lucky winner."

"I thought he was just propositioning you to be his next fling." Priya looked as though that wouldn't be a bad outcome.

"No. Although Charlie thought the same thing. Prince Arthur wants to marry a girl from the north to unite the country."

"That's a really odd angle for him to work," Priya said.

"He's really odd. He also said we could make history."

"What did *you* say?"

"I said I'd think about it."

"The gorgeous tragic playboy Prince wants to marry you and that's all you tell him?"

"I needed to figure out if I was crazier to say yes or crazier to say no."

"So why are you all sad and mopey today?" Priya gasped. "Tell me you didn't say no!"

"No," Amelia said. Though she wondered why she hadn't. "I'm annoyed. Because pursuing a destiny that will eventually make me the first northerner to sit on the throne since Richard III means coping with the *paparazzi*."

"You know Richard was kind of a prick, right?"

Amelia sighed. He had been. But history was complicated and York had so few heroes. "Not to York he wasn't."

Chapter 5

PAPS PURSUE POTENTIAL PRINCESS TO PUB

1 February
Year 21 of the Reign of King Henry XII

I am an absolute fool. After I got back from the gym I let Priya talk me into going out to the wine bar two blocks over for a change of scenery and also alcohol. We looked out the windows before we left and didn't see anyone outside except people going about their own business. We didn't see anyone as we were walking to the bar either. It was all fine and going to be a good night out, but someone at the bar recognized me and took my picture and put it on Twitter — I know, because I found it online later. When we left, a whole herd of paparazzi were waiting for me outside.

Priya beat them away WITH HER FLIP-FLOPS.

Amelia closed her diary — a pretty leather-bound book Nick had given her for her birthday last year — and laid down her pen. On the wall above her desk was hung her calendar through the end of term, with exam days and due dates inked in red. A framed photograph of her family, taken last Easter in the sitting room at Kirkham because the weather had been too appalling to venture outside, sat on the windowsill. In the center of the group stood her parents, smiling but reserved. Charlie and Jo had their arms around each other's waists. Their son Freddy was making a face at the camera, and their daughter Meg was half-hidden behind the huge clutch of flowers she was holding. Nick had his arm slung over Amelia's shoulder. She missed them all with a sudden intensity she'd not felt since her first month at university.

Priya, bored with the drama of Amelia's life when it was not taking the form of photographers shoving themselves into her face, took herself off to her room to do homework while listening to her boy band of the month. Now that Amelia had vented about her evening, she felt calmer about it. At least relatively speaking. At least with strangers no longer waving flashbulbs in her face she wasn't frightened.

She was, however, furious. Not just at the photographers outside the wine bar and her own lost sense of privacy. At Prince Arthur. He had handed her a bargain to change her life and her country, and then had left her to deal with the ramifications of that alone. Not a word of warning or advice about what was in store. Not even a peep to ask her how she was doing or to even acknowledge her existence.

The sane thing to do right now would be to call it off. To tell the Prince that she wasn't interested, that she liked her life the way it was, that she did not care for an existence where she was a prop and a model for any curious eye to see and own. It would be easy to do, too. The Prince, however baffling and infuriating he could be, was a gentleman. She was sure of that.

He would let her go and never breathe a word more about their brief non-affair to anyone.

But — and this was the thing that made Amelia pause, made her gaze shift from the photograph of her family to the London night outside her window — she didn't *want* to. Somewhere out there in the glitter and grime of London, was the Prince. And Amelia wanted to marry him. No matter how many photographers accosted her outside of however many different establishments. Even if Gary hadn't dumped her. Even if she'd gotten into grad school. She wanted *this*: Power and destiny and a future making history with a Prince who had keen brown eyes and a mouth too good at making promises.

But she wanted it on better terms than Prince Arthur had so far offered. She needed to know whether he really meant everything he had said. She needed to know if he would keep his word. She reached for her mobile and scrolled through her contacts to her eldest brother.

Charlie answered on the second ring. "What do you need?"

"I need a way to contact Prince Arthur," she said. "I can't just wait until he decides he wants to talk to me over tea again. You're one of his closest friends. You must be able to help."

❁

Two days later Amelia was met at the reception area of Buckingham Palace by the same footman as the first time and led upstairs, not to the reception room she'd been taken to before but to an office. The room was empty, and her escort shut the door after depositing her there, leaving her alone.

Arthur's public office here at Buckingham Palace, she assumed. It was a dreadfully impersonal place, richly decorated in deep blue velvets and a truly excessive amount of gold braid and gilt paint. She hoped he didn't spend a lot of time here, both because she couldn't imagine anyone doing actual work here and because she dreaded that the room had been decorated to his tastes. There was a desk, centuries old by the look of it, facing the windows that looked out onto the drab inner courtyard of the palace. Two armchairs and a sofa were arrayed around a fireplace, and there were somewhat famous and very boring landscape paintings hung on the walls.

Amelia wondered if she were allowed to sit. She wondered, for the hundredth time since she had received the Prince's invitation the day before, why she had been summoned here. In response to the letter she had sent him, of course. But what would the result of that be? The potential outcome was limited to two eventualities as far as she could tell: The Prince would continue with his scheme to marry her, or the Prince would end it. She had no idea which was about to happen.

She stared at the armchairs, at the fireplace, at the landscape paintings. None of them contained any clue as to her future. Amelia decided she would sit.

She was glad she did. A quarter of an hour passed before Prince Arthur appeared, walking into the room from another door, not the one Amelia had entered through, without knocking or being announced. She bolted to her feet and wondered when, if ever, she would be able to stop curtseying.

"Lady Amelia." The Prince acknowledged her with a nod. "I apologize for keeping you waiting."

"It's no trouble," Amelia said because she had to. Prince Arthur was holding something; with a jolt Amelia realized it was the letter she had written to him two nights ago.

"Will you sit? Shall I call for some tea?"

Amelia sat when Arthur did; he took the sofa, she took the same chair she'd been in. "No tea, thank you."

"Are you nervous?" he asked as if he were enquiring about the weather or her journey to the palace.

"Yes."

"You needn't be," he said with a smile that looked more like a grimace. "At least, no more so than I."

"Are *you* nervous?" It hardly made any sense. Either that the Prince would be nervous, or that he would be admitting it to her. The confession threatened to make her fond of him, which was either going to be useful or be a problem.

"Of course I am," Prince Arthur said. He laid Amelia's letter out on the table between them. "It's not every day I get a letter like this."

"Why am I here?" Amelia blurted.

Arthur looked surprised. "You wrote me a letter laying out your very legitimate claims on my time, and then you asked to see me. So, here you are. What do you need?"

Well. In that case. If he was going to ask, Amelia was certainly prepared to answer.

"My picture is in every paper, I can't sit through a lecture without someone making a disturbance, and a photographer caught me coming out of the gym at school. And then my roommate had to beat paparazzi off with her shoes!"

Prince Arthur blinked rapidly at the mention of Priya's defense of Amelia, but otherwise didn't seem particularly moved by the situation. "I'm sorry. People shouldn't do that."

Amelia scoffed. "And yet they do. I'm not sure you've ever had a normal enough life to know exactly how bizarre this is."

He inclined his head, a wordless acknowledgement of her point.

"And I haven't lied to anyone — not even my mother — yet, but I'm going to have to, soon, if things stay uncertain and unresolved."

"Why haven't you told anyone what's going on?" Prince Arthur asked. He sounded genuinely curious.

Amelia stared at him. "Since you are both royalty and a man, I suppose you wouldn't know," she said. "So I am going to tell you. If I am the princess-in-waiting, my life is the public's, not my own. I know that. I understand that, as far as that is possible for someone who was not born to the life you lead and never expected to be a part of it. I am, for some reason, willing to make that choice."

"York?" he asked.

"York," she agreed. "But if I tell the world I'm going to marry a prince, and then — for whatever reason — I don't, for the rest of my life I am the girl who is both a liar and the worst sort of climber. The only life I will ever be able to have will be on reality TV, preferably after a sex tape and an embarrassing episode involving addiction."

"Have you been talking to George?" the Prince asked.

"Pardon?"

"Princess Georgina. She said something very similar to me recently, about my options if I didn't marry."

"Ah." Amelia wasn't sure how to respond to that. She'd only ever seen the Princess up close at the garden party and had been gravely unsettled by her at the time. But she had no intention of letting Arthur derail her train of thought.

"I need you to say yes or no. I don't need a proposal yet. But I do need a plan. I can't endure the uncertainty of waking up and not knowing if I'm going to be a princess or a grad student. I could bear anything, even the paparazzi outside a wine bar, if it was going to be for the sake of something. But I can't bear wanting this and not knowing if I'm going to get it. I need our deal closed, or I need it gone."

"All right."

"Also," Amelia said. "I don't date people who don't give me their phone numbers, because I shouldn't have to come here to yell at you. If my irritation with you and the situation we've put ourselves in is treason, I want to be able to commit it *on the phone.*"

"It's not treason," Prince Arthur said calmly. "Although I think technically I can still have you executed, as long as it doesn't actually kill you."

Amelia stared at him.

"Sorry, constitutional monarchy humor," he said with a shrug. Amelia couldn't help but laugh — not so much at the joke, which was dreadful and not in the best taste — but at him, herself, and the absurdity of the situation they were now in. He caught her eye and grinned, a boyish look that made Amelia's heart speed up even as the rest of her relaxed.

Amelia had wondered, from the time she'd dropped the letter in the postbox right up to this moment, how Prince Arthur would react to her demands. She'd prepared herself, or at least tried to, for anger or rejection or even cold indifference. She was not expecting the way the Prince met her eye, nodded solemnly, and took her completely seriously. As if this were something they were really in together. As if, unequal as their stations were, he accepted her as a comrade in this mutual venture.

He held out his hand. "Give me your mobile," he said.

"I'm sorry?"

"Please?" he added. "I'm going to give you my number," he said, when she didn't move.

"We haven't agreed to anything yet."

"But we're going to. And if nothing else, you deserve to have my number so you can yell at me, or my voicemail, whenever you need to."

Amelia dug her mobile out of her purse, typed in her password, and handed it carefully across the table to the Prince with only the briefest stab of fear that he would find something embarrassing open on it.

He navigated to her contacts menu. "Now. Would you prefer I list it under 'Secret Royal Boyfriend' or 'Secret Royal Business Partner'?"

"How about secret royal codename? That way, if I lose my mobile, everything doesn't get worse." She didn't understand how a prince could be so bad at this.

"How's this?" Prince Arthur asked and slid the mobile back across the table at her.

Amelia glanced down at the entry he'd added: *Your Humble Servant*. That was workable, at least. And even sweet, if slightly inappropriate. "That will do," she said.

"Surely. At some point, we'll have to get you a more secure mobile. Also, I'll need your number, so I can make sure any calls you make actually go through to me."

"Don't you have it already? Somewhere in my file with my university address and my family tree and my now surely defunct career plans and everything else you found out without me telling you. Which is creepy, by the way."

"I do," he said. "But a prince should be a gentleman, and a gentleman asks."

"Next time a gentleman should ask first," Amelia said.

"Noted. Now. I don't want to rescind my offer to you. Do you wish to decline it?"

Amelia shook her head.

"Good. Shall we discuss terms?"

Amelia had the sudden thought that, someday in the probably not too distant future, she was going to have to go to bed with this man of the long fingers, infuriating habits, and impeccable posture. It would be a duty, perhaps, but not an onerous one. Not if he kept looking at her like this, with an intensity Amelia had never known.

She did her best to put the thought — and the accompanying thoughts as to what the rest of the Prince might look like under his gorgeous suits — out of her head as they worked their way through a shockingly comprehensive list of bullet points. Amelia wished she had brought something to take notes with, but the Prince didn't seem to need anything. If he was capable of keeping track of it all in his head, so was she. She wondered if there was going to be a formal marriage contract. Surely someone, somewhere, was already drawing up a prenup.

"If you're willing, we'll begin seeing each other," Prince Arthur said, "to ensure that we can stand each other in public — and that we don't hate each other in private — although I don't expect that will be an issue. We can both opt out at any time, but you should know that calling off our arrangement would come with its own costs, both for my family and for the north. And for you, as you noted."

"Is that a threat?"

"It's reality. Those costs increase the longer we wait. Think carefully before you agree. If you do, by this time next year — at the absolute latest — we both need to make a firm commitment to either go forward or call it off. It is my intent to be married within the next two years."

Amelia barely restrained herself from asking if this whole quest to get married was Prince Arthur's midlife crisis. But then, he was the Prince. He'd probably been having midlife crises of one sort or another since he was eighteen.

She was jolted out of that train of thought when he started talking about affairs. Specifically, he began talking about how they could and would each conduct them. And not affairs of state, either. Extramarital affairs.

"Excuse me?" Amelia said.

"A man has needs," the Prince said calmly. "And I don't want to assume you'll want to do more than your duty. Don't misunderstand me," he said. "You're lovely and I find you pleasing to look at. I'm sure we'll enjoy each other. But I hardly expect that we'll be the centers of each other's emotional and physical lives."

"Oh no. No no no. No," Amelia said firmly. "I know you haven't been celibate for the entire decade since Princess Imogene died. You've had affairs. I'm sure you have a mistress right now. Maybe more than one. But *please* don't sleep with other women while we're courting. Or engaged. Among other things, I found the stories about your affairs in the papers distasteful even before we barged into each other's lives."

"Why?" Prince Arthur was all curiosity. "You're a modern woman, surely you don't judge me for having sex out of wedlock."

"Hardly. What's distasteful is that the papers covered the matter at all. But your so-generous offer aside, there is a long and storied history of royal mistresses who are tolerated and even expected, and a much shorter list of scandals involving the flings of princesses and queens, which are not. My viable options are limited to you, and I'm giving up a lot for you to try me on. You can deal with not getting laid for a year."

He laughed, just a little, and Amelia was near certain it was at her expense. But because he didn't argue with her, she didn't care. She could accept that it might take time for a prince to understand she was the smarter of the two of them.

Chapter 6

STARGAZING OR STARCHASING? ROYAL LOVERS SIGHTED AT THE OBSERVATORY

17 February
Year 21 of the Reign of King Henry XII

Arthur sent me a list of suggested occasions to appear at together. By Palace courier. And told me to pick the one I liked best.

So for our first date he'll be taking me to the Royal Observatory. Except I'm fairly sure it's not actually a date, even if he does have plenty of reason to woo me. An agreement to marry if we can stand each other enough to make small talk for an evening is still not an engagement. And knowing what I want from him — a queen for my people and respect for myself — is not nearly the same as actually getting it.

In other words, I may be in over my head.

Priya was out at a speed dating night, so Amelia had the apartment to herself. She dressed with careful deliberation. This was her first public appearance with Prince Arthur, and she wanted people to remember her. Not just as the girl in the grainy pictures at the races or in the horrid photos from outside the wine bar, but as a girl the King and Queen spoke to at a garden party, a girl who looked like royalty already.

Amelia's hair was long and chestnut-colored, and she brushed it out and curled it into loose waves over her shoulders. Her eyes, like her mother's, were gray, and she did her makeup carefully — enough to look polished and effortless, not enough to look too young or incite judgment. That accomplished, Amelia wriggled into a wine-colored cocktail dress that showed off her figure without actually revealing anything. Amelia wasn't tall, but she liked the shape of her body — slim hips, round breasts, shoulders that slouched a little when she wasn't in public and didn't have to remind herself to stand up straight.

Her favorite piece of the ensemble was her necklace: a pendant with the white rose of York traced out in white gold and diamonds. Her father had given it to her for her sixteenth birthday. She smiled at herself in the mirror as she fastened it around her neck. If Arthur wanted to unite the country with their own personal union, people here in London would have to come to terms with her origins.

⁂

Amelia had been to the Royal Observatory before for school trips, but she'd never been there at night and never for an event like this. Certainly she had never arrived there — or anywhere — in a car with Prince Arthur, who had picked her up at her flat.

The Queen's House, built by a long-dead king for his wife, was down the hill from the planetarium and observatory proper and lit up against the dark evening sky. It held a distinct atmosphere of privileged and slightly secret sophistication. Such things weren't unfamiliar to Amelia, but as an earl's youngest daughter whose closest sibling was ten years older, she was more used to the idea of such parties than actually being in attendance.

The black and white tiled entrance hall had soaring archways cut into the walls, through which gleamed the sparkle of the ballroom lights and the bright jewel tones of women's dresses. After their coats had been taken, Prince Arthur put a hand on the small of Amelia's back and leaned to murmur in her ear.

"I'd take it as a favor if you called me Arthur tonight." Goosebumps broke out up and down her arms. "At least when speaking to me. I won't protest if you put on the show for other people."

Amelia turned her face up to him. He wore a dark grey suit that made him stand out amidst the staid black most of the men present had selected. The jacket was double breasted and somewhat old-fashioned, but appropriately dashing as any prince should be. "But you're the Prince of Wales spending time with a northern girl," she said. "Do you really want to give people something else to talk about?"

Arthur smiled, the fine lines standing out around his eyes. "Lady Amelia, you calling me by my given name is not going to change my awareness of that fact. Or yours, or anyone else's I'd imagine. I hardly ever get to be a man who's interested in things rather than the heir to the throne. Especially not in public." He glanced about the room. "And there are very few people I can ask to approach me as such. But it seems you might be one of them, so tonight I think it would be very nice to pretend."

"Does that mean I'm supposed to tell you to call me Amelia?" she asked, turning to face him fully. She was sad that he let his hand fall from her back, but tilted her head to look coyly up at him. "Or should we just skip straight to Meels?"

Flirting with the Prince of Wales was a new experience, but she couldn't fault it, especially when Arthur's eyes dipped down to her mouth before snapping back up.

"That, like the rest of this undertaking, is entirely up to you."

❀

With the cocktail hour before the meal in full swing, Amelia and Arthur followed the rest of the arrivals to the orangerie, which contained no actual orange trees that Amelia could tell. There were only slender marble columns and large dark windows that reflected the lights and colors of the room back at them.

Arthur acquired two glasses of wine and handed one to her. "Who do you want to talk to?" he asked, taking a sip from his own.

"I'm sorry?"

"I'm the Prince of Wales, people like to talk to me. If we must socialize, we might as well choose our company."

Amelia wasn't sure if Arthur's surliness was an affectation or not, but she was delighted nonetheless. "Well, who is here?"

Before Arthur could point anyone out to her, a couple swept up to them — the man with fine, thinning blond hair and the woman silver-haired in a rustling gold silk dress — to pay their respects to Arthur. Arthur gave Amelia a sideways look as he nodded in acknowledgement of their bows before shaking their hands, a look that clearly said, *see what I mean?*

Amelia found herself suddenly able to have conversations with people who ordinarily wouldn't bother speaking to her — because she was young, because she was merely a member of a minor northern family, or because she was just a graduate student. She wondered if this was why Arthur had selected this event as a potential first evening in public together. He could impress her, yes, but with the scientists in attendance he was also giving her access to something she cared about and could benefit from. He seemed to keep an eye on her, whoever she spoke to. Whether he liked what he saw, Amelia wasn't sure, but every so often their eyes met and he smiled.

Amelia was relieved. Her mother had made sure Amelia was well trained to be a pleasant and engaging conversationalist. But this was a dinner party in the grand formal dining room at Kirkham House, times a thousand. Amelia couldn't imagine the girl who wouldn't feel overwhelmed.

The feeling only increased when Arthur introduced her to the Duchess of Water Eaton, Helen Lawrence; the woman she'd seen come in off the balcony at the races, right before she herself had run into Prince Arthur. Amelia knew of her, vaguely — she and Charlie ran in some of the same circles, and the press talked about her now and then — but hadn't ever had a real conversation with her.

Helen shook Amelia's hand with pale, cool fingers.

"It's very nice to meet you," she told Amelia. Amelia responded in kind.

Helen gave Arthur a significant look that Amelia didn't understand at all.

"Who are you here with tonight?" Arthur asked Helen, putting his hand on the small of Amelia's back.

"No one, I'm stag tonight. I probably won't stay long, but I promised I'd come for a little while." She looked at Arthur coyly from behind the perfect cascade of her dark hair. The brightness of her blue eyes and the faintest of rosy blushes on her ivory cheeks made her seem as though she were glowing.

Amelia, who had been feeling rather good about her own ability to perform in public, was struck by the degree to which the duchess was in her element. Amelia may have been practiced in dutifully attending public functions, but the duchess inhabited her body and rank in a way that Amelia wondered if she'd ever be able to achieve herself — regardless of whatever that rank might turn out to be.

Once they were seated for dinner Arthur leaned over and whispered to her about those they were seated with. "Baron Rothwell, on your right," he told her. "Writes big checks but couldn't find the full moon in the sky."

"I thought, as the Prince, you were supposed to be nice," Amelia teased.

"No, not really." He shrugged and his shoulder brushed her arm. "Across from you, Viscountess St Quintin. Knows more than she'll ever let on. She used to be mistress to one of the American astronauts, although she's smarter than he ever was."

"Are you jealous?" Amelia murmured.

"She did sleep with an astronaut!"

Amelia couldn't help laughing. Arthur looked absolutely delighted.

After dinner, everyone was ushered to the undercroft, which had been set up for more drinks, more mingling, and also, now, dancing. When they reached the doorway, Arthur touched Amelia's elbow lightly. "This house boasts an operational telescope, and I believe it's open for use tonight. Would you like to investigate?"

The room watched them. Clearly, Arthur didn't care about the gossip that would ensue. Or perhaps gossip was his goal. As Amelia stood considering it, Arthur's fingers moved lightly on her skin. Perhaps Arthur wasn't looking to provoke gossip; perhaps he was actually interested in the two of them having time alone.

Amelia wondered if this was how Arthur behaved with all the women he dated. She also wondered if she cared. The Prince of Wales was offering to show her the stars.

"Yes. That would be very nice."

"Well then. Shall we?"

She took Arthur's offered arm. She was far too aware of the wool of his suit; nothing else existed but the pinprick of fabric against her skin. As they headed toward the telescope Amelia was shocked at how deserted the Great Hall had become in such a short time. Only the staff was there, busy with mopping up, and they threw glances at them as they walked, Amelia's heels clicking on the marble. She could hear the footsteps of the Prince's security behind them as well. She wondered how long it was supposed to take for her awareness of them to disappear.

The central staircase swirled up three floors in an elegant spiral that curled tightly on itself as it reached for the heavens. Arthur didn't let her arm go as they climbed.

"There's a ghost story about these stairs," he said as they passed the balcony on the second floor and continued up.

"Of course there is. It's a house in Britain," Amelia said.

He smiled. "There's a photograph. A shrouded figure, pursuing another figure, maybe two, up the stairs. The experts have declared it genuine."

"What do you think?"

"I think we wouldn't know what to do without our ghosts," Arthur said as they reached the top of the stairs and stepped out onto the third floor. It was an art gallery, carpeted and quiet, the windows night-dark. Across from the stairs a door stood open, revealing another set of stairs that presumably went up to the roof where the telescope was.

Amelia frowned. "Perhaps." Unbidden, the image of Princess Georgina rose before her, her face a living echo of the long-dead Anne Boleyn's. Amelia fought back a shudder. Arthur certainly wasn't wrong, either about the human species or their nation's fondness for superstition. "But we also might be free to do so much more were we to stop believing in them. The thing about science is that it exists whether we believe in it or not."

"Unlike everything else in the world, you mean?"

"Yes."

"Well," he muttered. "There's a new reason to hang on to the Commonwealth. Otherwise I might well go poof in a cloud of smoke."

Amelia giggled. If Arthur found her delightful — she thought she might sound charming — that would be a bonus. But her laughter disguised a moment of pure, unadulterated panic. Marrying Arthur to keep their country together would only solve one set of problems. They would still have to deal with several countries' recent and intense urges to leave the Commonwealth.

It was cold on the roof. Amelia drew a deep lungful of air, fresh after the heat of the party, and wondered if they should have gotten their coats. The dark sweep of the Thames and the lights of London were behind them. In front of them stretched a long hill, black in the night. At the top was the round dome of the great telescope. On the roof here was a much smaller one, tripod-mounted, pointed up at the sky. Standing by it was a staff member with a museum name tag pinned to her jacket. Amelia felt badly that she couldn't read it in the dark.

The docent, however, clearly recognized them, or at least Arthur, for she straightened immediately from a pensive pose at the railing.

"Good evening," Arthur said to her.

"Good evening, Your Highness. My Lady," she said, with a curtsy for Arthur and a nod to Amelia. "Here for the stars?"

"Yes," Arthur said, curtly perhaps, and with a nod to the telescope. "May we?"

"Sir, I can demonstrate —"

"I assure you, I won't break it," he said. "A Celestron Newtonian, yes?"

"Yes," she said a little hesitantly, but she stepped back all the same. "You know it?"

"I have one at Gatcombe," Arthur said, referring to his country estate. His astronomy habit was fairly well-known, although, unlike his horseback riding, less prone to produce photos Priya could put on the refrigerator. "Thank you," he said, clearly dismissing her, but polite. At least Amelia wouldn't have to call this whole thing off because he was the sort to be rude to waiters.

As the docent stepped back, she gave Amelia a sympathetic look. Amelia found it unnerving. The kindness, that was perhaps pity, could only be directed at what Amelia's life had already started to become. Still, compassion she would take.

Arthur bent over the telescope, squinting one eye closed as he twiddled knobs on the side, adjusting it.

"Here," he said, gesturing to her with his free hand, then straightening up to beckon her toward the eyepiece. "Take a look."

"What am I looking at?" Amelia brushed her hair over her shoulder to peer through the eyepiece.

"You can adjust the focus here," he told her, tapping a long finger at a wheel near her cheek. "As for what you're looking at, a fraction of what you should be able to see. The London light pollution is terrible. Marginally better in the winter, though not by much."

Amelia lifted her hand to the focus wheel and accidentally brushed Arthur's. A spark ran from her fingers up her arm, setting her nerves alight.

"Sorry," she said, jolting back as though she'd been burned.

At the same time Arthur said, softly, "Your pardon," and pulled his hand away.

"It's the Crab Nebula," he went on as she blinked into the eyepiece and shifted her focus to the tiny smears of light, brought into startling clarity. "It used to be a star. It went supernova a thousand years ago. And a thousand years before that was the last time your people had a queen."

He was standing next to her, not close enough to touch, but close enough that she could feel the warmth of him in the cold night air. His voice was low, probably to keep their conversation private.

"You're seducing me," she murmured.

"I should hope so."

There was humor in his voice — there was *always* humor in his voice — but Amelia had no idea what to do with the conversational cul-de-sac they'd arrived at. Was she supposed to declare her desire for him and the crown he had offered her? Were they supposed to kiss? With his security and the docent watching?

She turned her head from the telescope so suddenly and sharply she almost smacked herself in the face with it. Arthur, when her eyes focused on him in the dark, seemed unaware of her clumsiness. But he was smiling, something small and secret and, most importantly, as much at his own expense as at hers.

"The light — or lack of it — really is better out at Gatcombe," he said, deftly shifting the conversation to safer subjects. "That's where I first started learning about the stars. And I've always preferred it. Not just for the light. It's beautiful there."

"I miss spending time out at Kirkham House," Amelia said. "At Christmas it's a lot, with all my family there and all the neighborhood functions, but the rest of the year.... The land is so beautiful, but with school I hardly ever have the time."

"Perhaps we could go there together," he said.

Amelia's heart gave what could only be described as a flutter. Staged dates for the sake of public image were one thing, travels together outside of London were another. "If you're going to win my heart and sway my part of the country, I hope we'll be spending some time in the north," she said daringly.

"Certainly for official business. But we should go sometime, just ourselves."

"Is that even possible?"

"Easy, no. But it's possible." Arthur shrugged. "Our theoretical lives will be difficult enough. We might as well make the effort to take pleasure in them when we can. But," he added with an awkward laugh. "I'm getting ahead of myself."

Even in his awkwardness he was attractive. Amelia wrapped her arms around herself and tipped her head back to look up at the sky with her naked eyes. She needed a moment of not looking at Arthur before she was faced with the choice of whether to kiss the Prince of Wales on a rooftop.

"You're shivering," Arthur said.

"I'm all right."

"Still," Arthur said. "It's been a lovely evening so far. I'd hate to mar it by having you catch your death."

"Why?" she asked absently. "You could be cursed, and I could haunt the Observatory." Only then did she remember, although she was not sure how she ever could have forgotten, that Arthur was a widower. "I'm sorry," she said frantically, "I shouldn't joke about —"

"Death?" he asked mildly as he unbuttoned his jacket. "That would be like not commenting on the rain."

Amelia wondered whether Arthur was wonderful or just used to enduring terrible things.

"You don't have to —" she protested as he shrugged the jacket off. "I'm all right. Really. Also now you're in your shirt sleeves and the docent is staring," she said in a low whisper as he draped it over her shoulders.

"Let me be gallant." Arthur's voice was very near her ear. "There are very few people I get to take care of."

The jacket was warm from the heat of his body and smelled of his cologne. With one hand, Amelia held it closed over her throat and took a deep breath. What would it be like to be taken care of by this man for her entire life? She was struck by a sudden sense of want. Not just for a crown for her people, but for a lover for herself.

❁

As the car dropped her back at her flat, Amelia gave Arthur a little wave from the sidewalk before the driver closed the door again. Arthur raised his hand in farewell.

Amelia stood there for another moment as the car pulled away and faded into the anonymous London night. When she went upstairs this evening was going to end, and she was not yet ready for that to happen.

Tonight with Arthur had been nearly a fairytale, and tomorrow things were going to change. Not necessarily between herself and the man of whose intentions she was still uncertain, but between herself and the rest of the world. There had been photographs, official ones, at the Observatory, not of them happening to speak at a garden party, but of them at an event. Together. Whatever she and Arthur were doing, it was nothing she was going to be able to wave off — to her parents or anyone else. If she took five minutes to stand on the street and feel like a normal girl after a not so normal night out, Amelia thought she was allowed.

Finally, when it got too cold for her to stand, she let herself in and climbed the stairs.

Priya was still out. In her room, Amelia undressed slowly, re-hung her dress in her closet, and put her shoes carefully away. She gladly tossed her bra in her laundry basket and pulled on flannel pants and one of her brother Nick's old, worn rugby shirts. As she brushed her hair for bed, she caught a faint whiff of spice and musk and wondered if it was her imagination or if the scent of Arthur's cologne had lingered on her skin.

Amelia was grateful for the privacy and quiet as she sat down at her computer and opened her email.

Dear Mum & Dad, she started. *Sometime in the next day, you're going to see pictures of me. Maybe you already have. If you haven't, I'm sure they'll be easy to find. Yes, that is me and Prince Arthur together at the Queen's House at the Observatory. Yes, I was there as his date. Although we still are not dating. Not really.*

What is going on is much stranger than that and, in some ways, more traditional. Although it is going to end in much the same way. Possibly. I know this is nothing you ever wanted for me, likely because something this bizarre probably never occurred to you. I can only tell you that when someone offers you the opportunity to be part of the story of our country — both England and York — in this way, you say yes. And, so, I have.

Please, please don't call me freaking out.

She signed it *Love, Amelia,* and before she could lose her nerve, hit send.

"Are you awake?"

"I am *now,*" Amelia grumbled and tried to burrow back under the covers away from her very awake flatmate who had barged into her room. "Go away."

"Oh no. Not 'til you see what's going on outside." Priya bounced, heavily and repeatedly, on the foot of the bed.

"I don't want to see what's going on outside."

"Ohhh, yes, you do."

Amelia squinted an eye open. Priya was still wearing last night's clothes — a slinky black dress that Amelia could never have pulled off at the Observatory. Or anywhere. Her black hair was tousled and her smoky makeup was a bit smudged. "You look a mess. And why are your feet dirty?" Amelia asked.

"Actually, I look fantastic, and fantastically well fucked, thank you. Make up sex is the *best*." Priya smirked and bounced up again. "Come *on*." She yanked the blankets back.

"You were with Raveesh?" Still grumbling — and still wanting to know what happened to Priya's shoes — Amelia followed her out into the living room.

"Yes. We ran into each other at speed dating, and he was terribly sorry for any number of things and very willing to demonstrate that. *You*, on the other hand...." Priya dramatically pulled the curtain aside, so that she could look out and down.

"Oh my God." Amelia ducked below the windowsill and huddled on the sofa. Clustered on the sidewalk outside the flat was a mass of paparazzi, camera lenses all trained on the window or on the front door like they thought she might emerge at any moment.

"Mhmmmm." Priya climbed up on the seat of the sofa to get a better view. "I walked home this morning and snapped a heel two blocks from his place. So, I just took off my shoes. Until I got here and saw *that*, the most exciting thing happening this morning was the free samples at Costa Coffee, because I desperately needed that caffeine."

"Didn't you have your flip-flops?"

Priya turned over her shoulder to give Amelia a look of devastating scorn. "And be Flip-flop Girl Who Beats

Photographers for the rest of my life? Oh no. No more flip-flops."

Amelia groaned. "I'm going to take a shower. When I get out, they will all be gone, and I can go back to having a nice, normal life, yes?"

Priya tugged the curtain closed again, as if that could return Amelia's life to normal. "I don't think this is that kind of fairytale."

⚜

Amelia showered and dressed before she braced herself to turn her mobile, which she had switched off last night, back on. She immediately wished she hadn't. Scores of messages filled the screen. The green notification light flickered frantically…texts, emails, missed calls by the dozen. As she held it, wondering how to even start sorting through them, a call from her brother Nick came through. She fumbled to send it to voicemail. Nick never called unless he'd argued with Charlie or was drunk. It was unlikely he had done either this early in the morning, and Amelia did not want his surely amusing, but definitely annoying, commentary on her current situation.

She felt on the verge of panic. Excessive interest in her life history, as demonstrated by the articles about her immediately following the royal garden party was one thing. An army of photographers on her doorstep was another. There was no chance of getting anything done today; it would be impossible to focus on work with that crowd outside. She couldn't even run down to the corner shop, and they were out of milk.

Time to call in help. Her parents were out of the question; they would likely make everything worse. Nick was in town and definitely, judging by the number of times he'd called, very interested in the situation. But Charlie was the kindest, the one that knew Arthur, the one who already somewhat knew what was going on, and the one that had always been there for her. Also, he owned a car and could come pick her up.

He answered on the fourth ring. "Meels?"

"Hi. So, everyone knows I'm dating Prince Arthur, I'm trapped in my flat, and can you come get me? In your car? Priya has glued her face to the window and all the cameras are pointing up."

"Huh."

"Please?"

"This explains the eight missed calls from our parents that I've been ignoring because I was trying to have a quiet day with my kids," Charlie said.

"Why didn't you answer? Somebody might have died," Amelia asked.

"If somebody had died, they'd have called Jo."

❁

Amelia — and Priya, who was not about to turn down some Saturday morning excitement — lurked inside the vestibule of their building until Charlie texted her that he'd arrived.

As they stepped outside and into a burst of flashbulbs, Amelia considered pulling up her hood to shield her face. But she had absolutely nothing to be ashamed of and had done nothing wrong. She walked fast and frightened with her head held high to Charlie's car.

As the door shut behind her and Priya, Charlie pulled away from the curb. She slumped against the headrest and closed her eyes in relief.

While he navigated the streets to the mews where he and Jo lived with their twins, Amelia waited for her brother to say something. But he was silent and looked uncharacteristically grave. Amelia did not find it reassuring. She and Priya exchanged a glance but remained quiet. Everything was now beyond their control.

"Thank you," Amelia said sincerely when Charlie finally parked in front of his house.

"Come inside," he said in reply, grabbing her bag from where she'd tossed it into the front passenger seat. "Let's get you something to eat."

"Does Jo know?" Amelia asked, following.

"Jo has a Twitter account."

Jo met them at the top of the stairs with a worried frown and a hug for both Amelia and Priya. "So it's our new princess and her flip-flop wielding lady-in-waiting!"

Priya plopped down in an overstuffed armchair. "See? Told you it would stick."

Charlie and Jo's twins were spread out on the rug playing with Legos. Freddie's russet waves haloed the deep brown of his face. Meg's normally tightly-coiled curls had been formed into six braids, each fastened at the end with a plastic barrette bearing a white rose. Jo's doing, surely.

"Now are you going to tell me what's going on?" Charlie said quietly as he ushered Amelia into the kitchen and put the kettle on for tea.

"I'm dating Prince Arthur," she admitted.

"Yes, you said. But what does that actually mean? Arthur dates a lot of women."

"It means that we have common goals, and, if we get along and can work together, he'll marry me."

Charlie gave a sudden laugh that sounded more like a bark of terror. "So this is what everything at the garden party was about."

"I couldn't say anything then."

"No, I suppose you couldn't. I've known a lot of girls who've had to be quiet about the fact they're involved with Arthur." Charlie sighed and turned his face away from Amelia to rummage in the cupboard for tea bags. "They just don't normally expect to marry him. And they're not normally my little sister."

"To be clear," Amelia said, somewhat offended, "I'm not swooning over him and thinking too highly of myself. We have business meetings and find each other tolerably charming."

"How did this even happen? It's a done deal, is it?"

"I don't know," Amelia admitted before laying out the timeline of all that had transpired since the races. The more she explained, the more she felt herself swept up in the story. She realized how desperately she wanted this to work. Not just for York. But for herself.

Chapter 7

PRINCESS IS FOR THE BIRDS - GEORGINA CELEBRATES HER SEVENTEENTH BIRTHDAY AT SWAN SANCTUARY

23 February
Year 21 of the Reign of King Henry XII

Mum and Dad yelled. A lot. At least, Mum expressed her strong and conflicting emotions very loudly. Dad made unhappy noises in my general direction, which is mostly the same thing. But they finally calmed down, or maybe they just decided to stop yelling at the girl who might be their future queen.

Uni is no better. Since Monday photographers have been following me all over. Somehow, the ones that lurk in bushes are even worse than the ones that trail two feet behind me. They've started harassing other students for stories about me. And yesterday one of them climbed through the shrubbery and tapped on a classroom window to make me turn around so he could get a picture!

I assume all this is why the Collegiate Council asked me to a meeting tomorrow. Perhaps I'll be expelled.

❁

The meeting involved the Deputy Vice-Chancellor for the entire university, the Head of Amelia's college, as well as her own academic advisor. The Deputy Vice-Chancellor, who wore his academic gown to the meeting and frowned at Amelia over thick-rimmed spectacles, was definitely not pleased with the drama the press's response to Amelia had created. He blamed her squarely for the entire situation, which was so unfair Amelia didn't know how to respond. She was relatively certain she only avoided being slut-shamed because the Prince was involved.

In the end they agreed to increase security around the buildings she worked in and to be vigilant about paparazzi around university buildings in general. Amelia, however, had the sense that this fix had no real meaning, would not do much good, and likely wouldn't even last for long. She was glad she only had a month of school left.

She finally escaped only to have her mobile ring as she stepped outside into wan but welcome morning sun.

"What are you doing today?" Lady Kirkham asked when she answered.

"I've a lab due tomorrow. I'm finishing that," Amelia said as if this could possibly be a normal conversation about her life as a university student. "Why?"

"I'm on the train down. I tried to reach you earlier but you didn't answer."

"I was in a meeting, I'm sorry," Amelia said. Her mother always complained when forced to leave a message. Then Amelia registered what she'd just been told. "Wait. Why are you coming to London?" Unease was about to turn to alarm.

78

"I thought we might get lunch together."

"I have a lab due tomorrow," Amelia repeated as if an education was a reasonable defense for a possible princess-to-be. "And four hours on the train is a long way to come for lunch."

"Yes, and dating Arthur is a long way to go from —"

"Mother!" Amelia didn't actually know what her mother had been about to say, but she was sure she didn't want to hear it.

"What?"

"You're being familiar!" Amelia hissed.

"Oh for heaven's sake. I'm on a train. Do you want me to start shouting about his titles? He's been hungover in our sitting room, repeatedly, thanks to your brother and the horror of university, so I'll call him whatever I please."

Amelia met her mother in the dining room at a stuffy women's club Countess Brockett favored when in London. It wasn't technically her mother's club, but offered reciprocal membership with the club she belonged to in York. The interior decorating wasn't to Amelia's taste, but for once she couldn't lament the choice. Amidst the garish florals there was plenty of space between tables and a reasonable expectation of discretion from staff and members alike.

"How's Dad?" Amelia asked, once they'd ordered, trying to delay the inevitable crux of the conversation ahead.

"Not saying much. He spends most of his time reading the papers. Which don't usually contain photographs of his daughter with the Prince of Wales."

"Could you please pass the sugar?" Amelia asked. Maybe conversational blandness could save her.

Lady Kirkham passed it over to her, an amused look on her face, and waited until Amelia had stirred a spoonful into her tea before she said, "When were you going to tell me I'm going to be mother-in-law to a king?"

"It's not certain!" Amelia protested. "Before the wedding," she added when her mother gave her the keen look Amelia had often received as a child trying to talk her way out of trouble.

"Well thank goodness for that," Countess Brockett said drily.

Amelia and her mother had little in common, in terms of interests or the lives they led. Amelia's parents had never been wildly in love; they'd made a socially advantageous match, produced heirs, and kept up the honor of the family name. They didn't quarrel and seemed to enjoy each other as intellectual equals, but they also spent little time together. She'd never imagined herself in her mother's position. But then Arthur had happened.

"I want to say I hope you know what you're doing," Lady Kirkham intoned into Amelia's silence. "Except I don't think there's any way you possibly could."

"No. But I want to figure it out," Amelia confessed. Why did everyone think that knowing nothing about something was a reason to *not* learn more about it?

"Amelia," her mother said sternly. "This isn't some lab project. This is your *life*. You have so many plans. With your rocks and your bugs and your love affair with your career. I know you're upset about Gary breaking up with you and not getting into Santa Barbara, but is the solution to that really to marry the Prince and have his children?"

Amelia took a sip of tea and put her cup down again before she responded. "Marrying the Prince means that someday we'll have a northern queen again. And it will be me."

Lady Kirkham sighed. "I knew I should have sent you to school in London. You spent entirely too much time as a child rattling around Yorkshire and getting all sorts of ideas in your head."

"That wouldn't have changed who I am."

"No, perhaps not. But two months ago all you wanted to do was get your PhD. Now you're talking about...this."

"It was offered to me; I could hardly say no."

"Debatable," her mother said. "Learning how to say no when you need to — or want to — is the most essential skill for any woman. Your plans have changed overnight in a way I could have never, ever foreseen. What I mean is," she said as Amelia twisted her napkin in her lap. "If you really are going to marry the man who will be king, how could I not support you in that, if that's what you truly want? But you were going to get out of this nation of strife. Out of Yorkshire, out of Britain. You were going escape somewhere and make a life for yourself better than anything I, or even the King of England, could give you. I'm worried for you."

"Charlie says he's a good man." Amelia still couldn't bring herself to say his name out loud to anyone other than Arthur himself. Which was possibly a problem.

"I'm not worried for you in that way." Lady Kirkham waved a hand. "I'm worried about you being a lightning rod for hate the southerners have for the north and the hate nearly everyone has for women. The press will tear you apart for wanting things and getting them."

Amelia, for all her ideas and hopes for her people, could find nothing to say in response. Her mother *never* talked politics or feminism. To hear her speak of such things was as shocking to Amelia as her possible marriage to the Prince was to Lady Kirkham.

"And all for what?" her mother asked. "I won't gossip," she said, leaning forward over the table and dropping her voice. "But I know women. Who have been his...companions. Some for just a little while, some for longer. And you may be young and you may be lovely, but he is still a prince and does as he pleases. There's no delicate way to ask this." Her mother hesitated. "So you'll forgive me."

"What is it?" Amelia asked warily.

"Are you still a virgin?"

"*Mother!*" Amelia didn't need a mirror to know that her face had gone scarlet.

"If you think the papers won't be discussing your physical relationships, past, present, and future, I suggest you call the entire thing off now."

"And get me to a nunnery?"

"I'd sleep better at night knowing you weren't engaged to a prince, but that's up to you."

Amelia moaned into her hands. Maybe she could get her mother to stop talking by shocking her. "Mother, virginity is — it's a construct. It's an arbitrary label we slap on physical actions in order to control and shame women. It's not *real.*"

"And that's where you're wrong," Countess Brockett said. Amelia opened her mouth to protest, but her mother lifted a hand to quiet her. "I mean, yes, you are correct and I agree. But the first time you do anything — like be presented at Court, or get on a plane, or go to the theatre — it matters. Not just things that are physically intimate and can result in heirs to the English throne. But also those things."

"I'm not…I've done things."

"*Things*," Lady Kirkham repeated.

"Why am I having this conversation in this horrid club at one in the afternoon?" Amelia asked her silverware. "I have a lab due tomorrow."

Her mother didn't say anything further. Amelia looked up to see her watching her, waiting for an answer.

"It depends on your definition," Amelia said crisply. "In some ways, no. In a PIV way — yes."

"PIV?" her mother made a face.

Amelia's face flamed. "Please don't make me say what that means out loud. Especially not here."

"I know what it means. I'm just judging your choice of terminology. You've at least kissed, yes?"

"Not him, no."

"Amelia!"

Amelia leaned forward, hissing as quietly as she could, "Why is the scandalous thing in your mind that I haven't kissed the Prince?"

"Because this is the rest of your life," her mother said solemnly. "If you want to marry Arthur I certainly won't stop you. But if you are going through with this, please, *please*, sleep with him first. And for the love of God, kiss him, and soon. Don't make that kind of commitment until you at least know you're compatible in bed as well as on his arm. While you have his attentions you should at least enjoy them. Being a royal wife will be hard enough. Being a royal ex-wife…whatever the papers do to you now will seem kind by comparison."

❀

"And how was your day," Priya said drily when Amelia banged into their flat that afternoon. Priya was in pajamas and was stirring something on the stove that smelled heavenly. Amelia's stomach rumbled; for some reason, she hadn't had much appetite at the club.

"I had lunch with my mother," she said.

"How did that go?" Priya asked.

"She told me I should sleep with Prince Arthur before I agree to marry him."

"As if that's a question. Wait — " Priya stuck her head out of their tiny kitchen while Amelia unzipped her boots and threw them in the hall closet. "Is that a question?"

Amelia shrugged inelegantly.

"You're dating Prince Arthur. Who is hot and a total womanizer. *Why is this a question?*"

"Why does everyone keep calling him a womanizer? He's been single for a decade, he's allowed to date people." Amelia walked into the kitchen and hopped up on the counter next to where Priya was cooking.

"If he were a normal bloke who was single he could sleep with whoever he wanted and it would be fine," Priya said, suddenly serious. "But he's the Prince of Wales and he's been photographed all sorts of places with all sorts of women. All of whom he seems to happily set aside whenever the next girl to come around catches his fancy."

"So I should sleep with him before he loses interest is your logic," Amelia said flatly. Priya's view aligned appallingly with her mother's.

"Yes. If he bins you like the rest, you might as well enjoy the time you have with him. And if he *does* marry you, you may as well have the advantage on any other woman who catches his eye. Now or later."

"No pressure, then." The prospect was vaguely nauseating. Not the idea of going to bed with Arthur — though that made her nervous enough — but that her body could be a bargaining chip in whatever negotiations she had opened with the prince.

"You're hot, you'll be fine," Priya said. "Also he never seems to have gone for the young virgin thing before. The novelty might be interesting."

"Priya!" Amelia protested.

"What?"

"I'm making dubious decisions at every turn here. Sleeping with him is one thing I'd rather not screw up. As it were," Amelia said when Priya made a face at her.

"Is that a question of timing or a question of whether you'll be good in bed?"

"Yes," Amelia said miserably. She hadn't done much with Gary, and he'd never seemed particularly impressed with her in what little they did do. And Gary may have been an utter prat, but still.

"I know you're scared, but your mum's not wrong. You learn things about people in bed you don't anywhere else. Seriously. Don't get yourself into anything if you don't know what his dick is like."

"Please stop talking, and can we please take that off the fridge?" Amelia waved her hand at the glossy magazine photo of Arthur on his horse that was *still* on display.

"Oh no," Priya said. She swatted Amelia's hand away when she reached for the picture and the magnet holding it up. "That can come down when you've seen him naked. And reported back to me."

Chapter 8

A PIOUS PRINCESS FOR THE PLAYBOY PRINCE?

25 February
Year 21 of the Reign of King Henry XII

Arthur called me during lecture today. Arthur, the Prince of Wales himself, while I was trying to focus on wetland hydrogeology. The downsides of a Prince of the Blood having one's mobile number!

He was calling to invite me to Sandringham, or rather, to warn me that his parents are going to invite me to Sandringham next weekend. To go to church and meet the family…and run the gauntlet of royal approval, I suppose.

He asked me if I was busy. As if it mattered. There are few circumstances under which one can acceptably decline to obey the command of a royal invitation. Perhaps he was trying to be kind about my limited choices under the circumstances. Perhaps he forgot his own power. Either way, it's disconcerting.

The same day Arthur called Amelia at school, Priya discovered the part of the internet which was utterly and rapturously obsessed with the Prince's supposed romance and insisted on sharing it with Amelia. Which was how Amelia ended up sitting side-by-side with Priya against the pillows on Priya's bed. A bottle of gin and one of cranberry juice rested on the nightstand beside their two glasses. Amelia had refused to venture down this rabbit hole unfortified.

"You know," Amelia said as she opened a fresh Google search window while Priya topped up both of their drinks. "Of all the indignities I was expecting, the ability to play hashtag bingo with my life was not one of them."

"Ooh, I've got a winner!" Priya picked up her laptop, the bottle still in her other hand, and cleared her throat. "Hashtag, PetitePrincess. This time photoshopped in with no less than six world leaders at the trade summit last month in Berlin."

"They know I won't actually be involved in any international negotiations, right? Like, ever?"

"I think they're more on about how short you are."

"Please, internet. I know I'm short. No point for observation there."

"Do they get points for math?" Priya turned her computer around so Amelia could see her screen.

Amelia squinted to be able to read it and then groaned. *#17Years6months4days*. Because she apparently needed a hashtag to tell her how much younger she was than Arthur, too.

"I had to hang up on him today. At school," Amelia confessed. "He called to invite me to Sandringham."

Priya gave a low whistle.

"No, not like that. On Sunday. With his family. For church." While an amorous getaway weekend would have presented its own problems, these were not those.

"That is the opposite of royal sexy time," Priya pointed out, masking her horror poorly.

"That had somewhat occurred to me," Amelia said with a mix of disappointment and relief.

Amelia picked her mobile up off the arm of the couch before she could think better of it. She wasn't even sure if Arthur texted. Maybe he had a private secretary for that too. But after their rushed conversation earlier she wanted to reach out to him.

I'm sorry I couldn't stay on with you earlier. As soon as she sent it she put her mobile down and picked her laptop back up. She had no idea how long he might take to respond. But only a few minutes passed before her mobile buzzed.

It's quite all right, the message read. *I didn't mean to distract you from your studies.*

"Tell him I say hi!" Priya called. Amelia rolled her eyes, but she sent *my flatmate Priya says to say hello.*

My regards to Miss Joshi. Amelia supposed she shouldn't be surprised Arthur knew Priya's family name. That information was probably in the leather folio with all the other details of Amelia's life. Which Amelia found unsettling.

Trying to get that thought out of her head, Amelia tried to figure out how to ask Arthur what he was doing tonight without sounding like a pathetic teenager. Her mobile buzzed again.

Incidentally. All of these messages go into the official record of my correspondence, so we'll want to refrain from sexting.

"Oh my God!" Amelia dropped the mobile. While that was probably, on some level, good data to have, she had no idea what Arthur was thinking telling her that now. They hadn't even kissed yet.

"What?" Priya asked.

"Arthur is…oversharing."

"Oh, what's he saying?" Priya leaned over to get a glimpse of the screen.

"The opposite of anything interesting," Amelia said, showing Priya her mobile.

Priya cracked up.

How technologically minded of the royal historians, Amelia replied, torn between embarrassment and amusement. *That's…good to know.*

They're very into digital records. Anything to save them from microfiche, I think.

❁

The following day Amelia dug the invitation for the tea with Arthur out of the drawer where she'd stashed it and carefully dialed the number on the back. She had questions about her latest royal invitation and knew where to find answers.

The voice that answered, however, was different from the first one she had spoken to.

"Hello, I was hoping I could speak with Mr. Jones?" Amelia told the professional-sounding woman on the other end of the line.

"There are three Mr. Jones here, may I ask which one you're looking for?"

"I — he didn't give me his first name. But he called himself my royalty customer service representative?" Amelia said hesitantly, feeling somewhat ridiculous as she did so. She hoped she wasn't about to get him in trouble.

The woman gave a weary sigh. "That does, in fact, narrow it down. Please hold."

When the line clicked on again, there was the familiar friendly Welsh voice in her ear. "Hello, Lady Amelia. How are you today?"

"I'm well, thank you. You?"

"Recovering from the Princess Georgina's birthday celebrations." He did sound a little frazzled.

"Yes, I saw a headline. Something about swans?" Amelia asked. The Princess seemed a very strange girl indeed.

Mr. Jones gave a weary laugh. "Yes. Coordinating with the Plumage League was one of the highlights of my career so far."

Amelia tipped her head to the side. "I can't tell if you're serious."

"That's fine, neither can I. Now, how can I help you today?"

"I've been invited to Sandringham for church and lunch —"

"If you're calling to see if another invitation has been misdirected, I can assure you it hasn't."

Amelia found herself laughing at the gentle tease. "No. And I surely know what to wear for this, too. But I was just wondering — if there's anything you can tell me, that would be useful to know before I spend ten hours with Their Royal Majesties?"

"You want the Cliff's Notes of How To Spend A Day With Royalty Without Bollocksing It Up?"

Amelia stifled a giggle. "Does such a thing exist?"

"Not under that title at least. Nobody seems to want to take my suggestion. But there are some materials I can have messengered to you. If you want?"

Amelia did, desperately. But she had one question first. "Who on earth do those materials exist for?"

"I'm sorry?"

"How often does a situation like this come up?"

"Well," Mr. Jones said. "Over the course of centuries...enough."

"Centuries?!" Amelia asked.

"Oh yes. They get updated periodically, of course, but I never said they were very new."

Chapter 9

PRAYING FOR A PROPOSAL

3 March
Year 21 of the Reign of King Henry XII

The King's formal invitation for me to join the royal family at church this Sunday arrived. I was prepared for it of course, but now that it's in my hands…. A car's coming to pick me up. As we do these days. Cars, not carriages, just to be clear. It's like going to the airport!

I'm so nervous. I don't know what Arthur's told them. I don't know what they think of him being seen with a northern girl, and I really don't know what they think of me. This whole excursion feels like a test, and, as much as I want to spend time with Arthur, I don't want to go. It's terrifying. If I do anything wrong, or anything they — they, the King and Queen Consort of England! — take to be wrong, this entire adventure will be over.

At six o'clock in the morning and with the world still dark Amelia, tired and ever so slightly cranky, climbed into the sleek black Bentley sent to take her to Sandringham. She considered texting Arthur to ask how many dates they had to go on before she would be able to stay overnight in the same building as him, instead of a taking a too-early drive like this. She rested her head against the window and drowsed for much of the drive from London all the way up to Norfolk. Or at least tried to. Days to prepare and fret had not lessened her nerves.

It was fully light by the time the car pulled through the gate, past a security checkpoint, and up a long, winding drive toward the house. There was a figure standing at the end of it, peering down the road at the car.

As they drew closer, she could see it was Arthur. He stood with his hands in the trouser pockets of a blue suit shot through with cream pinstripes. Amelia didn't think princes were supposed to go around shoving their hands in their pockets. It made the fabric of the jacket pull across Arthur's chest, and as flattering as it was to his body, it couldn't have been good for the jacket.

"Lady Amelia," Arthur said, with a nod, as the driver opened the door for her and she got out.

"What should I call you today?" she blurted. His use of her title confused her.

"Just Arthur. Please," he said with a smile. Amelia realized he was only being playful. He fished his hands out of his pockets to take her by the elbow before she could curtsey and led them up the path to the house. "We are among family."

"Your family. My king and queen."

"If it's any comfort," Arthur said, his voice low and reassuring, "they're my king and queen too. Eventually they'll be your family."

Amelia was taken aback by the certainty in Arthur's voice. She felt duty-bound to remind them both of what still could go wrong. Especially here, on the very doorstep of the royal estate. The massive oak doors were covered by an even more massive stone portico, above which soared the red brick, absurdly turreted walls of Sandringham House.

"You mean if they like me, and I can get through today without embarrassing myself. Or you."

"Oh, I'm not worried about that." Arthur chuckled weakly and opened the door.

"Wait. Are *you* nervous?" she asked. It was hard to imagine. Amelia stopped awkwardly on the threshold to look at him; Arthur was forced to pause with one hand raised to keep the door from closing. Warmth swirled around them, creating eddies that lifted the ends of Amelia's curls as the heat tried to escape outside.

"My father is very excited to meet you," he said, nodding for her to precede him into the house. "Apparently it's been far too long since I've brought anyone home to meet him and Mother."

Amelia took a deep breath and finally stepped inside. Arthur followed. The door swung closed heavily behind them, and the foyer of the house stretched out beyond them, pillars arrayed down the hall like soldiers. The walls were painted a creamy, almost golden hue, and the floor was spread with colorful rugs.

It was on the tip of Amelia's tongue to ask if Arthur had ever brought any of his lovers to meet his parents. Surely, at least some of them had been vaguely possible wives, whatever the genealogists had to say. But before she could work up the nerve, a girl barely in her teens came skidding around the corner. Her face was terribly similar to Princess Georgina's, but where she was serious and thoughtful, this girl was aglow with delight.

"Hyacinth," Arthur scolded with a note of weary fondness.

"Uncle," the girl said.

This was not any common flower, but the Princess Hyacinth, second daughter of Arthur's sister Princess Violet, aged thirteen, and currently fourth in line for the throne. Her hair, darker than her sister's, was plaited over her shoulder though strands were coming loose. Her eyes were a merry hazel, and the smile she turned on them both was welcoming and happy.

"Your Highness," Amelia dipped her head to the girl.

"Please don't." Hyacinth interrupted her attempt to curtsy, holding out a hand instead. Amelia took it and was surprised by the firmness of the girl's handshake. She radiated a self-possession remarkable for someone her age and a distinct air of mischief that Amelia felt herself warm to immediately. "How do you do?"

Before she could reply, a woman's voice came from a room down the hallway. "Hyacinth, are they here? Don't leave them standing out there all day, bring them in."

Hyacinth waved at Arthur and Amelia both to follow her. Arthur offered Amelia his arm and an encouraging look, but Amelia was too nervous for it to be enough.

The royal family was arrayed around a sitting room bigger than the entirety of the flat Amelia shared with Priya. Books, newspapers, and even a few tablets lay scattered about on various surfaces. A fluffy ginger cat that had been curled up on a sofa bolted as soon as Hyacinth led Arthur and Amelia more than a few paces into the room. Amelia had apparently arrived in the middle of a quiet Sunday morning.

The woman who called Hyacinth in was the Princess Royal Mary Elizabeth Violet Anne, Violet to friends and in the papers. She greeted Amelia with a warm smile and, like Princess Hyacinth, waved off Amelia's attempts to curtsy and shook her hand instead.

"So here's the lovely girl." King Henry levered himself up from an armchair by the window where he'd been sitting working on an acrostic. He wore dark trousers, a crisp white shirt, and a waistcoat. A suit jacket was draped over the back of his chair, probably to the dismay of his valet.

"Your Majesty," Amelia said. The King, at least, allowed her to follow through on a deep curtsy.

"Lady Amelia." He took her hand and kissed it with what could only be described as a twinkle in his eye. "It's a pleasure to meet you."

"We've met before," Amelia said before she could help herself. "At the garden party at the palace."

"Oh yes, I know we did. But that's hardly meeting someone. That's a bunch of staged performances for the sake of gossip and intrigue. Only we don't really do court intrigue so much anymore; it's mostly just gossip these days. Pity." He tucked Amelia's arm into his own. Amelia glanced back at Arthur over her shoulder; he shrugged and gave her a miniscule smile.

And then the King of England, Scotland and Wales, His Majesty of Britain and all her Dominions, Head of the Commonwealth and Defender of the Faith, proceeded to introduce Amelia to everyone else.

Which was, to say the least, intimidating.

Queen Cecile, her soft silver hair swept up elegantly, wore a pale blue silk dress that would have looked a century out of date on any other woman but on her looked exactly right. Princess Violet's husband, Matthew, the Earl of Stamford, was a pleasant-looking man in his forties with reddish-brown hair flecked with grey and an easy posture that was nowhere near as perfect as Arthur's. He too wore a suit, though his tie was a bit loose and his bearing suggested a man who would always look slightly disheveled no matter how well dressed. This was odd perhaps for a royal but was part of what had charmed the country so thoroughly when he and Princess Violet married.

The Earl gave Amelia a hearty handshake and a look of solidarity that Amelia appreciated. It also calmed her somewhat; one person here at least knew what it was to run the gauntlet of meeting the royal family under such circumstances. And if Lord Matthew had survived, so too could Amelia.

The last was Princess Georgina who wore tweed culottes and a cabled wool sweater. Heels and her pinned-back hair prevented the outfit from seeming more casual than those of the rest of her family. Like her grandfather, she did not stop Amelia from curtseying to her. In fact, she rather seemed to enjoy it.

"Princess Georgina," Amelia murmured. Once she straightened up, the Princess did take Amelia's hand. Her fingers were cool and her grip was, to Amelia's surprise, quite delicate.

"Call me George." Her tone made it clear that it was concession as much as it was command. Amelia couldn't help but think what a queen this girl could someday make with her coolness and poise.

"Arthur's been a mess all morning waiting for you," Hyacinth interjected.

"Hyacinth," George and Princess Violet scolded at the same time.

"'Arthur's just taking a walk, leave him be,'" Hyacinth pitched her voice to match her mother's. "He was pacing. For an hour. Outside, where it's miserably cold."

Arthur finally stepped up beside Amelia. "Even princes are allowed to be nervous introducing their intended to their family."

❁

After a surprisingly pleasant hour sitting and talking in the drawing room at Sandringham, Amelia and the royal family walked to the church. For a building on the royal estate, it looked very much like any other village church Amelia had ever encountered. Constructed of grey stone with a solid bell tower rising to the heavens, the chill spring sun spilled through tall windows onto the ancient wooden pews inside.

Amelia spent the entire service intensely aware of the two inches between her body and Arthur's. She tried not to think about the entire congregation behind her analyzing everything from her posture to her choice of hat. To maintain an appearance of focusing on more godly matters, she counted the panes of glass in the window above the altar.

Eventually, unable to help herself, she turned her head slightly to gaze at Arthur. He was looking straight forward, his profile strikingly handsome. His high, broad forehead was creased slightly, as if he were concentrating fully on the sermon. The light caught in his eyes and made them shine like amber. Amelia allowed herself to stare only for a moment, lest she be caught out.

Beyond Arthur's profile was George's. Even at so young an age her face was sharper and prouder than Arthur's. But then, how could it not be? She was a young woman whose circumstances were as peculiar as Amelia's own. Perhaps more so; Amelia at least had been given a choice. Neither of them were people who should ever have had to consider the possibility of becoming queen.

As if sensing Amelia's thoughts, George shifted to meet her gaze. Her eyes narrowed. Arthur, between them, seemed oblivious. Amelia looked away quickly, turning her attention to her hands folded in her lap.

How could George make her so nervous? They were closer in age to each other than Amelia was to Arthur. Yes, George was a princess of the blood and soon to be next in line for the throne if Arthur never married or produced heirs. But beyond matters of rank, there was something to George that unsettled Amelia. She suspected, for no reason she could fathom, that her future with Arthur was, somehow, in this strange girl's hands.

While the rest of the family lingered outside the doors of the church, exchanging greetings with various members of the congregation, Arthur took Amelia's hand and walked on ahead, down the path that led to the house. When Amelia risked a glance back, only George was looking after them. She was frowning, but whether that was resentment or just a defense against the glare of early spring sun, Amelia didn't know.

Formal Sunday dinner back at the house that afternoon was pleasant on the surface, but Amelia spent the meal intensely aware that everyone's attention was at all times on her. She liked Arthur's family, especially the old King and the impish Hyacinth, but being under such close scrutiny was exhausting. She was relieved when they were done eating and Arthur asked if she wanted to take a walk with him.

Amelia tried not to notice the smirking glance Hyacinth gave George as Amelia and Arthur left together. She wondered if it was too early to wish the ground would swallow her up; apparently, her *intended's* niece thought they were sneaking out for a snog.

In the foyer Arthur helped her into her coat. When his fingertips brushed the back of her neck, Amelia felt goosebumps break out over her arms.

They strolled across the lawn to a gate into the back garden. "There's someone else I want you to meet," Arthur said.

"Is this where you reveal that your family secretly keeps a cousin locked up in a barn?" Amelia asked. It was a poor attempt at a joke, but Arthur seemed unperturbed.

"We don't tell secrets like *that* until you're much more committed," he said. As he unlatched the garden gate he pursed his lips and whistled.

Amelia heard the jingling first. Three of them, all English setters, bounded around a corner and skidded up in front of Arthur, quivering excitedly and eyeing Amelia with great curiosity.

Arthur crouched down and rubbed their ears. "This is Callisto, Ganymede, and Io."

"The Galilean moons of Jupiter?" Amelia asked.

"Three of them, at least. Given my circumstances, I couldn't quite call one of them Europa."

Amelia bent down carefully and offered Callisto a hand to sniff. The dog licked it in a friendly way and then sat thumping its tail in the grass. It grinned a happy doggy grin at Amelia.

"Do you mind if they join us?" Arthur asked, scratching his long fingers through the fur at the nape of Io's neck.

Amelia almost didn't answer. She was too distracted by the sight of Arthur with his dogs and the almost overwhelming warmth and fondness that bloomed in her chest.

"Not at all. I'd love it," she said eventually, when Arthur looked concerned at her silence.

Without bothering to put the dogs on leads, Arthur opened the gate again. He led them all out onto a path that ran back into the trees, in the opposite direction from the church.

"What did you think of the sermon?" Arthur asked as they walked. Alongside them the dogs sniffed at roots and rocks and scampered occasionally to keep up.

Amelia had a sudden stab of fear that Arthur was genuinely religious. "I'm not saying that this is the case, but what would happen right now if I said I wasn't paying attention and had no idea?"

Arthur clasped his hands behind his back and gave her a sideways look. "I'd be intrigued, because I've no idea what your personal views on religion are and that seems rather telling."

"Is discussing religion something we should be doing on the second date?" Amelia knew this was something they'd have to talk about at some point and at length, but she didn't feel ready yet. She barely had her feet under her in front of Arthur's family. She didn't want to risk tackling state religion or anything else of the sort until she felt more sure of herself.

"When the second date involves sitting three seats down from the current head of the Church of England, I would say yes."

If this conversation was happening, she needed information. "In that case, how would our children be raised?"

"You mean in regards to religion?"

"Yes."

Arthur hesitated before he answered. "Our eldest would be raised to be the head of that Church someday. As I was."

"How do you feel about that?" Amelia nudged at a stone in the path with the toe of her boot. She hoped turning the question around on him would buy her some time. Whether he truly believed or not, the burden must have weighed.

"I'm afraid I'm not very devout. A bit pagan, maybe, by some people's standards. And I'm spiritual …maybe. But a dead wife will do that to you," Arthur concluded casually. "My sister and I were raised in religion the same way we were raised in royalty. What's one more tradition and obligation when your whole life is tradition and obligation?"

"I don't believe in God," Amelia blurted. That seemed safe to confess, now she had Arthur's opinions. "I don't believe in ghosts either. I can't deny the power of myth or the belief in stories. But when it comes to a higher power, I've had too much training in science. If the data is out there, I haven't seen it. Or anyone who has."

She braced herself for a rebuke or a disagreement, but none came. "That's fair," Arthur said.

His answer was benign, but divulged little of his expectations of her. Amelia found the courage to plow forward. "When I look at you and myself and this situation in which we've found ourselves, I know I'm supposed to think

this is the way things are because this is the way God made us. Divine
right of kings and all. What I actually think is *there was last a
Yorkish queen in the north when Christ was alive.* It's quite odd."

"Our lives are very odd in most aspects. But that you've
thought about these things — and are at least trying to navigate
them — it's also brave."

"Thank you?" Amelia couldn't quite see how. People — in
York and throughout England and indeed through the rest of
the world — dealt with things every day that were far harder
than having thoughts about monarchy. But Arthur meant his
words to be kindly, and she didn't see the utility in pressing the
issue.

Arthur reached out a hand and took Amelia's in his own.
Amelia's heart jumped.

She stopped walking without realizing it, and Arthur
stopped with her. There was no confusion on his face, only
interest and curiosity and, just possibly, something warmer. She
had to use all her willpower not to grab his arm with her free
hand and curl close. She wasn't sure what his response would
be, and she couldn't bear the thought of him pulling away.

Her desire, however, was not misplaced. With his other
hand, Arthur tipped her chin up so that he could look directly
at her. The leather of his glove was cool on her skin, and
Amelia was struck again by just how much taller than her he
was.

He moved slowly, so she could have no doubt of his aim.
It was, she supposed, his way of asking permission, and she
appreciated it. This close, Amelia could see that his brown eyes
had the faintest ring of gold around the pupils.

Suddenly, terror overtook her. She couldn't believe her
own absolute stupidity in all of this: Demanding he stay

faithful, assuming this mutual duty between them could somehow be enough. If Amelia were honest with herself, she knew they'd been drawn to each other on some level that very first day at the races. But this was the first hint of the rest of her physical life, and she'd left herself no safety net. Her last frantic thought before his lips touched hers was *What if he's a bad kisser?!*

His lips touched hers, and after a few shocked moments she realized she had no cause for fear. The kiss was chaste, slow, and achingly deliberate. Arthur was giving them both time to test this and, perhaps, to savor it. His lips were warm against hers, his cheek cold where the tip of Amelia's nose was pressed against it. Arthur slid his hand into her hair and cradled her head. His fingertips were gentle on her scalp. She wished for a fleeting second that they would dig hard into her hair and drag her close.

She tried not to sigh as he pulled back. Definitely not an unmitigated disaster.

Arthur brushed a thumb over her cheek and looked as though he were about to say something. Suddenly, one of the dogs barked. Both Arthur and Amelia jumped and turned to stare at it.

"Come on." Arthur dropped his hand from her face to grab a stick off the ground. "They get cranky if they don't get enough exercise."

Chapter 10

ROYAL QUARREL? NO SIGHTINGS OF PRINCE ARTHUR AND HIS LADY

5 March
Year 21 of the Reign of King Henry XII

Back in London after spending the entire day with Arthur. Who, when he walked me to the car when it was time for me to depart, told me to call him by that name always, at least in private, promised to call me tonight, and then kissed me goodbye. What on earth am I supposed to write about that?

Amelia found that her nerves about the visit to Sandringham did not dissipate upon her return to London. She undressed, showered, and put pajamas on in an ever-increasing state of anxiety. It wasn't hard to pinpoint the cause: Almost immediately, she was waiting for Arthur to call.

Time crawled. Amelia tried to distract herself with a book, but it didn't work. She kept checking her mobile every minute, making sure she hadn't missed a notification. Waiting like this, like a teenager with her first crush, was ridiculous, and Amelia was annoyed with herself for getting so worked up.

They'd talked on the phone before. But never in a planned way — or when she wasn't angry with him. The truth was that his promise to call seemed like a suggestion that their relationship wasn't entirely for show. Some degree of intimacy could exist between them no matter how much their courtship was one of politics and convenience.

But, Arthur didn't call. Amelia's mobile lit up only with warnings for poor visibility due to fog tomorrow. Rationality began to return to her along with the promise of those clouds. Arthur had many obligations and a call the very same night as a second date was not standard procedure. Priya, were she home, would tell Amelia that surely.

❁

Amelia woke hoping for a text or some sort of message from Arthur, but there was nothing. She debated with herself for five minutes over whether she should text him and irritated herself so thoroughly in the process that she sent a simple *Good morning* to resolve the matter for herself.

There was no response. As the morning went on, and Amelia struggled to focus, disappointment gave way to worry and something very much like panic. Had she failed the test of God and family and kissing and all the rest? The stakes of the outing at Sandringham had been so high.

Everything had seemed to go well, but perhaps she'd been wrong. Maybe the King and Queen had objected to Amelia. Maybe George had decided that Amelia was not the right bride for Arthur. Or maybe Amelia had simply misstepped in regard to some arcane matter of etiquette or conduct. Whatever had happened, Amelia knew the outcome was likely all the same.

Silly. Silly. *So* silly. Except that it wasn't. The Prince of Wales, who offered to marry her to unite their houses and bring peace to the land, had promised to call her and then had not called her. Amelia was left with a cold feeling in her stomach and a litany of all of London's broken promises to the north running through her head.

❁

Five days passed with no word from Arthur.

Friday night she sat with her knees tucked up under the covers, staring at her mobile. She considered whether reaching out again was a good idea. Gary had done this, occasionally, ghosting her in some play for power or her attention. She didn't want to think Arthur was capable of that too. But…five days, a broken promise, and no word whatsoever.

She navigated to her contacts and hit *Your Humble Servant*.

He didn't pick up, though that didn't surprise her. As she waited for the tone, she climbed out of bed and went to her window.

"Hi, Arthur." She peeled back the curtain to look out at the London night, bright with light. Below, the flock of photographers huddled, determined as ever. Which seemed ironic, given her current predicament.

"Just calling to say hello," she said, trying to control any wobble of voice that would give away her nerves. "Which I think I am allowed to do, if we are planning a symbolic unification of the kingdom via our theoretical marriage. But really I just want to make sure everything's all right. And that Parliament hasn't declared an end to the monarchy or something. Although I'm pretty sure I would have heard about that. I'm thinking about you."

She concluded more wistfully than she had intended, but she was sure that call, at least, would garner some sort of response from him. Yet her mobile lay silent and quiet all that night and through the weekend.

When Monday came again, she fired off a string of texts to Arthur about various pieces of astronomy trivia; one of her professors had gone on and on about the latest findings from the new Mars rover. Surely, Arthur would be interested.

Her mobile chimed just as she was leaving the lecture hall, and her stomach lurched with excitement when she saw that Arthur had, *finally*, responded. She thumbed eagerly to the message.

Not now, please, read the text.

Amelia's heart plummeted, and angry tears — she refused to acknowledge them as hurt — stung her eyes. She switched her mobile to mute, shoved it in her bag, and hurried back to her flat.

❁

That Saturday morning — almost two weeks to the day since she had last seen Arthur — Amelia's mobile rang with the tone Priya had assigned him. Because *Your Humble Servant* was really not as subtle as Arthur may have thought, and *God Save the King* was really what Amelia needed blaring across the flat at eleven a.m. while she and Priya made brunch.

Amelia grabbed her mobile off the counter. "Hello?"

"Amelia. How are you?" Arthur asked.

"You remembered my phone number." It had been *two weeks*. Two weeks and nothing but a terse text message. She had used all her self-restraint to not chase the photographers outside her flat away with the announcement that Arthur had unceremoniously dumped her.

"I've been rather busy."

"I assumed. It was that or you'd fallen off the face of the earth."

"Well, I haven't done that."

"No," she said. Not even a word of apology! "Was there something you wanted to say to me?"

"No. Not in particular. I just — wanted to hear your voice."

Whatever Amelia had expected by way of response, it wasn't that. She took a deep breath to steady herself. "Is that supposed to make me feel better about you ignoring me for two weeks?"

"Probably not." At least Arthur now sounded somewhat guilty. Not that Amelia was mollified. Not after the worry and anxiety he'd put her through.

"Arthur," Amelia said, carefully. She'd had a long time to rehearse this speech. "We made a deal. I will be your wife and queen. If that deal is off, I need to know so I can make other plans for my life. If that deal is not off, then you don't get to ignore my existence as a human being. Whatever grand scheme of destiny you and I are enmeshed in, I am still a person and deserve to be treated as such."

"Yes. You do."

Meek agreement was not enough. Amelia needed to understand what had happened and if it would happen again in the future. "Then why didn't you call me for two entire weeks? If that's to be the frequency of our communications, that's one thing, but you said you would call. And then you didn't."

Arthur sighed. The sound made the line crackle. "Some time on Sunday after you left the estate at Sandringham, my father suffered what is called a transient ischemic attack, also known as a —"

"A mini-stroke," Amelia interrupted him, her stomach twisting unpleasantly. "Is he all right?"

"He is fine and spent these last two weeks recovering. Just this morning the doctors cleared him for light activities again. But I have been occupied with concerns for his health. Not to mention concerns about the nation, if I were about to become the bachelor king."

"I'm so sorry," Amelia breathed, in genuine sympathy. "But why didn't you tell me?"

"We didn't tell anyone," Arthur responded, rather more curtly. "We couldn't risk the news leaking to the press. Not in the current climate of political uncertainty."

Amelia frowned at the wall. "Are you calling me a security risk?"

"We couldn't tell anyone," Arthur repeated. Now that she was listening for it, he sounded exhausted.

"All right, then," Amelia said. "I'm sorry you had a truly awful two weeks. I'm glad your father is doing better."

"Thank you," Arthur said.

"But if we're going to do this," Amelia went on. "I need to know when I will have a right to know these things. And when things like this happen, I need some signal from you, even if you can't tell me what it is."

"I know," Arthur said. "This would all be a thousand times easier if you were by my side, but you're not. I'm just here doing what I can." He paused, but before Amelia could come up with any coherent response, he said, "Come to Gatcombe next weekend."

"What? Why?" First silence for a fortnight and now an invitation to his private estate?

"I'm trying to make up for ignoring you for two weeks. And I want to see you."

Amelia wanted to see him too. Which was annoying, given how upset she still was with him. "Can your father spare you?" she asked a little viciously, to give herself time and to make it clear she wasn't going to back down easily.

"He threatened to disown me if I didn't stop hovering."

"Can he do that?" Amelia gawked.

"Technically speaking, yes. Will you come?"

Gatcombe, Arthur's country home, stood overlooking a broad expanse of lawn. Behind it, trees stretched up the long, gentle slope of a hill. Much smaller than Sandringham, the house could even be called modest by royal standards. It might even have been been smaller than Kirkham House.

A large part of Amelia's lingering anger at Arthur faded as soon as she saw him standing in front of the house, watching the car as it pulled up the driveway, much like he had that morning at Sandringham. His posture was impeccable, but there was a set to his face that spoke of weariness and worry.

"I'm glad you're here," he murmured as Amelia stepped out of the car.

"I could have been here sooner," she noted more gently than she could have.

He gave her a wan smile and stepped close. Amelia's breath caught in her throat when he leaned down, but after a moment's hesitation he pressed a gentle kiss to her cheek, not her mouth.

"Do you want someone to show you to your room so you can rest?" he asked. "Dinner will be soon."

"It's a drive from London, not a cross-country carriage trip. And I didn't even do the driving. I don't need a nap." Now that Arthur was including Amelia in his life, she had no intention of hiding away.

"Yes, but you're about to spend two days trapped in a house with my closest compatriots. I offer what escapes I can."

As a footman took Amelia's bags out of the boot of the car, Arthur turned as if to walk back up to the house. Amelia stopped him with a hand to his arm.

"I haven't studied up. And you hardly provided details beyond logistics," Amelia said. "Who is here this weekend? Besides us."

"And this is why I generally do things through my social secretary." Arthur sighed. "I invited a number of my friends because it's been some time since I've seen anyone except my family and my staff. And you. Who have been furious with me, so I thought that, well, I should ask you too. But it seemed cruel for you not to know anyone here except me, and Violet surely wanted a break too. So I invited my sister and my brother-in-law and told them to bring George and Hyacinth."

"What should I read into the fact that my brother is not amongst those here?" Amelia knew Charlie had spent many such weekends with Arthur and his friends.

Arthur looked embarrassed. "I did call Charlie. But he was angry with me because I had upset you. He told me I would have to work matters out myself, without him intervening. And Jo wouldn't have come anyway."

"Because of the horses?"

"Because of the horses." Arthur tipped his head toward the house and held his arm out for her. "Shall we?"

❈

As Amelia was led upstairs by a footman, she realized she should have inquired of Arthur if she was being given a room of her own or expected to share his. If they were sharing, Amelia hoped Arthur would have warned her, but recent events made her wary of assuming. She could have just asked, but didn't know how without sounding — and feeling — immensely awkward.

It wasn't until she was ushered into a lush but anonymously appointed room that she was certain she would be sleeping alone. She was relieved. Kissing Arthur, and thinking about doing more than kissing him, was one thing. But this weekend was going to be overwhelming enough without adding sex into the mix. If he could kiss her and then not speak with her for two weeks — not even to offer an explanation as to why — could she trust him to pay her any more attention after they slept together? She wasn't certain and that uncertainty made her nervous.

After she changed into a knee-length skirt in a deep plum and a buff-colored silk blouse she still had plenty of time before dinner. Amelia figured she might as well use it productively. She ignored the somewhat ancient-looking desk beneath one of the windows in favor of curling up on the lush tester bed with green velvet hangings. She fished her tablet with some readings for her next lecture out of her bag.

The work steadied her nerves and for a while almost made her forget where she was. Which was wonderful until she happened to glance at the clock. She should have been downstairs for dinner ten minutes ago.

She lost another minute checking her hair and makeup in the mirror and then got so turned around in the corridors she couldn't immediately find the stairs. Her relief when she did quickly turned to dismay. From halfway down the staircase, she had a view of the dining room through the thrown-open French doors. Everyone was already seated around the table and to a one had an excellent view of her.

Including Arthur, whose eyes met hers immediately. The other guests stared at Amelia. Whispers broke out among them. Arthur rose from his seat at the head of the table. Rescue, Amelia hoped.

Never taking his eyes off of her, he navigated his way around the room to her, reaching the foot of the stairs at the same moment she did.

"I'm sorry I'm late," she whispered.

Arthur said, "I'm glad you're here." He took her hand and led her into the dining room and to the empty seat at his right — the place of honor.

The room was large and yet more comfortable and less ornately appointed than Amelia expected. Golden-brown curtains contrasted with the dark blue walls and white crown molding for a look that was elegant without being stuffy. The furniture — walnut sideboards and chairs, not to mention the table — was simple and tasteful. Candles in plain silver holders marched down the center of the table and were clustered on the sideboards, giving the room a festive air. Amelia wondered which of these choices Arthur had been responsible for or if they were the product of tradition and history.

There were a dozen people seated at the table: Princess Violet, Lord Matthew, the Princesses Georgina and Hyacinth, Helen the Duchess of Water Eaton, and seven others — four women and three men — Amelia didn't know. Lord Matthew caught her eye and gave her a conspiratorial smile. Hyacinth, sitting next to him, did the same. Princess Violet merely nodded to her in greeting.

At the foot of the table, in hostess's place, sat George. The girl wore a dark green dress that brought out the color of her eyes, and her hair was pulled back into a low knot that allowed it to gently frame her face. But her eyes, as they fixed on Amelia, were not soft. In her still-lanky teenager's body, she was as possessed and graceful as any woman Amelia had ever seen

Across from Amelia on Arthur's left sat the Duchess of Water Eaton. Amelia wondered what Helen thought of a low-ranked girl from a northern family being seated above her. Whatever her opinions, she was at least pleasant.

Sitting next to Arthur like this was not a pleasure Amelia would have for long. Once they were married, it wouldn't even be a possibility. As hostess she would take George's seat at the foot of the table, far away from her prince. Perfectly serviceable for a loveless political marriage, but not quite the intimate companionship Amelia might have once craved for herself. Still, she thought, as the soup was served, it was how her parents did things, and they were happy enough.

Conversation around the table was stilted throughout the first course. Amelia wondered if that was because of her presence, her tardiness, or if something had happened before her arrival.

"Did you see what Canada's done?" Helen asked into an awkward silence as the soup was cleared and the next course was brought.

"The new Prime Minister?" Amelia had seen the headlines but hadn't paid much attention beyond that. Between school and her strange courtship with Arthur, she hadn't had time.

Arthur groaned. "I've had people fretting at me for the last week about that. As if there's anything I can do."

"The new Prime Minister," Helen said, for the benefit of a few confused looks around the table. "Is rather enthusiastic about forging Canada's course in the world. Alone." She threw a teasing glance at Arthur. "Without her historical ties to the Commonwealth, Britain, and the Crown."

"Oh," Amelia said. She hadn't realized the situation was as bad — at least for Arthur — as that.

"Yes." Arthur gave an exasperated smile. "Oh. He's being quite brilliant about it, really. His cabinet picks are exceptional, and he's making good on his campaign promises. The people adore him, and they'll follow where he leads."

"It also doesn't hurt that he's very handsome," Helen said with a sidelong glance at Arthur.

Arthur sighed. "No, it does not."

Amelia looked at Arthur consideringly. For all that he was the Prince of Wales — and for all his declarations to her that they'd make history together — he was essentially a powerless man bound to an institution that, some days, seemed to be kept around more out of habit than for any practical purpose.

"Would you rather have the Prime Minister's job?" Amelia asked. She was genuinely curious.

Arthur chuckled. "Considering I think he'd rather my job didn't exist at all...." he trailed off. It wasn't an answer. As Amelia filed it away to explore more later, she caught Helen giving Arthur a look of sympathy mixed with compassion. When Helen noticed Amelia's eyes on her, she shifted expressions swiftly and dove skillfully into a new conversational topic. Amelia filed that away too.

❁

In the post-dinner milling about, Amelia lost track of Arthur as she got caught up in conversation with Helen and Lord Matthew. When she found him again, he was in one of the drawing rooms on a sofa near the windows, looking out into the dark. He seemed, for a moment, so profoundly alone that Amelia couldn't help but feel an overwhelming surge of sympathy. No wonder he had been something of a playboy between Imogene's death and Amelia's own arrival on the scene. Who wouldn't in such circumstances seek connection desperately?

Arthur glanced over at her as she sat down next to him. He gave her a tired smile when she didn't leave the two or three inches between them she might otherwise.

"Maybe this was too much with everything else going on," he said quietly.

Amelia tipped her head to the side. It wasn't an apology for ignoring her for weeks, but she appreciated him at least acknowledging the situation.

"Maybe," she said slowly. "But I'm here now. What do we do?" Perhaps he was as uncertain as she was about how to make sure she was included in his life in the future.

Arthur didn't answer. Instead, he curled a hand around Amelia's where it rested on her knee. He lifted it and pressed a kiss to her knuckles. His mouth was warm; Amelia had to bite her lip not to gasp. Such a small touch, but it set every nerve alight.

"I am sorry," he said, his voice barely above a whisper. His breath ghosted over her skin. "I knew I was out of practice at letting people into my life, but I didn't realize how much."

Amelia tried to will her mind to work clearly. She could either declare that she didn't want this anymore, or she could let it go and judge him by future actions.

"It can't be easy," she finally said. "Your life and the rules you live by are hardly normal."

"No," Arthur said. "But I can do better."

Someone coughed delicately. Amelia and Arthur looked up. People had filtered into the room and they hadn't even noticed.

Arthur scanned his eyes over the throng and frowned. "It's been a long day." He dropped her hand and stood before speaking to the room at large. "I'll see you all in the morning."

Amelia also rose, as was protocol. Once Arthur was out of the room, the Lady Olivia Beaumont of Stoughton Grange, who'd stared at her all through dinner — approached. She was a tall woman in her late thirties with rich auburn hair and flawless makeup.

"His Highness does have a type," she observed, her tone casual and her eyes judgmental.

"I beg your pardon?" Amelia hovered on the edge of dizziness. Whatever was about to happen next was going to be terrible and she had no idea how to stop it.

"Oh, I assumed you knew. It's hardly a secret in these circles. The Duchess there and His Highness used to be...*involved.*"

The people nearest them stopped their conversations to listen. Helen, on the chair nearest Amelia, froze. She looked absolutely mortified. Amelia was torn between discomfort — knowing Arthur had had liaisons was one thing; meeting the object of one of those affairs was apparently something else — and sympathy for Helen, who looked as though she hoped the floor would swallow her whole. On the other side of the room, George watched with a hawkish curiosity as the conversation unfurled.

"I hadn't expected him to take up with a girl quite so young," Lady Olivia went on. "But needs must, I suppose. And I can see how the Duchess could have been a problematic choice...." she trailed off theatrically.

"You'll excuse me," Helen said before Lady Olivia could finish and vanished before anyone could say a word to stop her.

Amelia considered standing her ground. It was certainly the brave thing to do. But the thought of remaining in this room and hearing what Lady Olivia or anyone else had to say was unbearable.

"You'll excuse me as well," Amelia said. "I should go check on the Duchess."

She never got there. In the corridor she ran smack into someone. Apparently, this was becoming a theme. She stammered her apologies and took a step back. The man, whoever he was, hadn't been at dinner. This, combined with his look of mild neutrality — despite the fact she'd nearly run him over — led Amelia to assume he was a member of the household staff.

"Lady Amelia." He addressed her with a slight nod.

"Sir. I'm sorry. I was just — escaping." She waved a hand back at the room she'd just come from.

"Ah." He peered over her shoulder, though the door had already closed behind her. "Given that the Duchess of Water Eaton just made her egress through this same route, I must guess Lady Olivia."

"Is she always like that?" Amelia asked in a low voice.

The man chuckled. He was older than Arthur, perhaps sixty or so, with a shock of brilliant silver hair and a friendly face. His eyes took in Amelia and the situation keenly. "Not always. But she chooses her enemies relentlessly and not always wisely. No one ever profited by insulting His Highness's favorites."

"So why are they friends?" Amelia asked before she could think the better of it.

The man looked amused at her asking. "His Highness admires her ambition and honesty. Unfortunately, she's also the sort who mistakes being unkind for demonstrating wit. Which isn't a problem until it is."

"I'm sorry, I'm afraid I don't know your name." Amelia was glad for an ally against Lady Olivia but not quite sure how she felt about being called a favorite. Flattering, yes. Useful in the long run? Perhaps less so. The unpleasant suspicion that perhaps Helen had run after Arthur, and was with him even now, snuck into her mind. She tried to ignore it.

"Baron Vyvian Fuller of Inner Temple," the man said with another incline of his head. "His Highness's valet, at your service, ma'am."

❀

In her room, Amelia was grateful beyond words to finally be alone. But when she changed into nightclothes and crawled into bed, the solitude instantly became oppressive. She turned out the light and the room went dark except for a strip of moonlight coming in through the curtains. She stretched under the covers. The bed was so big she couldn't reach all the edges of it.

This could be the rest of her life: Dinners with people she barely knew, evenings of excruciating conversation, accusations whenever she was out of Arthur's protective sight, and then nights in a giant bed, all alone, with Arthur asleep in another wing — possibly with someone else.

She thought of texting Priya for a friendly presence. But Priya had her own life; Amelia already pestered her too much. Besides, she would surely tease her and tell her to go find Arthur in his rooms. While that wasn't a bad choice, it wasn't one Amelia felt prepared to act on.

❀

She wasn't sure what she would find the next morning when she went downstairs to breakfast, but only Hyacinth and George were seated at the table in the bright solarium.

"Where's everyone else?" Amelia asked as she sat down with them.

"Sleeping off last night," Hyacinth said as she spread jam on a piece of toast with terrifying precision. "Why are you awake?"

"I thought more people would be around and that I should be up for that," Amelia admitted.

"You mean so they can't talk behind your back too much?"

"Hyacinth!" George scolded.

The younger girl made a face at her sister. "What? It's true."

"That people are talking behind my back, or that I'm trying to prevent that?" Amelia asked.

"Yes," Hyacinth said. "Also, if you're looking for my uncle, he and Dad went out walking earlier. You've already missed them."

"Oh. Thank you." Amelia wasn't sure whether she should confirm or deny Hyacinth's assumption.

"Amelia," George said, with some urgency. "About last night. I know you were being polite, but no one would blame you for showing your teeth from time to time."

"I was given to understand princesses should only do that when they smile," Amelia said in startled response. George had never spoken so many words to her at one time before. She hadn't expected them to be on her behalf.

"Then smile when you do it." George smiled herself. Before Amelia could respond to or even process this support from the strange Princess, George flicked her eyes up over Amelia's head.

She looked over her shoulder. Arthur was standing directly behind her.

"I thought we might find you up," Arthur said. If he had any idea what had happened last night after he'd left the room, he gave no sign of it. In fact, he bent to kiss Amelia easily on the mouth before sinking into the chair next to hers. "How did you sleep?"

"Well, thank you," Amelia said. "But tonight I'm following your lead and going to bed before everyone else."

"It has its advantages." Arthur reached across the table to pour himself a cup of coffee. Amelia wasn't sure if he meant to imply that she should go to bed *with* him or was just making a simple statement of fact. Given the uncomfortable look George and Hyacinth exchanged, she wasn't alone in her uncertainty.

"George and I are going riding this morning," Hyacinth said into the awkwardness. "If either of you would like to come, we'd be glad of the company."

❀

The air was damp and cold with the first hint of spring as they rode out of the gate and onto a faint track that led over the fields, followed by one of Arthur's equerries. Amelia hung back a little as Arthur bantered with his nieces. It seemed right to give them some sort of space for whatever freedom they all found in riding and being outside, and it gave her the chance to look her fill at Arthur.

Arthur was posting as he rode, unnecessarily at this speed, but Amelia wasn't about to complain. Perhaps he was showing off; perhaps it was merely long habit. Either way, the action highlighted his exceptional thighs. Amelia could tell he was eager to push the horse into far more than a slow trot, but anything faster would no doubt make conversation difficult and perhaps offer too much challenge to Hyacinth. A girl her age could be very skilled with a horse or not at all.

Eventually, George and Hyacinth moved ahead of their uncle together, leaving a space next to Arthur. Whether it was by design or just two sisters caught up in their own conversation, Amelia was glad of it.

Arthur gave her a broad smile when she rode up beside him. She was reminded of when they'd first met at the races. His smile, with fine lines crinkling at the corners of his eyes, made Amelia's stomach swoop.

"You have good form," he said. Amelia couldn't help but notice how his eyes tracked up her body. Nor could she help her own blush in response.

"You sound surprised. I did tell you I could ride."

"You'll have to show off your jumps to me some time," Arthur said flirtatiously.

Had they been alone — and not on horseback — Amelia would have liked to kiss him. "I'd be happy to," she retorted. "If you'll show me yours."

Arthur laughed, a sound of pure delight.

Before Amelia could say anything else, Hyacinth called back to her over her shoulder.

"Yes?" she answered distractedly.

"Do you want to race us?"

Amelia gave Arthur a questioning look.

"Well, do you?" he asked.

Amelia wanted to stay and continue this discussion, but perhaps riding with the Princesses was not the place for it. She did relish the chance to show off her skills. Amelia grinned at Arthur and nudged her horse to catch up to George and

Hyacinth. Once they'd agreed on a finish line Arthur counted them off.

It was sheer joy to race through the fields. The horse Arthur had leant her was strong, fast, and responsive. The two princesses were skilled as well. Amelia could hear the hoof beats of Arthur's mount following close behind, and if she rode a little more flashily than she might have otherwise, she could hardly be blamed. She was good at this, and a prince was watching.

Suddenly, Hyacinth's horse stumbled and reared up. Hyacinth fell off the gelding and hit the ground with a sharp cry, rolling wisely out of the way. She didn't hit her head, at least as far as Amelia could see, but she was curled on her side in evident pain.

George and Arthur, along with Arthur's equerry, were off their horses in an instant attending to her. While their own mounts were relatively calm, Hyacinth's horse had now bolted and was headed rapidly toward the woods.

"Am I useful here?" Amelia shouted down to Arthur and the girls.

"I don't see how," George snapped.

Oddly, Amelia had never been so happy for the unpleasantness of teenagers or the awkwardness of her own circumstance. She kicked her heels into her horse's sides and drove quickly into a gallop after Hyacinth's horse.

When Amelia returned to the stable yard leading Hyacinth's horse beside her, almost an hour had passed. She was tired, cold, and very in want of a bath. She was also increasingly worried about the Princess, if for no other reason than a total lack of information.

She turned the erstwhile runaway horse over to a groom who came out to meet her, relieved to have help with the difficult animal. The stable yard was otherwise mostly empty, except for a man on the other side of it brushing down a horse. With a jolt of surprise she realized it was Arthur.

He looked over when she rode up to him and swung down.

"You caught him," he said, nodding to Hyacinth's horse.

"Yes. Eventually. He ran into the woods. It took forever. Is Hyacinth all right?"

"For the most part. Broken wrist. Our physician took her to A&E, much to her displeasure. She'll be back in an hour or so with X-rays and a cast. Could have been much worse."

Amelia blew out a relieved breath. A broken wrist was an annoyance, particularly for the active Hyacinth, but it was much better than the dire scenarios she'd been spinning in her head.

"The horse is all right?" Arthur asked.

Amelia nodded. "Perfectly fine and not even sure what all the upset was about. Damn skittish though."

Arthur raised an eyebrow as she removed her own horse's tack and saddle.

"Why do you look surprised?" she asked.

Arthur shrugged. "You're a small girl. This part's a lot of work."

"And you're the Prince of Wales, doing it yourself. Isn't this what you have people for?"

Arthur ran a hand down his horse's neck. "This is one of the only things people leave me alone to do."

"I bet it took you a while to train them into that."

"It did."

They fell into silence after that, both of them focused on their horses. But whenever Amelia glanced sideways at Arthur she caught him staring at her.

"This weekend is a bit of a mess," Amelia said mildly into the silence which was beginning to grow awkward. "One of the Princesses fell off a horse, the other hates me; your friends think I'm a child and a fool who can't even make it to dinner on time; and it's only Saturday morning. You want me to be queen, I think, but no one else here seems to know that and they'd probably be appalled if they did."

"I don't really care about what other people think. Do you? Or was this just a game until it got hard?"

"Other people are not what make any of this hard. What makes this hard is you and your inability to be consistent or transparent about anything. Including whether you want me around."

"I wanted to call," Arthur said quietly. "When my father was ill."

"So why didn't you?" Amelia demanded. Maybe now they could be done with this argument once and for all. And maybe Arthur would finally say something that could make her understand him and his wretched mercurialness.

"Enough awful things have happened in my life. You're one of the good ones. I didn't want to drag you into a crisis."

"If you want me to be your partner, you need to treat me as such," Amelia said. "I won't break because the world is hard to live in sometimes. If I'm going to go through with this, I'm not doing it alone."

"So you are going through with this?" Arthur asked. He turned to look intently at her.

"That was the deal."

"Good. Will you marry me?"

Amelia blinked. "What?"

"I said, will you marry —"

"No." She took a step back, panicked. "Not like this. You can't ask me like this."

Arthur looked around, as if he had just realized where they were. "We can go inside?"

"That's not what I meant."

"Then what did you mean? You're clearly not doing this just for your health," Arthur looked nervous, Amelia noticed in an abstract way.

"Without me, your crown, or at least your legacy, is forfeit. I'm barely more than a child who is about to be abused by media all over the world. The least you can do is kneel." Amelia had no idea where the words came from. She hadn't rehearsed them, indeed had never imagined this moment, not like this: standing in the Gatcombe stable yard in the cold damp of an English spring.

Arthur smiled at her, almost proud. Then, he strode the two paces to where she stood and sank to one knee before her, right there in the dirt. His horse whickered softly as he took her hands in his.

"Go on," Amelia said. "Both knees." She could hardly believe her own daring, but Arthur had always seemed to enjoy it when she pushed. She would have so little power in their lives going forward, he could at least give her this.

Arthur seemed to agree, because he shifted his other knee under himself as well.

At the sight of the Prince, on both of his knees for her and at her command, Amelia realized with a startling clarity that she was absolutely and completely in love with him. Well then.

"Is this all right?" he asked, with an amused tilt of his mouth.

It took Amelia a moment to find her voice. "Yes."

"Lady Amelia Brockett. Of Kirkham. Of York. Of all my supposed enemies." He looked her straight in the eye. "Will you marry me?"

Amelia nodded.

Arthur squeezed her hands. "The least you can do," he said, "Is actually say yes. Aloud. Please."

"All right then," she replied, laughing just a little. "Yes, Arthur, I will marry you."

"Shit," Arthur said.

"Excuse me?"

Without a word, he stood, grabbed Amelia by the wrist, and strode off to the house, dragging her after him.

"Arthur!" she demanded, as he banged in through the side door and tromped through the atrium and then the sitting room, past a handful of people who broke off conversation to stare after them. "Where are we going?"

"I don't have the rings," Arthur said as he reached the stairs and started to climb, two at a time. Amelia had to run to keep up.

"You forgot?"

"I wasn't quite planning on…." Arthur trailed off as they reached a wing Amelia hadn't been in yet. He fumbled a door open and pulled her inside. For a moment their bodies were pressed together, and then the door closed again with a muffled bang of heavy oak.

Arthur finally dropped her wrist. "Wait here," he said and vanished through another door.

Peering after him, Amelia could see the corner of a four-poster bed and a high window with a view of the field where they had just been riding. She hardly had the chance to take in the rest of her surroundings — solid wooden furniture, rich leather chairs, a fireplace that was empty now but would surely be cozy when lit — before Arthur was back, holding something in his hand.

"You weren't planning on proposing?" Amelia still felt strange. Was this how myths began? She didn't feel mythical; she felt like an awkward girl standing in a dimly lit sitting room.

"No. Not right then at least." There were spots of color high on his cheeks. "Do you want me to kneel again?"

"Your trousers are muddy."

"And I'll catch hell from my valet for that, I'm sure. Is that a yes or a no?"

Amelia let herself laugh and shook her head.

"There are two rings," he said slowly, and the mood was suddenly serious again. "One belongs to the Crown," he said with a hint of bitterness. "But I thought you wouldn't stand for not having something your own."

He grabbed her left hand, gently uncurled her fingers, and turned it over. "There's some fascinating history to this one, but we can talk about that later. Or you can look it up yourself," Arthur said. There was the sensation of cool as he slipped the first ring on her hand, a solitary ruby surrounded by a halo of smaller diamonds. It was beautiful.

It was also red. The color of Lancaster. And the south.

Amelia tilted her head at Arthur. "You're promising me I'll be the first queen of my people in nearly two thousand years with a ring that claims me otherwise."

The corner of Arthur's mouth quirked up. "But it's surrounded by diamonds. White stones, for the white rose of York."

"That can't be what this ring meant when it was made."

"But it's what it means now." Arthur smoothed his thumb over the back of her hand. "I've another for you. It's new, I had it made. Welsh gold. Conflict-free diamonds from the Commonwealth. I wanted you to have something all your own from the very beginning." He took a step closer to her and slid a second ring, a circlet of diamonds, onto her finger. "No matter what happens after today," he said, his voice very near her ear. "This is yours. A symbol of my regard for you. And my promise that before you are a symbol of anything, to anyone else, you will always be a person to me. My wife and partner."

"How did you know my size?" Amelia asked.

"Charlie. A pair of your gloves. And some very good guesswork."

"So you planned some of this at least?" She wanted the whole of her body to feel the way her small hand felt enveloped in his.

"Some," he said. "You took me by surprise."

"I fail to see how this is my —"

Arthur cut Amelia's words off with his mouth. This time, unlike in the park at Sandringham, the kiss was not tentative. Or chaste. When Amelia made a soft sound of surprise, he dropped her hand and grabbed the back of her head instead.

She was suddenly acutely aware that they were standing in Arthur's rooms, feet from his bedroom, and with a heavy door between them and the outside world. She was an adult, and on her finger now were rings meant to serve as insurance against a marriage gone wrong. She could sleep with him without consequences.

Arthur was clearly thinking along the same lines. His hand not tangled in her hair began to unfasten her riding jacket. Amelia's breath hitched — nerves or desire or both — and Arthur's hands faltered. But then he slid both of them under her coat, beneath the shirt that had pulled out of her trousers over the course of the morning. His fingers spread warm and strong against her back.

"I'm sorry," he murmured against her lips.

Amelia made a questioning sound, and Arthur pulled back further. His dark eyes were wide, and his lips were a deep red. The spots of color on his cheeks had spread. Lancaster, her mind supplied unhelpfully. But it was a good look on him. Amelia wanted to put it on his face more often.

"There's an announcement to make and logistics we need to attend to. Immediately."

"Oh." Amelia could hardly argue with the dictates of royal protocol. Just…why *now*? Surely five more minutes wouldn't hurt. Or ten. Or an hour. But Arthur was already pulling away from her, tugging her shirt back down and straightening his own coat where Amelia's fingers had wrinkled it without realizing.

After that, things happened at an alarming pace.

Once they'd made themselves decent, Arthur summoned his equerry and told him to assemble everyone downstairs in the drawing room. As he and Amelia walked back downstairs hand-in-hand, Amelia was intensely aware of the weight of the rings on her finger. She'd worn fine jewelry before, but never anything so heavy and bold. The rings marked her out, not just as victorious in a game she had never wished to play, but as different from other people, intended now for something less than mortal.

She was glad she hardly had to say anything when Arthur led her into the drawing room and announced their engagement to the other guests gathered there. Only Princess Violet, Lord Matthew, and Hyacinth — just then returned from hospital and with her arm in a cast — looked pleased. Lady Olivia looked murderous. Helen smiled, but it was tight and the expression didn't reach her eyes. George's face was unreadable.

And then, in front of everyone, Arthur kissed her. This time it was chaste and very much for show.

Luncheon was as awkward as dinner the night before had been. By the time it was over, the head of royal public relations, Beatrice Slingsby, arrived from London. She was followed soon after by Arthur's solicitor, because there were legal matters to settle. Namely the prenuptial agreement.

Arthur holed himself up with the solicitor in his study. Which left Amelia to meet with Beatrice alone in the sunroom. Amelia couldn't help but apologize for ruining her weekend, but Beatrice tutted and flapped her hands.

"This is much better than many of the weekends I've had ruined in service to Their Majesties." She gave Amelia a meaningful look.

"You've been in this role a long time?" Amelia asked carefully.

"I always prefer announcing weddings rather than funerals," Beatrice said in confirmation. "Besides." She pulled out a massive binder which she dropped loudly on the table between them. "You shouldn't worry, I'm here to ruin your weekend too."

Amelia eyed the binder warily. "What's that?"

"Something the chief steward should be delivering to you, but as I am present, and he is not…. Here, have a princess manual." She pushed it across the table.

"Are you friends with Mr. Jones in the household office?" Amelia blurted.

"Pardon?"

"Mr. Jones. He calls himself my royalty customer service representative. It just seemed to go with the princess manual," Amelia said.

Beatrice's raised an eyebrow, and Amelia realized that almost certainly she was *not* friends with Mr. Jones.

"I'm sorry," she said. "This is making perfect sense in my head and probably none to you."

"No matter. Big day, and we try to develop a sense of humor about our jobs where we can. But your job is now very important. And this," she reached her arm down the table to tap at the binder with one perfectly manicured nail, "will help you get it right."

❀

By the time Beatrice released her for dinner, hours had passed. Amelia startled as she exited the sunroom and shut the door behind her. Arthur was leaning against the wall in the hallway outside.

"Were you waiting for me?" she asked.

"I wanted to make sure you survived." Arthur gave a tired smile. "Although you're in very good hands with Beatrice."

"She seems lovely," Amelia agreed because doing so seemed appropriate. "Although I don't think anything could have prepared me for the horrible necessity of discussing my wardrobe for an hour and a half."

"I'll trade you arguments over heel heights for the prenup negotiations."

Amelia thought about asking, but then decided she didn't want to know. "There's no way all of this gets sorted before the end of the weekend."

"I'm afraid not."

"What do we do?"

"We have a few options. Most everyone will leave tomorrow night to go back to their own homes. You and I and my people can stay here to finish the planning. It's certainly the more scenic option and will afford us some respite from the rest of the world. But to be honest, all will be easier if we return to London. You could stay with me at St. James's Palace; it will be simpler to have you close to hand. The announcement of our engagement itself will be made from Buckingham, of course."

"Of course," Amelia echoed dully, feeling overwhelmed already.

"Will that interfere with your studies?"

"No," Amelia said, chagrined Arthur had remembered what she herself had forgotten in all the activity of the day. "No, it's reading week."

"Good."

"Although, I have a question," Amelia said before she could lose her nerve.

"What is it?" Arthur asked gently.

"We're engaged now. But I don't know what you want or expect or if there's a page in the princess manual back in that room that will tell me if I'm supposed to sleep with you tonight."

Arthur looked away. "Whatever you want."

That wasn't an answer. Though it did serve the purpose of reminding Amelia where they'd left things that morning in Arthur's rooms, before he'd pulled away and the rest of the world descended on them.

"Nothing you do is solely about what you want, or you wouldn't be marrying me," Amelia said. "Now we share that burden. Clarity would be helpful, I think."

"We hardly need to get started on producing an heir before the wedding," Arthur said. His hand twitched before he lifted it and traced a fingertip along the cuff of Amelia's sleeve. "So you must tell me what you want instead."

Amelia had to tear her eyes away from the sight of his hands if she was going to do anything but fall into his arms right now. Or demand that he answer the question first. She took a deep breath. "I became engaged to the Prince of Wales today. I'm already more than a little overwhelmed, and I feel the attention of your guests keenly. Perhaps too keenly. Can we just not tonight?"

"Of course," Arthur said.

Amelia thought he looked almost relieved. But his fingertips lingered at the inside of her wrist.

Chapter 11

PRINCE ARTHUR AND LADY AMELIA PLAY HOUSE AT ST. JAMES'S

20 March
Year 21 of the Reign of King Henry XII.

It's four a.m. Can't sleep. At ten, we leave for London. To finalize the prenuptial agreement, to present me to the King and Queen as the future princess, for the official announcement, and for the rest of my fairytale life.

Charlie's meeting us at St. James's Palace. Where I'll be staying for the next week. With Arthur, because it's his royal residence in London. I told Charlie not to tell anyone, not even Mum and Dad, that he was coming. I couldn't tell him why, but I'm sure he knew.

❁

"You have to read it," Arthur said, not for the first time. He brandished the tablet at her. Behind him, mud-colored fields sped past the windows.

"Do I have to read it now?" Amelia pushed the tablet — with the wretched prenuptial agreement — back at him.

"No, but it's been two days. You haven't even looked at it."

"I haven't needed to, because every time he thinks I have a question, your solicitor explains things to me. In very small words." Amelia wanted to discuss none of this. Especially not in the back of the car that was driving her and Arthur to London, privacy screen between them and the driver or no.

"And I know you're clever enough to understand it all, which is why I'm telling you to read it."

"No. Also, you're a fool, because I may be very smart but I'm not a solicitor."

Arthur gave a sigh of exasperation and tossed the tablet down between them. "Fine. It can wait 'til we're in London."

"Thank you." Amelia had no intention of reading it once they were in London, either.

She turned her head to look out the window so she wouldn't have to look at Arthur. Now that they were leaving the relative safe haven of Gatcombe to return to the capital, everything that she had agreed to this weekend seemed more overwhelming by several orders of magnitude. It may not have been fair to blame Arthur entirely, but as far as she was concerned, the entire situation was completely his fault.

"Oh." Arthur touched her hand lightly to make her look at him.

"Yes?"

"If you don't like to read in cars — if you get carsick — you could have just told me."

"I don't get carsick," Amelia said shortly. "I just don't want to read it. It's bad enough that I'm signing my life away for the sake of destiny and my people. I understand this is a deal with the devil, but I don't need to be saturated in the revolting and surely insulting terms of it."

"I'm hardly the devil."

"No. Not you," she admitted. "Not entirely, at least, Lancaster aside. Just — everything else."

Arthur didn't say anything, but he curled his hand around hers. Amelia felt her cheeks go hot and looked out the window again. Her desire and affection for him were necessary to ensure her future would not be miserable, but those feelings were also inconvenient. She wanted to stay annoyed with him, but he was rubbing small circles into the back of her hand with his thumb. His touch sent frissons up her arm and into her stomach where they bloomed, warm and pleasant like a drug against the impending public relations nightmare.

❁

Amelia had passed St James's Palace many times, but she had never had occasion to enter before today. As she got out of the car, in the shadow of the looming red brick clock tower, she suppressed a shiver of unease.

Another of Arthur's equerries fell in beside them as they entered the palace. Arthur had little to say to Amelia — and Amelia had nothing to say at all — but Arthur and the equerry spoke in low, urgent tones about meetings and timetables.

Quickly, they left the public, newer, and gaudier parts of the palace behind them. Red carpet and gilt furnishings gave way to plain dark walls and chill stone floors. It was like going back in time, centuries of British architecture and history giving way beneath Amelia's feet. Some of this palace was as old as Kirkham House; some of it was much older.

At the door of a formal sitting room the equerry stood aside to let Arthur and Amelia enter first. Charlie was there, and, as soon as she and Arthur stepped inside the room, he leapt to his feet. He bowed to Arthur and strode over to Amelia, grabbing her into a tight, enveloping hug. She clung to her brother and the simple relief of having him there.

"You must tell me if you're happy," he whispered urgently in her ear.

Amelia gave a shaky laugh. "I'm finally suitable for something better than the children's table."

He held her at arm's length to look at her. "Amelia."

"It's all a little overwhelming," she admitted. "I will be, how's that?"

"Completely wretched," Charlie said, "but I can hardly declare I don't trust you."

"Or one of your dearest friends," Arthur added from where they'd been ignoring him.

"Yes, that too," Charlie said. After a moment of hesitation, he reached out a hand to Arthur, who shook it with apparent relief. "But I'd be lying if I said this whole thing weren't requiring a lot of calming breaths."

"Yes, well, join the club," Arthur said. "Will you sit? And get my fiancée to read the things I need her to read."

"I really don't need to read it," Amelia said plaintively to Charlie. "What am I going to do, negotiate?"

"That is generally how these things go, yes," Charlie said.

"But I'm not trying to better my position and I don't need to better my means," Amelia said. "My God, I sound like I'm in a Regency novel — *He has five hundred a year!* Five hundred what?! — None of this means anything to me. I can feel all right with this, but then his solicitor starts telling me about baby bonuses. If you want me to be happy, either of you, don't make me read that thing."

Charlie and Arthur exchanged a look over the top of her head. She hoped it was about how she was correct and not about how she was approaching a panic attack.

"She's been like this all morning," Arthur said.

Charlie shook his head. "I'm not surprised."

"Okay, how's this," Amelia said. "Charlie, you're a solicitor. And my brother. You read it and tell me whether to sign it or not. And I authorize you to negotiate on my behalf, I guess. But please don't, really, because I'm not a thing or a service, all right?"

"I spent the weekend trying to make this document more favorable to you," Arthur said quietly. "But there are some matters about custody of any future children, should our union be dissolved, that I would appreciate you being aware of before the public announcement." He looked at his hands for a long moment before he looked back at Amelia. "If you prefer Charlie describe those sections to you, rather than read them yourself, I won't object and will leave you two alone to do so."

Amelia considered for a moment that Arthur might actually be ashamed.

❁

Once Arthur and his equerry left, Charlie and Amelia sat on opposite ends of a sofa while Charlie scrolled through the agreement on the tablet.

"That's not a good look," Amelia said, trying to keep her voice light as the crease between Charlie's eyes deepened.

"He's right," her brother said. "You need to know what's in here."

"Tell me then," Amelia said. She crossed her legs at the knee and clasped her hands over them.

Charlie glanced at her hands, then away; she wasn't wearing her rings yet. She wouldn't, outside the privacy of Gatcombe, until the official announcement. Too many staff to see, too many people who might call the papers.

Charlie took a deep breath and plowed ahead. "In the event of the dissolution of your marriage —"

"Would you just say divorce? Please?"

"All right. If you get divorced. Arthur retains custody of your children. You would have periodic visitation rights, which will be negotiated with his social office and —"

"No."

Charlie looked up at her.

"No I will not give up custody of my children," Amelia said. "And I will absolutely not discuss with anyone except their father whether and when I get to see them. I don't care what they're heirs to. Does Arthur really think I won't love my children?"

"Amelia, where is this coming from?" Charlie said softly. "Your concerns are reasonable, but you're not convincing me you're fine or that you know what you're getting into."

Amelia brushed her hair out of her face and stared at the wall. "I'm scared," she admitted.

"You'd be a fool not to be."

"No," Amelia said. "No, you don't understand."

Charlie shifted closer to her on the couch and put an arm around her shoulders. Amelia stiffened against the touch.

"Arthur's lovers have been excoriated by the press for years," she said. "The tabloids only don't go after his nieces because they're not eighteen yet. And I remember — I remember what people said after Imogene died. How everyone wondered if it was a conspiracy. If Arthur really loved her."

"As one of Arthur's — and Imogene's — best friends, I can assure you he did. Very much."

Amelia nodded slowly. "But I don't even have the protection of Arthur's love. All I have is some jewelry and a legal document that claims my children will not be *mine*."

"That's not quite what it's saying."

Amelia ignored his words. "My legacy as a Yorkish Queen is nothing if I can't raise my children to know and love and be of our home."

"I understand that, but —"

"Elizabeth of York was once meant to be queen, too, you know. Then she lost her head." Amelia smiled as if the cruelties of history were truly a joke. "Sometimes I wonder if that's going to happen to me. Not literally, of course, I don't think." She looked her brother in the eye. "But the effect to my reputation, to my ambitions, to my hopes for our people, could be the same."

"Surely you thought of all this before you said yes. I tried to talk to you about it; I'm trying now. I know mother warned you, too."

"It seemed less real then," Amelia admitted. "But I still can't say no, Charlie, *I can't*. This is about our family. About the people we grew up with, went to school with, live next door to. It's the history of everyone we know, wronged before any of us were even born. It's about what we could be, if just given the chance. And if we took the opportunity." She took a deep breath and hated the way her shoulders shook.

"You frighten me," Charlie said, his voice as steely as Amelia's own.

Trapped in this ancient room, she felt claustrophobic. She needed her brother's help, not his doubt. She stood and peered down at him. One day she would rule over him. She pointed at the tablet. "Negotiate that. I need to some air."

Amelia took a deep breath when she finally made her way outside into the courtyard, but she was not alone.

Aside from guards standing outside the doors, a man in a crisp dark suit strode a dozen paces behind her. His bearing was erect, and he was on clear alert, his gaze sweeping the otherwise deserted courtyard. He followed her when she turned down a path lined with a low hedge. An uneasy chill crept down Amelia's spine.

"Excuse me," she said, turning around and biting the words far more sharply than was polite. "Would you kindly stop following me?" At least she had resisted cursing at him.

The man drew to a stop and met her eyes easily, with no attempt to hide that he'd been stalking her. "I'm sorry, Lady Amelia, I'm afraid it's my job. I could maintain a slightly more discreet distance if you'd like, but I was concerned you might get lost out here."

"It's your job to stalk me? Also, we're in a courtyard, where do you think I could even go?"

"I'm security."

Amelia threw her arms wide in disgust. "First they think I won't love my children and now this! I'm not going to murder the Prince in his bed; you needn't worry."

"No, no, no," he said kindly. "I'm security *for* you. Not the threat of you, although you make a very convincing one."

Amelia sagged with the weight of her own foolishness. "Are you just today's lucky winner or do you come with the rings I'm not yet supposed to mention?" she asked in a desperate attempt to be slightly more amiable.

"Come with the rings, ma'am." He smiled at her poor humor. Of course, he was paid to.

"Are you allowed to walk with me, or do I have to pretend you're not there?" Amelia asked.

"I can walk with you if you wish."

She beckoned him over. "Come on then. What's your name? And your entire life story. I need to be distracted from my woe, and I assume you already know everything about me."

The man tipped his head to the side before jogging a few steps to catch up with her. He was maybe a handful of years older than Arthur and nearly as tall, although stockier. "My name is Edward Glynne."

"What should I call you? I'm not accustomed to having a bodyguard."

"Edward is just fine."

"All right. Will you call me Amelia, then?" She'd not asked Arthur to call her that so quickly. But she was desperate for any human connection that made her feel less like wheat to be ground in the royal wheel.

"Perhaps, Lady Amelia."

So much for that hope then. "And now, your life story?"

"I've been in His Majesty's service for, oh, about as long as you've been alive, I'd wager."

"I'm not sure which of us should be more depressed by that."

He chuckled. "I know at least thirty ways to kill a man in under thirty seconds, so I feel all right about it."

"Can you teach me some of them?"

He raised an eyebrow at her. "Maybe once you start looking a little less murderous. I like my colleagues; I'd rather not make their jobs harder by setting you loose in the palace."

"Do you have a wife? Children?" Amelia asked, desperate to keep the conversation focused on Edward and away from herself.

He hesitated. "No."

"Perils of the job?" Amelia was aware she was prying, but she also didn't care. Plus, Edward's voice contained the softest touch of a northern accent. Perhaps he really was on her side.

"I have a boyfriend," he said with some amount of caution. "We both have nephews, but no children."

"How long have you been together?" she asked, not skipping the beat he seemed to expect her to.

"Oh, goodness. Ten years? Fifteen?"

"You don't keep track?" The question wasn't the most polite, but this was not a high-achieving day for Amelia's manners.

"I'm afraid the start of our relationship was rather nebulous. We've never quite agreed on a definitive anniversary."

"Nebulous for five years?" Amelia couldn't help asking.

"Lady Amelia, if I may be impertinent. You're not the only one to have ever struggled with a change in your relationship to the world."

By the time Amelia — with Edward beside her — went back inside, she was feeling far more rational about the situation at hand. No matter what her heart did every time she looked at Arthur now, theirs was a political arrangement. They had agreed on that from the start. And such arrangements required negotiation. This was merely a part of that.

She could hear voices coming from the room where she had left Charlie as soon as she turned the corner into the hallway. Edward immediately fell back a few paces.

"I didn't write it," Arthur's voice came through the door. "And it's to protect her at least as much — if not more — than me."

"You could have chosen someone else," Charlie retorted angrily.

Amelia stood outside the door, hand raised to knock. She wondered whether she should wait and continue to eavesdrop or if she should turn tail and head back outside.

Whatever Arthur replied, she couldn't make out the words, but Charlie's response came loud and angry. "'She said yes' and 'I don't love her' are *incredibly* awful reasons to put someone through this!"

Amelia glanced sideways at Edward. He stood placidly with his hands behind his back, examining the further end of the corridor with the greatest apparent interest. She took a deep breath, blinked the tears out of her eyes, and opened the door.

Arthur stopped talking mid-sentence. He looked absolutely distraught.

"Amelia," Charlie said from where he was standing by the window.

"Have we made any headway?" she asked. If this was going to be all business, so be it. She would grieve later and briefly.

Charlie and Arthur looked at each other; Charlie made a *go ahead* gesture when Arthur hesitated.

"Shared custody in the event of divorce," Arthur said. "You would be provided a house in London as well as one in reasonable proximity to my own country estate."

Amelia looked at Charlie.

"It's your decision," he said.

"I know that," she snapped. "What's your advice?"

"As your solicitor, in these circumstances, the terms are generous and you should take them. As your brother, these are terms which would mean I don't have to punch my very good friend right before I am inevitably arrested for treason."

"Ideally, though," Arthur said. "We wouldn't get divorced at all."

"Well, yes," Amelia said. That much was obvious. "You don't want that kind of complication in your life. Plus it would be terrible for the country."

"It would be." Arthur conspicuously ignored her tone. "But I'd hate to have uprooted your life for nothing."

"Not entirely nothing," Amelia said. She was unable, in the midst of the ongoing emotional whiplash that was life with Arthur, to resist gibing him. "I'd still be Queen Mother eventually."

Charlie let out a long-suffering sigh. "Speaking of children, I'd like to get back to mine sometime this week, so if you two are done?"

"If we're done? Are you sure you're done yelling at the Prince of Wales?" Amelia asked.

Charlie and Arthur exchanged a look that Amelia couldn't interpret.

"For now, yes." Charlie set the tablet with the agreement on it down on the table. "I leave you to do with this as you will."

"Will you come down for the announcement? With everyone?" Amelia asked. The prospect of facing something so momentous without her family beside her was terrifying. She didn't know if her parents would approve or the consequences if they didn't.

"I think that depends on whether your fiancé has any intention of doing our parents the courtesy of not surprising them with this news." He turned to Arthur. "I know you couldn't have asked for my father's permission —"

"Don't be medieval, Charlie!" Amelia exclaimed.

"— But now might be the time to extend some courtesy. Given my wife's vociferousness on Yorkish independence, my family has a track record with marriages the media has too much opinion about. It's only fair to give my parents time to brace themselves for round two." He turned to Amelia. "I have no idea how you turned out to be the most stressful member of our family."

"Will you bring said wife?" Arthur asked blandly. "I am fond of Jo."

"I don't know," Charlie bit out. "That depends on how she's feeling about horses."

❁

That afternoon, Arthur and Amelia signed the agreement. After the Crown's solicitor whisked the formal papers away into his briefcase, Amelia stared at Arthur, who was staring at a painting on the wall.

"Are you up for one more obligation tonight?" Arthur asked, turning to look at her.

"Do I have a choice?" Truth be told, Amelia was exhausted, but she now served, like the rest of the palace, at Arthur's pleasure.

"You always have the choice. But my parents have invited us for dinner."

"When did they do that?" Amelia blurted.

"A courier came while you were walking in the gardens," Arthur said blandly, as if that were a normal way for one's parents to issue a dinner invitation and as if he weren't perfectly well aware she had stormed out of the room.

"I don't have anything to wear," Amelia protested.

"I sent people 'round to your flat to pick up whatever you might need for the next few days."

"That's not creepy." Amelia wondered what Priya had thought of the intrusion. She should call her tonight, if she was ever given a moment to herself. Amelia hadn't talked to anyone outside of Arthur's circle for days.

Arthur continued as if she hadn't interrupted. "They've brought your things already to your rooms here. If you'd like me to show you to them?"

"Surely a member of your staff can do that," Amelia said. "Playing tour guide is below your station."

"It's my home." Arthur took her hand.

"One of your homes, you mean."

Arthur chuckled. With his touch, Amelia could almost forget Charlie's words through the door of the meeting room.

"But also my favorite, at least in London. And the one we'll spend the most time in. If you enjoy it too."

Arthur led her by the hand down halls, around corners, and up staircases. Eventually his three dogs appeared from down another hallway and trotted on alongside them, sniffing happily at pillars and baseboards.

"Why did you pick St. James's to live in?" Amelia asked.

"Its age and its lack of pretensions," Arthur said without hesitation. "It's a palace because we call it a palace, not because it's particularly large or grand. After growing up at Buckingham and Balmoral, it was somewhat of a relief to come here."

Amelia nodded. "You might like Kirkham House. If you're still willing to travel north?"

"Of course," Arthur said. He might have been trying to placate her after the tensions of the morning, but Amelia thought she had earned it. She squeezed his hand, and Arthur responded faintly.

"Anne Boleyn stayed here, the night after her coronation," Arthur waved at a passage.

"That's not very auspicious," Amelia said, wondering at the point of Arthur taking them the long way to her own chambers.

"No?" Arthur turned his head to look at her. "She was already pregnant with Elizabeth at the time. The greatest queen England's ever seen."

"Yes, and Anne lost her head. Literally."

"Beheadings are rather out of fashion these days. So is trying women for witchcraft."

"And thank God for that."

"Do you know," Arthur said, his voice teasing as they mounted a narrow flight of stairs, the worn stone steps carpeted with a deep red runner. "That my niece likes to say she's a witch?"

"George?" Amelia guessed, horrified by the segue.

Arthur nodded. Amelia thought of the paintings she'd seen of Queen Anne. There was something of Anne in George; the pale narrow face, the sharp hooded eyes. And why shouldn't there be? Anne was George's grandmother, many centuries removed, the line of Lancasters unbroken from the defeat of Richard III to the present day.

"Why?" Amelia asked. At the top of the stairs they emerged into a corridor even quieter than the one below. Pale sunlight fell through the windows onto wood-paneled walls. Motes of dust swirled lazily in the light as they passed.

"She was born with a caul. My sister told her, when she was little. She thought it was an interesting fact, something George would like to know as a matter of scientific curiosity."

"And George decided it meant...."

Arthur nodded, both grave and amused.

"She's a strange girl," Amelia said cautiously. It wouldn't do to criticize a princess she was now in the process of ensuring would never be queen.

"George is all sorts of things you wouldn't expect. She likes to tell me her dreams. They were all about Imogene, after she passed. Or about our birds dying."

"I didn't know you kept birds," Amelia said. She'd only met Arthur's dogs.

He shook his head. "The Crown's. The swans. The ravens at the Tower of London. The ones they say the throne will fall without," he added. Amelia remembered talking about those ravens the day she and Arthur had first met. She shivered.

"Are you all right?" Arthur asked, concerned.

"Just a draft," Amelia said. That was better, surely, than to admit she could be affected by dreams and auguries and long-dead women.

"Here we are," Arthur said as they reached a door halfway down the long gallery. "Not the rooms Queen Anne stayed in, if it's any comfort."

Chapter 12

RAVEN GONE WALKABOUT? BIRD MISSING FROM TOWER OF LONDON

21 March
Year 21 of the Reign of King Henry XII

It turns out that one does not get used to having dinner with Their Majesties the King and the Queen Consort of England at Buckingham Palace. Not that I expected to. They're charming people. But — especially with the trappings of a palace about them — it's impossible to forget what they are. Or what their son is.

At this point I've met, I think, every single member of the royal staff. Except my Mr. Jones. I'm not even sure where they keep the Royal Household Office. And I've hardly had time to ask in between meetings with the rest of them. The chief steward. The Lord Chamberlain. The Head of G Branch. Every one of them has been very clear about what they need from me as I begin to perform the role of princess in waiting. Most of them have given me timetables. Some of them are color coded.

People keep checking to see if I've read the princess manual binder from Beatrice. Yes, I've got it. No, I haven't read it yet. No, your sitting there to make sure I do is not an acceptable option. Oh, and by the way, if you have anything worthwhile for me to read, about how to actually be an effective princess instead of a pretty dress-up doll who says all the right things at receptions, I would be most grateful.

I've been too busy to check the internet to see what it has to say about me being at Gatcombe and now at the palace. Which I'm certainly taking as a blessing.

❀

Tuesday evening, Amelia let Arthur ring her parents and break the good news to them. He had offered, and while it may have been the more cowardly route, Amelia thought that he owed her. She found it deeply satisfying to sit next to Arthur in his private sitting room while he called her parents *Sir* and *Ma'am* and was in every respect the perfectly-mannered suitor.

It also kept her from dwelling on the news coverage of the day, which had heavily featured a raven missing from the Tower and what its disappearance might mean for the Unified Kingdom. Particularly when the Lancastrian Prince of Wales had brought a Yorkish girl to stay with him in St James's.

When it was her turn to speak with her parents, Arthur handed the mobile over with a distinct look of relief.

"You managed to get engaged this year after all." Her mother spoke in an exceptionally dry tone.

"Thank you, Mother." Amelia couldn't help but echo her tone.

"Are you all right?"

Amelia wondered when people would stop asking her that. That they cared about her well-being was a positive, but that people felt the need to make that inquiry in response to an engagement was not, on the whole, reassuring. "All things considered, yes."

"Have you slept with him yet?"

"Mother!" Amelia looked at Arthur, certain he could hear both sides of the conversation. He stared back at her placidly, but that was no denial.

"You've been living in the same house as him for days. Surely you've had opportunities."

"Mother, I am not discussing this with you," Amelia protested, though both she and her mother were laughing. "Can you hand me to Dad so he can scold?"

"In a moment," her mother said more solemnly. "I want you to know I'm proud of you."

❁

Amelia woke on Thursday, the morning of the announcement, to gloomy skies and unsteady nerves. Her rooms in the palace, low-ceilinged and dark-walled, seemed small despite its luxurious furnishings and the delicate cream color of the bed hangings.

She wondered how Arthur could stand to live in a place this dark. Modern LED lighting and strategically placed mirrors only did so much in such an old building. But perhaps the moodiness suited him, the habitually mournful Prince of Wales. Although, surely, he hadn't been perpetually sad when Imogene was alive and lived here with him.

When Amelia arrived downstairs to the breakfast room, Arthur was already there. One of his dogs was curled up at his feet and perked up its ears at the sight of her.

"Good morning," Arthur said warmly, folding his newspaper as Amelia took her seat. "How are you?"

"Wishing I could go back to sleep and wake when all of this was over." Amelia surveyed the spread of food on the table and decided to stick to coffee.

"You're going to be fine," Arthur said.

"Yes, all I have to do is stand there and look pretty," Amelia noted more sharply than she had intended. Beatrice had briefed her thoroughly — and firmly — on what was expected of her today. Namely, smile, wave, and say absolutely nothing. Her worries were not about her own performance, but everyone else's reaction to it.

"You should eat something," Arthur said after several moments of Amelia staring at her coffee cup and neither of them speaking.

"Can you not?" This time, Amelia intended every bit of her sharpness. She was barely holding it together as it was; she did not need Arthur attempting to take care of her.

"Of course. My apologies," he said, his tone as mild and unoffended as if Amelia had merely spoken of the weather. "Have you heard, they found the missing raven?"

"No, I hadn't." Amelia held her breath for a moment in order to avoid sighing with relief. She may have been joining the mythology of her nation, but she was a scientist and had no intention of succumbing to superstitious nonsense about birds. "Where was it?" she asked mildly.

"Down at the pub. Again."

"This happens a lot?"

"More than you might think." Arthur was clearly on the verge of laughing himself. Amelia was relieved he didn't believe. "Apparently it's quite the lush."

"George must be pleased."

"She is. She never believes me when I tell her they'll turn up. She always thinks it's going to be the end of the world."

❀

At the appointed time, Amelia and Arthur went to the car waiting to take them to Buckingham Palace. That there was an event scheduled at the palace, following a weekend spent by Arthur and Amelia together, had hardly been kept a secret from the public. Even so, Amelia was startled to find the short drive along the Mall from St James's to Buckingham lined with people watching the cars as they passed. Some waved and tossed flowers; others stood unsmiling and impenetrably grave, as though the motorcade was something between a wedding and a funeral procession.

She wore a simple pale yellow dress with a navy blue jacket. In other circumstances, she might have liked to have worn a dress to match the stone in her ring. Except that stone was red and Amelia had refused to wear the color of Lancaster. Beatrice, instead of fighting with her, had declared that 'it wouldn't do to have her standing next to the Prince and looking like a whore.'

Amelia still wasn't quite over the horror of that Pyrrhic victory, even if it did mean she didn't have to wear a red dress. At least she had exceptional shoes to make up for it. They were sage green, with two-inch heels and two narrow straps across the ankle. The colors of her ensemble suited the early spring perfectly.

As they stepped into the palace, Amelia was whisked aside by a very determined assistant from H Branch for touch-ups on her hair and makeup. Amelia could perhaps put her foot down about the color of a dress, but there was no avoiding having her face powdered and her curls arranged over her shoulders. The whole world would see the pictures from today's announcement.

At last she was released and led by another member of the staff back to the rest of the proceedings. Amelia could hear the babble of voices as she approached. When she rounded the last corner and the room came into view, Arthur was already waiting there, surrounded by a fluttering gaggle of aides and assistants.

Her heels clicked on the slick stone floor, and it might have been that that made Arthur turn to look at her. He nodded at her, a small gesture, and Amelia expected him to turn back to his people. But he kept his gaze fixed on her, watching her walk all the way down the hallway.

Arthur's face was pensive. When she finally reached him, he held out a hand for her. She was surprised to find his fingers were cold.

"Are you ready?" he asked.

"To be honest, I don't think so."

"Do you want to go in there anyway?" He tipped his head toward the presentation room in which the media waited.

She tightened her hand in his. Arthur seemed to understand and share everything that was difficult about this road they had chosen to walk together. Moments like this had made Amelia fall so unwisely, so unrequitedly, in love him.

"Yes," she said.

Arthur nodded to a footman, who pushed the door open.

Amelia had been put through her paces by the Crown's publicity team for this moment. She had rehearsed the choreography of it: Walk into the room, hold Arthur's arm, stand still and smile while he spoke and answered questions. But what rehearsal could not prepare Amelia for — what nothing could prepare her for — was the onslaught of light when she and Arthur crossed the threshold.

Flashbulbs went off, what seemed like thousands of them. Amelia couldn't see anything and was desperately grateful to be holding on to Arthur. She didn't understand how anyone could ever acclimate to this, and her encounters with the paparazzi now seemed tame by comparison. She wished fiercely that Priya was here beside her.

Arthur's statement was brief, doing little more than announcing the engagement and thanking everyone for coming today. The press, however, were not satisfied and immediately started hollering questions. Arthur answered them all calmly.

No, they hadn't set a date yet but were planning on something this coming fall. Yes, Amelia was wearing two rings, the ruby ring and the diamond eternity band because they wanted to have something between them that wasn't a part of their royal roles. Yes, Amelia was from York, but her allegiance was to the whole of the kingdom and the wedding would take place at Westminster Abbey, as was traditional.

"Lady Amelia, how does it feel to follow in Princess Imogene's footsteps?"

The question, shouted over the end of Arthur's words, was shocking. Arthur's arm, which Amelia still held, jerked almost imperceptibly. She had to employ all her inner discipline not to gape. Considering that Imogene was dead, following in Arthur's dead wife's footsteps wasn't something she was in any hurry to do quickly. And with Arthur right there, the question was just cruel.

"I know Prince Arthur still cherishes her memory, as does the kingdom. I feel very grateful that he has room in his heart for me after so great a loss," she said. "I will be paying my respects at her gravesite." Amelia felt strangely far away from herself as she spoke. She'd never been trained to be any sort of public figure, yet she knew what to say. Her words were surely a far better choice than her and Arthur hurrying away in the face of an awkward question. "You're very brave for asking."

Arthur clasped his hand over hers where she clung to his arm and squeezed. They smiled for yet another dizzying volley of flashes and then someone from the public relations team announced the event over.

The second they had retreated back out to the corridor, Amelia felt her legs go weak. There were too many people about for her to just collapse on to the floor of the palace, but she was only still standing because Arthur was holding her up.

They rounded a corner, and then he was pushing her into one of the antique, red velvet, and hideously uncomfortable chairs that lined the hall at intervals.

He crouched in front of her, still holding her hand. "You did very well," he said.

"Even if you were wildly off script," Beatrice said as she came clattering around the corner. Amelia still couldn't see properly — her vision was a haze of yellow and purple spots from the flashes — but Beatrice's voice, and the irritation in it, was distinct. "Now we're going to have to arrange a visit to Princess Imogene's gravesite. We'll need to release a photo or two, but due to the sensitive nature we can keep most of the press away." She turned to Arthur, "I'm sorry, sir, I know this must be difficult for you."

"It was an expected question." He dropped Amelia's hand and stood. "We should have been prepared."

❁

That evening, Amelia and Arthur had dinner with the King, Queen, Amelia's parents, Nick, Charlie, and Jo. After the events of the day, Amelia wanted a bath and a nap, not a formal dinner for which she would have to be alert and attentive. But this was her life now, and so she sat and talked and ate, all the while keeping her posture perfect despite desperately wanting to slouch.

After the meal was finally over, and after Amelia had hugged her parents goodbye and promised to come home soon to visit, Arthur stepped up beside her.

"Can I see you to your rooms?" he asked.

"I thought we were driving back together?" She needed to stop assuming; logistics were a thing that happened to her now, not something she had any say in orchestrating.

"We could, if you want," Arthur said. "But it's a lovely evening. I thought you might enjoy the walk."

"A walk would be lovely," Amelia said, though the offer still puzzled her. If Arthur didn't love her, there was no reason for him to go out of his way to spend time with her out of the limelight and away from their families.

There were only a few hundred yards along the Mall from Buckingham to St. James's, but they walked slowly. Amelia thought Arthur might want to talk about the day, but he was silent, apparently enjoying the quiet and relative solitude. Amelia, as full as her mind was, could think of nothing to say. The footsteps of security fell behind them at a discreet distance, their figures barely discernible as shadows against the lamplit trunks of trees.

They entered the gate of St. James's together, past guards that saluted smartly to Arthur. When they reached the ancient oaken door that led to the residential wing of the palace, Arthur stopped.

"On second thought," he said. "Could I invite you to come up?"

"To your rooms?" Amelia was more surprised now than she had been at the offer to walk her home. This amount of attention was completely unnecessary and left her confused. She wondered if she needed to say yes. She was exhausted, and if Arthur didn't love her and their engagement was now official, what did she have to lose by saying no?

Her own happiness, a traitorous voice inside her whispered. Arthur didn't have to love her for any number of forms of satisfaction. He just had to pay attention to her. Which he was trying to do now. Amelia would be a fool to turn that down.

She realized that Arthur, awaiting an answer from her, was now babbling. "Or your rooms, if you'd rather. But I'm fairly sure I have a better stock of scotch. Assuming that's to your taste?"

"I grew up with Charlie. It most definitely is."

"Well then." Arthur nodded at the door. "Shall we?"

Amelia gamely slipped her arm into Arthur's. "Is this where you show me your etchings?" If there was truly nothing to lose, there was no reason not to be bold.

He gave her a sly but cryptic smile. "If you'd like."

The private sitting room he led her to was furnished in much the same style as Gatcombe — dark leather and warm wood — only with a few more ornate a touches, as she supposed befitted the residence of a prince in his palace. On the wall was an ancient tapestry, which Amelia wanted to take a closer look at, but Arthur waved her through the sitting room, on through another door, and into a study.

Here the walls were a light grey, and the furniture was sleeker and more angled than Amelia had seen elsewhere in St. James's. Navy and silver accents around the room made it look modern and livable, not like the stuffy scarlet and gold that overwhelmed Buckingham.

"You like it?" Arthur asked as she took it all in.

Amelia pursed her lips consideringly. "It's a little less fairytale prince than I was expecting."

"Is that a good thing or a bad thing?"

"Since I don't immediately think that everything in the room, including you and me, is a royal treasure, we'll say good thing." She still wasn't sure what Arthur's plan was for this evening, or if, in all his mercurialness, he had one.

Arthur busied himself with a decanter while Amelia studied a series of photographs on the wall. They were all black and whites in plain black frames, depicting everything from sweeping cityscapes to a macro shot of a rusted hinge on a wrought iron gate.

"These are beautiful," Amelia said when Arthur handed her a tumbler.

"Thank you. Imogene took them."

"Oh! I didn't know she was a photographer."

"I'm not surprised," Arthur said. "It was one of the things she liked to keep for herself."

"I suppose this is all very odd for you." Amelia was glad she could keep staring at a picture of a swan on the wind-ruffled surface of a river rather than look at Arthur.

"On the contrary," he said quietly. "Getting married ten years after my first wife died is probably one of the most normal things I've ever done. Even if it is to you."

"Er, thanks?"

"You really did do a fantastic job today. That's why it's always had to be you. You're never afraid."

Amelia laughed, low and dark. She took a long swallow of her drink. "On the contrary. I'm always afraid. I just keep going is all."

"Why?" Arthur sounded genuinely curious.

At that, Amelia turned to face him. "Because I'm *Lady* Amelia, daughter of York, and that's what I was taught to do. Isn't that what you were taught to do? As a prince and a son of Lancaster and all that?"

"Mostly the all that," Arthur said, looking at the glass in his hand. "Military life was helpful. Although I dreaded the specter of it as a child."

"Why?" Amelia asked.

He chuckled. "Oh, I didn't like people then either. And the army seemed to have rather a lot of them."

"Did you like it once you were in it?" Amelia asked.

Arthur shrugged. "It was useful. I could be useful. Which is a rare enough feeling around here. But then my grandmother died, my father ascended the throne, and I got pulled from active duty in the Balkans and shipped back here to be invested as the Prince of Wales."

There was bitterness in his tone as he spoke, and he waved a hand to take in the room, the palace, London itself. Amelia tried to do the math. Arthur would have been no older than she was now.

"I couldn't look my friends in the eye anymore," Arthur went on. "I've had nothing real to do since."

"Just the fairly minor task of keeping the country afloat?"

"Parliament and the Prime Minister do that well enough without the monarchy," Arthur said. "Although, speaking of that," he hesitated, then cleared his throat. "Since we're talking about awkward things."

"Yes?" Amelia asked with some trepidation.

"We haven't discussed our own physical relationship. Beyond your perfectly fair desire to wait until some future unspecified date."

"Do we need to discuss it beyond that?" Amelia was dismayed. Engaging in pleasant banter was one thing, but perhaps her earlier flirtatiousness had been too much. Having an actual conversation about sex was not something that felt appealing in this moment.

Arthur gave an awkward laugh. Amelia wanted to dissolve into the floor. Anything would have been better than explaining to Arthur that she didn't want to wait because she was uptight about sex, but because she felt overwhelmed and uncertain in the face of what her life had become.

"I thought we should talk about it sooner rather than later," he said. "Surely it's better for both of us if it's not a black box."

Her mother's — and Priya's — opinions on the matter came back to her. They weren't wrong, but knowing that didn't make this moment feel any easier. She nodded in vague agreement that yes, they should probably talk about this.

"Please," he said. "Don't be offended, but you're a virgin, aren't you?"

Amelia's cheeks burned, and she resisted the overwhelming urge to cover them with her hands. She made some sort of noise that Arthur was decent enough to take as a yes.

"May I ask why?"

She side-eyed him. "I think that's fairly clear," she said. "Logistically, I mean. I am because I am."

"Amelia," he said.

"Arthur."

"If heirs were not a necessity I wouldn't worry about it, but I also wouldn't be marrying you. And while there are many ways we could enjoy each other — or not, as you prefer — heirs are a necessity. I should really ask...is sex, that kind of sex, something that interests you?" he asked hesitantly. "I just —"

"...should stop talking?" Amelia offered.

"I just want to know anything that might make this easier for you. Or better. Or more enjoyable."

"Or you could keep talking." Amelia threw herself down onto one of his couches. If they were going to have this conversation, she would at least slouch for it.

The cushion dipped slightly as he perched carefully next to her.

"How would you like me to ask this question?" Arthur asked gently.

"Like we're equals," Amelia said, staring at one of Imogene's photographs instead of looking at Arthur. "Like I'm not some poor stunted girl you have to make sure doesn't panic because you need babies. Maybe you're a terrible lay.

Maybe you have freaky kinks. Maybe you can't get it up. I have no idea why you and Imogene never had children."

"We kept putting it off." Arthur's tone was perfectly easy, as if he had terrible conversations like this every day. Perhaps he was trying to be kind to himself as much as her. "Our lives had so many external interruptions. We wanted some time for just us, and we kept wanting it, until we didn't have it anymore."

"Oh." What else could Amelia say to that?

"So no, as far as I'm aware, I have no problems in that regard." There was a smirk in his voice now that made Amelia's cheeks burn again, but she wanted to laugh, too. How could he be so wonderful about driving her mad and putting her at her ease at the same time? Especially when he didn't even have feelings for her.

"All right," Amelia said, now willing to rise to the challenge. "Keep telling me about yourself. Because I — perhaps foolishly — wasn't planning on having this conversation tonight. But if we're going to, you might offer me something other than the vague sensation that I'm pathetic."

"Well," Arthur said blandly, although his cheek twitched and Amelia thought he was trying to hide a smile. The situation *was* funny, if mortifying. "Once I got tied to the bed with one of my ties."

The image that presented was so absurd Amelia laughed before she could stop herself. She clapped her hand over her mouth in horror.

"I'm sorry. I shouldn't laugh. I didn't mean —"

Arthur, though, was chuckling. "No, by all means." He leaned back against the other end of the sofa, one long arm stretched out across the back. "Whatever you're imagining, the reality was just as absurd."

Amelia let her hand fall from her mouth. Impolite as her outburst had been, the last of the awkwardness between them seemed to have been dispelled. That — combined with Arthur's easy, open, posture — made her feel bold again. Perhaps this time she could face the consequences of that.

"When did you lose your virginity?" she asked.

Arthur didn't blink at the question. "I was eighteen, maybe nineteen. It was my first year of university. With Imogene, if you can believe it."

"That's incredibly romantic and not at all a promising sign," Amelia said.

Arthur gave her a baffled look.

"Everything in the papers just been lies, hasn't it? You have no idea what you're doing."

Arthur rubbed his hands over his face. Amelia was glad there were aspects of this conversation that made him uncomfortable too.

"Imogene and I were together a long time. And yes, there have been lovers since. Not as many as the papers think but more than any of our parents would likely approve."

"Helen?" Amelia pulled absently on a loose thread from a pillow.

"Helen is a complicated case. Did she tell you?"

"No. She was lovely to me. Lady Olivia told me. Helen was suitably mortified."

Arthur frowned. "That certainly clarifies a number of my friendships."

"Why didn't you decide to marry one of them? Surely a real friend is preferable to a stranger."

"You're hardly a stranger anymore," Arthur said fondly.

Amelia felt her breath catch, but she forced herself to ignore it. "I was three months ago. Some of those women you've known for years."

Arthur reached out a hand and, when Amelia didn't pull away, traced his fingers along the lines of her palm. "Most of them didn't want it. Some of them aren't suited for it. The few that do and are — aren't the right fit for me. They know it, and I know it. You get to be a very good judge of people in a life like mine."

"So why me?" Amelia asked. She tried not to stare at their hands as he pushed his fingers through hers. There was something obscene about it and highly arousing.

"Why not you?" Arthur asked. "You keep showing up. You talk to me like I'm a person. Like you said, you get scared and you keep going. It's a very small thing, but it's also everything."

"Was it easier with Imogene?" Amelia realized with a jolt that she was quite possibly the only person in the country, maybe in the world, who could ask Arthur such terrible questions and expect to receive answers. But even if he weren't the Prince of Wales — even if they'd been the most ordinary of couples — she would still want to know. She wanted to know everything about him.

"Yes and no," Arthur replied after taking a moment to think. "We had more history. But it was like the military when I was a child. I knew what was coming for both of us. Mostly, it really was a long time ago. I do miss her, some days very badly. But that doesn't mean I can't move on or care for other people deeply as well."

Amelia smiled weakly. He was so politic. Perhaps, in time, she would learn from him. "I'm sure Charlie has told you, or the people you had look into my background and *eligibility*. Maybe my mother was kind enough to volunteer this information," she said. "But I had a boyfriend. A serious one, for what I thought was a long time."

Arthur nodded. While he almost certainly knew that Gary had existed, Amelia appreciated that he was letting her tell the story. "So it's not that I didn't have opportunities. And I did things. I'm not a complete innocent. But we tried, a few times, and it wasn't good at all and didn't exactly work." Amelia sighed. "He was a jerk about it and he dumped me right before Christmas. Because of that. I think. And then I met you."

"Sometimes that happens," Arthur said thoughtfully. "It could be that you weren't comfortable. Or a medical issue. That's quite common."

Amelia blinked at him. On one level, she was impressed that he knew something about the lives of women. On another, she was far from interested in having her own experiences mansplained to her. "I know. I even went to the doctor. But it's just..." she shrugged. "One of those things. Congrats on being the lucky winner." She trusted Arthur with many things, but she still worried he would be angry at her lack of full disclosure on this particular point.

"We'll figure it out when it's time to figure it out," Arthur said easily. "Thank you for telling me."

"I...you're welcome?" Amelia was relieved he wasn't angry, but she also hadn't expected him to be so easy and lovely.

Arthur laughed. He really was astonishingly handsome when he laughed; the fine wrinkles at the corner of his eyes deepened, his teeth showed, and something almost carefree suffused his face. Amelia wanted to imagine a life where she could always make Arthur laugh like that, but it was too unlikely. She had a job here, and it was not to make him fall in love with her. Over time he would necessarily ignore her in favor of other interests and duties. The prospect of her own heartbreak, if she got too attached to his smile, was something she would have to come to terms with.

"So," Amelia said, ready to turn the conversation — and her thoughts — to other subjects. "You got tied to the bed with one of your neckties?"

Amelia smiled when Arthur laughed again. "I'm rather sure you don't want the details of that."

"Probably not. But making you squirm is entertaining."

Arthur narrowed his eyes at her. "Charlie warned me I might be getting in over my head with you."

"I have two older brothers. I'm not completely helpless." She said it to remind Arthur as much as herself.

"No," Arthur said, his smile fading. "No you are not." He leaned down, his arm braced on the back of the couch, and kissed her.

Amelia was glad her earlier confession hadn't made him retreat. For a moment they stayed there, eyes closed, breathing softly. Arthur's lips were gentle and warm. She could hear the rustle of his suit jacket as he brought his other hand up to cup her cheek.

"You feel like the movies," she whispered.

He deepened the kiss, sliding the hand on her cheek up into her hair, surely destroying whatever was left of her curls from this morning. She sighed in the quiet, and he took the opportunity presented, touching his tongue to hers tentatively before his grip tightened in her hair and the kiss turned forceful.

She slid a hand under his jacket, eager to feel the muscles of his shoulders shift as they kissed. With an astonishingly clever movement and without breaking the kiss, Arthur took the hint and shrugged off the jacket.

Then he wrapped an arm around her waist and scooped her upright. Amelia fell against his chest and curled her hands in his shirt. The warmth of his body bled through the fabric. She wanted more of it and knew this was her time to take the initiative.

She swung a knee over his legs to straddle his lap. She realized too late that the position made her dress ride up her thighs more than she intended, but she was here now and could feel Arthur's hardness pressed against her.

His pupils were so wide, his eyes were nearly black. Color was high on his cheekbones.

"Are you all right?" Arthur asked. His voice was breathless.

She gaped at him. "How do I *look*?" She shifted her hips against him to make her point.

He gave a breathless, gasping, chuckle. He lifted a hand and ran it through her hair, his fingertips lingering on the side of her neck. "I want to hear you say it."

"I'm perfect," she said, and it was true. "With you, I'm perfect."

Chapter 13

PINING FOR HER PRINCE

24 March
Year 21 of King Henry XII

*I didn't go to bed with Arthur. I think I could have, if I'd wanted to.
I did want to. But he's too much a gentleman and while I was bold, I
wasn't bold enough. Despite that, it felt like it would have been easy, and
I'm not sure I can trust anything in this process that feels that way.*

*At some future date — I don't even know when the wedding will be!
— I'll go back to being a princess living in a palace. But for now, I've
been released on my own recognizance. God, it's good to be home in my
own flat, with my own bed, and no staff about constantly. Except, of
course, for the security desk the Palace set up outside in the hall.*

❦

"I still can't believe you didn't tell me," Priya complained.

She and Amelia were in the tiny sitting room of their flat,
wearing pajamas, and curled up under a fuzzy blanket Priya had

dragged out from her room. It might have been nearly April, but the nights were still cold.

"I thought about it," Amelia said. "But I couldn't tell anyone. I'm honestly surprised Arthur didn't take my mobile when he gave me the rings."

"Okay." Priya flapped her hand and reached toward their coffee table to pour herself more vodka. "Time for terrible questions."

"I am afraid," Amelia said, holding out her own glass for Priya to refill.

"Drink more!" Priya insisted.

"I'm drinking, I'm drinking!"

Priya tucked her legs more snugly under herself. "Question number one, have you banged him yet?"

Amelia put her hands over her face and moaned. Since she was still holding her glass as she did so, her drink sloshed onto her lap. She swore.

"See, I don't know if that's a yes or a no," Priya said.

"Nooooo," Amelia moaned.

"Amelia." Priya disapproved. "You spent a week with him and still didn't get into bed with him?"

"It wasn't a whole week," she said defensively.

"Do you not want to bang him?" Priya sounded concerned. "Because if you don't, that's okay, but maybe you should have considered a different career path?"

"Why is everyone so understanding and so infuriating?" Amelia was starting to notice a pattern. Everyone kept pretending both that she had choices she didn't and that she didn't have the choices she did.

"That sounds intriguing. You should tell me more about that."

"So last night, we…." Amelia wasn't sure how to put it.

"Fooled around?" Priya offered. "Did some heavy snogging?"

"What decade are you from? No. We kissed. Or. Well. We made out? I guess? For a long time. And, I was on his lap. And I could feel his —"

"— Dick? Prick? Cock?"

"Priya?"

"Yes?"

"You are the worst human being."

"I'm really not, but do go on. If you want advice, you've got to learn how to say these things."

"Fine," Amelia snapped. She was relieved to have someone to talk to, but also mortified. "He was either really big, or really hard, because oh my God," Amelia finished in a rush and downed her drink.

Priya refilled her glass. "Which one of those scenarios is supposed to be the problem again?"

"I don't even know what to do."

"Yes you do," Priya said. "It's not like you and Gary were celibate, and it's not like you hated it all. This also isn't one hundred percent your job."

Amelia sighed. "I know. You're right. But I'm twenty-two and incredibly inexperienced. He's thirty-nine and was married. And he's had a lot of affairs."

"Did he tell you how many?"

Amelia smiled with the memory of the conversation. "He said less than the papers had reported, but more than anyone's parents would approve of."

"Quite the diplomat you've snagged then," Priya observed.

"I should hope; he is going to be the King of England!" Amelia took a sip of her drink. "I made him promise not to sleep with anyone else. For now, at least. No pressure, or anything!"

Priya frowned.

"What's that face?"

"For someone who keeps saying she's scared and doesn't know what she's doing, that's awfully strategic of you."

"Wrong choice?" she asked, uncertain.

Priya shook her head. "Probably right choice. At least he'll be desperate."

"Wow, thank you for that staggering vote of confidence."

"I talk you up, and you're not going to believe me. Plus, every fairytale life needs realism, don't you think? You've signed up for a job, Amelia. No matter how fit your prince is. And since it's a job, yours is mostly to lie there."

"Not helping!"

"Then why are you doing this?" Priya set down her drink. "When it seems actually romantic, you get scared. When it seems like your dutiful destiny, you get scared. If there's no version of this mess you like, and you're too timid to talk about it, I don't understand."

"You and I talking about it now," Amelia said meekly.

"Barely."

"And he and I actually had a really nice conversation about it," she confessed. "Even if it made me blush scarlet. He told me he got tied up with one of his ties once."

Priya snapped her fingers and pointed at Amelia. "Now that is something we can work with."

Amelia gave a little shrug. "He didn't seem particularly enthused by the experience."

"No, but talking is the first step. And that he shared something silly and maybe even mildly embarrassing with you, that's good. He's not expecting you to be perfect. He doesn't seem like he's even expecting himself to be perfect. Now, being nervous about the next step is totally normal, but believe me, that is a feeling that passes once you actually do something."

Amelia narrowed her eyes.

"Look." Priya leaned forward earnestly. "I was really afraid of sex until I wasn't. Both the act and everyone's expectations of me regarding it. Boys, friends, my mother, aunties —"

"Always the dread aunties," Amelia said.

"You don't even know; I undersell it." Priya took a gulp of her drink. "But yes, sex is a big deal, but it's also totally not a big deal. Your prince is either going to deal with you as little as possible outside of getting you pregnant, or he's going to spend all the time in the world making his precious prize exactly what he needs her to be. Neither of those sound like terrible options. But I sort of hate you, because I wouldn't be able to stand either of them."

"Why not?"

Priya shrugged. "No internal sense of discipline? No tolerance for rules I don't personally see the point of? Who knows. Doesn't matter. Not my life."

"I'm sorry," Amelia said softly.

"Ugh, why?"

"I don't know." Amelia looked at her hands. "One day I'm going to be queen. It seems like a thing worth apologizing for."

"Well if you *must* apologize," Priya said, with a grin that told Amelia everything really was okay, at least between them. "Duchies are a nice way to say sorry."

Amelia did the only logical thing, which was to whack Priya with a throw pillow. "Enough about me. Tell me about Raveesh."

Which Priya did. In great detail and with a vulnerability Amelia knew she preferred not to display. As Priya related a conversation she and Raveesh had had about their futures — and about what their parents thought of their on-again off-again relationship — Amelia thought that maybe being physically intimate wasn't just a way to connect with Arthur. Common ground that she could still share with Priya, even when everything else in her life was changing, was incredibly appealing.

Much later, when they'd finished the bottle of Priya's no-longer-ex's vodka and retreated from the living room, Amelia lay on her back on Priya's bed, staring at the ceiling. After days of being surrounded by strangers and nights alone in a bed that wasn't hers, she craved the familiar company.

"The worst part," Amelia said quietly to the ceiling. "Was that I wanted more." Next to her, the blanket-covered lump that was her friend stirred questioningly.

"How is that a bad thing?" Priya mumbled sleepily.

"Because he was wonderful. And didn't treat my body like something he owns. Or that I owe him. Except, it's like you said. This is a job, and I wish it weren't."

If Amelia feared that Arthur would, once again, pull away from her now that she was out of his constant sight, she need not have. She woke the next morning to a text message. It was only a simple *good morning*, but it was an acknowledgement. She smiled in relief as she tidied the living room after last night's drinking.

"Hey!" Priya interrupted her train of thought, sticking her head out of the bathroom. "Can I try on your rings?"

"Um, sure?" Amelia said. "Just be careful. One of them was his great grandmother's."

"I'm already Lady Flip-flop. I'm not going to be Lady Loses the Royal Engagement Rings Down the Sink, too."

Amelia leaned against the doorframe of the bathroom as Priya fished the rings out of their little glass dish on the counter.

Priya made cooing noises over the rings and rightfully so. They were lovely when one could forget the weight of what they represented. Amelia was not, however, prepared for the sight of them on Priya's hand.

She wasn't jealous. Rather, Amelia was confused. Arthur had told her that one of the rings was for the realm and the other for her. But now, seeing the rings on Priya's hand, none of that felt real. Did these jewels really mean anything? Or were they just a prop, designed to make her something she wasn't at all suited to be. Amelia doubted she would ever truly be princess — or queen — any more than Priya was in this moment.

"Oi, er, Meels?" Priya said.

"Yeah?" Amelia jolted out of her reverie.

"I can't get them off."

"You're kidding."

Priya held out an already-red hand; the rings bit in around her knuckle. "I really wish I were."

Amelia was about to say something reasonable despite the creeping panic clawing up her throat when her mobile rang. She yelped.

"It's Arthur," Amelia hissed. She nearly dropped the mobile in the process of trying to answer it.

"I'm afraid you're going to be angry with me," Arthur said as soon as she answered and fumbled it to her ear.

"What? Why?" Amelia asked.

"What's he saying?" Priya asked, still tugging at the rings. Amelia waved a hand at her to be quiet. Priya leaned into Amelia's space to eavesdrop on the call.

"I'm leaving on a state trip," Arthur said. "Tomorrow," he added. He sounded apologetic.

"Oh. All right," Amelia said neutrally. Arthur was informing her of his plans; this was a step in the right direction. She put her hand over Priya's to stop her tugging at the rings; they'd get this solved as soon as she got Arthur off the phone. There was just one thing she needed to know first. "Where are you off to?"

Arthur cleared his throat awkwardly. "Australia."

"*Australia*?!" Amelia almost dropped her mobile again. Priya jumped back from the outburst.

"It is a member of the Commonwealth," Arthur said gently.

"He's going to Australia, and he's not taking you?" Priya hissed.

"Shhh!" Amelia flapped a hand at Priya while Arthur made indignant sounds about her shushing him. "No, sorry, not you, Arthur. How long will you be gone?" she asked.

"Six weeks."

"Six *weeks*?" Amelia fairly yelled.

"It's some distance, and there's a Commonwealth to be saved."

"We'll have time to get the rings off," Priya frantically whispered.

"Not the important thing!" Amelia whispered back. She returned her attention to the call. "And you didn't bother to tell me this before, because why?"

Arthur, Prince of Wales, Duke of Lancaster, and heir apparent to the throne of England, muttered something unintelligible.

"I'm sorry, I couldn't understand you," Amelia said crisply. "Say that again?"

"So you are angry with me."

Amelia turned away from Priya and stalked into her bedroom. "Please don't make this about my reaction to your behavior."

"I'm sorry," Arthur said contritely. "I just — want things to be all right with us."

"Before you leave for six weeks to the other side of the planet!"

"I'm a public figure, Amelia. With duties and obligations to the Crown. Whether I want them or not. You've had the opportunity to say no. I never did."

"I know. *But,*" Amelia said. How could he be so reasonable, so infuriating, and still sound so wounded, all at the same time? She wished he was standing in front of her right now, not on the other end of the line. "We were just starting to figure out how to do this...*thing* together." She couldn't bring herself to say *relationship* since it wasn't; there was no forgetting what Arthur had said to Charlie. "But now you're leaving. I don't know what you want from me, and I don't know where this leaves us. I don't know where this leaves *me*." Amelia winced. She had said too much and no doubt sounded needy in a way a prince did not need.

"You've every right to be upset," Arthur said. "I meant to tell you, I did. But everything happened so quickly — my father was ill, and I invited you to Gatcombe on a whim. I was going to tell you then, but then I proposed to you, also on a whim, which got very chaotic very quickly. And that's a terrible excuse, but I rarely know what I'll be doing seventy-two hours in advance. I know you're surprised I'm going to Australia but frankly, I'm surprised I'm going to Australia too."

"You forgot you're going to Australia?!"

"Yes?"

Amelia laughed; perhaps she was not the least competent person in this whole affair. "No wonder the Commonwealth is falling apart."

"I'm not going to tell them I forgot."

And there it was, that note of camaraderie, of shared amusement at everything difficult in their lives. Amelia clutched at it and pressed her mobile more tightly to her ear. "You're a dubious prince and a terrible boyfriend," she teased. The sentiment was true and safer than saying anything she really felt.

"I know. I'm a little out of practice. I really am sorry."

Amelia knew there was nothing for it; she would have to be brave. "I'll see you when you get back?"

"God, yes. Of course," he said with a vehemence that startled her.

"I'll count on it then," Amelia said, hope flaring in her breast. "Travel safely."

"I will. Good luck on your exams."

"Thank you."

There was a pause. What else was she supposed to say before she hung up? *Good bye? Good luck? I love you?* Those last three words would have felt natural, but Amelia feared the result would be her mortification.

Finally, before the silence became even more terribly awkward, she settled for a soft *goodbye* and clicked off.

Priya was in the living room, dressed now, the rings still on her hand and Googling on her laptop for ways to get them off.

"You have freaky tiny child hands," Priya declared. Apparently she wasn't going to ask anything further about the call with Arthur for which Amelia was grateful. She might need to talk about it at some point, but for now they had other things to attend to.

Arthur may have been going to Australia for six weeks, but her rings were stuck on Priya's hand. Neither of them could leave the flat while this condition persisted. Amelia wanted to cry, but that didn't mean she wasn't going to find a solution.

"I have an idea."

"Where are you going?" Priya demanded.

Amelia strode to the front door, unlatched it, and stuck her head out into the hall. Thankfully it was Edward, not one of the rotating night guards, who was there at the impromptu security desk.

He stood immediately. "Lady Amelia. Can I assist you?"

"Do you know how to get stuck rings off of hands?"

Edward didn't blink. "I can certainly do my best."

Amelia led him into the flat. He entered deferentially, not like a bodyguard who had a right to go anywhere Amelia did, but rather as a guest who had been invited. In the midst of her embarrassment and anxiety, Amelia appreciated it.

Priya was standing in the kitchen, wringing her hands.

"Good morning, Ms. Joshi," Edward said politely, taking in the situation with a glance.

"Hi, Edward."

He gestured to her hand. "May I?" he asked Priya. At her nod, he took her hand in his and examined it. "Ah yes. I wondered if this might happen." He sounded amused and nodded to the counter next to the sink. "Come on, up you get."

Priya obeyed. Henry draped his jacket over a kitchen chair, rolled his sleeves up neatly, then soaped Priya's hand.

"We can never tell anyone about this," Amelia fretted, doing her best not to hover. Edward's easiness did little to dispel her own worry.

"Are you kidding?" Priya kicked her heels against the counter happily. "I'm getting an amazing hand massage from a royal bodyguard. This is going *everywhere*. Truly excellent."

"Priyaaaaaaaa."

"I can assure you of my discretion, Lady Amelia," Edward said, though he and Priya exchanged a wink.

He gave the rings one last wiggle, and they slid off into his palm. "There we go," he said. "Crisis averted."

Chapter 14

PRINCE ARTHUR WINS AUSTRALIA'S HEART

26 March
Year 21 of the Reign of King Henry XII

I have a crush on my fiancé who doesn't love me. He is also the Prince of Wales and on a state trip to Australia.

Technically, this is a better situation to be in than the one where Gary dumped me and MIT rejected me. But those things still happened, and my comeback plan has downsides. The photographers camped outside — beyond the perimeter security is maintaining — aren't helping.

Arthur sends me a text or email every few days. Nothing earth-shattering or intimate, but he's staying in contact, and that's nice. He even sent me flowers. Rather, he called or emailed someone to send me flowers. I came home from lab to find them on the table. An entire vase of white roses, with one red one in the center. What it's a gesture of, I'm not sure. An acknowledgment of our scheme? This mutual destiny we've given each other? Perhaps it's a symbol of our friendship, an echo of my rings. Or, more darkly, a reminder of the way Lancaster always spoils everything.

Someday, if we both work at it, I think we could love each other, the way family does. Or the way friends do. But loving someone and being in love are two different things. He needs to feel more. And I need to feel less.

I also need to go visit his dead wife.

❁

As soon as Monday came, Amelia called Beatrice, the royal public relations head, to ask her several questions, and then she called the household office. This time, when she identified herself and asked for Mr. Jones, her royalty customer service representative was immediately put on the line.

"What can I do for you?" he asked, as sunny and competent as ever.

"I have a question." Amelia had dozens of questions. Hundreds perhaps, but right now there was only one she was worried about.

"I'll do my best to find an answer. What do you need to know?"

"Later this week I'll be traveling to Princess Imogene's grave. To pay my respects. I want to bring flowers to leave there, but I don't know what's —" Amelia flailed for the word. "Proper? Appropriate?"

Mr. Jones hesitated. "I can forward you to the G Branch office; they can coordinate a bouquet or a wreath for you to bring."

"No. I want to organize this myself. I'm not sure flowers mean very much if someone else does all the work. Please. I want it to be personal. Not just a photo op."

"I'm certainly happy to help you, but this is rather above my paygrade, and we do have people who are paid to do things like this."

Amelia wondered if she were asking too much or if Mr. Jones just wanted to make sure she got the best service possible. "I know, but I want it to be you. Everyone else scares me," she admitted with some degree of shame. What kind of princess was frightened of her own people?

"Hmm, all right, then. Roses are always a good choice. Although maybe not the best, given your circumstances."

He said it wryly, but Amelia couldn't help but be stuck on the notion of York as *circumstances*, as if the place of her birth was a dreadful condition. Though she did see Mr. Jones's point.

"Hardly appropriate for me to lay a wreath of white roses on my predecessor's grave," Amelia said, as if flowers could conquer the already dead.

"Quite. I recommend lilies. And if I can suggest, since you don't want us to handle them for you — get them somewhere busy enough that you're sure to be seen doing it. I know crowds probably aren't your favorite right now, but it'll make a lovely story."

The day Amelia and Arthur's sister, Princess Violet, went to Imogene's gravesite in one of the Crown's chauffeured cars was unseasonably warm and sunny. Outside, the landscape was beginning to bloom into spring. In her lap Amelia held a bouquet of lilies.

Amelia had been twelve when Imogene died, and she still remembered it clearly: From coming downstairs one morning to find the television on and her mother in tears, to attending the state funeral and watching the hearse make its slow, somber way through the streets. She remembered, too, Charlie's quiet, awful grief. He and Imogene had been friends before Imogene and Arthur had even begun dating.

Now Amelia was part of that sad, strange saga as well and in a way she could never have foreseen. Not when she was twelve and not even a few months ago. How quickly a life could change. A skiing accident. A bit of clumsiness at the races. A moment of errant bravery.

She and Violet didn't talk much in the car and not at all on the walk to the grave. They were flanked, as always, by Edward and by Violet's security. Amelia was grateful for the silence, even as she was aware that Violet was studying her.

Imogene's grave, alone on a quiet hilltop, was surrounded by a low stone wall with just one gate and a guard meant to keep out the more casual visitors. Violet didn't even glance at the guard, and Amelia tried to follow her lead. Ahead was a photographer, as had been arranged. For royalty, grief was as public an emotion as any other.

The grave itself was simple, just a white plinth carved with an inscription. As she laid the flowers she'd brought, Amelia thought of the woman she'd once known only in photographs and from television. Now, she had some slight sense of her from Arthur's words as well.

She hesitated before she pressed her fingertips to the stone engraved with Imogene's name and the verses a national poet had written for her. Even in the spring sunshine, the stone was cool. If Amelia had been religious she would have whispered some promise to the dead princess whose place she was taking, some lofty declaration of duty and devotion.

I'm sorry, she thought instead. *This life should have been yours. You may not have wanted it, but I never longed for it.*

❁

Back in the car, Violet turned to Amelia, deliberate in putting the somber mood behind them. "What kind of work do you want to do once you're married?"

Amelia wasn't expecting the question. "I thought princesses didn't work? It never occurred to me that would even be possible —"

"Charity work," Violet clarified. "Committees and such. To be honest, I'm surprised you haven't a charity you're involved with now, being an earl's daughter. Or is that not done in the north?"

Amelia stammered at the ignorance. Of course the north had charity! Without it her people went hungry. But she was a student and had always hoped to help in other ways.

Violet continued, cheerfully oblivious. "George does work, of course."

Amelia hazarded a guess. "With the swans?"

"And the ravens. She worries about them very much. And, as odd as it seems, rightfully so. They are our legacy."

Amelia decided not to mention the conversations she'd had with Arthur about the ravens. She was uncertain as to whether she was supposed to know of George's belief in herself as a witch or the fact that their most recent missing raven had turned up at a pub. Just because Violet was surely aware of her own daughter's strangeness — and the somewhat prosaic habits of the ravens — didn't mean it was polite to discuss.

"I'm an earl's youngest daughter," Amelia said. "And I'm in university, working on plate tectonics."

"Environmental causes are perfectly acceptable. We're not like the Americans; we know global warming's real."

Amelia stared. She knew women like Violet often did the work of CEOs and MBAs for free. But she had never imagined herself joining their number. Of course, it was logical. As princess and eventual queen, what else would she have to occupy her? She wondered if this were one of the topics covered in the binder she continued to refuse to read.

"Since the engagement's been announced," Violet went on as if Amelia were keeping up. "You really should put something together. You can't just be some student Arthur picked up — although, to be fair, of his many vices, youth's never been one." She sighed. "You're more than welcome to come to events with me, and I'm sure my mother would say the same."

"What causes do you support?" Amelia asked, glossing over *just*, *picked up*, and Arthur's *many vices*.

"All the family charities, of course, and the Lady Exeter talked me into some borzoi rescue group nonsense that has dog fashion shows."

"Dog...fashion...shows."

"Yes, there's a runway and everything. It's absurd. I also write a number of large checks to various domestic violence shelters. But I don't talk about those in public."

Amelia must have looked as startled as she felt, because Violet gave her a sly smile, not dissimilar to her brother's.

"This work can seem empty-headed. It's not. But no one wants a monarchy that makes them sad. Sometimes I can help with my presence. Sometimes I can help with my money. Sometimes neither is enough. And I suppose saving the borzois doesn't feel frivolous to the dogs."

"This must all be odd for you, too," Amelia said. "Arthur marrying again. When you were so close with Imogene."

Violet gave her a considering look. "From the moment Imogene died, we all knew he was going to have to remarry."

"If he didn't, you could be queen," Amelia blurted.

"Yes," Violet said with a serious nod. Amelia wondered how much trouble she was going to get in for being impertinent and possibly treasonous. "But I don't want to be queen."

"Why not? There's so much work you have to do, and you'll never be on the throne like Arthur."

"It can be difficult, being a royal child," Violet said. "Nothing about your life is normal, and it takes you years to realize how different you really are from other people. Not in any innate quality, but in what is expected of you. I had more freedom than Arthur when we were young, but only a little." She brushed a few strands of hair of her forehead. "Do you know how my parents made sure I wasn't jealous of him, of the titles he had and I would never? Of the crown that one day would be his?"

Amelia shook her head.

"They taught me that for me to be queen my brother would have to die."

"Oh," Amelia said quietly.

"Even when I was very little, I knew I didn't want that. This job demands sacrifices from all of us, but that was never one I was willing to make."

"I don't think many people would say a prince marrying a girl seventeen years his junior was making any particular sacrifice." Amelia tried for humor.

"We both think more highly of my brother than that." Violet smiled. "I know how difficult this life can be. I know the one you're going to have is not one I want for myself or that my daughters want for themselves. I also know Arthur doesn't want to inflict that life on anyone, much less someone he cares for. Why do you think he waited this long to remarry?"

❀

A week later, with Arthur still in Australia and her lectures very nearly over, Amelia met with Violet in her office at Kensington Palace, where she, Matthew, and the two young Princesses lived, to discuss charity work. Her offer of help was not one Amelia felt she could refuse. After drawing up a timetable of activities and engagements, Violet turned to the topic of attire. Which was apparently more important than anything Amelia would ever say at the meetings.

"The honeybee society," Violet announced, flipping through an elegant leather-bound notebook of the sort her entire family seemed to favor. "Lady Bowyer has a loathing of purple. And you mustn't wear a vibrant red before you turn fifty — at least half these women will be dead by then — and yellow is too on point."

"Because of the bees?" Amelia asked dubiously.

"Because of the bees," Violet echoed. She squinted at Amelia. "Must you really wear that necklace?"

Amelia frowned at her.

Violet held up a hand placatingly. "I'm only asking because Beatrice is going to make you take it off."

"She can try. I won't."

"It makes you look like a radical."

Amelia couldn't wait to tell Jo of the inadvertent compliment. "It's a piece of jewelry. And if I take it off, I'll look like a hostage. At least to York."

Violet smiled and tipped her head. "Point."

The next day Amelia — dressed in a light springtime blue — sat beside Violet at one of the six tables for eight at the Royal Society for the Protection of Bees. Which at least was somewhat relevant to Amelia's interest in science. On a low stage was a long table with three women at it. One of them had a gavel.

"They tried to make me the chair once, because of my position." Violet whispered to Amelia. "When that happens, and you don't wish to, you explain that you're here as an observer and to provide support but that your royal duties preclude you from being able to be as fully dedicated to the cause as you might like. Then you write another check."

Back in her room in her flat, Amelia pulled out her mobile and flopped on the bed. It was the middle of the night in Australia and Arthur was surely asleep, but she'd had been an aggravating day and wanted to reach out.

I don't know how your sister doesn't go mad, she texted Arthur. *Or anyone forced to sit through a bloody committee meeting on saving the bees.*

She was surprised when a reply came almost immediately. *Bees are very important.*

I know that. You know that. I don't need a committee meeting to tell me that.

Surely it wasn't that bad, Arthur replied.

She was eventually going to have to have a talk to him about minimizing her reactions to things. *There were sandwiches shaped like bees.*

After a moment, her mobile chimed again. *Where are you now?*

At home. Why?

May I call you?

Amelia stared at the mobile for a moment. Since his departure, they'd exchanged texts, but nothing more. Her traitorous heart leapt at the chance to hear his voice. *Yes, I suppose so.*

Her mobile rang almost immediately. She had to change Arthur's ringtone to something other than *God Save the King*.

"I didn't think you'd be awake," Amelia said by way of greeting.

"Between jet lag and my schedule, it'll be months before I'm back on a normal sleep cycle," Arthur replied, his voice warm in her ear. "But now, let's talk about the damned bees."

Amelia opened her mouth, then closed it again. "Before we get this conversation underway, you should probably do me the courtesy of reminding me that this call is recorded for posterity and we shouldn't be having phone sex," she said. Arthur's admonishment regarding sexting so many weeks ago still made her cheeks warm.

"Actually," Arthur said. "No."

"No?"

"No, these calls aren't recorded."

"Oh." Amelia's cheeks burned with mortification. She'd been joking about their distinctly non-private lives. Would Arthur now think she was coming on to him in a completely inappropriate and ill-timed manner?

But her prince went on like nothing remarkable had been said. "If you're interested, I can help you make some of what is expected of you less shallow and more genuinely compelling. I don't want you withering away to nothing."

"Sometimes if feels like nothing is exactly what I'm supposed to be," Amelia admitted with a bitterness she'd so far managed to keep out of her conversations with Violet.

"No. No, no, no, no, no," Arthur said firmly. "You are now my partner in this ridiculous venture. I want you to be as content as you can be. Which likely includes being proficient in charity work. My life — our life together — will be more pleasant if you're not miserable. Especially when I've contributed to your misery. I owe you. Let me help. I've more practice at this."

Amelia slumped back against her pillows. He wanted her to be happy, and he wanted to help make sure she was. That was kind — and she was grateful — but his very good points about why his concern had nothing to do with any possible feelings for her were not cheering. She decided to focus on her most immediate problems. "I'm staring down a month of exams, a summer full of wedding planning, and then a life I still can't fully imagine. I don't even know where to start."

"Amelia." There was a note of exasperation in Arthur's voice. "Someone else will be doing most of the wedding planning, and in a few months you will be one of the most powerful and influential women in the world, with more financial resources than even an earl's daughter could dream of. You can, almost literally, do anything you could want or imagine. What does this country need that you care about and that it doesn't have? Whatever it is, you can make that happen."

"Science education. For girls," she blurted. If she couldn't build her own career in the sciences — and that was a loss she was still learning to navigate; she hadn't even gotten a final acceptance or rejection from Santa Barbara — perhaps she could build someone's else's. Several someone's. Hundreds of someone's. And for girls in the north the opportunity — the wealth — such a program could bring would be huge.

"There you go," he said, and Amelia could hear the smile in his voice.

Chapter 15

THE PRINCE OF WALES STOLE MY GIRLFRIEND!

17 April
Year 21 of the Reign of King Henry XII

I got an email from Santa Barbara today. They've accepted me after all. Brilliant, useless timing, that. I wonder if they ultimately took me simply because they kept seeing my name in the news.

In any case, I accepted the offer with a deferred admission to next fall — not this coming one — just in case it turns out I need a backup plan. There's no harm in making sure I have options. I feel like I'm tempting fate to let my old life go quite yet.

In her first year at university, Amelia had been a frequent dinner guest at Charlie and Jo's house. She'd been homesick, no good at cooking, and uncomfortable living in a new city so far from her own people. As school got busier and she adjusted to life in the south, her visits had become less frequent. Thus, it was somewhat of a surprise when Charlie called and announced that Amelia was long overdue for a Sunday night dinner.

"Do I have to?" Amelia asked. It wasn't that she didn't want to see her brother, but quiet evenings at home with nowhere to go and no chance of being photographed were something she treasured.

"I'm pretty sure being engaged to Arthur means you sort of outrank me, so no."

"I don't have any rank except my own until the wedding." Amelia said. That was one of the things the Lord Chamberlain had made very clear to her.

"Then that means I still get to boss my baby sister around," Charlie said.

"I have to study."

"A three hour break won't kill you. Bring Priya too, if she wants. And do tell us how much security staff we'll be feeding."

"I'll let you know," Amelia said drily.

"Excellent. Eight o'clock?"

"I'll be there."

Which was how Amelia and Priya, escorted by Edward, arrived at Charlie and Jo's in a chauffeured car. Amelia braced herself for incessant curious questions about processes and plans and the circus that her life was now. But her brother simply asked her how school was going and Jo asked Priya about Raveesh.

When Meg asked if she could be a flower girl in the wedding, Jo changed the subject before Amelia could respond. Amelia was glad; wedding attendants had not yet crossed her official agenda, and she had no idea how much control she would be able to exert in that arena.

"Do you want to take a walk?" Charlie asked Amelia after dinner.

"Walk, yes. Be followed around your block, no."

"Fair enough. Garden then?"

"Please."

"Priya?" Charlie asked.

Priya shook her head. "Jo and I are going to have some girl talk that has nothing to do with royalty while you two bond."

Charlie and Jo's back garden was lovely in the spring twilight, even with Edward looming in the shadows. Charlie fetched drinks, and Amelia happily sprawled on a bench and looked up at the sky without a worry about being snapped in such an undignified position. The *Daily Observer* had questioned her femininity and propriety enough.

After a quarter of an hour spent in peaceful silence contemplating the emerging stars she had once looked at with Arthur, Amelia said, "I don't know how to talk about any of it, if that's what you're after."

"What I'm after is a quiet evening in my garden having drinks with my sister." Charlie grinned at her with a smile that reminded her of childhood. Charlie had been her dashing big brother then. Now, she was less impressed but she still felt safe with him.

"Everyone has opinions," Amelia said. "*Everyone.* I'm just trying to study enough so I don't fail my exams. Not that it matters, because I'm probably never going to school again, but I've worked too hard to let it all go now. I try not to get distracted by *it* or *him* but he's in Australia for six weeks, and I wasn't supposed to be this girl."

"Which girl is that?" Charlie asked.

"The one who pines after a boy."

"So call him," Charlie said, in the voice that meant he thought she was being ridiculous.

"He's the Prince of Wales. I text. He initiates calls."

"Be that as it may, that has not stopped you shouting at him before."

Amelia chuckled darkly, remembering the demands she had made of Arthur after paparazzi had caught her and Priya at the wine bar. "He told you about that?"

"He did. He was rather impressed."

"What did he say?" Amelia sat up a little.

Charlie held up his hands, his glass still in one of them. "Oh no."

"Charlieeeee," Amelia wheedled.

"No. Arthur's been my friend for a very long time. I'm happy to be his confidante. I'm happy to be your confidante, too. He can vent to me, and you can vent to me, but I am absolutely not sharing either of your confidences with the other."

"Is Arthur venting to you about me?"

"If you want to know what's in the man's mind, ask him yourself."

Amelia may have lamented not yet having the courage to take Charlie's advice, but it was just as well. The next time she spoke to her fiancé was at the Palace meeting to determine the date of their wedding.

At Buckingham Palace, Amelia sat at a table with a representative from Parliament, the head wedding planner, Arthur's social secretary, Beatrice, and the chief steward, as well as half a dozen other people she didn't know but also had pressing opinions to contribute on the matter. A conference room phone sat on the center of the table, the sleek technology at odds with the rich woods and velvets of the rest of the decor.

Arthur's voice crackled out of it. "Good morning, everyone."

"Your Highness," the wedding planner said.

"Is Lady Amelia there?" Arthur asked.

"I'm here." Amelia raised a hand even though Arthur couldn't see her.

"Good," he said. "Because it's four in the morning, my body thinks I'm in Hawaii, and I'm ready to come home. I don't want to suffer this alone." His tone was warm and fond, but he did sound exhausted.

Amelia wanted, suddenly, to be in bed with him. Not for sex, but to wrap herself around him and listen while he talked about his flight and dozed off from the jetlag. The fantasy was far from Amelia's current reality, but indulging it was preferable to focusing on the bureaucrats wrangling over the date.

The biggest consideration in determining the date of the royal wedding was tourism. September would be best, apparently, because that would allow sufficient preparation time. It would also still be warm enough for people to sleep outside along the carriage route the night before. As which particular date was most suitable was debated with little input from Arthur and none at all from her, Amelia wondered why she was in attendance. Wouldn't it be easier to forgo the illusion that she had a say in these sorts of state decisions?

After two hours, the assembled agreed on September 1. Amelia nodded because it seemed appropriate to. She had a wedding date, but she found it hard to care at all.

"Is that everything you need from me?" Arthur asked after the final decisions had been made.

"Yes, Your Highness," the wedding planner said.

"Good. I'm going to go back to sleep now. When are we announcing?"

"As soon as you're back in the country, sir."

"Of course. Need to give everyone a chance to plan their holidays around the big day." Arthur chuckled. "Amelia, are you still there?"

"Of course I am." Amelia noticed he didn't use her title this time. She counted it a small joy in a tedious day.

"I'll see you when I get back," he said warmly. "The rest of you, have a lovely day."

❁

As she waited for Arthur's return, Amelia stumbled through her double life as student and royal-to-be. Her first exam fell on a morning early in May, with the second following that afternoon. She considered going home between the two tests, but time was short, so Amelia detoured to the dining hall to eat. She had set down her bag at a table and was taking off her cardigan when she accidentally elbowed someone walking past.

"Oh, I am sorry." She looked round at whoever she'd banged into. She tried not to startle when she saw who it was "Oh. Hello. Gary."

"Amelia."

Amelia hadn't seen her ex from anything but a distance since their breakup just before Christmas. He was as good-looking as he'd ever been — medium height, a little lanky, with a sporty tan and brown hair that flopped into his eyes in a calculatedly careless way. Confronted with his continued existence she was overwhelmed with emotion: Anger at him for dumping her, nostalgia for when her life was a normal sort of disaster instead of a royal one, and terror at not knowing the right sort of small talk to make with him.

She turned back to the table and began digging through her bag as if looking for something. He didn't go away. She looked up and did the only thing she could. "How have you been?" she asked.

"Great. Getting cuckolded by the Prince of Wales has been exciting." His voice was louder than what was appropriate for normal conversation. Not that this was normal.

Amelia laughed nervously. Surely he was joking. "Gary."

"What? Are you embarrassed?"

Amelia glanced around and saw that they had begun to draw eyes — and ears — all over the hall. Some people had their mobiles out. Ready to film the excitement, probably. She felt ill. "I am embarrassed that you are making a scene."

"Hardly. You're the one who decided to make a social climbing spectacle of yourself," he said.

"I didn't seek these circumstances out." Amelia wondered if Gary had always been this awful. Surely he must have had redeeming qualities at some point.

"Really? You've always been ambitious, Meels. You saw an opportunity, and you took it."

"Don't call me that," Amelia snapped. "And what's wrong with opportunity? My very peculiar life started after we broke up. It has nothing to do with you, and I think we would have had to have been married for that word to apply." She couldn't bring herself to repeat it.

"You'd also have to be willing to do something other than suck cock."

Amelia would have laughed hysterically had it not been so awful. She drew herself up to her full height of five feet and almost three inches. "I'm going to walk away before I slap you."

"You wouldn't dare."

Amelia raised her eyebrows. Gary had just said the absolutely wrong words. On the heels of a number of other wrong words. She was almost disappointed when Edward appeared at her elbow and gripped it tightly.

"Can I be of assistance, ma'am?" His voice was a study in neutrality, but his eyes were fixed on Gary and threatened danger.

"No. No, we're just fine here, thank you, Edward." She put a hand on his arm as a giggle threatened to burst out of her. Edward really was here to protect other people from her; without his presence she definitely would have slapped Gary. "I know we're due back at Buckingham for more meetings soon. I'll be with you in a moment."

He released her and slipped away but maintained a far less discrete distance than before. Amelia was thankful.

"I think we're done here, Gary?" she smiled and shouldered her bag again before turning away.

"I guess I shouldn't be surprised by your thing for older men," he called after her.

She turned around, oddly delighted that he felt the need to continue the fight. "Pardon?"

"You were always a child," he clarified.

It was the perfect set-up, and Amelia beamed. "But unlike you, I grew up!"

❁

Edward followed her as she made her way outside. He stayed a respectful distance behind, as he always did, until she turned, grabbed his elbow as he had hers earlier, and drew him forward. "We don't need to go to the palace. I just wanted to be mean," she said, as if Edward weren't well aware of her schedule. "But I really do need a sandwich or something. Do you mind if we stop?"

He murmured something polite and agreeable and let her hold his arm as if they were out for a lunchtime stroll together. It wasn't until they were in line at a Pret that what had happened with Gary truly sunk in.

Amelia took a shuddering breath and barely resisted the urge to hide her face in Edward's chest.

Edward, because he was wonderful, curled a soft hand around hers on his arm. He said nothing until she had collected sandwiches for both of them and they were walking back to the university. Amelia still had to take an exam this afternoon.

"I think Gary broke up with me because I wouldn't let him fuck me," Amelia said, chagrined at herself for her language choices.

"Ah?" Edward asked, as if she had just commented that she thought it might rain tonight. Amelia wondered if being this calm in the face of emotional intransigence from one's charge was part of his training, or if that was just Edward.

"For twelve hours it felt like the end of the world, when he dumped me. And then I decided I was well rid of him. Until my mother lashed out about it at Christmas. Then I met Arthur." Amelia picked the crust off her sandwich. "This is going to be a mess, isn't it?"

"I'm afraid so."

She was going to have to make so many phone calls to head this off. *God*, what was Arthur going to do?

Back in the flat, Amelia dialed Beatrice's number and paced the kitchen floor as she waited for her to pick up.

"There's a situation you should be aware of," Amelia said when she answered crisply on the fifth ring. The woman was disconcertingly quiet as Amelia explained as succinctly as she could what had gone on in the dining hall. Amelia couldn't stop her voice from faltering uncertainly as she finished.

"This is not good, Lady Amelia," Beatrice said in a stunning declaration of the obvious. Amelia flinched as though she'd been scolded. "The press will love this, but you will not. Our media is going to twist Mr. Hendley's words and make them worse. You'll be blamed for all of it."

"Naturally," Amelia said wryly.

"You'll apologize, of course."

"I'll — what?"

"Apologize," Beatrice repeated, as if Amelia hadn't heard her. "For the scene caused. And for your indiscretions."

"There were no indiscretions." Amelia had done nothing wrong whatsoever. The outburst had been all Gary; he'd made the spectacle — and at her expense.

"There was a public discussion of sex acts, which is certainly unbecoming —"

"No."

"Excuse me?"

"No one, at any point, has so much as suggested that my engagement to His Royal Highness requires I be a virgin as pure as the driven snow."

"Surely you must —"

Amelia ran over Beatrice's words. If she'd been angry with Gary, it was nothing to the rage she felt now. "And even if I weren't at least one of those things, I would not apologize. A woman does not apologize when a man harasses her for having a relationship with someone who is not him."

"Lady Amelia —"

"A woman does not apologize for private activities that hurt no one and violate no promises. And no matter what the papers print tomorrow, I would be setting a terrible example if I did."

"Ma'am, it's my job to —"

"No. I have literally never said this in my life. But I outrank you. Even without my upcoming marriage. And short of an order from the King, Parliament, or my fiancé, your words are just advice. Come up with another plan." The speech came easily in her fury.

"You're not a princess yet," Beatrice said darkly.

"Was that a *threat?*"

"It's a statement of fact." Beatrice's voice was clipped. "Arthur's engagement is a matter of political expediency. The new princess is meant to strengthen the image of the Crown around the world, not create petty tabloid headlines."

"The Crown, including the current Prince of Wales, has a history of making plenty of petty tabloid headlines without my help. Good day, Beatrice."

Amelia's cheeks burned with anger as she hung up. Immediately she scrolled to Arthur's number in her mobile.

When he didn't pick up, Amelia slumped down at the table. He was either asleep, ignoring her, or already on a call with Beatrice.

"Hello, Arthur," she said to his voicemail as politely and calmly as she could. "When you get this, please give me a ring." She considered saying more, but wasn't sure she could remain calm enough to do so in the face of this ridiculous, awful, infuriating situation. "Hope your day is going well."

❁

Amelia's mobile rang with Arthur's ringtone at five that the afternoon.

"Amelia. Is now a good time to talk?" It was two in the morning in Australia, but Arthur sounded wide awake and sterner than she'd ever heard him. His tone made it clear that was less a question and more an instruction to make it a good time to talk. Amelia's heart sank.

"I've been waiting hours for you to call, I clearly have nothing but time."

"Up to and including time to get into a fight on YouTube."

"Yes, because I scheduled that, invited cameras, and oversaw the uploading," Amelia snapped. She hadn't expected Arthur to be thrilled. But she also hadn't foreseen having to fight him about this.

"Beatrice called me."

"I'm sure she did," Amelia said. "Right now I'm angrier at her than Gary."

"So she said."

"Did she say *why?*"

Arthur sighed. "I'm going to tell you what I told her. Which is that I'm not a referee and you're not a child. But I need you to trust her expertise."

"She told me to apologize!"

"You two did make a scene." Arthur tried to reason.

"No. I was trying to get lunch. He accosted —"

"He hardly accosted you, Amelia."

"*He accosted me*, cast aspersions on us, and aired my personal history with him. And Beatrice wants *me* to apologize?" Amelia kept her pitch low, restrained, and furious.

"It didn't make you look very likable."

"Arthur!"

"Yes?"

"Will you listen to yourself? Beatrice is asking me to make a public apology because a man I used to date, and who dumped me, approached me in public, yelled at me for moving on with my life, and then tried to slut-shame me for not having sexual intercourse with him. You never asked me if I was a virgin until after we were engaged —"

"I didn't care. In some ways, I'd rather you weren't."

"This is not the time to examine that." Amelia couldn't believe any of this was happening. "Beatrice is asking me to apologize for being a real girl. One who's too slutty to marry you and not enamored enough with men to keep every single one she's ever met happy. And then she threatened me! Regarding you...us."

"She didn't —"

"She did!" It was an effort to keep her voice restrained, but she managed. "I understand you just want this to go away. So do I. But if the reason she wants me to apologize is that I'm supposed to be a role model, apologizing is the worst thing I could do. And I won't. Women shouldn't have to apologize when men treat them badly. Or when their perfectly reasonable private lives are made public because people are malicious, puritanical busybodies."

For a long moment Arthur was silent. "I don't know if I've mentioned this before, but you really do give magnificent speeches."

Amelia smiled in spite of herself and was glad he couldn't see it. A compliment would not deter her. "Do I have to apologize or not?"

"No," Arthur sighed down the line. "You don't have to apologize. I'll speak with Beatrice. Although I do owe *you* an apology. I'm sorry."

"I didn't do anything wrong," she repeated. Needing, against all good judgement, not just his acquiescence, but his support.

"Well," he said, trying to lighten the mood. "Other than saying yes to me, probably not."

Chapter 16

PRINCESS PRIMPS AT PRIVATE RETREAT WITH QUEEN

1 May
Year 21 of the Reign of King Henry XII

I have no idea what Arthur said to Beatrice, but whatever it was, I think it worked. I haven't heard anything from her about apologies or anything regarding Gary at all.

The papers have been less lenient, and the internet has been a disaster. I finally had to block news sites and social media so I wouldn't see people talking about how terrible I was to Gary or how terrible I'll be for Arthur.

I've had a few defenders here and there — women who are as angry about having to apologize for existing as I am. But as glad as I am for them, reading anything about the incident makes me feel ill.

I'm trying to forget it happened. I'm trying to remember I have people on my side. And I'm trying to pretend there aren't more unintended consequences ahead.

Amelia slept in gloriously late the day after she finished exams. By the time she got out of bed, in the early afternoon, there was a knock at the flat door. The security detail must need something from her. As she answered it, Priya peered curiously over her shoulder.

On the other side of the door was not Edward, nor any other member of the security staff, but a young man dressed in the drab uniform of a palace messenger — navy blazer, regulation tie, and clunky shoes made for walking. The messenger bowed to Amelia, offered her a heavy white embossed envelope, nodded to the security guard, and departed.

"That's never not going to be weird," Priya said.

"He didn't even speak," Amelia agreed.

"What is it?" Priya tapped at the delivery with one perfectly manicured pale blue nail.

Amelia turned the envelope over in her hands. The royal crest was on the back, but who would be contacting her in this manner? Arthur was still in Australia. Violet would have called. Beatrice wouldn't use a messenger for anything less than a stack of binders Amelia didn't want to read.

Amelia slit the envelope open. The card that dropped out of it into her hands was almost identical to the one she had received inviting her to that first tea with Arthur and, later, to the garden party. This one, however, had not been issued on behalf of the Prince of Wales or the chief steward. It was from the Household Office on behalf of Queen Cecile. And it wasn't regarding a simple afternoon event. No, Amelia was being invited to spend three weeks at Sandringham.

Priya let out a low whistle and snatched the card out of Amelia's hands. "So I guess they're not kicking you out of the princess business?"

Amelia grabbed the invitation back. "Maybe it's a typo," she said doubtfully.

Priya walked into the kitchen and flipped the kettle on. "It's hand calligraphed. Those people don't make typos."

"They could."

"They don't. At what point are you going to stop thinking this is a dream you're going to wake up from?"

Amelia frowned and sat down at the table.

"Why the glum?" Priya asked. "Isn't this what you wanted?"

Priya was right. But from the first this entire experience had been a case of careful what you wish for. She knew it would add new and strange features to her life, but she hadn't understood all the ways in which it would interfere with all the things she loved best.

"It's three weeks, Priya. Three weeks! With the Queen of England! Who is a real person. Who I apparently know! Even though I am human disaster and a possible traitor and Arthur and I are…whatever we are. It's like I'm sitting an examination every minute of every day, but no one has told me what the questions are. I'm going to have to be on my best behavior the entire time."

"And this is why I don't like visiting my gran. What are you going to do?"

Amelia fidgeted desultorily with the edge of the card. "There's nothing I can do. Who says no to the Queen?" She looked up at Priya and the tea she was making. "I wish you could come with."

"So invite me."

"It's not like I've got a plus-one."

"You're an earl's daughter and engaged to the Prince of Wales. I'm fairly sure you can do whatever you want. They probably expect you to come with a retinue. You get ladies-in-waiting, right?"

"You are not my lady-in-waiting."

Priya made a dismissive noise. "Obviously. Twenty-first century and all that. But if you want me along for courage, you're going to have to have some courage yourself. Now call that royalty customer service whatsit of yours and get us sorted."

Two days later, Amelia and Priya climbed into one of the royal Bentleys to make the three hour drive up to the royal residence at Sandringham. Summer had finally arrived in England, which was quite the change from when Amelia had last taken this journey in a cold, uncertain spring. As they made their way out of London they rode with the windows down, their hair whipping toward the lush green fields that glowed in the warm sun.

As they laughed over the small luxuries of the royal car — sparkling water, fresh fruit, fancy jammie dodgers — Amelia couldn't help but worry. The invitation may have been a sign of her inexorable progress toward being Arthur's bride, but with Priya by her side, the journey away from London and the life she once thought she'd have seemed clearer than usual. But no one else seemed to understand.

Her parents, when she'd called to tell them her return to Kirkham House for the summer would be delayed, had been delighted. At least her mother had been. Her father had said as little about it as he had about anything else in this venture. Arthur's response to Amelia's email about the trip had been downright bland, which did nothing to lessen her sense of merely being a box to be checked.

Amelia and Priya straightened up as the car began the winding climb into Sandringham. Remembering the ravages the breeze had wrecked on their hair, Priya rolled up the window and repinned hers. Amelia tried to smooth her own into place as she adjusted her hat.

The car pulled to a stop. As the chauffeur hurried around the door and handed Amelia and then Priya out, a pair of footmen darted out of the house and to retrieve their belongings from the boot.

Amelia looked up from tugging her skirt straight to see Queen Cecile standing in the shade. She felt as if she'd been caught out, but she wasn't sure at what. She tugged at Priya's elbow. "Come on, we can't curtsey from here."

"Why not?" Priya hissed. "And why is she waiting for us?"

"Because we're her guests," Amelia hissed back. "Are you nervous?"

"Of course I'm nervous; she's the Queen. Doesn't she have anything better to do?"

"She's also a person," Amelia said, but Priya had a point, if not about Queen Cecile, then about the role she filled. The King was power. The Queen was all that was good and right and proper about a British woman. Amelia was fairly certain that neither she nor Priya lived up to that ideal. She'd never felt it more acutely. It must have shown on her face.

"Are you scared?" Priya asked.

"No," Amelia lied. Lately, she was scared of everything.

❧

Queen Cecile greeted them both warmly and interrupted their curtsies before they went too deep. She seemed unsurprised by Priya's presence and greeted her by name. Mr. Jones had saved her once again.

"Girls. It's so good to have you here. And Amelia, I am glad you've realized this journey you are on is not one to be undertaken alone."

Amelia bit her tongue. The knowledge was hardly new. Not when the whole of the kingdom cared about her every move and Priya had once had to defend her from the press with shoes.

"Thank you, Your Majesty, for being amenable."

The Queen waved a hand in a manner that reminded Amelia of her mother. "I believe we're scheduled to take tea together to go over the itinerary for your stay, but surely you want to see your rooms and freshen up first?"

❧

Despite her earlier visit to Sandringham, Amelia had not seen this part of the house. The apartments she and Priya had been assigned were luxuriously appointed with heavy, ancient furniture that bordered on the oppressive. Dark oak dominated the living and dining areas. The bedrooms, which had an adjoining door between them, seemed tiny under the command of ancient tester beds with heavy velvet canopies. Amelia had loved such beds as a child, the curtains keeping her from the prying eyes of the adult world, but now they struck her as claustrophobic. Like coffins.

Their luggage had already been brought up, and Amelia took a few minutes to unpack, hanging her clothes in a truly magnificent wardrobe. The windows by her dressing table were open, and the warm springtime breeze ruffled the curtains.

As Priya busied herself with her own preparations, Amelia went to the bathroom to check her makeup and fix her hair more thoroughly. When she emerged back into her bedroom, she shrieked.

Two minutes ago her bedroom had been empty. Now, it was full of birds. Pigeons to be precise. Perched on the tester canopy, pecking at her hat on the dressing table, striding about on the floor as if they were the masters of the house. One particularly plump specimen on the windowsill ruffled itself and cooed.

Priya barged in through the adjoining door. "What the bloody hell?"

Amelia gestured to the birds, which were too alarming to summon words for.

A frantic series of knocks came from the door leading out to the hall. "Lady Amelia?" came the voice of a worried footman. "Lady Amelia, are you in need of assistance?"

She knew the birds were not her fault — how could they be? — but she felt embarrassed nonetheless. She was like a magnet for bad, awkward, vaguely spooky misadventure.

"What do we do?" Priya asked.

Amelia made a wordless noise and flapped her hands at the invading birds. One, settling itself on her pillows, flapped back.

Priya grabbed a throw blanket off the back of a chair. "Shoo!" She waved it at the birds.

The birds remained unperturbed.

The knock came at the door again, louder. "Lady Amelia! Is everything well?"

"There are pigeons!" she shouted, having finally found her voice.

The door opened, and one of the footmen who had led them upstairs hurried in through the sitting room to her bedroom. He stopped at the sight before him.

"Ah. So there are. Pigeons."

Amelia clapped her hand over her mouth to keep from laughing at the absurd understatement. Her mobile chirped with an alert in her bag. She scurried to dig it out, if only because she could respond to a text; she could think of no response to an invasion of pigeons.

The message was from Arthur and included a picture. He was at some nature preserve, holding a koala. It was hard to say who looked more unimpressed: Arthur, or the koala.

Making great friends with the wildlife here, the accompanying text read.

What timing, Amelia texted back, and then snapped a picture of her bedroom at Sandringham covered with pigeons.

✿

Once the footmen had escorted Priya and Amelia to the safety of the hallway — and their belongings had been rescued — Queen Cecile herself led Priya and Amelia to their new rooms.

"I'm sorry the beginning of your stay here has been so disruptive," she said, ever serene, as she navigated through the hallways. "And I am sorry to have to move you from those rooms; they do offer the best view of the grounds."

"It's no problem, ma'am," Amelia said. Priya nodded fervent agreement.

Queen Cecile, however, continued with her explanations. "The groundskeeper was not willing to make any promises as to how long it would take to safely remove the birds. And then, of course, the rooms will need to be…cleaned," she finished delicately.

"Does this sort of thing happen often?" Amelia ventured to ask. "If I'd known, I wouldn't have opened the window."

The Queen shook her head. "No. Hardly ever, in fact. And when it does, it usually involves my granddaughter."

"Princess Hyacinth?" Amelia guessed. She could easily see the mischievous Princess conspiring to bring wildlife into the house.

Cecile shook her head. "No. Of course not. Hyacinth's a normal girl. I meant George. Our little court witch, obviously."

Amelia and Priya exchanged a look.

"Now, I want to apologize again for the rooms I must give you."

"I'm sure they're fine, ma'am," Priya said. "This is Sandringham after all."

The Queen fixed her with a keen eye, such that Priya shrank back against the wall.

"No, listen to me. These are the only rooms we could put together in such short notice. And they have a history."

"Murder?" Amelia blurted before she could think better of it. The birds had clearly shaken her self-control. Arthur might be used to her outbursts, but the Queen wasn't.

Cecile, though, smiled. "No. Not really."

The footman opened a door and flicked on the lights. The rooms were as beautiful, if not more so, than the set the pigeons had invaded. Heedless of any concerns related to birds, the Queen entered and pulled up the sash.

"Bosworth Field is two hours off that way," she said. "Some of the wounded straggled up by the lake before this house was even here. Periodically the land, or the groundskeepers, or the royal archaeologists turn something up."

"I'm London-born," Priya volunteered. "Makes no difference to me."

The Queen turned toward Amelia, clearly expecting a response.

"I'm quite used to living with my history," she said with as much magnanimity as she could muster. She was uncertain if the Queen were trying to be kind or cruel in mentioning the site of Richard III's defeat.

"I'm sure you are. But we've had many a guest — partial to all sorts of roses — complain that in these rooms they could hear the sounds of battle, wounded men and dying horses. I shouldn't want you to be so uncomfortable that you would prefer to sleep with the birds."

Eventually, their belongings were delivered, the Queen departed, and Amelia and Priya were left alone.

The light and breeze of the countryside filtered into the room as if nothing remarkable had occurred. But even through the vast windows the outside world seemed unreachable in the haze of peculiarity at hand. There was a creak as the house settled, and Priya grabbed her hand.

"Are you sorry you came?" Amelia asked. Everything that had happened since they'd arrived was some mix of embarrassing and frightening. Amelia felt desperately at fault for it, as if her northernness had summoned George's birds or the rumored ghosts of Richard's dying horses.

"Yes. No. I don't know." Priya shook her head. "I wouldn't have believed you if I'd not seen it with my own eyes." She slipped her hand out of Amelia's and sat down on a sofa. "You're the womb and I'm the womb's faithful servant. The house is full of birds. The Princess is a witch; the Queen is quite possibly mad; and a ghost army might be massing on the shores of that pathetic little lake out there. Meanwhile, your fiancé is gallivanting about with koalas, which definitely seems like best choices. But I get to go home in a week, and this — or places like it — will be home for you forever."

"Can I ask you something?"

"You hardly need my permission, *Lady Amelia.*"

"And you hardly need take that tone with me, *Lady Flip-flop.*"

Priya gave her a weak smile. "I don't actually like being called that, but what is it?"

"I'm sorry," Amelia said automatically. "If it had been you that met him at the races, and got sucked into this...."

"But it wouldn't have been, would it?" Priya pointed out. "I'm not a neat little package of political expedience, am I? No well-connected brother, either. So. "

"I wish you wouldn't —"

"This was going to be hard on our friendship eventually. Let's just acknowledge it and move on." Priya's voice was anything but conciliatory and fairly so.

"All right. Yes. It's horrible. But it shouldn't have been me either. And I need to know, if this had happened to you, what would you have done?"

For a long time Priya said nothing. "You won't like this, but I wouldn't have told anyone. And I would've said no."

"Why?" Amelia asked.

"Because if I won't let my family get involved in my personal life, why on earth would I let my country, and all its centuries of bad behavior, do so instead?"

The rest of the evening and next morning passed without further dramatic incident. In the early afternoon, as she and Priya were investigating books in the library, Amelia was informed by a footman that the Queen desired her presence.

She threw Priya a questioning look.

"Well go on then," Priya said. "It's not like you can say no."

"You'll be fine?"

"I'm a big girl. If I get lost or am subject to a pigeon attack, I'll yell."

Amelia followed the footman out of the library and through meandering corridors to a door that opened onto a study. There, amid light woods and furniture upholstered in cream and mauve, the Queen sat at a desk writing a letter. As soon as Amelia was ushered into the room, she set down her pen.

"Amelia. Thank you again for coming. I trust your rooms are comfortable?"

"Yes, ma'am. And I'm pleased to report the night passed with no ghost activity."

"I'm glad to hear it."

The Queen offered Amelia a seat at the low sofa under the big window, called for refreshments for the both of them, then sat down next to her. She kept up such a run of pleasantries and small talk until the tea came in that Amelia barely had to think of what to say at all. She was astoundingly grateful.

"Before we get started on anything else," the Queen said, holding a fine bone china cup and saucer in her pale, slender hands. "I wanted to say how much I admire you for the way you spoke to that young man. And the way you stood up for yourself to Ms. Slingsby. It was very brave of you, and all the girls of England need someone who will remind the world of their worth and the respect they are due."

Amelia nearly dropped the sugar spoon she'd just picked up. "Are you saying," she blurted before she could think better of it, "that you invited me to Sandringham for three weeks because I yelled at my ex-boyfriend and at the head of royal public relations?

Queen Cecile gave an enigmatic smile. "No. Bringing you here is a tradition of long standing. Imogene came, before she and Arthur married. I came in my turn, when I was engaged to our king. So have all the women who have married into the family since this place was built."

"Is this one of those things that gets mentioned in the princess binder?"

"Yes. In some detail."

"I haven't read it yet," Amelia confessed.

"I know." Cecile looked amused at Amelia's ignorance, but not upset. "But that manual can hardly teach you all you need to know. Which is where I — and these three weeks — come in. I know Princess Violet has been helping you figure out what sort of work you want to do after your marriage. But *Her Royal Highness* is not the last job title you will hold. Even my own daughter cannot help prepare you for the burden you will carry, when my son is crowned king."

"Three weeks is hardly long enough," Amelia said.

The Queen laughed with good grace. "That is true, and it is best you know it. But you are capable and determined. And if you are willing to work hard, I know you will be able to use any tools I can give you to the best advantage of yourself, your husband, and the kingdom."

❁

The Queen had a timetable prepared for Amelia and Priya both. Amelia's days were consumed with lessons about etiquette on the international stage, the management of royal residences, and the difficulties of raising children in the public eye. Priya, meanwhile, got to spend her days skeet shooting and playing garden croquet when she was able to avoid the clutches of the Queen's mistress of the robes, who was determined to involve Priya in any and all preliminary wedding preparations.

Each night, Amelia returned to their rooms with the books, journals, and letters Cecile suggested she read. They exposed less the practical lessons Amelia was struggling to learn and more the personal costs that came with the crown.

As she and Priya perused them, Amelia no longer wondered why her friend would have said no to Arthur's offer had their situations been reversed. The life she had signed up for would be luxurious yes, but worthy of much complaint; the surest way for her to receive no succor would be to vocalize any of it. Her comforts would be history, friends who would hopefully stay beside her despite her change in circumstance, and a spouse far more wedded to the nation than to his bride. Amelia couldn't help but note how the King was not present in these days, but on his own holiday at Balmoral Castle, four hundred miles away.

❁

"Think you'll survive on your own?" Priya asked.

Amelia stuffed a lemony iced cake in her mouth, heedless of the crumbs that dropped onto her pajamas. Priya would leave in the morning, but for now lay side-by-side with Amelia in her bed, as ladies-in-waiting once did to keep their mistresses warm. The pigeons had not found their new rooms, and the sounds of battle had not been heard, but Amelia still dreaded the prospect of being alone here. She imagined the work of this trip — and the circumstances of it — would only become more difficult without her friend by her side.

"Better than I would have been had I come alone. How's that?"

"It'll have to do," Priya said.

"It will, won't it?"

Priya rolled onto her side to face Amelia. "Will you promise me you'll leave if things get odd?"

"Things are odd now."

"More odd. Like, really, really odd."

Amelia promised. She couldn't blame Priya for worrying. Anything seemed possible here and not in a good way.

They didn't fall asleep until long after midnight. When they did, Amelia dreamed of a raven, huge and solitary, watching her.

The following afternoon, after one of the Crown's ubiquitous black Bentleys whisked Priya away down the drive, the Queen's chief lady-in-waiting announced that the King was due for dinner, and Amelia was expected to meet with him after.

❁

"Lady Amelia." The King held the door to his study open for her. He seemed as kind and as welcoming as he had upon their first meeting, and Amelia found herself returning his smile instinctively.

He waved her into the seat across from his desk and crossed the room to a sideboard where several decanters and bottles were perched. This room was about the same size as Cecile's study, but paneled in dark wood and furnished with heavy leather furniture. The contrast was striking, but each room seemed to suit its inhabitant perfectly.

"Drink?" the King asked. "Arthur tells me you're fond of scotch."

Amelia thought that was a rather unladylike thing for the King to know about her, although she was grateful for the thought of a drink. Why — and when — had they been discussing her drink preferences? "What else has Arthur told you about me?"

The King handed her a tumbler and retreated behind his desk to sink into well-worn leather. "Many, many things," he said. "All of them good. And I know my wife's spent a lot of time with you these last few days, teaching you about being a queen."

"Yes, sir. As much as such a thing can be taught." She considered confessing her fear of not being able to fill the role laid out for her, but decided against it. Doing so would only relieve her own discomfort temporarily and would benefit the King — and the country — in no way at all.

"Indeed." The King nodded and took a sip from his glass. "I'm afraid there's very little I can do for you, at least in the way Cecile can. I know all that she does and very little of how she manages any of it. My power in most things is of a much less practical nature. However there are some very practical things I can do for you, and we should talk about that."

Amelia took a sip of her own drink. The scotch was of a very good quality, and the silky burn of the alcohol helped ground her. "Like what, sir?" She could hardly ask the King to get to the point.

"What do you wish to be called, after your wedding?"

"I'm sorry?"

"Your name. I, as King and Fount of All Honours, can and will give you the titles you deserve, but in order to pick the right ones, I should know. What is it you would like to be called?"

Amelia stammered. She hadn't known there were options. "My family calls me Meels, but I imagine that's not what you mean."

The King smiled at her. "By default, upon your wedding, you will no longer be Meels. Or even Amelia. You'll be Arthur, Princess of Wales."

"That's...." Amelia tried to think of a polite way to put it. Slightly satisfying, if people saw how horrible it was. Otherwise, just plain horrible.

The King nodded in understanding of her unfinished sentence. "A statement of sorts, but one you may not wish to make. If you're amenable, I will invest you as a princess in your own right, and then you can use whatever name you choose. What is your full name?"

Amelia grimaced slightly. "Amelia Sarah Anne Proserpina Brockett."

"You have plenty of names to choose from. And we are always fond of Anne in this household. But, this assumes you don't wish to pick an entirely new one."

"I hate my name." Amelia admitted. "Not Amelia. But the rest of it. Sarah's fine. Anne is fine if I don't think about it too hard. But then my mother decided I needed to be named after Persephone, too."

"The girl from Greek mythology?"

"The one who fell in love with Hades and went to join him in the underworld. Yes."

"That's the polite version of the story," the King said.

Amelia looked him in the eye. "Yes. I know. But she was also strong and did what was necessary."

The King held her gaze for a long time. Amelia wondered what he was seeing there. "Perhaps your mother knew exactly what she was doing," he finally said.

"Your son is far kinder than Hades."

"This is true," the King admitted, but Amelia could hardly take it as a retreat.

"Are you saying Arthur is the god of death, then?" The conversation had turned too dark all because of a name Amelia had never liked, and she had no idea how to rescue it.

"No. I'm saying the life of the monarch exists apart from the world of the living."

The sky outside the windows was now fully dark, and there was only one light on in the room, a small green-shaded lamp that lent the King's face an almost sickly cast.

But then His Majesty shook his head and the effect vanished. Amelia blinked.

"Don't listen to me, what am I talking about?" the old man said. "Yes. I'll make you a princess on your wedding day. And you'll be invested with the standard family honors. You just have to decide what name. You have time, so think it over, but do let me know."

"Thank you, sir," Amelia said. At the King's nod, she stood, glad to leave the suddenly chilly room.

"Amelia," the King called to her as she reached the door.

"Sir?"

"You're marrying my son in three months. Do call me Henry."

Try as she might, Amelia could not relax that night. As far as she knew, there were no other humans occupying this wing, but the house seemed alive with their absence. She made herself comfortable in the sitting room — which felt desolate without Priya's things scattered about with her own — and tried to read a book.

Her distracted thoughts were interrupted by a knock at the door. Goosebumps broke out up and down Amelia's arms. It was nearly eleven, surely no one would approach her door this late in the evening. But the knock came again, louder, and the familiar voice of the one footmen called her name.

Amelia pulled her dressing gown tighter around herself and opened the door. "Yes?"

The footman inclined his head. "I'm sorry to disturb you, ma'am, but Her Majesty has requested your presence."

"Of course," Amelia said tightly. She wondered what crisis had broken out for her to be summoned like this. "Let me get changed."

The footman led Amelia, fully dressed now in day clothes, through the corridors to a wing that housed the King and Queen's private apartments. He knocked on the door and opened it at a summons from within. The Queen, still in her clothes from dinner, lingered by a fireplace in a sitting room. Amelia was glad she'd bothered to redo her hair.

"Thank you," the Queen said quietly. The footman withdrew, shutting the door behind himself.

The Queen turned to Amelia, who was trying and failing to hide her unease. "And thank you, Lady Amelia, for coming to me so late at night. I hope I did not wake you?"

Amelia shook her head "No. I hadn't gone to bed yet. I couldn't seem to want to sleep."

The Queen gave a sad-looking smile. "I'm not surprised. Even aside from the ghosts. The King told me of your conversation earlier today. The one about your name."

Amelia glanced around the room, but there was no sign of the monarch. "Oh."

"Will you sit down?" the Queen indicated a pair of armchairs. "I remember the conversation I had, with the queen — this king's mother — when I was going to marry Henry," she said as Amelia sat. "Of all the preparations I had been making to give up my old life it was that one that felt the most strange."

"I thought it was just me."

The Queen shook her head. "In this life you are never alone. No matter how much it may seem you are. That's part of what I've been trying to teach you. Even if you can never speak with them — in this lifetime, at least — there are women who have come before you, who have suffered all the indignities you will suffer. Many of them worse. I find it helps, sometimes, when things are very strange and I am very lonely, to remember them."

"How do you do it?" Amelia asked. They had come close to this issue, in their lessons and conversations, but had always retreated. Perhaps Cecile had only been waiting for this moment.

"Now, I'm quite happy," the Queen said. "I know it must be hard to believe, but it's true. After fifty years of this life, I can't imagine any other. You make friends, of a sort. You enjoy your occupations. You love your children. And, in time, your marriage finds its rhythms. Henry and I weren't a love match," she said.

"You can't tell," Amelia blurted.

"Yes. That's the point, which you'd do well to remember. But we were friends and fond enough of each other. When he asked for my hand I knew I would be a fool to say no, though

I feared — as you must for yourself and my son — what the future might hold. He did what he could to make me happy. I tried to lessen, if I could not share, the burden of his royal obligations. We adored our children. And I found, in time, that we loved each other. Not the passionate first love of youth, perhaps. But love that had grown out of our shared struggles and been strengthened by time. I do not think we have wound up anywhere much different than most couples do after so long a time."

Amelia looked the Queen in the eye in the same forceful and perhaps impertinent manner she had used with the King earlier. She may not have been made for patience and duty, but such was now the shape of her life. In time, perhaps she could learn to be grateful for the rewards that would eventually come of it.

CHAPTER 17

PALACE PARAMOURS REUNITED

22 May
Year 21 of the Reign of King Henry XII

I am learning there is a certain rhythm to the cloistered life of a member of the royal family. I cannot say that I am suited to it, as hypnotic as it may be to follow protocol and to act in a manner that is always mindful of history.

Arthur returns from Australia soon, and I feel a quiet, nervous anticipation at that fact. Does he expect this time here to have changed me? Because I am not certain it has. I am myself, always. Which seems not entirely suitable for a girl who will, one distant day, be queen.

The most delightful thing about Sandringham is also its most insidious. There is no such thing as a general public here. Papers arrive late. Televisions are few and far between. No wonder the north has been so mistreated. No one knows anything beyond these gates exist.

As the King departed once again the following week, Arthur arrived back in England. And so, at a dreadful morning hour, Amelia followed instructions and journeyed to the airfield at Sandhurst. She wore a cream-colored suit, a hat with a chocolate brown flower on it, and her rings.

No one from the royal family accompanied Amelia to meet Arthur's plane. It was only her — and the waiting crowd of functionaries who were apparently necessary to welcome the Prince of Wales back to English soil — that watched the dramatic sight of Arthur's plane land and taxi in.

She held her breath as stairs were rolled up to the plane and the door was finally opened. Amelia just wanted to be a girl welcoming her fiancé home. A girl whose fiancé happened to take chartered jets to countries that still recognized his father as their God-ordained king, but still.

Arthur, when he finally emerged from the jet, looked around as if startled to find himself on solid ground. After the twenty-six hour journey from Melbourne, Amelia could hardly blame him.

When he finally reached the bottom of the stairs and passed the various officials arrayed to greet him, he stopped in front of Amelia. He looked more exhausted in person than he had sounded over the phone last they spoke. Amelia had to suppress the urge to touch his face and soothe the lines of worry between his eyes.

He took her hands, and for a wild moment Amelia thought he might kiss her right here on the tarmac. Surely that would make excellent press after the debacle with Gary. But he dropped her hands and gathered her up in a hug.

Amelia closed her eyes and pressed her face to Arthur's chest. He was warm and smelled of stale airplane air and just the faintest whiff of his cologne. Amelia knew this was an entirely platonic gesture, but Arthur was holding her in his arms, trusting her. The intimacy of it took her breath away as Cecile's words echoed in her ears. Arthur might not love her now, but perhaps he would, someday.

❀

After the long drive back to Sandringham and luncheon with the Queen, Arthur invited Amelia to take a walk with him in the grounds.

"Don't you want to sleep off your jetlag?" Amelia asked, even though her heart leapt at the offer.

Arthur shook his head. "It's easier if I push through."

Arthur's dogs had arrived at the estate by car from London shortly after he had landed. Now they frisked joyfully around him as Arthur offered Amelia his arm and led the way outside.

"Have you enjoyed your time here so far?" he asked.

"Yes and no," Amelia admitted. "I've learned a lot, though." She wondered if she should bring up the pigeons. Or mention the battle ghosts. She decided against both.

"Then we'll call that a success. And now, for a brief matter of business — since I'm back home, the wedding preparations begin in earnest. Later this afternoon the designer for your wedding dresses will be here."

"Wedding dresses?" Amelia repeated.

"You'll need at least two," Arthur said.

"*Two?*"

"One for the ceremony. And another — at least one, maybe more — for the receptions."

"Oh." The excess was absurd. But Amelia supposed she should have expected it.

"For more details, you'll have to ask the designer. Or my mother."

"Oh, I will. Do you have to wear multiple suits?"

Arthur shook his head. "Uniforms." Of course; he'd served in the military. "But, effectively, yes. To be honest it's nice to be able to change as the day goes on. Things get sweaty."

It was absurd and funny, and Amelia was glad to be back by his side. They walked on mostly in silence, following the path that led through the formal gardens down to the woods. Arthur threw a stick for the dogs to chase. While Io and Ganymede ran off after it, Callisto stuck to Amelia's side.

"I think you've stolen the affections of my dog," Arthur said, amused.

"Her affections are her own," Amelia said tartly. "She can give them wherever she wants."

"True enough. But in that case, she's given her heart rather firmly to you."

"She just missed you," Amelia said, as they came upon a moss-covered stone folly. Grecian-style columns in a circle, three meters across, supported a domed roof that dripped ivy.

Arthur led the way up the steps. "And you? Did you miss me?" he asked.

Amelia stared at him. "What kind of a question is that?"

"An honest one," Arthur said. There were stone benches inside, but he didn't sit. "You had a hell of a time on your own while I was gone, with your ex. You might fairly blame me for it and want nothing more to do with me."

Seeing Arthur unsure of himself was somewhat a new experience "If I didn't want anything more to do with you," Amelia said, a bit archly, "I would have let you know."

"I suppose you would have." Arthur chuckled. "So you did miss me?"

Somewhere in the distance, a bird trilled with pleasure. The shadows on Arthur's face were green in the light filtered in through the ivy. His eyes glittered at her. She realized he was now standing very close to her. He hadn't often shown her this much affection.

"More than I thought possible," she confessed.

"Me too," Arthur said. "I don't want to go so far without you again." And then he kissed her.

Making out with the Prince of Wales in a garden folly on the Sandringham Estate was yet another new experience for Amelia. And not a bad one. Arthur pushed her back up against the cool stone of one of the pillars. He cradled the back of her head with one hand and gripped her waist tightly with the other. Amelia whimpered into his mouth and wondered whether they would finally go to bed together tonight.

One of the dogs barked sharply.

Arthur broke the kiss and stepped back hastily, his eyes wide. "I'm sorry," he whispered.

"I'm not," Amelia shot back. "But someone might come." She levered herself up off the column. "How's my makeup?"

Arthur lifted a hand and wiped what Amelia assumed was a smear of lipstick from the corner of her mouth. "There. Now you're perfect."

❁

When Arthur had mentioned meetings with the dress designer, Amelia had not realized that she would be sitting across a table at Sandringham house with the head of a very chic, very famous fashion house. He greeted her warmly as though he met with royalty all the time — which perhaps he did — and unpacked a thick folio of sketches, photos and fabric swatches.

"Sorry I'm late," Arthur said, opening the door without knocking and then closing it again behind himself. The designer stood and bowed to him, which Arthur acknowledged with a nod before sliding into the seat next to Amelia.

"Are you even supposed to be here?" Amelia asked him, surprised. When they'd parted at the edge of the garden she hadn't expected to see him until dinner.

"Yes, I'm afraid. I won't see the final dress before the big day, but," Arthur tipped his head toward the growing pool of pictures on the table, "protocol demands some sort of involvement from me. Mostly so that if anyone tries to make a fuss about the suitability of the dress, they can holler at me and not you."

"Is that likely to happen?" Amelia asked with a frown.

Arthur didn't answer. He nodded to the sketches instead. "Take a look."

Amelia, with a glance for permission at the designer, took the one closest to her and spun it around to look at it. And then she looked at Arthur.

"Did you know about this?" she asked faintly.

"I had a few ideas. But I'm not the creative genius in this room, no."

Amelia looked at the drawing in her hands and then at the others scattered across the table. Arthur wasn't any sort of genius at all. The sketches showed dresses made of different materials, with different necklines and sleeve lengths and silhouettes, but on all of them, on the bodice or the skirt or the sleeves or the train, were roses: white…and red.

"Can you even put color on a royal wedding dress?" Amelia asked, to mask her reaction, which was horror. To marry Prince Arthur, to stand in Westminster Cathedral and give up her name and her old identity — she was prepared for that. As prepared as anyone could be. But she didn't think she could do it in a white gown dripping with red.

"Long story short, yes," Arthur said. "I was worried it might be a bit too on the nose with the symbolism, but I think all of these have tremendous potential."

"You've seen these before?" Amelia asked, not sure if she should be affronted.

"There were a lot of car rides in Australia," Arthur said. "It's a very spread out country. I had to do something."

"Did you think about the symbolism?" Amelia focused her attention on Arthur, not the designer. None of this was his fault; he'd just done as he'd been told.

"The symbolism of our two houses uniting?" Arthur asked mildly.

"Of me walking down the aisle in a dress that looks like it's covered in blood."

"I hardly think —"

"That's what this looks like!" Amelia exclaimed.

"If I may —" the designer began, desperate to intervene, but Arthur talked over him. "It's a wedding dress. With roses on it. White for York, and red for Lancaster. And also, red for love and passion and any of a half-dozen other things the color and the flower mean."

"It looks like I've been shot with arrows!" As far as Amelia was concerned this was worse than the pigeons and the ghost battle combined.

"Amelia," Arthur said, his voice stern. "If you don't like the idea, we can adjust it, but we are marrying to bring our houses and our people together. We can't do that if you pretend mine don't exist."

"Can I acknowledge your existence in a way that doesn't look like blood?"

"I suppose that depends what you think looks like blood."

"Perhaps," the designer broke in again, "we could remove the roses on the bodice and skirt. And limit them to the train." He pushed another sketch toward Amelia. "Something like this."

"So you can drag my roses through the dust?" Arthur asked in a mutter.

"They're *our* roses, or will be," Amelia snapped back. She looked at the sketch and then turned toward the designer. "Red roses on the train and perhaps a few on the veil?" She was not going to let Arthur have the final word on this point. "If," she said, turning to Arthur, "you come to York with me."

Arthur blinked. "I beg your pardon?"

"You heard me."

"If you wanted me to go to York with you, all you needed to do was ask."

"And all you needed to do was ask how I felt about red roses on my wedding dress and now here we are."

Arthur's eyes narrowed. "Yes."

"Yes, what?"

"Yes, I'll come to York with you. Even though I'm not convinced you have any idea what the consequences may be."

"Protests, abusive headlines, and scoldings by your ministers and my city council?" Amelia offered.

"More or less."

"Brilliant," she said. "Let's go. And I'll wear your roses." Internally, Amelia sighed. She and Arthur were definitely not going to bed together this night.

❁

To Amelia's disappointment, Arthur did not appear at the breakfast table the next morning. She had hoped for something that might pass for domesticity, at least while they were staying under the same roof. Their disagreement about the dresses had probably made that out of the question, however.

The Queen, who Amelia breakfasted with, made no mention of her son. She carried on as though nothing at all was amiss, talking with Amelia about the weather and the headlines in the morning's paper. Her calm presence was a reminder to Amelia that this — mornings alone over the breakfast table — was one more part of the life she had signed up for. She could be sad about it, or she could be interested in the weather and the news, too. She had to learn to be content with her own company, or at least without Arthur's.

Still, she couldn't help asking, as their plates were cleared away, "Do you know where I might find Arthur this morning?"

"He's out and about with his equerry, I believe," Cecile said. "Not to worry, though, you'll see him for dancing lessons."

"Dancing lessons? But I know how to dance," Amelia blurted.

"Of course," the Queen said. "This isn't a sign of our lack of faith in your ability. But everything does need to be perfect."

Amelia hadn't seen Arthur since their fight in front of the wedding dress designer yesterday. Faced with the prospect, she would rather not see him at all today than have to dance with him. Her emotions were still too high, too confused, to be that close. She wanted to spend time with him, but memories of Arthur kissing her in the folly hours before springing that monstrosity of a dress on her still made her cheeks burn with fury.

But she'd made her bargain and now here she was.

❁

Arthur was waiting for Amelia in the ballroom when she arrived. He wasn't wearing a jacket, a state of undress Amelia had almost never seen him in. Standing in a bright shaft of sunlight and dipping his head to talk to their dance instructor, he wore nothing more than trousers, a shirt and a waistcoat. He was devastatingly attractive, the very picture of a modern storybook prince.

"Lady Amelia." Arthur offered a polite nod of his head, but there was nothing of warmth in his tone and it made Amelia quail. Was he going to make her pay for her outburst yesterday? It was definitely within his power to do so, whether in the design of her dress or his agreement to come to York.

This was not the time to sort the matter out, however. At their teacher's instruction, Arthur wordlessly offered Amelia his hand. She took it just as wordlessly. If he wanted to pass the time in silence, she could match him.

As an earl's daughter, social dancing was a required skill for Amelia. Growing up she had taken ballroom dancing classes at her mother's insistence. Arthur was surely at least as well trained and likely in better practice. But they could not find their equilibrium. Not with any sort of waltz, and certainly not with anything more complex. Time and again their instructor made them stop and start again, with admonishments to think less and trust each other more.

Good advice, to be sure. And, in the moment, impossible to take. Yesterday's conversation about their houses had seen to that. How could she follow a man who had been made her enemy long before either of them had even been born?

"My father told me he asked you what name you want to use, as a princess," Arthur said, halfway into yet another failed attempt at a Viennese. Amelia had no desire to swoon in his arms on command.

"He did," she said cautiously. She wasn't sure where this was going, or what fresh demand Arthur might be about to make. She just knew she didn't want to deal with it while he was spinning her about the ballroom at Sandringham.

"What name do you want to use?" Arthur asked.

"Why do you want to know?"

"Because it will be your name. Your public one, at least. I'll have to know eventually. More importantly, since it matters to you, it matters to me."

If that was meant to be an apology, it was a paltry one. But Amelia had already embarrassed herself by shouting at the Prince of Wales in front of a fashion designer yesterday. She wasn't going to compound the issue by moving on to a dancing instructor.

"I don't know," she admitted. "I've never had to decide something like this before. No one's ever called me anything but Amelia."

"Which you may retain if you wish and if you so choose," Arthur said. "You could be Princess Anne or Sarah or anything else you wanted."

"Even Princess Arthur?" Amelia asked archly.

"Even Princess Arthur." To her surprise he smiled and squeezed her hand. "And no one could call you Amelia ever again without your permission." "

"You mean, no one but *you* could ever call me Amelia again," Amelia said. Arthur would always outrank her, and their lives would always be such where that would matter.

"Would that be so terrible?"

She flushed at the tone in his voice; he was too clever with it. Within her anger and a strange, almost intrusive, sense of intimacy warred. He was manipulating her now as surely as he had with their excursion to the folly before the disastrous dress meeting.

But he was also pointing out a truth. There was something erotic to the thought of her name as it stood now belonging only to the man that would be her husband. With that thought, they fell into to step. The dance worked, and the counts of their instructor faded into the distance, unnecessary.

She was charmed and dismayed and very much in danger of swooning until she remembered to think beyond Arthur. Without breaking step, she punched him in the arm, hard. "And your father and your mother! Yes, it would be terrible! And you just set me up."

Arthur laughed.

Amelia stopped and broke their embrace. "You're horrible," she said. "And just for that I shan't ever use Princess Arthur. Even though it was passive-aggressively tempting."

"You really are delightful when you're angry," he said.

"Yes, and you really are very patronizing!"

They smiled at each other like feral creatures. Arthur took a step toward her and extended his arms in the shape of the dance's embrace. A challenge. She stepped forward into his hands.

"You're much more appealing when you're asking for my consent than when you're being a bully about your royal status," she said.

"Would you believe me if I said it were mischief? Not everything I do is about what I am."

"Would you believe me if I said I didn't care?" Amelia asked. "I'm out of my element, Arthur. For better or worse, you are the only ally I have. I need you to act like one."

"You're right. I'm sorry." Arthur had the good grace to look abashed. "I'll do my best, but I do find the best ally is an adversary."

She would not take up the incredibly tedious argument Arthur was asking her to have. "Then you really will come to York? Like you said?" she asked instead, hating herself for how hopeful she sounded.

"Of course I will," Arthur said. "I keep my promises. Always. Especially the dangerous ones, very much including you and your precious York."

"Good." Amelia liked being thought of as dangerous. "Because I have a feeling there might be riots."

Chapter 18

A KING FOR EVERY COUNTRY...EVEN YORK

5 June
Year 21 of the Reign of King Henry XII

I survived princess camp! Despite pigeons and ghosts and my utterly intolerable and mercurial fiancé. I had thought that afterwards, I'd return to my flat and life would continue as normally as it could under the circumstances, but that was false optimism.

I've been moved into Buckingham Palace from now until my nuptials. While I'm here, I'm taking up a massive suite of rooms with footmen and ladies-in-waiting to attend any and all of my needs. To me that seems excessive, but I'm still creating less of a logistical headache than needing to be regularly transported across the city for meetings. Maybe it's because I've grown up seeing Buckingham on TV, but this palace feels less haunted than St. James's or Sandringham. I can't say that I mind.

I see Arthur every third or fourth day when he comes for meetings or meals. Occasionally he invites me to St. James's for same. Perhaps I am finally letting go of what we don't have and thinking about what we might. I'm trying at any rate.

Priya and I have given up our flat. We were planning to at the end of the summer anyway, but I still miss it. Priya has moved in with two of her other friends; they found a deal in Whitechapel and are now more fabulous than ever. I haven't been to visit yet. I wonder if the Palace will even allow it.

Planning a wedding, even a royal one, isn't a full-time endeavor — at least for me, the bride. But there is a veritable army of people working nearly around the clock to make sure everything goes perfectly in September. With my own copious free time I've begun preparing for our royal trip to York. The distance between us aside, Arthur has been true to his word.

❀

Amelia had taken the train between London and York more times than she could count. But she'd never done so in such pomp and style. The royal party had two entire carriages to itself. Arthur, Amelia, their staff and their security were more than comfortable for the express ride north.

Despite the lush accommodations, the mood in the royal cars was that of people bracing for a storm. Amelia didn't feel any more placid. She was excited to be going home for the first time in months, but the stakes were high, and there was much that could go awry. She would also be seeing her parents for the first time since the engagement announcement. She had no idea what to expect from them.

"Sir?" Vyvian, Arthur's valet who she'd first met at Gatcombe, appeared, interrupting her line of thought. He looked worried.

Arthur, in the seat next to Amelia, looked up from the brief he was reading. "What is it?"

"Sir," Vyvian said again. His gaze flickered to Amelia and then back to Arthur. "There's just been a message from the Tower. I'm afraid I have some bad news. About the ravens."

"Oh for heaven's sake," Arthur rolled his eyes. "Don't tell me one's gone missing again."

"I'm afraid one has."

"The Tower should just install a Yeoman warder down at that blasted pub those damn birds seem to like so much. It would save significant effort. And my niece a great deal of worry," Arthur said irritably.

"I'll let them know," Vyvian said drily.

"My life would be much easier if no one took all this myth and superstition seriously," Arthur said once his valet had left again. He spoke lightly, but his forehead was creased with worry.

"But if they didn't, then you'd have no reason to exist. Or marry me."

Arthur considered that. "Yes, there is that." He wrapped an arm around her shoulders and tugged her to him.

After a moment's surprised hesitation, Amelia went willingly, until her forehead nestled against his chest. That they both found the world they faced together strange was the sort of common ground that gave her hope. At least it did when they weren't shouting at each other.

"I think Beatrice is glaring," Amelia mumbled into Arthur's shirtfront.

"Beatrice is always glaring."

Amelia knew Arthur was right. Ever since the incident with Gary and the apology Amelia had refused to make, Beatrice hadn't been a fan of hers. She wasn't rude — Amelia's titles present and future protected her from that — but there was an iciness now that hadn't been present when they had first met.

❁

When the train began to slow Amelia stood to get a better view as they pulled into the station. Arthur's arm seemed to drop from her shoulders reluctantly, but perhaps Amelia was merely feeling the hope of being home.

The brakes squealed as the train came to a halt. Amelia turned to gather her things and found herself toe to toe with Arthur.

He smiled at her. "Are you nervous?"

"No," Amelia said. It was even true. She knew York and York knew her.

"Really? I am," Arthur confessed.

"Whyever so? You're the Prince of Wales." Amelia only half meant it as a tease, but his honesty and awareness of what York could bring might serve him well.

"You're their princess." Arthur nodded out at her city beyond the yellow brick of the station. "I'm just the Londoner who's marrying you. I think I'm allowed my nerves."

Amelia was struck with fondness. If Arthur could learn to love her, the way King Henry learned to love Cecile, her life would be good. On days like this it even felt possible.

She reached for the small enameled white rose pinned to the breast of her dress and unfastened it. Daringly, she reached up to Arthur to affix it to the lapel of his suit.

He looked at her questioningly.

"There, now they have to like you," she said. If he would make her wear red roses, then she would make him wear white.

❁

As she stepped off the train behind Arthur, she looked for the defaced poster about British unity she had seen after the races at Kempton last December, but it was gone. Instead, the station was festooned with white bunting. White tissue paper roses and Roman and Viking-style banners were draped incongruously next to each other. The timing of their visit may have coincided with the Yorkshire Heritage Days, but no such decorations had been present in previous years. With a shock, Amelia realized that they had been put up for *her*.

She and Arthur approached the welcoming committee side-by-side. A little girl greeted Amelia with a curtsy and a bouquet of white roses. Also welcoming Amelia back to her city were the Lord Mayor of York, her consort, the head of the York Archaeological Trust, and her parents.

Amelia knew enough protocol that she had no problem speaking with the Lord Mayor. But formally greeting her father and mother as if they were not blood relations was peculiar. They outranked her, of course, except for that little matter of her being engaged to the Prince of Wales. Her parents clearly didn't know what to make of the situation. Amelia was unnerved. She had never seen them at a loss for words before.

Before they could find their way to small talk, Amelia was shepherded out of the station and into a car with Arthur, the Lord Mayor, and the head of the Trust. Before the door was closed after them, the head of the Trust was already talking at full speed about a recently-begun archaeological dig near the walls which they were now en route to tour.

All statements about the significance of the dig were directed at Amelia. Except for surprised glances at the white rose pin, the other occupants of the car all but ignored Arthur's presence. The focal point of the research was a two-thousand-odd-year-old building from when York had been called Eboracum and a center of power and trade in the Roman world.

Amelia hoped Arthur was at least vaguely intrigued, but in truth she couldn't wait to talk all of this over with Jo. It was impossible to be from York and not take pride in its history.

Amelia smiled as the car passed under the bar at Monkgate and then turned into one of the little side streets that were so familiar to her. Amelia had come to love London, but York would always be home.

They parked on the side of the road near the dig. She and Arthur were led round the corner of a building toward what had formerly been a carpark and was now an excavation site. In heels as always, Amelia concentrated on carefully picking her way over broken pavement.

She was startled when they came in view of the wall and there was a great roar. At first, because of the sheer volume, Amelia thought something was terribly wrong. Had there been an explosion of some kind?

But the sound went on and on. Eventually Amelia realized she was hearing not cries of alarm, but joyful cheering. She looked up from the cracks below her feet and saw people — *thousands of people* — lining the walls above the dig; they crowded the balconies and windows of the surrounding buildings. Some were even perched in the trees.

Amelia turned her face up to look at the crowd. When she raised her hand to wave, the crowd roared again. These were the people she had grown up with from the great distance of Kirkham House. Now they were cheering for her return as something quite different than when she had left. For the first time in her life *breathtaking* was not an abstraction.

As she stared at her people silhouetted against the sky, something fluttered across her vision. Amelia turned her head to see a bird, huge and black, take off from a tree and circle the gathering from the air.

Amelia grabbed Arthur's arm. "Arthur, look," she hissed as she pointed.

But the Prince had already seen it. As they and the crowd watched, the raven let out an unearthly cry and wheeled away into the sky.

Beside her, Arthur stood frozen. Amelia felt sure she could feel his pulse beneath the fabric of his jacket, hammering like a rabbit.

"What have you done?" His voice was full of wonder. And maybe fear.

She looked around at the walls again, at the people and at the sky where the bird had faded from sight. "I don't know."

❁

The rest of the day was filled with events that served to emphasize how ecstatic York was about Amelia…and how little its misgivings about Arthur and his family had changed. No one mentioned the raven, but the bird was present in every pause and silence.

At luncheon Amelia addressed a group of schoolchildren. Arthur also gave a few words, but where Amelia was greeted with wild applause, Arthur was met with stony silence. No matter how ill that boded for everything she and Arthur must do in the times ahead, Amelia couldn't help but be charmed.

There was nothing so fierce as the hard frowns and tiny fists of Yorkish children who knew who their rulers were and weren't.

Back on the train that night Arthur paced back and forth the length of the car. He had every cause; York's reception of himself had been anything but royal. Or even cordial.

"Are you angry?" Amelia asked.

The rest of their staff had retreated to the other car, likely to strategize; only Edward, Vyvian, and Arthur's bodyguard were left. They sat by the door at the opposite end pretending not to listen.

Arthur stopped pacing and sat down heavily in the seat across the aisle from Amelia. "No. I'm not angry. I'm at a loss." He gave a weak sort of chuckle. "George is going to have a thousand questions about that bird. The whole country is. She'll have been beside herself with worry. Though I suppose she'll be impressed with it for getting that far north so quickly."

"They're sure it's the one from the Tower?" It was too strange; too fearful an omen to really believe. All day Amelia had almost wished it were an ordinary raven. Or better, just a crow.

But Arthur nodded. "I got word before we left. It was apprehended by a local falconer just outside the city. Its leg band confirms it. Definitely from the Tower."

Amelia knew better than to express a certain sense of satisfaction at a Yorkshire falconer being the one to capture the London bird. A smile must have twitched at the corner of her mouth, however.

"Today was quite the coup for you," Arthur said sharply before he sagged back against the seat, his broad hands splayed on his knees. He squinted at her, his eyes keen, his face softening. "They'll use that word in the papers, you know."

"They already are," Amelia said, handing Arthur her tablet. The London papers hadn't hesitated to imply Arthur was a traitor for following his northern princess to the wall. The Yorkish ones had flat out called Amelia the same for bringing him there. The crowd today may have loved her but the media — and the rest of Yorkshire — weren't as sure.

Arthur scrolled through the various headlines, then looked up at her. "Do you want to back out?"

"No." Amelia's voice was firm.

Arthur blinked at her.

"I can't go back. Not to what I was. My own parents greeted me like a stranger on the train platform of the city I was raised in. There's no returning from that. So I'm in this. With you. And we're in this together. Shared work. Shared struggles." Amelia believed in her words, but she also knew Henry and Cecile had never faced anything like this.

"I thought you might say that," Arthur quietly.

"And?"

Arthur stood from his seat across the aisle and dropped into the one next to Amelia. "It's what I hoped you were going to say. Ghost stories and birds and an angry populace — I can't do this alone either."

This time when he put an arm around her shoulders, Amelia didn't hesitate; she immediately curled into his embrace.

❁

Some time later Amelia was shaken awake. She opened her eyes groggily and mumbled unhappily at the brightness of the carriage lights.

It was Edward. "I'm sorry, ma'am." His voice quiet. "We've just reached London."

Amelia lifted her head from where she'd been leaning against the window. There was no sign of Arthur anywhere.

"Where is His Highness?"

"I'm afraid I don't know." Edward's face was lined with weariness and strain. He was northern; he knew how momentous and possibly disastrous the events of the day had been. "He went on ahead with his staff."

Amelia swallowed down the miserable lump in her stomach and reached to pick her mobile up from where it had slid onto the floor. It was then that she realized that there was something in her hand. As Edward moved away again, Amelia uncurled her fingers. There, in her palm, was the white rose pin she had fastened to Arthur's lapel.

Chapter 19

PALL CAST OVER ROYAL NUPTIALS

25 August
Year 21 of the Reign of King Henry XII

Since we've returned from York nothing has been quite right between Arthur and I. He can say he's not angry about what happened; he may even think he's telling the truth. But he's upset. Whether because he believes whatever George pronounced about me and the power of the north, or just because our mutual bargaining has opened up some very real political headaches, I don't know.

In any case, southern politicians are declaring the appearance of the raven as a sign of London's dominance over the North. York is divided between claiming it as a sign of true British unification and claiming the raven's capture by a Yorkish man as a sign of York's eternal independence from London. I and the whole country fear we're only a hair's breadth away from something terrible happening. All because of birds. It would be funny if it weren't so dire.

The wedding is two weeks away. Arthur's come to stay at Buckingham Palace until then. Now I live only a staircase and a short stretch of hallway away from him. And he's hardly touched me. Nothing more than a brief kiss in farewell after we eat a formal dinner together.

The outside world debates ravens; the Palace debates flower arrangements; and I debate with myself how many mistakes I've made.

❁

Five days before the wedding, Amelia attended another meeting of the Royal Society for the Protection of Bees. Beatrice and the head wedding planner surely would have preferred if Amelia had stayed at Buckingham to address a myriad of final details she had no real say in, but for a palace with so many rooms, Buckingham could be incredibly suffocating. And so, when Violet had more appointments in one day than she could attend by herself, Amelia was more than happy to go in her stead.

Today the Society was debating which bees should appear on their annual bee calendar. Some of the most spectacular specimens might appear frightening to some of the populace, while some of the most benign looking bees were less critical to the sustainable agriculture of the kingdom. Amelia tried not to appear irritated as the gathering of noble women debated the media readiness of at least a dozen bee species.

At the end of the afternoon she was in the hallway, chatting with one of the committee members about the emotional resonance of the Bombus muscorum and praying for a polite escape. Suddenly Edward appeared and drew her away from the conversation with a hand on her arm.

"Oh thank God," she said as he led her away at a pace faster than was comfortable. "I thought she'd never stop talking." Then she noticed that Edward's face was drawn, his eyes moving too quickly about them as they hurried down the hallway. "Edward? What's wrong? Is there a threat?"

"Lady Amelia, I am very sorry to be the one to bear such news." He spoke softly and without breaking his stride. "The King is dead."

Amelia went cold. She would have stopped in her tracks if Edward had not had a firm grip on her elbow. He was practically dragging her along the corridor.

"What?" she asked blankly. "I saw him at breakfast this morning. He was fine."

"The public will know in thirty minutes if we're lucky and in five if we're realistic. We need to get you back to the palace."

"Why?" Amelia asked. She wasn't even the King's daughter-in-law yet. She was, as far as a royal death was concerned, no one.

"For your safety." Edward gave her a sidelong look that made Amelia feel even colder. They were at the door now, and he stayed close to her side as they clattered down the steps to the waiting car.

"What do you mean?" Her voice was barely audible over the sound of their footsteps.

"There may be those who will blame a northern princess-to-be for the death of their king." He gave her a fleeting look of sympathy.

Amelia stared at him. All these months people had told her she maybe wasn't prepared for this. That she underestimated the burdens this life would place on her. Somehow, even with Edward at her side every day, even with the security desk that had been set up outside her old flat, even with everything that had happened in York, she had never quite realized that her life might be in danger.

"Oh."

Edward said nothing as he handed her into the car. What was there for him to say, anyway?

As they crawled through London's afternoon traffic, the church bells began to ring. First one and then another clanged until every church in the city was pealing mournfully for the dead King. The hair stood up on Amelia's arms.

She would not be getting married next week. And her fiancé was no longer the Prince of Wales. He was the King of England.

❀

There must have been a bustle going on somewhere at Buckingham Palace. But if there was, it was far from the main hallways as Amelia was whisked up the stairs and to Henry and Cecile's private living quarters. Amelia was too shocked to feel capable of tears. They would come surely — she'd been fond of the King — but for now she just felt overwhelmed.

She was announced with almost no reaction from the room's occupants. The rest of the family had come over from Kensington Palace. Matthew was on a sofa, with Violet on one side and a red-eyed Hyacinth on the other. George stood at the window looking out at the gardens below. Her face was not visible but her hands were clasped too tightly behind her back.

At the head of the room Arthur sat in a chair with his back to the window. His head was turned away from the door Amelia had entered through. His face, visible in profile, was pale and drawn. His gaze was somewhere very far away.

He only turned to look at Amelia when she entered his peripheral vision. She had spent the better part of a year working with him, loving him, and falling, foolishly, in love with him. Never had he seemed so remote.

"Your Majesty." Amelia dropped into a deep curtsy — deeper than she would have had he been standing. She reached for his hand such that she might swear him proper fealty.

Arthur all but tore his hand away from her. "Don't."

The family stared. Even George turned her head to watch.

Amelia recoiled as though struck. He was the King now, and she could hardly shout at him or demand to know what he was thinking. Not with his family here. Not with his father dead.

She straightened up and took a step back. Arthur turned his head away again. She looked around for an empty seat. The only furniture currently unoccupied was the chair next to Arthur and the sofa by the door, apart from the rest of the family.

So she sat on the sofa, clasped her hands in her lap, and waited. For what, she didn't know, but there was nothing to do until someone told her what to do next. All the princess camp in the world — with its pigeons and ghosts — could not have prepared her for this.

❀

People came and went: aides with food or a note for Arthur, always read, frowned at and not spoken of. At one point Hyacinth asked to be excused and was told no, not by her mother, but by George. Eventually one of the notes for Arthur was enough to pull him out of the room. Amelia couldn't help but wince at the urgency of his stride. She was used to a certain languor from Arthur, but as King, everything about him was a stranger to her.

Thirty minutes later a footman came for her. She was hurried through the halls to a meeting room. There, Arthur and various members of the royal staff sat at a long table.

"The wedding's going to be postponed," Arthur said as she walked in.

"Of course." She bobbed her head, although she was not sure whether in agreement or acquiescence. Either was a better option than pointing out that she'd figured out that piece of news hours ago.

"We'll hold the funeral that day, since everyone will already be here," the chief steward clarified. "The wedding will shift to the spring."

"How fortunate we are in catastrophe." Amelia wished someone would give her permission to sit down.

"Amelia," Arthur said. His tone was not quite scolding, although she felt sure he wanted it to be.

"Your Majesty?"

"The formal accession will take place tonight at eight o'clock. I'll be taking the name Gregory. What it is you feel so duty bound to express to the Crown can wait until then."

Arthur turned to one of his advisors and resumed some discussion that obviously had nothing to do with her. Amelia knew she had been dismissed. Another footman hurried her back to the rest of the royal family.

"Should I tell them?" she asked as they walked. "About the accession?"

"They've already been informed."

When Amelia returned to where the family was gathered, everyone looked at her.

"They told you about the wedding?" George, still at the window, asked.

"Yes."

"I'm sorry."

"It's hardly the worst news anyone has to deal with today."

"Royal weddings, like royal funerals, affect more lives than you might expect. Even if it's a wedding half the country doesn't want to happen." George gave a sad, cryptic smile. Amelia struggled to remember that this girl was years younger than her.

Not knowing what to say in reply, Amelia nodded and returned to her seat.

Eventually, Hyacinth came to sit beside her, tablet and a pair of earbuds in hand. "Did you want to watch it on the news?" she asked.

"Do you watch it on the news?" Amelia countered.

"I find it provides a valuable perspective." The young Princess offered an earbud, and Amelia took it with gratitude. The news was familiar in its way. Curled on a couch with Hyacinth, Amelia could almost ignore that her purpose in life was now largely to prevent this child from being second in line to the throne.

❁

Amelia was finally able to leave the room only to shower and change before the accession. A woman from H Branch did her hair and makeup, and Amelia didn't miss the extra time she spent dabbing concealer under her eyes. The clothes she was given to wear she had never seen before, and she wondered if they'd been purchased at the same time as her attire for the engagement announcement. The Palace was always prepared.

She stood, clad in black and very much in the background, while Arthur, in a somber dark suit, sat at a table in the middle of the room and signed the papers that acknowledged him as legally, officially, King. He didn't look at or talk to her before or after. Even the flutter of camera shutters and the light of flashbulbs seemed to fade in the somberness of the occasion.

George, who looked so regal as to be inhuman in a black dress and hat with a short veil covering half of her face, stopped Amelia in the hall afterward.

She glanced around, as if to make sure they could not be overheard, before she said, low and urgent, "You must swear fealty to him."

"I know. I would have. He stopped me," Amelia said. George had been there; she'd seen the whole thing.

"You must make him accept you. Both as his subject and as the woman who will be his queen. Especially after what happened in York. The raven…. If you don't kneel to him people will fear the return of ancient treachery and doubt my uncle's reign. It would be disastrous for you both. For all of us."

Even if Amelia had been less steeped in the history of the country than she was, she couldn't help but recognize the monarchy, especially upon the king's death — *long live the King* — as something ancient and primal. She knew this, not despite her own now-neglected training as a scientist, but because of it. George had always been an uncanny young woman, and in this moment, Amelia was terrified of her and her pronouncements.

"It would have been you," she said. "It still will be, if he doesn't marry me."

"Or if you don't produce an heir. Yes," the girl said gravely. She squeezed Amelia's hand with cold fingers and then left her alone in the corridor.

Amelia waited for Arthur to exit the room.

"Sir," she said when he finally appeared.

He looked at her distantly, as though she were just another member of his staff, someone in his way from one meeting to the next.

"I'm sorry." Amelia took a step closer to him and kept her voice low. There were any number of witnesses about, but it was Arthur who had refused to let her do this in private. Perhaps, it occurred to her now, to force this very moment and provide evidence of northern loyalty. Someone raised to power was maybe not always as kind as she oft liked to think. "Princess George told me I must. And she is not wrong."

She took his hand and bent to him. Arthur's fingers flexed, tense in her grasp, but he did not pull away.

"Long live the King," Amelia said and kissed his hand.

When she straightened, there was a flicker of something in Arthur's face that Amelia couldn't read.

"Lady Amelia." His voice was nearly a whisper.

Amelia thought he tightened his fingers around hers ever so slightly before she stepped back.

"We will speak of this later," Arthur said, and then he was gone.

Chapter 20

WEDDING JOY TURNS TO FUNERAL MOURNING

29 August
Year 1 of the Reign of King Gregory I

I was supposed to spend this week attending to last-minute wedding details. Instead, I'm dealing with last-minute funeral details.

I haven't seen Arthur in days, except in passing if I'm needed to be in the background when he appears in public. There was a whole day's worth of meetings about that. Half the staff finds the idea of a would-be Yorkish princess unseemly. Half the country is frightened and angry that the old King is dead. The other half is frightened of what's going to happen to them now that the political situation is more unstable than ever.

My heart is with the north, but I can't blame the south for their anger. The King was ill and they weren't told. Now the world they knew has been turned upside down. Parliament is demanding an investigation. Of what and who, I am not sure anyone knows.

The raven that flew to York was returned to the Tower weeks ago, but now all the ravens have been caged to keep them from escaping. Just in case.

❁

As was expected of them, Amelia's parents, along with the rest of the peerage, came down to London to express their appropriate public grief. Even Nick was going to join them at Westminster Abbey to pay his respects.

Only over the strenuous objections of the Palace was she allowed to meet them for dinner at Charlie and Jo's house the night before the public viewing. In the end she was only able to go because Arthur interceded on her behalf after she agreed that they would keep the drapes closed and avoid any boisterous activities that neighbors could comment on.

Conversation around the dinner table was stilted. It was plain her family wanted to discuss the immediate political situation plus what it meant for Amelia's future, but no one seemed to know how to bring it up. Edward was there as ever to protect her, but it was plain no one trusted him as he sat on alert by the front door. Amelia was miserable.

Eventually she dropped her fork with a loud clatter onto her plate. She wondered bitterly if the sound was too boisterous for the Palace. From the looks her family gave her, she felt sure it must be.

"Go on," she goaded. "Say it. Any of you. Whatever it is. That I don't know what I'm doing it or should quit while I'm ahead."

Nick looked up from where he'd been sawing his roast into bits, his eyes sparkling with interest. "Don't think you're ahead at all," he mumbled.

"Thank you," Amelia said with disgust. Was that really the most courage she was going to see from her family? "Anyone else?"

Charlie raised his hands in a placating gesture. Amelia turned on him.

"Don't you," she hissed. "Always so reasonable. Always so London with your crisp little vowels."

"Amelia," Lady Kirkham scolded her daughter.

"Mother," Amelia shot back in the same tone. "For the love of God and country won't one of you just ask me if I poisoned him already and get it over with!"

"All right, that's enough." Jo pushed back from the table and grabbed Amelia by the elbow to hoist her out of the chair. "The radicals are going to go have a chat in the kitchen. You lot try to be normal."

"She was at the bee charity." Edward's voice, calm, collected, and sad — and as northern as Amelia's own — came from his seat by the door.

Everyone turned to look at him.

"Our late king and Lady Amelia were very fond of each other. And she was at the bee charity that day. Things are plenty bad, Amelia, without you needing to make them worse."

"Oh my God." Amelia's mother stood and pressed her hand to her breast as if she might faint, the very picture of a horrified doyenne in a regency novel. "He's going to report your outburst to the Palace."

Nick snickered. Charlie remained frozen.

Amelia felt Jo's hand tighten on her arm, and wisely so; she'd never felt so furious at the woman who had mostly hired other people to raise her.

"I'll do no such thing." Edward also rose to his feet. "I was born and raised in Gunnerside, as northern and maybe as Roman as any of you. Amelia's my queen, and I serve her, maybe not in a palace of our choosing, but in one of hers."

"Well, that's the most treasonous thing anyone's said all day," Jo remarked before finally hauling Amelia off to the kitchen as she had promised.

Jo moved to the stove to start putting away leftovers. "Are you all right?"

"Not really," Amelia said. "I know no one expected this to happen. But now that it has, I didn't expect to feel this utterly alone."

"That's all well and good, but you can't go saying what you said —"

"I really was at the bee charity."

"Be that as it may." Jo set a pan in the sink with a clatter. "Trying to hurt yourself before Lancaster hurts you is just doing their dirty work for them. If you must lose your temper, you can't lose it like that."

"I know, I'm sorry," Amelia said. She'd let Jo down. And Edward too. She felt less bad about her sharp words for her brother — although she knew he was, like any of them, doing the best he could with an odd hand in strange times.

"Thank you," Jo said, "but it's not the apology any of us need. This is politics, Amelia, now more than ever. And you must be politic to survive it."

"I don't know how. They've done so much to try to teach me how to be a princess — and it's all been peculiar. Having a monarchy is at least half mad if it's like this —"

Jo interrupted her. "You do know I'm not really allergic to horses?"

"Pardon?" Amelia asked, startled by the non sequitur.

"You know how Charlie always attends the races and weekends at Gatcombe and all the other things we're expected at, and I never go?"

"Oh. Yes?"

"I'm not allergic to horses."

"I don't understand." Amelia frowned in confusion, unsure of what, if anything, this had to do with the maelstrom of royal mourning they'd all been caught in.

"What I'm allergic to," Jo said slowly, "is the south and their racist inbred faces. If I can keep my family alive and well and happy — despite what people think of me here — and still do everything I can for my home, you can stop acting like your grand scheme to give us a queen again is some terrible thing that's happened to you."

Amelia nodded slowly, more than a little ashamed.

"I'm not saying what you've chosen for yourself is easy or wrong. But you did choose, all on your own. Even if no one expected this turn of events quite so soon," Jo said. "You have an opportunity no other woman in your generation will have. Be sad if you need to. But you can't be afraid."

"I'm trying."

"Try harder. You carry all of us with you whether we like it or not."

❁

As Amelia readied herself quietly to depart her brother's house, Edward stood near, silent and watchful.

"You shouldn't have said what you said," Amelia told him quietly.

"And you shouldn't have said what you said. But the facts remain. You were at the bee charity, and you are who I serve."

Amelia nodded and took Edward's hands in hers. For the first time she understood perhaps why Arthur had refused to let her swear fealty to him the night his father died. There was a burden, a shock, to being presented with that sort of unearned love and service. Any sane person would refuse it, but to do so was — she knew too well — also unkind.

"I understand. Thank you. Shall we go to Westminster Abbey tonight then? It seems I have more courage for my duty than I knew."

❁

While she had first been informed that it would be acceptable for her to pay her respects to the dead King during the family-only hours on the first night of the lying in state, Amelia had discovered she was incapable of making herself go. No one in the royal family had truly invited her, and Arthur had not asked for her support. No one, she had reasoned, could call her usurper if she didn't claim to be family she wasn't yet.

But Amelia had put off this act for too long. Jo's words tonight — and Edward's — made that clear to her now. She must follow protocol, and invent it when it was absent, if she was to be seen as worthy for the task that now lay before her. It might not be enough — for her or Arthur or York or even the whole of the Unified Kingdom. But if she had been sincere in any of this, she had to try.

This late at night the public wasn't allowed inside the abbey, but the strange collective grief of the nation was not something that slept. Outside there was the loud murmur of black-dressed crowds and news trucks against the ambient rumble of the London night. Amelia watched from the car as two police officers drove off a souvenir seller with some violence.

Inside the abbey, time had paused. Candles flickered in the darkness as Henry's people gathered to pay him their respects. Standing vigil around the casket were four members of the royal family: Arthur; two royal cousins, and George. She was dressed in a smart black trouser suit, her hair pulled back severely. Her parade rest was as perfect as the others. Amelia wondered at George's strange freedoms. Who allowed her them? How had George bargained? And why?

Amelia slipped into a pew a few rows from the front. She would walk by the casket, bow her head, and offer some approximation of a prayer, but she wasn't about to do it while her fiancé was standing vigil. She glanced around the abbey, because looking at Arthur — *the King*, she reminded herself — was disconcerting; he felt so far away and not hers at all. But then, he never had been.

The abbey's columns soared to the ceiling, lost in darkness. It was not as large as the Minster in York, and it felt colder. Though perhaps that was just the dark. To Amelia's right, across the aisle and several pews closer to the front was Helen, Duchess of Water Eaton. Amelia was surprised to find her there. Though perhaps she shouldn't have been, considering the duchess's past relationship with Arthur.

Amelia couldn't help but admire her profile in much the same way she had always admired Arthur's. Helen was what a queen looked like, proud features and exceptional posture. This was not a woman who ever had to watch her feet when she descended a staircase. Amelia didn't understand how she could feel so different from Helen when she knew they must have been raised much the same. She also didn't understand why

Arthur hadn't chosen her. Her poise was effortless, and her accent and blood were London and the south through and through.

Maybe, Amelia thought almost viciously, *she couldn't have children.* But her sharpness wasn't meant for Helen, so much as herself, too convenient, too useful to be remembered in these terrible days. If anything, Helen was perhaps as much a victim of circumstance as herself.

After twenty minutes the guard changed. Four soldiers appeared to replace the four royals, and Arthur and his relatives vanished down the side aisle and through a door that closed silently behind them. With Arthur off the scene, now seemed the best moment for Amelia to pay her respects. But just as she was about to stand, he strode back out of the same door with George hot on his heels.

"I'm not going to argue with you about this over my father's dead body," he said. He spoke softly, but the space was nearly empty except for a dead man and his guards. His words carried. Amelia thought he sounded darkly amused, but that didn't change the degree to which he looked as if he was running away from George.

"Is it because you think I'm a girl or because you think I'm a child?" George said. She didn't sound like either. "Or is it because I'm a witch?"

"It's because all of this is already irregular enough." Arthur softened.

"I'm still the heir to the throne. After my mother."

"That's very nice, George. I'm still the King. Witchcraft isn't real —"

"They caged the ravens. To protect you. You know it is!"

Arthur let George's feelings about the supernatural pass without comment. "And your mother will have my head if I let you spend the night in a creepy old abbey standing guard over your grandfather's casket, so if you could please let it —"

"Arthur."

Amelia's head turned as Helen stood and called to him. He went easily, smiling through his general grief and his very specific frustration with George. George, for her part, rolled her eyes like the teenager she was and stormed back up the aisle, muttering about those that did not heed omens. Amelia watched as Arthur kissed each of Helen's cheeks in greeting and then leaned his face against hers. They weren't of a height, but they were much closer than he and Amelia.

After a long moment they broke apart and Arthur slipped down the aisle and through the side door again. Amelia, finally, stood to walk to the bier to pay her own respects. Henry had been a real man she had known and would miss in her own life, not just that of the country. But it was hard to remember the man who had been so kind and warm to her in the face of the almost unearthly majesty of the casket surrounded by candles and draped with his royal standard.

For the first time, Amelia fully understood what it would be like, to be a part of Britain's history in the way that she would. It wasn't just about absurd charity events or even the dangerous ongoing struggle between north and south. It was this — the cold, echoing abbey, the guard standing silent and mournful, the hymns that would be sung. Someday Arthur would lie here on a bier like this one, and someday Amelia would be laid to rest beside him. Because being a part of history meant to one day depart from it and let the next generation carry on.

She stood with her head bowed for a long time; she only became aware of how much time had passed when her body gave an involuntary shiver in the chill. She turned down the aisle, moving as quietly as she could in her heels. She was ready to leave this cold, dark place.

Before she reached the abbey doors, a shadowy figure stepped out from behind a pillar. Amelia nearly jumped out of her skin.

"I'm sorry, I didn't mean to startle you," Arthur's voice said as the shadow resolved itself into the shape of her fiancé.

"It's all right." Now was not the time for teasing, or pointing out that lurking in the dark was not a good way to keep from startling people.

"Thank you for coming," Arthur said. "I wasn't sure if you would."

Amelia, cold, unable to see very well in the shadows, and now spooked by the entire evening, wanted nothing more than to go to Arthur and let him wrap her up in his warm still-very-much-alive arms. But she had no idea how he would react — were Arthur and she allies struggling with this sudden turn of events or had the King's death put them at now insurmountable odds? Amelia didn't know, but she couldn't bear to be pushed away, not tonight.

"Of course I came." Her duty done, it was time to leave. "Goodnight," she said and slipped away from him through the doors to where her car was waiting to take her back to Buckingham.

❁

The funeral passed like a dream. A heavily scripted, organized, and well-documented dream. Instead of walking down the aisle at Westminster Abbey on her father's arm, Amelia walked beside Arthur, in black instead of white, holding no flowers and not touching him. Hymns were solemn instead of joyous, and of all the tears shed that day, in the abbey and across the country, none of them were happy.

Amelia expected to feel some sort of relief when it was all over. But after she and Arthur returned to Buckingham Palace, Arthur disappeared into his rooms. The now-Queen Mother Cecile retired into her solitude. George and Hyacinth went back to Kensington Palace with Matthew and Violet. And Amelia, for the first time in a week, was left entirely alone.

There was nothing to do: No meetings scheduled, no public appearances demanding her presence. She undressed slowly. Tonight was supposed to be her wedding night. As she laid aside her clothes she couldn't help but be painfully aware of her own flesh. Not as something inherently sexual, but as something inherently *alive*.

She went to bed naked, perhaps in deference to the night this now wasn't. But she couldn't sleep. The bed was too big, too cold, and too empty. After hours of tossing and turning she couldn't stand it anymore. She might not be able to escape her life and her choices, but she could at least escape her bedroom for a little while. What was a castle for if not haunting its halls?

She didn't bother to get fully dressed, throwing on a nightgown instead. No one would be up at this hour, and, if they were, they would hardly dare bother her. In the name of royal propriety, she pulled on a dressing gown on as well and stepped out into the hallway.

The palace was entirely different at night. By now Amelia had seen these corridors and galleries both bustling with people and empty, but now, after the events and emotion of the day, it felt like the moon. Cold, foreign, and remote, with silver light streaming in from the outside.

When she saw the figure standing by a window she almost turned back, but then the person turned at the sound of her footsteps. It was Arthur. Neither of them said anything, and for a long moment they just stood and looked at each other.

The King was dressed in the uniform trousers he'd worn at the funeral, though not his jacket. His shirt collar was unbuttoned and his cufflinks were missing. Amelia wrapped her arms around herself and wished she'd worn proper clothing.

"Are you cold?" Arthur asked.

"No, sir."

"I wish you wouldn't call me that," he said.

"I've hardly had a chance to call you anything at all." She took a cautious step toward him and, when he didn't retreat, another.

"I've been busy," Arthur said. He didn't sound weary as much as exhausted.

"What should I call you now? Gregory?"

He shook his head. "Arthur will do just fine. As it always has."

"All right."

"Do you know why my parents named me that?" he asked.

"I wouldn't presume to guess," Amelia said. She stopped barely a foot away from him.

Arthur gave her a ghost of a smile that came nowhere near to reaching his eyes. "Because I could never use it as a regnal name. Could you imagine an actual King Arthur? It's absurd."

"That seems an odd trick to pull on you." Amelia had no idea why they were talking about this, but it was the first time they'd spoken at any length since Henry died. She wasn't about to walk away from him now.

Arthur shook his head. "It was a kindness. I can never be King Arthur. I can be King whatever else I want, though. Gregory does as well as anything. And that means that I will always have space between who I am as a man and who I am as a king."

"And you don't want me to treat you as a king, is that it?"

"I still remember the moment I truly realized that one day my father would die and I would succeed him. I was eight. I don't know how to explain the sensation. It was as if all possibilities — all chance of a life that was not prescribed for me in its entirety — had been taken away. When you are to be king, no one treats you like a man. Not really. No matter what they call you. Imogene was my one escape from that. My friends — like your brother — were too, to an extent. And then there was you." Arthur sighed and looked down at his hands.

Amelia held her breath. These words, this conversation was everything she had been waiting for. She needed to understand Arthur even more than she wanted him to love her.

Arthur continued. "Imogene has been dead eleven years. The only person who touches me every day is my valet when he helps me dress. Now that I am king, no one has touched me in the last week at all except to swear that they are my humble subjects. I'm amazed the dogs still come to me. I couldn't bear that. I can't bear any of it. Least of all from you."

"It was unkind of you to make me a scandal by refusing me," Amelia said. He was so fragile and beautiful to her, but he still had to know what he'd done.

"I am sorry. It was not my intent."

Amelia realized that she had closed the remaining distance between them. For the first time she wondered if Arthur had refrained from touching her these past months not because he didn't want to, but because he was not sure how to.

She lifted a hand and held it mere millimeters from his face. "May I?" she asked, the words barely a whisper on her lips.

His nod was so small that had she not been standing so close, she wouldn't have seen it. The air between his skin and her fingertips burned as she finally pressed her fingers to his cheek.

Arthur's eyes fluttered closed for a moment. When he opened them again his pupils were dark in the moonlight coming in from the window and his gaze was focused entirely on her.

Amelia took her time. She ran her fingertips over his cheekbone and pressed a palm to his jaw and the end-of-day stubble there. She brushed her thumb over the fine lines at the corners of his eyes and ran the back of her fingers across his forehead, brushing into the hair at his temples. The silvery light made it look greyer than it was. Then she traced her fingers down his cheek and to the corner of his mouth where his face wrinkled up when he smiled.

Of course, he wasn't smiling now. But when she pressed her thumb to the very corner of his mouth and lifted her eyes again to his, he met her gaze.

"Please," he said, the word a warm breath against her skin.

Amelia took another half-step closer. Their feet now were touching, and she could feel the leather of Arthur's shoes against her bare toes. In the shadowed hollow of his throat his pulse sped up as she traced her first two fingers over his lips, touching his mouth, exploring the dips and lines of his lips. She thought her own heart would beat out of her chest when he swallowed and the very tip of his tongue brushed her fingertips.

She stood on her tiptoes and pressed her other hand to his cheek as well. He dipped his head slightly, but Amelia met him more than halfway.

The kiss was unbearably intense. Amelia felt as though she were going to melt from way his breath went unsteady against her mouth. She suspected Arthur felt the same way.

He let her lead. Just when Amelia was beginning to wonder if she should pull back before Arthur had the chance to push her away again, he wrapped one strong arm around her waist, shoved his hand in her hair, and took control of the kiss for himself.

He licked into her mouth, his tongue looking for every kind of touch he'd been denied since the last time they'd kissed, weeks ago. His hands tightened almost painfully in her hair. She wondered if he even recalled they were in a semi-public hallway. Although, to a king, definitions of public and private might well seem different. Wasn't that the point, of everything they'd said to each other tonight? Of Arthur's very name?

Chapter 21

QUEEN IN WAITING…AND WAITING…AND WAITING

1 November
Year 1 of the Reign of King Gregory I

It's been a long time since I've written. I haven't been able to find words for the last two months. After a while, mourning turns to depression. Resilience fades.

The papers have covered most of it: The country grieves in the face a new king with no queen; the Commonwealth is trying to shiver apart at the seams now that their beloved Henry is gone; and no one can decide what to do with me.

I'm frightened. No one on Beatrice's team seems to know if I should be seen in public. I've hardly been outside since Henry's funeral. I get air of course, but on the grounds here, far from the fences and cameras with all their zoom lenses. The outside world knows I'm here, but no one — including me — knows if that's a permanent situation. Every day I don't venture past the gates seems one day closer to this entire adventure coming to a tragic and medieval end. The princess in the tower.

I still get visitors. Priya comes by at least once a week. Charlie and Jo come occasionally too. It's hard for them, though. They're my brother and sister-in-law, which is enough for the papers to print all sorts of terrible things about them.

I've been moved into the apartments adjoining Arthur's at Buckingham. His new rooms, that is. Queen Cecile has all but permanently retired to Sandringham, and Arthur's been moved into the monarch's chambers. We now share an interior door, but much like my relationship with the outside, I do not pass the threshold. I rarely see him, and never, as I had once hoped, at night.

A new date for the wedding has been set for this coming spring. Arthur's coronation will transpire the same day. Logistically, it's easier to have everyone come to London for one major royal event. I say Arthur's coronation, and not our coronation, because it's not clear yet whether I'm going to be crowned. At the same time as Arthur, or at all, assuming the marriage even takes place.

In retrospect, everything was so simple when I was merely marrying the Prince of Wales. Comparatively, no one minded — much — having a Yorkish Princess of Wales. Which seems strange to say now; everything was difficult back then too. But having a Yorkish Queen Consort of England, with the country divided, on edge, and perilously afraid of its own ghosts, is turning into a much different matter. There are protesters outside the palace gates almost every day.

I sold my life to be queen. And now, even if I do marry Arthur, I may never become one.

Arthur's been in meetings on the matter for months. I'm not allowed to attend, and he doesn't tell me how they're going. George does, though. God knows who tells her. Maybe Arthur. Maybe her ravens. I certainly don't know why she tells me.

She says Arthur's being pressured to set me aside, to pick a bride from a more suitable family. A southern queen. Because the easiest solution to the problem of a Yorkish queen no one wants, of course, is to not have a Yorkish queen at all.

I want to think Arthur would never agree to such, that he would keep the promises he made to me. But he has also made promises to his people just by the fact of his birth. Perhaps he will think those are more important. Perhaps they are.

❁

Within the privacy of the palace, ancient traditions mattered even more than they did outside. Invitations to dinner with the King were generally handled formally. Amelia received one from Arthur in early November, written by his steward and delivered to her by messenger. What might have once felt promising — Arthur reaching out to her — in the current crisis merely felt ominous. What were the odds that this dinner was good news when it was much more likely that he had finally reached a decision on what to do with her?

Amelia spent a long time getting ready. If this was to be the last time they spent together, she wanted to do it in the style of one who would have been queen. She put on a dark grey sheath with a black lace overlay and a lace collar that came up to her throat. The dress satisfied every demand of modesty, and yet — especially when paired with nude heels and a pair of pearl earrings — was predatory in its sensuality. Even if everything between them was about to fall apart, it couldn't hurt to remind Arthur that he had a body and that she had one too.

Her brain reminded her unhelpfully that her choices were not so different from what Anne Boleyn had tried in her final days.

A formal invitation meant a formal arrival, and Amelia was shown out of her own quarters, down the hall, and to the door of Arthur's. He stood in greeting as she was announced. Amelia curtsied as soon as the door shut behind her.

Arthur stopped her with a hand on her elbow. He slid his grip to her fingers and then raised her up. Their eyes met, and Amelia found she couldn't look away as he bowed his head. His lips were soft and his breath warm against her knuckles. This was more tenderness than she had expected. Was he trying to woo her? Or say goodbye?

"At some point, you're going to stop doing that, right?" he asked.

"Is that a command?" Amelia retorted. Apparently, she was going to be foolishly brave right up until the very end.

"It would ruin the point if it were," Arthur said. He didn't smile, but the corners of his eyes crinkled up.

Amelia's heart clenched. If her tenure as princess that never was came to its conclusion tonight, how much would she miss this man? The palace, the promised titles — she would regret the loss of none of it, except the chance to make a difference for her people. But losing Arthur too — he was still holding her hand and gazing into her eyes — it would be too much to bear.

"You look beautiful tonight," he said before he remembered himself. He cleared his throat and dropped her hand. "Shall we go in to dinner?"

Whoever had set the table had arranged their seats at adjacent corners and placed candles so that the space felt intimate, even romantic. This was counter to the most basic household protocol and could only have happened at Arthur's request. But what did it mean?

Arthur was in no hurry to enlighten her. He was courteous, made small talk, and mentioned nothing of significance. He also looked exhausted, though that was neither new nor surprising.

Their plates of roast duck were cleared away and their wine refilled before the footmen retreated to their posts. Arthur gestured to them to leave. At their departure, he sat back in his chair, his long fingers on the stem of his wineglass.

"I have something I want to talk to you about," he said.

Amelia felt her heart skip a beat. Arthur's tone, low and silky, suggested he wanted to coax her into something, but whether that would be a good thing or a bad thing, she had no way of knowing.

"Go on then," she said and was glad that her voice did not shake.

"I want to talk about our wedding. And the coronation."

Amelia's heart sank. Arthur looked far too serious for whatever he was going to say next to be good news.

"What do you mean?" she asked.

"I want this to be your choice," he said, "and I know you may not want more of the public spotlight on you than is unavoidable, but the more I consider our wedding —"

"Do you consider our wedding?" she blurted, unable to help herself.

"I do," he said. "Constantly. Among many other things. Like what purpose this monarchy and all our myths serve, assuming there is any at all. But that's a matter for another day. I've come to believe that you should be crowned too."

"You have?" Amelia said, her throat tight.

"Yes." Arthur dipped his head in a nod. "Not privately, not quietly. But next to me and with me. And not as Queen Consort. As something new."

Amelia was sure she looked as confused as she felt. Arthur wasn't making any sense. "That's not possible."

"I've spent a lot of time these last few weeks, talking to scholars and lawyers and people whose job it is to know these things, because I want my reign to be different. My father's death has shown me things need to be different — from what's happened in the streets to what's happened here at court. I made you a promise. Now," he said, as Amelia opened her mouth to interrupt again. "Do you want to hear the offer or not?"

"Tell me," Amelia demanded. Of course she wanted to hear. She wanted Arthur to let her in again. And she wanted to lead her people. Even if the cost was going to be high. It already had been, and that was no reason to stop now.

"I can't make you Queen Regnant. And believe me, I spent a lot of time trying to find a way. But I can't, because in so doing I would demote myself, and then Parliament would go mad, and we'd all be fucked."

Amelia giggled. She'd never heard Arthur curse like that before. For him to reserve it for this particular moment delighted her.

"But what I can do," he continued, "as Fount of all Honours, is assign you all the rights and privileges of a queen regnant, just without the name. With the exception that when we disagree, I break ties. At least in public."

Amelia opened her mouth, but couldn't find any words with which to respond. What Arthur was offering her was immense, bigger than anything they'd even vaguely discussed before. And so was the danger of him even suggesting it. If there were protests at the mere idea of a Yorkish queen, what would happen when the public learned of what Arthur was planning?

"Queen pari passu," Arthur said solemnly.

"Queen with an equal step?" Amelia took a stab at the Latin.

Arthur nodded. "More or less. Queen on equal footing. Queen by my side. Imogene and I were equals in our private lives due to circumstances that are not the ones in play here. But I can't marry someone the world sees as my subject —"

"The king can only marry someone the world sees as his subject. The sovereign outranks everyone. That's what being king means," Amelia protested.

"I don't mean historically. I mean me. Personally."

"Your people won't like this," Amelia said, mostly to stall for time as she processed what he was telling her. "There's no precedent. To bend everything for...." she couldn't make herself finish the sentence.

"A northern traitor?" Arthur asked with a smile.

"This is dangerous," Amelia insisted. She didn't know how she would ever say no. Her only hope was to make Arthur take it back.

Arthur shrugged. "That's why it's your choice. I imagine some people will have strong feelings about it."

"Are you even allowed to make this offer?" Amelia asked.

"I'm King, they aren't. And this isn't political, which means I'm not barred by Parliament."

"Everything about me is political," Amelia said. "As is everything about you and your rank."

"Yes. Everything, but only by implication. Not fact," he said with a level of enthusiasm Amelia knew not every woman would find flattering. "I know I've been distant. I know none of this, especially the last few months, has been easy for you. But I've been trying to survive a thousand crises of which you and George and ravens have only been a fraction. The Commonwealth —"

Amelia drew herself up to her full height, regardless of it being unimpressive. But Arthur was on the verge of rambling. "You can tell me about the Commonwealth after you get to the point."

"I needed to survive the immediate crisis so I could keep my word. I promised you I'd make you a queen for your people. And mine. Now I've found a way; let me keep that promise."

"You've raised the stakes," Amelia said softly. "Tell me what you're leaving out."

"You don't trust me."

"I don't trust a lot of things."

"What is it you're afraid of?" Arthur asked.

"What am I afraid of?" Amelia echoed incredulously. "I'm afraid of the southerners who will lose their faith in you if you do this. I'm afraid of the northerners who will see this as their excuse to claim Yorkish sovereignty. I'm afraid of what happens to a king who angers his people, and I'm afraid of what's going to happen to the queen he does it for. I'm afraid of the wars we all pretend are over. I'm afraid of George's prophecies. I'm afraid of you. I'm afraid of me."

"When has that ever stopped you?"

"There will be protests."

"There have been protests for months. We'll put an end to them."

"They'll get worse."

"We have police. And laws. We can't bow to violence."

"We also can't encourage it. They'll call us traitors."

"They'll be wrong."

"You're rewriting the constitution for me!" Amelia found that she was on her feet. And that she was shaking.

"I told you we'd make history together." Arthur stood too, graceful like a hunting cat.

"You never said it would be like this."

"I didn't know." Arthur's voice was low and very close now. "I couldn't know, what you would be."

"Queens have died for trying to be the equal of kings," Amelia protested. She managed to keep her voice firm, but she clasped her hands together to still their trembling. It didn't work, and Arthur noticed.

"We don't behead women for being ambitious anymore." He seemed to loom in front of her: a king tall and proud and stern. The lamplight turned the edges of him gold. "If you don't want this, for yourself or for your people, say so. I'll let you go."

"I don't want to," Amelia breathed.

"You don't want to go, or you don't want to stay?"

"Go."

His arms were suddenly around her. "Tell me yes," he said, his voice in his ear.

Amelia turned her head to meet his mouth. She nipped at his lower lip. That was the only way to seal a pact like this. In blood.

Arthur groaned low in his throat and chased her mouth as she pulled back.

"I have to go," she said. Further consummation of their relationship, of all their plans, would have to wait.

❁

The next morning Amelia set to work. She would need allies beyond Arthur. She would need a staff. So she called the household office. These days, she didn't need to specify which Mr. Jones she wished to talk to. Everyone who worked there knew who to transfer her calls to.

Mr. Jones greeted her as sunnily as he always did. Amelia wondered if he was truly perpetually cheerful, or if it was just a very effective mask he put on to deal with the world he worked in.

"What can I do for you today?" he asked.

"I have a favor to ask," Amelia said.

"You've only to name it."

Amelia already owed him near a lifetime's worth of favors. She wished she could even begin repaying him.

"I'm not sure this is proper, so you'll forgive me," she said "But could we meet? In person?"

"In what context?" Mr. Jones asked. She detected a note of caution in his voice. As well he might, given the maelstrom of controversy that surrounded her. Little did he know how much worse it was about to get.

"I need some advice on some social matters. And don't say there are people more qualified than you, you're the one I trust." Amelia needed advice on much more than that. But calls could be recorded, and she couldn't risk providing details over the phone.

Mr. Jones, apparently, questioned none of it. "I'm very flattered, ma'am. Where would you like to meet?"

Amelia floundered. She wasn't prepared for this question, although she should have been. "I don't have an office. Yet."

"You should get one of those, you know," Mr. Jones said. "I mean, as a suggestion."

"You're right." Amelia knew he was, but that was a problem for another day. She didn't even know how to go about getting an office. She assumed one would eventually be assigned to her, just like her rooms and her staff and her wardrobe. She told Mr. Jones as much.

"Until that happens," he said slowly. "We could meet in a public area of the palace. Like the staff cafeteria."

"That may not be the place for an extensive conversation," Amelia said carefully.

"No," Mr. Jones agreed. "Alternately, we can meet in your apartments. I'm sure you have any number of staff members in and out at all times. You taking a meeting with someone from the social office wouldn't cause comment. Not much, anyway."

"All right," Amelia agreed. Someone might take a young man visiting her rooms to be someone she was dallying with, but she couldn't shape her life around avoiding gossip. Not all of it, anyway.

"Excellent. Then I will assume, with your leave, that I should show up at your rooms at a time you appoint with coffee in paper cups and then you can ask me or tell me whatever it is that has at least one of us slightly concerned."

"It's not bad, I promise," Amelia said.

"You'll forgive me, ma'am, that's the least reassuring thing you've ever said, and we've spoken several times when you've been in tears."

❁

Amelia watched as the man who presumably was Mr. Jones was shown into her rooms by one of her footmen, holding two cups of coffee and with a leather folio under his arm. He wasn't overly tall, but he had strong shoulders and a trim waist, as though he spent his off-hours playing rugby. His face was as cheery as she had imagined, with pleasant blue eyes, dimples, and sandy hair that threatened to flop down into his eyes when he attempted to set down the coffee and folio all at once.

Amelia stood and tried to help, but only succeeded in making sure half of one of the coffees spilled on the table instead of either of them. As it spread to take up the largest surface area it could, Mr. Jones bowed to her.

Amelia scoffed. "Please don't. We've spoken a million times, I'm not anyone really, and I've just spilled your coffee."

He paused just a moment to consider her before producing a wad of napkins from his pocket and doing his best to mop up the spill. "Macsen Jones, at your service, ma'am."

"Thank you for figuring this out," she nearly whispered, although she wasn't quite sure why. Mr. Jones tossed the soaked napkins in the rubbish bin discreetly tucked behind a chair.

"Now that I'm here, what can I do for you?" he asked pleasantly.

Amelia opened her mouth and closed it again. She and Mr. Jones were clearly close in age. While he would listen politely to anything she said and work diligently to provide whatever she needed, she felt terrible about the burden she was about to place on him. Speaking of Arthur's offer to her aloud was dangerous, possibly for both of them.

"I need to ask you not to discuss what we talk about here outside of this room."

Mr. Jones bobbed his head. "Of course, ma'am. You can be assured of my discretion."

"You may feel less like being discrete when you hear what I have to say. My only safeguard is I suspect no one would believe you if you did talk."

As Amelia told Mr. Jones of Arthur's idea for queen pari passu he sat very still, except for his eyes, which grew wider and wider as she spoke.

"And that is why I called you here today," Amelia finished. "I don't want to make assumptions about your heritage or your allegiances. But you are from Wales. You understand the position of the north."

Mr. Jones nodded slowly.

"I'm surrounded by people in this palace who think I'm the gravest of enemies and that my people are all traitors. But we're just hungry and resentful. Honestly, we want to be a part of this kingdom too. If I'm going to succeed — never mind if I'm going to survive — I need friends by my side. Friends like you. Who understand that things aren't as simple as those in the south — or in the north — may think. Who would help this new endeavor at least stand a chance."

"With all due respect, ma'am," Mr. Jones said. "I am from Wales, and while our sympathies aren't with the south, we generally like to leave well enough alone."

"Which is why you're in London, working at Buckingham Palace?" Amelia said.

"A job's a job."

Amelia nodded but stayed silent, hoping — praying — to draw him out further.

"But I couldn't say no to being in the thick of things."

Amelia's nod turned enthusiastic. "Yes. Exactly. And if you truly don't want to be involved, I don't blame you. And you won't have to do anything. But you've helped me so much. I know you care. If not about politics, then at least about making sure I won't lose my head — metaphorical or otherwise — in the days to come. And if you do want to be in the thick of things there's no better place than here, with me, doing this."

"But what would 'this' entail, exactly? I don't work with the press and I have nothing to do with policy. I'll be your friend, but you don't need to pay me for that."

Amelia tried not to feel pathetic in the face of that kindness. "You can organize things, yes?"

"They've not sacked me from the social office yet," Mr. Jones allowed.

"You manage dates. And events. Details. People. All sorts of things. You even survived Princess George's birthday at the swan conservatory," Amelia reminded him.

"Barely," Mr. Jones muttered, but at least he smiled.

"I'll need someone like that, to manage the details and logistics of my life. My public life, at least. All the grand strategy in the world won't mean anything if I don't have someone who can make sure it gets carried out. And with any luck, I may soon have a people to win over."

"You want me to be your private secretary?"

Amelia nodded. "Yes."

Mr. Jones hesitated. "You know I am woefully unqualified. On paper, at least. I know I can do the work you want me to — at least, I think I can — but the hiring is traditionally done by the chief steward and H Branch."

"I'll be the Queen of England, can't I just ask for you?"

"You could, but generally you'll be given a list of the most plausible candidates and —"

"You can learn on the job," Amelia said decisively.

"It's not that sort of —"

"I'm learning on the job," Amelia cut him off. "I'm so unqualified it's ridiculous. Every time I think I've got the hang of this something else terrible happens. But I can't keep bobbling through this alone. Be as brave as me and say yes."

"Is no one else teaching you how to do any of this?" Mr. Jones sounded appalled.

"No. Not in the way that matters. Lots of people are telling me how to be an acceptable queen. Fewer people are interested in helping me be an effective one."

"All right, ma'am," he said. "Offer accepted."

Impulsively she grabbed his hand. "Please call me Amelia."

"If you call me Macsen," he shot back.

"Brilliant. Thank you," she said, feeling awkward all over again. "I have one other request."

"Now I'm really nervous," he said with a laugh.

"I would like you to come to the wedding."

"The whole world will be at the wedding, ma'am. Amelia," he corrected, when she twitched her fingers in his.

"I mean I would like you to be in the abbey and come to the reception and have a proper invitation. I couldn't have done any of this without you, and I would like you there. Can you please tell me where to have such an invitation directed and if you have a girlfriend or a boyfriend or —"

"I've an ex and a dog," Macsen cut in.

Amelia frowned thoughtfully. "We'll just say *and guest* then."

"Aren't you worried I'll bring the dog?" he asked.

Amelia leaned forward conspiratorially. "I would be delighted if you brought the dog."

Chapter 22

KING GREGORY I PREPARES FOR HIS FIRST CHRISTMAS ADDRESS

20 December
Year 1 of the Reign of King Gregory I

Having never previously been at Buckingham Palace at Christmas, I don't know what it usually looks like for the holidays. I feel safe in assuming that it is not normally as grey and cheerless as this. The royal family is still in official mourning, and so there are no decorations: No trees, no candles, no festoons of pine boughs. It's rather miserable. But no one asked for my opinion, so I'm ignoring the season lighting up the rest of London and readying for the coming storm.

Arthur, after his grand and terrifying suggestion of queen pari passu, has been as distant as ever. Hopefully, that's because he's trying to figure out how to make this work and not because for the rock of the land he's as changeable as the wind.

There was a knock on Amelia's door one morning a few days before Christmas. She opened it to find George on the other side. She was casually dressed in slacks and a soft green sweater. In her hands, she carried a box of delicate silver and gold paper.

"What can I do for you?" Amelia asked warily. George rarely sought her out, unless it was to give her news of meetings that Arthur wouldn't. Those conversations were often brief and cryptic, so much so that Amelia still wasn't sure if George was an ally or not.

George looked around the room, as bare of decoration as the rest of the palace. "Will you make snowflakes with me?" she asked. Amelia could hardly believe this was the same young woman of the garden reception, of Arthur's accession, of the vigil.

"It's not much," George added when Amelia didn't say anything. "But it's cheerier than nothing."

"That would be lovely." Amelia stepped aside to let George in. Even company she was uncertain of was still company. Life in the castle, and in her circumstances, was lonely.

She and George sat at the same table where Amelia had convinced Macsen to join her cause. Together, they spent the morning folding and snipping little squares of craft paper into snowflakes.

"Don't you want some of these for yourself?" Amelia asked as they began stringing them onto threads.

George shook her head. "I have lots, mostly from years ago. Hyacinth and I do this every Christmas, whichever residence we might be at."

"A princess's rooms must surely always welcome more decoration," Amelia tried. As long as they were discussing holiday snowflakes she was spared anything more serious.

"Who says I'm a princess?" George retorted.

Amelia startled and put the scissors down. "Are you renouncing your title?"

George pursed her lips. "No. I'm just not a princess."

"I don't understand."

"I'm not a girl; I don't like being called *Princess* or having to wear dresses; and if there had been a chance of being bowed to as King or Witch — with a capital-W — I might view your future child as competition. But as it is…." George trailed off and shrugged expansively.

"What would you prefer I call you?" Amelia asked. Royal life had taught her to take refuge in the niceties.

"George, as you do. I'm genderqueer and like it well enough. Protocol allows for no freedom in my title and honorifics. Adjusting my pronouns in my situation would be difficult. And we all have enough difficulties right now."

"You mean me," Amelia said glumly.

"I do."

"But if you could have things as you wished them," Amelia led.

"If I could have things as I wished them, my pronouns would not be my main concern," George said. "I am a singular creature, but not a single creature. What pronoun would you use that could encompass me and the birds and all the witchcraft and auguries of the land?"

"They?" Amelia suggested.

"Maybe one day, but I would prefer you not get ahead of me."

"She for now?" Amelia clarified.

George nodded. "She for now. But we'll make Arthur, Fount of all Honours, do something about it once we get your situation solved, won't we?"

Amelia hastily agreed.

George lapsed into silence. Even doing nothing more than shaking out bits of cut paper from a finished snowflake, she exuded something unsettling, but Amelia understood it was not the young royal's gender; it was the rest of situation. Had the birds that invaded her rooms at Sandringham been part of George's collective witchcraft? To share a room with what Amelia — despite her science training — now had to accept as magic was exhausting. But George shared a body with it; surely that was harder.

"I want you to know," George said eventually. "That I'm glad for queen pari passu."

Amelia's heart sped up. "Arthur told you?"

George shook her head. "Arthur asked me."

"Asked you what?" In spite of her anxiety Amelia felt her hackles rising. For a youth who didn't want the throne, George always seemed to be judging Amelia's path to the same.

"If it was a good idea. If it would harm the ravens."

"You mean if the kingdom would fall," Amelia clarified.

George shrugged. "If you'd like. Arthur does not always know what to make of me."

"Well?" Amelia prompted. What Arthur thought of George was hardly the point right now.

"After my uncle, Britain won't have another king." George smiled apologetically.

Amelia's fingers froze. The paper swan she was folding fell from her numb hands to the table. She fumbled to pick it back up.

"Don't look so fragile at it," George said. "There aren't many people who can endure my family or our circumstances," George continued. "You caught my uncle's eye and made a bargain with him. The people will have to deal with the consequences of that. You are not exempt."

"I'm trapped in a palace and the whole nation hates me. Believe me, I don't feel exempt."

George continued as if Amelia hadn't spoken. "He went to York with you."

"He said you'd be furious, after what happened there," Amelia said after an uncomfortable pause. She could hardly get into a debate with a Lancastrian heir over the symbols of their respective families and their blood-soaked history.

George shook her head. "Not furious. Frightened. People are often unskilled at interpreting the emotions of those they consider women. Besides, it looks the same on me. It's the eyes," she said, pointing at her face.

Remembering the portraits of Anne Boleyn that so resembled George, Amelia wondered if anyone had been able to tell the difference between anger and fear on the face of that long-dead queen at her execution. Too, Amelia wondered, if Anne had dreamed, like Arthur's niece, of ravens.

❦

Once George had left, Amelia sat in her sitting room for a long time, deep in thought. *After my uncle, Britain won't have another king.* Did Arthur know? Had George told him? Was he reconsidering queen pari passu? Should he?

The contemplation got Amelia nowhere. Her confusion over Arthur — his generosity and his distance — would be eternal if she never asked. Besides, she could hardly blame him for not using the door that adjoined their rooms, if she never did either.

She had to move an armchair over a foot to even stand in front of the door properly. Once she did, she hesitated. She didn't know which room of Arthur's the door led to, or if he was in his rooms at all.

There was nothing for it but to try. She raised her hand and tapped the heavy oak with her knuckles.

For a long, drawn-out moment Amelia thought Arthur hadn't heard or wasn't there. But then there was the faintest sound that might have been footsteps, the scrape of something heavy being moved across the floor, and the squeal of a long-unused lock being turned.

The door opened.

Arthur stood before her in his shirtsleeves, lit from behind by soft lamplight. It fell in a warm beam across the floor, reaching across the wood and carpet into Amelia's own sitting room. She realized belatedly she hadn't turned on the lights, even though it had grown dark outside. Arthur wore his reading glasses, behind which his eyes glinted brown at her.

"Amelia?" he asked, looking worried when she didn't speak.

"I'm sorry. Am I disturbing you?"

He shook his head and stepped back to let her in. "No. Not at all. I'd forgotten this door was here," he added as she crossed the threshold.

This room, too, was a sitting room. Judging by the decor, Arthur hadn't had it redone to his own tastes since he moved in. The cream-colored walls, gold moulding, and rich crimson velvet of the furnishings and drapes were nothing like the cool blues and greys he seemed to prefer at Gatcombe and St. James's.

On one of the armchairs, pushed close to a fire that crackled warmly in the chill that never seemed to leave the palace, was a yellow legal pad and a stack of printed pages, all well-thumbed. On a little table next to the chair was a cut glass decanter and tumbler.

"I've interrupted your work," Amelia said awkwardly.

"No. Well, yes, you have. But I'm glad you came." Arthur moved the stack of papers from the chair to the table and gestured Amelia to sit down. He took the seat opposite her as if having an unscheduled private conversation was completely ordinary for them. Then he seemed to hesitate. "Why did you come? Are you all right?"

"I don't need something to be wrong to talk to my fiancé," Amelia said. Nerves made it sharper than she meant it to be,

"No, of course not."

"But I do want to talk to you," Amelia said.

Arthur gestured for her to go on.

"You told George what you're planning?" Amelia asked. "You — rather — asked?"

Arthur looked at her over the top of his reading glasses and then took them off. He dangled them from his fingertips as he answered. "Yes. I did. Does that bother you?"

"No," Amelia said. She didn't say that she'd thought for ages that George hated her. "It surprises me a little. You haven't told your sister. Or I imagine your mother."

"George has known almost from the beginning." He chuckled, a little self-deprecatingly, but his eyes were very serious. "I could hardly make a decision like that without the permission of my court witch."

"Did George tell you...." Amelia began and then trailed off. George's pronouncement about the future was too terrible to say out loud and she had no idea what Arthur knew or felt about the matter of her gender.

"I've been perfectly aware of any number of things about George for a long time," Arthur said.

"And you're always trying to convince me you don't believe in witchcraft. Yet you go to all the birds and magic of England for your advice."

Arthur laughed. "If you had George at your disposal, wouldn't you?"

Amelia sighed. "I was supposed to be a scientist."

"And now?" Arthur asked.

"Now I want to know if she told you what she told me."

"Which is?"

"That if you married me and made me queen pari passu Britain would never have another king."

Arthur nodded. "She told me that too."

"What are you going to do?"

Arthur shook his head. "There doesn't seem to be much I can."

"Other than not marrying me and making me this strange new kind of queen," Amelia pointed out. Someone had to say it.

"I promised you."

"You did. But you also promised the realm you would take care of it. That's why we're doing this — all of this! — to make this a place where her king speaks for all her people. But now George says you'll be the last and what would be the point?"

"Perhaps we'll only have daughters. Perhaps the monarchy has done more harm than good. Perhaps an asteroid will hit the earth. A witch, regardless of what either of us thinks a witch is, riddles."

"But —"

Arthur held a finger to his lips to silence her. "Did George tell you not to marry me?" he asked.

"No."

"And she didn't tell me to refrain from making you a strange queen. I've learnt many things from having George in my life. Among them, that there are always more possibilities than I can imagine." Arthur gave Amelia his fondest smile, the one that made them conspirators and convinced her he might one day love her. "Therefore, after everything, don't you want to see what will happen?"

Whatever her fears and reservations, Amelia still didn't have a no for this man. She nodded, and Arthur picked up the pad on the table next to him and handed it to her.

Amelia leaned forward to take it from him. "What is it?"

"The announcement. Of queen pari passu."

"A speech?" Amelia asked.

Arthur shook his head. "The king doesn't make speeches. Except on Christmas," he said ruefully. "And I will give a speech then, but not about this. A speech would attract all the wrong sort of attention. Screaming curious crowds, analysis on the news of how strong my voice is as if that's a measure of my conviction. This will be a decree in the papers. Let them try to argue with words printed in black and white if they can."

"You sound confident," Amelia said. She didn't feel the same. Arthur surely underestimated all the ways an unhappy public could tear apart anything they wanted to. His words were the least of it.

"I am. Go on, read it."

Amelia looked down at the pad and Arthur's precise, looping handwriting. It laid out everything Arthur had told her about the kind of queen he would make her. Softened, for public consumption — Arthur couldn't very well come out and *say* 'And now I'm making chaos for the good of our realm' — but firm and clear in its intent. There would be no doubt in anyone's mind that Arthur was turning the world upside down.

"What do you think?"

Amelia swallowed. Holding these words in her hand, what Arthur was doing for York — what Arthur was doing for *her* — made it feel more real than it had the night he first offered it. Perhaps he was onto something, wanting to print this.

"I think it will do what you need it to do. What — we — need it to do. I still don't know what's going to happen next, though."

"In life one rarely does. Sometimes that's terrible and sometimes that's good, but one never knows until the attempt has been made."

"What does George think?" She still couldn't believe Arthur's niece had accepted this.

"She gave her approval. Unlike either of us, I suspect, she's not frightened."

"Is she frightened of anything?" Amelia asked.

"The day Imogene died," he said, with only the slightest hesitation. "She was inconsolable. Hardly a wonder — she and Imogene were very fond of each other. But how many six-year-olds grasp the idea of death so fully? She went to bed sobbing that all the ravens would die."

"And then?" Amelia asked, knowing any story about George was unlikely to end there.

"And then in the morning she woke up, calm as a mill pond. She got out of her rooms and found me in the gardens. I'd not slept all night, and she looked like a ghost child rising out of the path in front of me. Like the child Imogene and I would never have. But she took my hand and told me that it would be all right. That I would find a queen again. I convinced myself for a long time after that, that some well-meaning chaplain had gotten to her and that she meant my wife, in the afterlife. Now, I think she meant you."

Goosebumps broke out up and down Amelia's arms. "That doesn't feel comforting."

"No. It didn't then and it doesn't now."

Amelia was silent. What was there to say to that?

After a few moments she realized that Arthur was looking at her. Staring at her, really, his eyes intent as she sat, her head bowed over the decree that would make her — very nearly — the equal of a king.

She flushed under his stare. But rather than change the topic or flee as she had so many times before, she let herself savor the sensation, the warmth spreading from her cheeks and down her throat to the rest of her body. Her entire being felt alight under Arthur's gaze.

This wasn't her imagination; she couldn't have dreamed his gaze. This was not how one looked at a business partner or a political ally.

Arthur suddenly cleared his throat, the sound harsh in the otherwise still room.

"I'm very sorry, but I'm afraid I have other business to attend to tonight."

"Oh." The dismissiveness, the carelessness, of Arthur's tone was like a bucket of cold water. She stood so quickly she nearly stumbled over her own feet. She had grown too susceptible both to Arthur and his family's magic. Fairytales existed for a reason and that was to tell little girls like her that to be under a man's sway was not the same as having his love.

Still, she couldn't help asking, "Can I see you? Later, tonight?"

Arthur raised his eyes from his hands to her face. For the briefest of moments he held her gaze. The intensity she thought she had seen there before remained, but she was no longer sure of its meaning. If George was a witch, then Arthur was too. But he was of a different sort entirely. He was a banked fire made flesh, a man waiting to turn the very air to flames.

He was looking at Amelia now like she was that air.

"That wouldn't be a good idea," he said. He cleared his throat again, and the spell broke. He was once again a normal man with very little interest in her. "I have meetings early tomorrow. I shouldn't stay up."

Chapter 23

ENGLAND ERUPTS IN RESPONSE TO KING'S PROCLAMATION

28 December
Year 1 of the reign of King Gregory I

The decree announcing the creation of queen pari passu was in the paper this morning.

Since noon there have been crowds outside the gate shouting. Some in joy. Some for my head. My actual head this time; I'm not just being paranoid.

I don't think Arthur planned for this.

If Amelia had once been trapped in the palace by public relations uncertainty, she was now trapped by sheer practicality. The streets of London were filled with protesters, while news broadcasts kept her up to date on the ugly things they were saying about her, York, and a king who would take such a queen.

The newspapers were hardly better. There, lengthy opinion pieces criticized Arthur's decision about queen pari passu and predicted the fall of the monarchy. Meanwhile, matters that should have received news coverage — debates in Parliament over things that actually mattered like jobs, schools, roads — devolved into shouted arguments about tradition, mythology, and ravens.

⚜

Amelia approached the conference room for a meeting of the wedding planning committee with reluctance. It seemed crass to debate decorations when she had thrown the country into turmoil.

Everyone in the room stood when she entered. Even Arthur. Disaster may have been at hand, but there was a force to her presence now. She nodded to the assembled and took her seat at the corner of the table next to Arthur, expecting the usual round of boring logistics she wasn't actually invited to have an opinion on.

"We must talk about the dress," Beatrice said.

"What about the dress?" Her dress had been done for months. What was there to discuss now?

"We have to do something about the roses," the steward said.

"I don't understand," Amelia said.

Beatrice shot Arthur a grave look.

"Arthur?" Amelia turned to him, her voice rising slightly in anxiety that had nothing to do with the aesthetics of the flowers but everything to do their symbolism.

"It seems our staff," Arthur emphasized the word almost cruelly, "is concerned about public sentiment regarding our wedding."

"What do you mean?" Amelia asked.

"We've decided the design previously approved for the dress is no longer appropriate given the current political climate and His Majesty's recent proclamation," Beatrice said. "There is still sufficient time to create and approve another look. Designers are lining up for the chance."

"But the roses were supposed to represent the unification of our houses, of the whole country. I even agreed to red roses along with the white," Amelia said numbly. She felt as though the rug was being pulled out from under her. Again. Although not by Arthur this time. They had fought over the dress and come to an agreement; Amelia had been proud of that. She had even grown to love the design of the gown, both for its own sake and for what it symbolized.

"You can, of course, have roses in your bouquet or the arrangements," Beatrice said, her voice a parody of placation. "Just not white ones. We've decided a pale blush would be appropriate."

Amelia looked helplessly around the table. How mad would she sound if she objected to pale pink roses? In other circumstances pink would have been fine, but at the moment the symbolism of the blood of Lancaster tainting the white rose of York was too grotesquely literal to bear.

"No."

Amelia sagged with relief at the sound of Arthur's voice.

"Roses at weddings are ordinary," the King said. "The absence of them is not and will create new problems, not solve old ones. If Lady Amelia would like roses on her wedding dress, she shall have roses on her wedding dress as previously agreed upon."

"But sir —"

"The Crown may be upheld by superstition, but we do not bow to it. Nor do we make decisions based on the whims of people standing outside my home with tagboard signs threatening my wife-to-be. Now, do we have any real business to attend to?"

Amelia turned to Arthur to mouth a *thank you*. He graced her with a tiny nod.

The committee turned to discussing the order of ceremony for the wedding itself. The Archbishop of Canterbury would perform the service, and Amelia had nothing to add as the staff debated amongst itself over music choices.

She spoke again when the chief steward mentioned the presentation of the ring.

"I'm sorry," she interrupted. "Don't you mean the presentation of rings?"

"It's a single ring ceremony, ma'am."

"I don't understand." Unlike the mess about the roses and the ravens, this time, she truly didn't.

The steward slid his eyes toward Arthur rather than answer. Amelia turned to look at her fiancé, too.

"I won't be having a wedding ring," Arthur said quietly.

"Oh." There was nothing else Amelia could say, not in public and certainly not surrounded by people who didn't like her. Not about how a wedding ring, if Arthur didn't have one too, felt not like a symbol of commitment but a mark of her as his possession.

"I apologize for the interruption," she said to the chief steward. "Please, continue."

❦

When the meeting was over, Amelia stopped Arthur with a hand on his arm before he could escape. "Can I talk to you a moment?"

Arthur gave her a considering look. "Come to my office."

Amelia might have wished for a more neutral location but as long as he was king, there was no neutral ground for her in all of England. With a sigh she followed and took a seat across the desk from him when he sat.

"No one told me it was going to be a single ring ceremony," she said.

Arthur sighed and shifted a paperweight on his desk. "It's tradition. Surely you know that."

"You're breaking thousands of traditions with queen pari passu. Why not with a ring as well? It's only a symbol."

"Symbols are important," Arthur said.

"You just told a roomful of your advisors — and mine — that we do not bow to superstition."

"And yet." Arthur gave her a look that was almost regretful. "The ravens are still caged."

Amelia was not going to stray down the witchcraft path with Arthur again. Not now, not when the very real shape of her future marriage was at stake. "How can I ever be your equal if I must wear your rings but you don't wear mine? Is everything just clever words to you no matter the consequences?"

"We can't have all things all ways," Arthur said. "There's a limit to what the people will tolerate."

"Yes, and I'm fairly sure the scene outside indicates we've already passed it."

"The protests will settle down," Arthur said. "The tabloids will grow tired of this story and find something else to sensationalize. But understand that roses for a day are one thing. A ring for a lifetime — that makes me yours before I am this kingdom's — might ruin everything."

"I can't be your equal if I'm also your possession," Amelia said again. There was no rationale Arthur could offer that would change that. If she had to, she would keep saying so until he understood.

"And you can't be my equal at all if the country cannot adjust. I know nothing but this life, Amelia, but I know that it is often the small things that are a step too far. I'm sorry, but there's no other way."

Overnight protest crept toward riot. Outside the gates of Buckingham Palace the outraged were more orderly than elsewhere, only carrying signs and shouting. But clashes between supporters of York and Lancaster were spreading. In Leicester, there were arrests; in Manchester two people had landed in hospital.

No more kings, George had said. Had she thought it would happen like this? In blood and violence? Amelia had no way of knowing. The young royal was securely tucked away at her home at Kensington. All Amelia could do was carry on without her guidance and wonder if the ravens knew how to pick locks.

Each morning Macsen, now her private secretary, briefed Amelia on her schedule and what was happening both inside and outside the palace. She had brought this about — she and Arthur. It was her duty to see it through.

It took less than a week for headlines about how much half the country wanted a different queen to be joined by photographs of Helen Lawrence, Duchess of Water Eaton, being ushered through a side door of Buckingham Palace. Speculation spread like wildfire. Amelia wanted to trust Arthur, but Helen appearing at the palace wasn't good. Not for Amelia, at any rate.

❦

That night, the ministers came under cover of darkness. Amelia watched from her high window at Buckingham Palace as they scurried across the gravel in their black, rain-soaked trench coats and matching, inadequate umbrellas. They'd come to scold — maybe even threaten — Arthur for finding loopholes in the very constitution of the land.

Amelia thought of George and her ravens and wondered, not for the first time, if she herself might be beheaded.

She was startled by a knock at her door. She crept toward it cautiously; there would be a guard standing outside, hopefully, but who would come to her this late at night? And for what reason?

To Amelia's surprise it was George, as if Amelia's thoughts had summoned her. Her honey blonde hair was damp and escaping its usual confines, curling around her ears.

"What are you doing?" Amelia asked.

"I came to see you," George said, as if that wasn't obvious and as if appearing at eleven on a miserable night was perfectly normal.

"How did you get here?" Amelia stepped back to let George into her rooms. She was glad she hadn't undressed yet, uncertain if she could have faced George only in sleep clothes.

George looked confused. "I walked."

"From Kensington Palace?"

"From the Tower, actually."

"The Tower of London?" Amelia was shocked.

"Yes, of course."

"You can *do* that?"

George gave a small, elegant shrug. "I needed to check on the ravens. Who's going to stop me?"

Any number of people, Amelia wanted to say. Her parents. Her guards. Arthur. But George obeyed no laws except her own. "How are the ravens?" she asked.

"They're not happy. They don't like being caged."

"I'm sorry."

"Whatever for?"

"It's my fault they were locked up."

George looked at her keenly. "Actually it's my uncle's for choosing you. It's not your fault other people are afraid of you."

"There's no reason to be afraid of me." Amelia was quite sure she was the least frightening person in this room.

George waved her reassurance away. "I came to talk to you. Are you well?"

"I'm not sure," Amelia admitted. She led George to the window and nodded at the grounds below, where another clutch of ministers huddled by the gate. "They've been coming and going all night."

"They blame you for pari passu. They want my uncle to set you aside."

Amelia nodded. She'd been able to figure that out for herself. "And yesterday, the Duchess of Water Eaton was here."

George tipped her head to the side. "What does that have to do with anything?"

"The entire south prefers her to me as a potential queen," Amelia offered.

"That's because they know her. They don't know you yet. They haven't wanted to." George shook her head. "But they will. The duchess isn't your rival. Or your enemy."

"What would happen to the ravens if he did set me aside?" Amelia asked.

"I don't know." George nodded to the men below the window. "They're ravens too," she said in a voice that frightened Amelia; it was not the young royal's own.

"Pardon?"

"Caged. Humiliated. Pinned. They don't like it either, when you cut off their options."

❁

The following day Amelia was summoned to Arthur's office.

She wanted Arthur to rise from behind his desk, take her in his arms, and hold her against the storms that threatened both of them. But she didn't expect it, not really.

Although Arthur stood when she entered he did not come out from around his desk. At his gesture, Amelia took a seat in the chair across from him.

"Will you come to Canada with me?" Arthur said.

"I'm sorry, *what?*" Of all the many things Amelia had imagined hearing in this moment, Canada had not been amongst them.

Arthur continued as if his invitation were in no way peculiar. "It's been decided that my first state visit as king will be to one of our recalcitrant Commonwealth countries. To show that they are important to us and to cool things down here by getting me out of England. The media could use a distraction. I've just been to Australia, and Canada is nearly as irritated with us as our own little island, so Canada it is."

Amelia was furious. "Irritated?" she asked. "*Irritated?* There are ministers visiting you in the dead of night telling you to set me aside! You're having meetings with the Duchess of Water Eaton who more than half of the country would prefer you marry! The nation is moving toward violence, and you ask me to come to Canada?"

Arthur had the good grace to look pained. "I can't do anything about my ministers demanding an audience with me. I also can't do much about the violence; although some decent and fair policy out of Parliament might help. Which is only going to happen if everyone stops being distracted. What I can do is normalize your presence by my side in social as well as public matters. Also, there's the possibility that Canada will be charmed with a woman who's young, beautiful, and somewhat an outcast — as they are themselves."

"You're using me to manipulate Canada to stay in the Commonwealth and avoid your responsibilities here!

"If we can make the Commonwealth like you we might just be able to pull queen pari passu off."

Amelia stared at him disbelievingly.

Arthur raised a shoulder. "I never said this would be easy."

"No," Amelia said cautiously. "You also never said it would be bizarre."

"Perhaps not," Arthur said. "But do you want to get out of here with me? Just for a little while?"

"I don't like the idea of running away from our problems. Or the kingdom's."

Arthur frowned slightly. "About that...."

"What do you want me to do?" Amelia asked. Arthur was up to something, and she wasn't sure she was going to like it. As usual.

"You have to do something for the south."

"Because giving up my life and my name and my dreams aren't enough?"

"Amelia —"

"The people making noise now are the ones who think London should conquer York once and for all, restart the wars, summon an army!" Amelia stood up in her shock and her upset. "Three hundred years ago they would have had my head on a pike! You want me to do something for them?!"

But even as she spoke, she knew Arthur had a point, little as she wanted to admit it. And little as she expected anything good to come of Arthur's suggestion. Or, frankly, the excursion to Canada.

A muscle in Arthur's jaw twitched. "Is that your only objection?"

"My only objection! Arthur, three days ago Parliament voted down a bill for funding schools in Yorkshire because they don't like me. Last week it was jobs. God only knows what it will be next week. How many objections do you want?"

"Do you remember what I said to you, the first time I asked if you wanted to marry me?"

"I'm not likely to forget," Amelia didn't sit down. She couldn't bear to give up even that slight bit of ground.

"I told you I'd make you a queen for your people. But I also said we'd unite our houses for the first time in centuries. Which means I have to make concessions for you. But," Arthur said, when Amelia opened her mouth, "it also means you have to make concessions for me. Which you did once, when you agreed to red roses on your wedding dress. But I need you to do it again."

"It's always me," Amelia muttered, mutinously.

"Yes, that's why I offered you queen pari passu," Arthur shot back. "Hear me out. I have been living this life for decades, and I know how this works. The people will never accept you if you can offer them nothing but discord, a few roses, and a banner they don't understand any more than you understand theirs. And why should they? So let's offer them something. Show them why they should want a truly unified kingdom, with you by my side at its head. Help me keep the promise we made each other and our people when we first started this adventure."

"What kind of concession?"

Arthur shook his head. "That, is up to you. And York."

❁

Back in her rooms, Amelia stared at her mobile. She didn't know the answer to Arthur's request, but she knew he was right. George's words came back to her. The southern ministers felt trapped and blamed her. If she could alleviate the pressure on them, she could in turn preserve her position and help her people.

She needed advice, but how could anyone know what she could give the south to save them all? Priya, like Macsen, had already expressed more than reasonable distaste for this particular national drama. Charlie would be angry and afraid — for Jo and for his children, all stranded here in the unkindness of London and Lancasters. Nick could navigate the business world but had never given Amelia a piece of useful advice in her life. Her mother, who had led through a good marriage a life of very successful survival, would also be of no help.

Which left only Amelia's father — silent, distant, and careful. Like Arthur, he had seen decades of politics come and go. He'd kept his counsel and survived them.

She called the number that went directly to his study at Kirkham House. Either no one would answer or he — not staff — would.

When he picked up, he sounded worried. "Amelia? What's wrong?"

"I need your help," she said.

"Amelia —"

"I'm fine. But things have come to a place, and I think maybe you have the answer."

"For over a year you've been courting the King and never once you've called me for advice." He was neither scolding nor proud; he was simply stating fact.

"Well, now I need to court the south. And I don't know how. The whole nation thinks I've wronged it just by falling in love." She hated herself for saying it. It was, after all, half a lie. She and Arthur had made a plan. She had gotten in too deep, and together they had made a mess. "Arthur says I must win them over and that charm is not enough."

"It never is," her father said, "but I know what we shall do."

"You do?" Amelia was surprised to have a solution offered to her so easily.

"The Tower Crown."

"What about it?"

"We give it back to the people Richard III took it from. It is theirs, after all, no matter how long our family has held it."

Amelia was shocked. That heirloom had been in their family for centuries, as much their property as her parents' home and estate. People travelled to Kirkham House to see it. How could her father talk about giving that away?

"That's too much to surrender," Amelia said.

"No, it's not. Just because we have lost many things doesn't mean this should have ever been ours."

"But it's buying my safety," Amelia said firmly. Giving away that crown would have a tangible impact on the resources available for Kirkham House's upkeep. "Mind, this shouldn't even be about my safety. It's just a wedding…it shouldn't matter."

"We're not buying your safety," her father said. "We're ending the wars once and for all. And we're putting you on the throne."

⚙

The day before Amelia and Arthur were due to leave for North America, the clouds scudded low and angry across the London sky. Amelia stood in a small antechamber on the first floor of Buckingham Palace waiting for her father. He'd left York that morning by train, accompanied by two members of the royal security detail to ensure that no harm became him or the artifact he carried.

Arthur, waiting with her, wore a grave expression and a heavy, dark grey overcoat over his suit. Amelia wore a black wool coat and white scarf, hat, and gloves. Nestled beneath the scarf was her white rose of York necklace.

The somberness of their attire matched the mood of the room. A small handful of advisors and officials also dressed for the cold milled about. George was there too, elegant in a dove-grey coat. No one spoke, except when aides appeared into the room to offer an update on the earl's progress.

It was a strange prelude to the Canadian visit. Amid the unrest, newspapers had been covering the King's upcoming trip abroad with some excitement. The announcement that Lady Amelia's father would be visiting the palace for a significant public ceremony of unknown subject had only confused the national mood further.

The public, eager always for a spectacle and new angles on the ongoing crisis, queued up by the thousands in front of the stage that had been set up outside the palace. They didn't know what they would witness, but hoped it would be history in the making.

In the antechamber, an announcement was made that Lord Kirkham was on the grounds and headed to them directly. With a look, Arthur dismissed his advisors to the other side of the room. When George hesitated, he nodded her in their direction as well.

"Keep an eye on them," he murmured.

Lord Kirkham entered with an erectness of bearing Amelia had rarely seen her father demonstrate. He was flanked by the two guards and carried a metal box.

He bowed to Arthur, just a dip of his head, and Arthur nodded in acknowledgement. The two men held eye contact for a long, charged moment. Amelia wished she could have spoken or touched one or both of them.

"How was your trip?" Arthur asked after some silent accord between them had been reached.

"Uneventful, Your Majesty. I didn't expect so much attention from your men, but they were very helpful."

Amelia wasn't sure her father entirely meant his words. Perhaps, like her, he had been frightened by this pass to which they had all come. But that was the advantage of speaking as little as her father always had; if he'd been scared, no one would ever know.

"Did anyone bother you?" Arthur asked.

"No. Not at all. Of course, I don't think anyone knows why I'm here." Amelia's father turned to her and said her name with a warmth and focus that surprised her.

"Father."

"How are you?"

"At some point, people are going to stop asking me that, yes?"

"Only when they stop caring about you. So, I think, no," he said with a smile. He cleared his throat and glanced around the room briefly. His eyes momentarily settled on the small group of people trying not to be obvious that they were straining to catch every word spoken.

He held out the metal box for her to take. "Amelia," he said. "My father, when he died, passed on this treasure to me; his father had passed it on to him. And now I give it to you, to do with as you think best for your future and that of our country."

The remarks for the ceremony itself had been written in advance and vetted with Crown officials, certain members of Parliament, and even the Prime Minister himself. But no one had planned a speech for the simple act of a father handing his daughter a family heirloom. Amelia found herself incredibly moved.

"Thank you." Her eyes stung in spite of her attempts to remain composed. "I'll do my utmost to do right by our people."

Her father smiled. "I know you will."

"Sir, it's time," said an aide by the door.

❁

The stage had been set up outside on the gravel between the palace wall and the gates, on the very ground the ministers had crossed in the night to try to negotiate with Arthur. Amelia had seen the crowd grow from the windows all day, but that was nothing to stepping onto the stage beside Arthur, her father, and George and being greeted by the uneasy roar of the crowd.

Arthur stepped up to the podium. The crowd fell silent.

"Thank you for coming today," he said, "and for standing side-by-side with your fellow citizens in a time when that has not, I know, always been easy. The truth, however, is that such disunity is nothing new for our so-called Unified Kingdom. The wounds we have laid open in each other are deep and ancient and cannot be healed in a day or in a season. And while I know — and all of you know — that symbolism and intent are not, and can never be, enough, they are a valuable sign of commitment and of new beginnings." He paused. The crowd didn't make a sound. They, like Amelia, were holding their breath.

"Five hundred years ago, Richard III killed our young and rightful king, Edward V, and his brother in the Tower of London and took his crown — both literally and figuratively. While the Wars of the Roses ensured that the Yorkish line of kings ended with Richard, the boy king's crown remained in York, a symbol of the conflict we all know has not yet truly ended between the houses of York and Lancaster." A gust of wind tugged at the flags on the stage.

"Today, my fiancée, the Lady Amelia Brockett, daughter of York, comes to return that crown."

The crowd reacted in shock. There were no shouts, but a current of whispers ran through the assembled masses.

Arthur stepped out from behind the podium, which was Amelia's cue to stand beside him again. The whispers died away, leaving only the hiss of the wind.

"Your Majesty," Amelia said. Strategically placed microphones caught and amplified her voice without her having to raise it. Which was fortunate, because it felt like the wind was trying to tear the words from her mouth. "Wars have no winners and deserve no trophies. On behalf of York I return to you what was stolen, so that we might heal and one day celebrate a victory of true unity."

She held up the box for Arthur to take. Their fingers brushed. Even through both their gloves it sent a shockwave of heat up Amelia's arms. Her cheeks flamed. Arthur met her gaze, his eyes steady and very serious. For just a moment, as the box passed from York to Lancaster, they were the only people in this frigid wind-swept place.

Amelia dropped her hands. Arthur expressed gratitude and appreciation for what the north was returning. Amelia waited 'til he was done and counted five to make absolutely sure every eye was pinned on her and what she would do next.

She curtsied, the full, deep, ancient curtsy no one performed anymore. Her father bowed as well.

Amelia stayed there, knees bent, head bowed, and waited for the world to change.

Please, please let this work she prayed to God, to George's ravens, to a million things she didn't believe in.

The crowd broke out in loud, confused, but mostly happy-sounding shouts. It wasn't the roar of approval she had received in York simply for being there, but it was something. This was the sound of a new beginning, of hope. But even though the crowd's reaction had been the point of this humiliating exercise, Amelia couldn't move until a sign came that it was safe for her — and for all of York — to rise.

The sign was George. The child who would have been queen, cool as a marble statue with her pale skin and grey coat, stepped forward. She took Amelia's hands and raised her from her curtsy, the faintest smile on her face.

"You did well," she murmured and drew Amelia into a brief, affectionate embrace and kissed her cheek.

❁

The four of them dined together that evening. After the meal, before he departed for the car that would take him back to the train station, Lord Kirkham drew Amelia aside.

"I brought something else from York," he said.

"What is it?" Amelia asked with a frown. Today had been a success by all accounts. She couldn't imagine another Kirkham treasure needing to be sacrificed to king and country.

"Your mother tells me you'll be travelling with His Majesty on a tour of the Commonwealth."

"No tour, just Canada, but, yes."

"If you're going to appear at the side of a king, you should look like a queen, whether he's given you a crown yet or not. Your mother and I, we want you to have this."

With that, he drew a flat, square box from the folds of his bulky overcoat. "It was highly useful, having those bodyguards on the way down. Otherwise I can't imagine the headache it would have been getting this to you."

Amelia opened the box with trembling fingers. Inside, nestled in velvet at least as old as the building they were standing in, was the Kirkham tiara. Amelia remembered her mother wearing it on a small handful of very formal occasions; there were photographs of her grandmother and paintings of her great-grandmothers wearing it displayed in the house.

"Joining our families together doesn't mean losing our history," he said. "Your prince isn't wrong. A unified England that acknowledges York and all our history will be a beautiful thing. And never, until he took the throne, did I think it would ever be possible."

Chapter 24

CANADA CELEBRATES ROYAL COUPLE

12 January
Year 1 of the Reign of King Gregory I

The return of the Tower Crown has lifted a weight from me. Perhaps because we believe it has cooled the chaos brought about by the announcement of pari passu; the evening news — and the morning papers — in both York and London were favorable at least. But perhaps I have also been relieved of a burden that lay hidden in my blood. Only time will tell, at least as regards our ultimate success.

I had hoped a transatlantic flight would give Arthur and I the opportunity talk about the ceremony yesterday or what we're going to do in Canada, or...anything really. But he's holed up with his equerry doing I don't even know what — history suggests this only leads to chaos. Meanwhile, I've been left to my own devices. At least Edward and Macsen are along for the trip, or I'd go crazy for no one to talk to.

So far into this adventure I shouldn't feel like I'm still auditioning for this life. But I still do.

Will I ever not?

❁

They landed precisely on time, as if even jet streams bent to royal will now that the great houses of England had made their tentative peace. Standing at the plane door, waiting to descend the stairs to the tarmac, Amelia wished she'd chosen to sleep more during the flight. They'd been given their itinerary for the day, and it would be hours before they would reach the hotel. She tugged at her gloves.

"Are you nervous?" It was the most Arthur had said to her in hours.

"Yes," she said. "It's my first official visit as whatever on earth it is that I am."

"You are Lady Amelia," Arthur said simply, as if that were all would matter. As the big door was opened, he offered his arm to her. "Shall we?"

❁

They were greeted by the Canadian Prime Minister and a phalanx of adorable schoolchildren, all of them bundled in parkas and holding flowers. Amelia could almost feel the entire country swoon when Arthur gravely accepted a clutch of red and white roses from a little girl in a white coat and bright red hat. Twined around the stems was a ribbon printed with *Toronto*, *York*, and *London*. Amelia smiled to herself. The red and white of the Canadian flag were certainly convenient. Whatever Beatrice and the chief steward tried, her roses couldn't be hidden. They were everywhere.

After that, the day passed in a blur. Amelia and Arthur lunched with the Prime Minister — who was even more handsome in real life than on the television — before Arthur went to meet with officials at Queen's Park. Amelia, meanwhile, visited science classrooms at a girl's school. It seemed so long ago that she'd told Arthur she wanted to improve science education for girls. Perhaps when and if all the clamor over her very existence finally died down, she could get back to work that could do some concrete good. But first, she was due to attend a cocktail party for Toronto's own bee charity.

She and Arthur weren't reunited until ten o'clock that evening when they finally arrived at the hotel from their separate appointments. Their luggage had already been delivered, but both hotel staff and their personal staff were nowhere to be seen. She was left standing across from Arthur in the suite they'd be sharing for the duration of the trip.

There was a dining room, a sitting area, and a fireplace. Two doors on opposite walls led into separate hallways. Arthur's master suite was on one side, Amelia's was on the other. She wondered how many people believed they truly weren't sharing a bed.

"I know things have been difficult recently." Arthur walked around the sofa toward her. "The pressure on us both is considerable. But I at least feel better to be far from home."

"You rule the Commonwealth. This is your home."

Arthur laughed tiredly as he came to stand in front of Amelia. "You know what I mean. What happens if we try to enjoy this? Take a break from everything that makes our lives difficult?"

"You can't take a break from all of that unless you abdicate. Which I don't think you're interested in doing."

"True," Arthur allowed. "But the protesters outside Buckingham Palace can't reach us here, and there are no ghosts of dead princes haunting these halls. I'm also fairly sure even you can't summon a raven all the way across the Atlantic."

Amelia smiled wanly. "I've asked Macsen to keep me closely updated on the situation in both London and York. I won't celebrate our absence from a crisis, only the absence of a crisis."

"You're a queen already."

"I'm not, but thank you," Amelia said. "Now. What did you have in mind in terms of enjoyment?" Amelia asked. This far from home, she felt bold.

Arthur smiled. "Many things. But not tonight. You must be exhausted."

"And you're not?" she shot back.

"Oh, I am." He leaned forward quickly, before she was expecting it, and pressed a fleeting kiss to her lips. "But we'll both enjoy this trip more after a decent night's sleep."

Before Amelia could protest, he was gone.

❀

She saw Arthur only briefly in the morning. They ate breakfast together, though it was hardly an intimate affair. Arthur had his equerry and his valet and an aide briefing him on his schedule and going over final details. The bustle around Amelia was less complicated, but only marginally.

Macsen sat on a stool next to her at the table, reading her headlines and tweets about the situation at home and the royal visit — people seemed to be reacting favorably — and briefing her on her own schedule for the day. An assistant provided by the Canadian government hovered at her shoulder, making final adjustments to her hair and clothes. It was like four weeks' worth of events in London packed into seventy-two hours. Amelia was dimly aware that she was already tired, but she'd been tired for months. Now, at least, she was exhilarated too.

She spent the day at more schools, taking tours, giving talks, and being shown all manner of science projects and experiments. She was applauded everywhere she went, and while that might have been politeness, Amelia thought it might also contain some actual enthusiasm.

Students' eyes lit up when she took the time to examine their projects and ask questions. Teachers and administrators were happy, even eager, to discuss their programs. What they had, what they needed, and what they hoped for.

While Amelia listened, Macsen, at her elbow, scribbled down notes. Amelia wasn't going to just smile and nod and leave; she was going to take what she heard and do something about it. *This* was what Amelia had dreamed of, back when Arthur first made her his offer. One day soon, she'd be able to do this same thing in London, and then, most importantly, in York.

When the school day ended, Amelia was hurried back to the hotel to get ready for the state dinner being held that evening. She crossed paths with Arthur, who was leaving the suite just as she entered it. He was dressed already, in a tailcoat decorated with all the requisite medals and honors for such an occasion.

"You'll have to excuse me," he said. He looked tired and distracted. "I have one more thing I have to attend to. I'll meet you before we have to leave." He strode off down the hallway, his medals clinking softly over the sound of his and his security's footsteps.

Amelia barely had time to wonder where he was going. As soon as she stepped inside the suite she was whisked into her room by her assistant.

Macsen pressed painkillers and a glass of water into her hand even before they started on her makeup. When Amelia protested that she was fine, he shook his head.

"You've got six hours of schmoozing and dancing in heels and a tiara ahead of you. If you don't have a headache now, you will."

"What do you know about any of that?" Amelia asked.

Macsen laughed. "Trust me."

"How are things at home?" she asked.

"Quieter," he said softly. "Edward says there were no arrests today and only two dozen protesters at Buckingham."

By now it was almost routine to sit in a chair for hours while she was transformed into the image of a storybook princess. But she'd never worn the Kirkham tiara before. She thrilled as she watched the assistant nestle it on top of her curls and then hold it in place with all sorts of ingenious hidden pins and elastic bands. Made of diamonds and Whitby jet set in gold, the tiara was unique and — thanks to the jet — unmistakably northern.

❀

Arthur, despite his promise, was late. Amelia spent a quarter of an hour sitting in the car, perched uncomfortably on the seat so as not to crease the skirt of her gown or crush the petticoat, and getting increasingly annoyed.

Finally the door opened and Arthur — and a blast of cold air — slid in.

"Did you get lost?" Amelia asked, her voice dry as the door was shut behind him and the car began to move.

"Fortunately no. Although it was touch and go for a while there. I was starting to be concerned that if we wandered even a little off track I'd wind up on the tundra with only the stray polar bear between me and the North Pole."

"I'm glad you made it. Although perhaps if you got lost in the wild the Commonwealth would stay together out of sheer guilt."

"Can you even imagine the apologies Canada would make?"

Before Amelia could react, Arthur's mobile chirped. He dug it out of his pocket to check the message. Amelia frowned. What disastrous thing had happened back home?

"What is it?" Amelia asked, as Arthur typed a reply.

"Just a moment."

Amelia waited, not at all patiently. Arthur poked at the screen some more, before he handed the mobile to Amelia.

Amelia felt her mouth drop open in shock.

THE FIRST QUEER PEER, the headline read. HELEN LAWRENCE, DUCHESS OF WATER EATON, ANNOUNCES HER BETROTHAL TO MARGARET EVELYN, BARONESS OF GODSTONE.

Amelia had to read it twice and skim through the first paragraph of the article before she looked back at Arthur. He was sitting back in his seat, legs crossed at the knee, hands folded easily in his lap. He looked smug.

"Why didn't you tell me?" she demanded. Of all the pieces of news she had anticipated, she had never expected this to be the coda to all her fretting about Helen.

"Tell you what?"

Amelia waved her hands to indicate the mobile, Arthur, herself, and possibly all of existence. "This!"

Arthur shrugged. "It was hardly my information to share."

"The papers were full of people who wanted you to set me aside — for her!"

"And that wasn't going to happen," Arthur said. "No matter what they wanted. Or what you feared."

"Why was she at the palace?"

"Ah yes, that." Arthur looked somewhat pained. "Helen wanted advice about rolling out this information. I needed advice on how to handle Parliament threatening to refuse my choice of bride. My reputation as a womanizer has been convenient to me — and to Helen and Margaret — in the past."

"But not to me!" Amelia wasn't angry so much as annoyed at Arthur and at herself.

"I know. And I'm sorry for that. We tried to be discrete. But it was one good thing I could do that wouldn't cause any more protests or controversy. They'll be the first same-gender marriage amongst the British peerage, with the full affection and support of their king."

Amelia's irritation drained away, leaving her with the realization that she and Arthur weren't so different after all. Amelia could listen to teachers and schoolchildren. Arthur could do this for his friends and for his people. Little things in the big picture, perhaps, but not to the people whose lives they affected. She felt a wave of respect for him.

"I suppose," she said as the car turned a corner and brought the lights of the evening's venue into view, "that this announcement will also further distract the public from your marriage to a certain northern girl."

Even in the dim light of the car, she could see Arthur's smirk. "I would never have asked them to plan their announcement to suit my convenience."

"No?"

"Not in a thousand years." The car drew to a stop under the great house's portico. "Helen offered."

Amelia laughed.

Arthur smiled at her and grabbed her hand where it was resting in her lap. "And now," he said, as attendants approached the car to open the doors. "Let's go show Canada what an excellent idea my marriage to a certain northern girl is."

❀

Snow was falling when they stepped out of the car. Flakes landed in Amelia's eyelashes. She blinked them away as she took Arthur's arm and proceeded down the red carpet with him. Combined with the camera flashes going off it lent a magical, if blinding, air to the whole evening, though Amelia was glad when they were inside where it was warm again.

Dignitaries and their spouses filled the foyer, the men in white tie, the women in gowns that glittered under the lights. Amelia watched as Arthur had to reenact handshake after handshake for the sake of the official photographer. They couldn't go two feet without being stopped to take a picture with another guest. She kept waiting for someone to ask for a selfie. She wondered if saying yes to that sort of thing was allowed.

"Ready to dazzle them all?" Arthur bent to whisper in her ear as they waited to be announced to the ballroom proper.

Amelia shivered at his breath against her ear as they were waved forward to the top of a staircase. The doors opened, and her reply caught in her throat at the sight of the crowd in the ballroom below and all the upturned faces gazing at her and Arthur as they appeared.

"His Majesty King Gregory the First," a deep voice intoned. "And the Lady Amelia Brockett."

❁

Arthur and Amelia were seated at dinner with the Prime Minister and his wife, and the Governor General and her husband. Amelia made charming small talk, quickly deflected queries regarding the protests and felt, finally, as Arthur excused himself from the table for his speech, like someone capable of being queen.

Arthur's speech quickly caught and held the attention of the entire ballroom. He was very, very good at this. Amelia supposed she shouldn't have been surprised considering how recklessly, but ultimately deftly, Arthur had maneuvered them through all the crises of her northernness. Here, in a recalcitrant Commonwealth country that didn't want him to be their king, Arthur could so easily look pathetic to be pleading for his relevance. But instead he was dashing as he invoked the great and special relationship between the British and Canadian peoples and any number of things about the fundamental wonderfulness of the Commonwealth.

When he finished, the audience applauded enthusiastically. As Arthur took his seat next to Amelia again she couldn't help but lean over and whisper *well done* in his ear. In return he grabbed her hand and kissed the back of it, his eyes crinkled up in a smile.

"Next time we're here, you get to make the speech."

"Ohhh, no no no no no no," Amelia demurred, although she suspected, in time, she would relish the opportunity.

"They'll get tired of my charms soon enough. But I quite think they'll like yours." Arthur was clearly riding a bit high on the attention and success of the evening.

She gave him a smug smile. "You're in a room full of people who love you and you're enjoying every moment of it."

As if to prove her point, Arthur left the table soon thereafter to grace the other tables with his presence, and, she supposed, to advocate for the Commonwealth. He only returned when the music from the small orchestra began.

"Lady Amelia," he said, that glint of fun still in his eye. "May I have this dance?"

Amelia expected Arthur to make conversation with her as they danced. Surely he wanted to discuss the progress of the evening or what they'd done during the day. But he didn't say anything, just looked at her with that intense gaze he had occasionally turned on her but never entirely followed through on.

They'd danced together once before when she'd been at Sandringham learning to be a princess. That was before Henry had died and the world had become so difficult. Since then Amelia had hardly had a moment to relax. But she was relaxed now, happy and easy in Arthur's arms as he led her around the dancefloor. For the moment, there wasn't anything to hope for or fear from the future. There was only now and Arthur's eyes intent on hers.

They were both wearing gloves, thanks to the dictates of a white tie affair; their skin wasn't even touching. Still, Amelia was acutely aware of every point of contact and was nearly out of her mind for wanting to do away with all of the layers that were between their bodies.

Before she could do anything regrettable, like kiss the King of England at the state dinner held in his honor, she cast about for a conversation topic. Her gaze fell on the young Prime Minister, dancing with the Governor General.

"Do you wish it was you?" she asked, remembering their long-ago conversation about him at Gatcombe. She nodded her chin over Arthur's shoulder. He turned his head slightly to see who she was talking about.

"I wish a lot of things. But living out life as more than a lightning rod for superstition would be nice."

"That will calm down eventually." Amelia said. "Although perhaps only once we both decide where we stand on those very superstitions."

"Indeed," Arthur said wryly. After a moment he spoke again. "We should do this more."

"Attend state dinners in Commonwealth countries?"

"Dance together."

Amelia was aware that they were attracting eyes beyond what it was reasonable to expect given that the King was dancing with his fiancée.

"Everyone's staring," she whispered to him as the song ended. She expected him to drop her hand and for them to go their separate ways. He always did right as they started to connect.

"I hadn't noticed," he said and whirled her back onto the floor.

❁

As soon as they entered their suite back at the hotel room, Arthur dismissed their staff for the night. Macsen and Edward both hovered for a moment in a kindness that moved Amelia deeply, but this was not the time for their protectiveness. She signaled them to go as well.

Arthur and Amelia stared at each other from opposite ends of the room. Arthur took a step toward her. Amelia's heart beat so loudly she was sure he could hear it.

And then, suddenly, he stopped and turned away.

Amelia's heart quivered with confusion. What could have possibly gone wrong? She had been so sure that this time all of Arthur's hot and cold would be replaced only with desire for her and a celebration of the budding success of their partnership. "Arthur?" she asked.

"Just let me deal with all this," he said softly. He lifted the collar and badge of the Order of Canada over his head and placed them on the desk, wincing as they clattered. When he shrugged off his tailcoat there was a faint rattle and clinking from the honors pinned to it. After that there was the sash. He laid it all aside with an ease that spoke to long practice. Amelia was riveted.

"I didn't know it was all so jangly," she said, needing to break the silence.

"Shhh."

"Are you *embarrassed?*" Amelia was too astonished at the idea — and Arthur's odd insistence on something like modesty — to follow his directive.

Arthur shook out a sleeve to undo the cufflink. "I don't want it to come between us."

His voice was so low Amelia could hardly hear it. They'd been dating, of a sort, for over a year; they'd been engaged for months. They'd weathered all manner of crisis together and had kissed desperately more than once. They had also fought and been strangers to each other. Never had they had a moment that felt as intimate as this. And they weren't even touching...yet.

Amelia's mother and Priya, and even Arthur, had been correct. Virginity was a big deal, and yet, it wasn't. Not at all. She'd once expected to meet this night with resignation, or with unrequited love. But now, certain of what was to come no matter how unexpected, she felt neither of those things. She was happy. She enjoyed Arthur's company. The situation wasn't perfect, but it was good. He was kind. They made each other smile, and they made each other burn. And someday, possibly sooner than she had once thought, it would be even better.

She crossed the room to stand in front of the sideboard with the big mirror over it to divest herself as well. She had to take off her rings to get her gloves off, and they caught the light fantastically. Amelia took a moment to admire them — Arthur had chosen well — but she left them on top of her gloves.

The tiara was more complex. She breathed a sigh of relief when she untangled her last strand of hair from it and could finally set it aside. She was just reaching for her necklace when Arthur appeared in the mirror behind her.

"Allow me," he said softly. The first few studs of his shirt were undone, exposing his throat, and his sleeves were rolled back to the elbow. Amelia met his eyes in the mirror and nodded.

He carefully unhooked the clasp and laid it with her other jewels. Amelia thought he might unfasten her dress, but Arthur touched her hair instead.

With deft fingers he took down what was left of the elaborate knot it had been twisted into. He didn't pull at all as he tugged out hairpins and untwisted curls, which was more than Amelia could say for her own abilities. When that was done he ran his fingers through it until it fell in neat waves down her back, then gathered it over one shoulder to kiss the nape of her neck.

Amelia shivered.

His fingers hovered above the fastenings of her dress. He wasn't touching her, but she could feel the heat of his skin.

"Go ahead," she breathed.

"Are you sure?"

"If I wasn't before, your striptease with the medals certainly convinced me."

"Amelia," he said, breathless and gently chiding. "You said, before, that you were nervous." His fingertips brushed her skin. Goosebumps broke out over Amelia's skin.

"Since then I've faced death threats, angry crowds, witchcraft, and the possible end of our country," she said. "I can handle you."

The soft breath of his laugh tingled against her cheek. "Tell me what you like. What you want." He unfastened the hook and eye at the top of her dress. His fingers brushed over her skin as he toyed with, but did not actually lower, her zipper.

"I want you to take me to bed."

"That's not very specific." Arthur's dark eyes glinted at her in the mirror.

"You have to present me with options before I can choose," Amelia challenged.

They stared at each other for a moment in the glass. Then Arthur spun her around and kissed her.

The kiss was sharp and nearly bruising. Amelia gasped into his mouth before she lost her breath entirely. There was only Arthur and his hands as they held her; one grasping her chin to tilt her head back, the other sliding down her back. Any restraint he had previously exhibited was finally, blessedly gone.

When his hand reached the dip in her waist he pulled her against him sharply, Amelia could feel the hard length of him against her hip.

"All right?" Arthur pulled back enough to whisper against her temple.

Amelia responded by shoving her hands into his hair and pulling his mouth back down to hers.

Arthur smiled against her mouth and turned her away from the sideboard. Still kissing her, he walked her backward.

In Arthur's arms she felt as cared-for and well-led as she had all night as they'd danced together. She pressed a smile into Arthur's chest when she realized she had not merely succumbed to metaphor; he actually was leading her in a dance, humming under his breath to keep time.

She looked up at him again when the backs of her knees bumped up against the bed in his room. He smiled at her, soft and wondering.

His fingers found her dress's zipper again. He sank to his knees as he pulled it down, revealing not just her skin but perhaps his nature. He reached up and tugged at the shoulder of her gown. The cloud of violet organza slipped down and puddled at their feet.

Amelia ducked her head with an awkward smile. "I'm sorry."

Arthur paused with his hands halfway under her petticoat. "What on earth for?"

"There's more architecture involved in this dress than the Tower bridge. It's not exactly appealing."

"And that, is where you're wrong." Arthur's clever fingers traced over her ankles and up to the backs of her knees. "Any man with sense knows a good dress is a work of art and appreciates what a woman has to do to wear it."

Amelia tried not to laugh as Arthur managed all the hooks and straps of her undergarments far more deftly than she herself had when getting dressed for the evening.

"Do you think women would wear such dresses if it was not a joy to divest them of all their secret layers," Arthur asked as he undid her garters and rolled down a stocking. Inch by inch, garment by garment, he revealed her.

He pressed a soft kiss to the inside of her thigh as the last of her undergarments were discarded. She had barely stepped out of her knickers when he dragged his mouth the rest of the way up her leg. He parted her with his mouth.

Gary had done this, of course, but not often, without complaint or, frankly, well. Arthur was clever with his tongue and possibly smug. He hummed against her clit.

"Arthur," she tried to say with a sharp tug on his hair. It came out of more of a breathless keen.

Arthur made an inquisitive noise but didn't stop his ministrations. The vibration shot through her body.

"If you keep — I can't stand up."

She wasn't sure how intelligible that was, either. But one moment she was standing, holding on to Arthur for dear life, and the next she was on her back on the bed, Arthur hovering over her, pressing kisses to her throat and breasts and stomach. The fine fabric of his clothes scratched against her skin, lighting up her nerves with an eager heat.

Amelia whined and tried to push him lower, back to where she really wanted him, but he sat up.

"Wait," he said, one hand on her hip.

"For *what?*"

Arthur hung his head sheepishly. Amelia narrowed her eyes. "What?" she repeated.

"I'm afraid I didn't come prepared for any sort of, well. Tryst."

"You don't have condoms," Amelia interpreted and barely refrained from commenting on *tryst*.

"Afraid not. Although I could send someone —"

"Arthur…."

"There's no point in having a staff if I can't send someone to fetch —"

"No," Amelia said.

"No, don't send someone, or no, you don't want to…?"

"Don't send someone." She reached out a hand and hooked her fingers in the open collar of Arthur's shirt.

"Amelia —"

"No. I mean it." She was surprised to find that she did.

"There are any number of things we could —"

"Do you not want to?" Amelia asked.

Arthur looked at her helplessly.

"We both want this," Amelia said. "We've survived the political nightmare we created together. And we're getting married in a matter of months anyway and condoms have nothing to do with why."

The corner of Arthur's mouth quirked up. "That's true."

"And now we've cleared up the misunderstanding about Helen, I feel confident you're not going to be taking any risks with my health. At this point in time or any other. Although you are a terrible womanizer for not having condoms on you at all times."

Arthur laughed.

"What?" Amelia poked him in the side with her bare toes.

"You." Arthur leaned back over her, his weight braced on one arm. "Only you would rattle off a list of evidence for why I should fuck you like you're presenting a paper."

"So are you going to?" Amelia started in on the infuriating studs still holding Arthur's shirt closed.

"That depends on whether you're ever going to manage to get my clothes off."

"Help a little, would you?" she hissed.

Arthur sat back on his heels again, Amelia's hands sliding away from his body. She watched as he worked, his hands efficient with practice.

"Will it always be this awkward?" she asked as Arthur stood to divest himself of his trousers.

He paused with his hands at his waistband. "This isn't awkward, Amelia. It's companionable."

She considered the statement as he skimmed out of the rest of his clothes. She knew he was fit, but it was something else to appreciate his body beyond the abstract. His arms were toned and his chest was broad and defined, with a light dusting of hair. She reached out a hand to skim over his well-muscled thigh. Riding and military service together had done wonderful things for his body.

Suddenly everything Amelia had been worried about for months seemed absurd. Not because Arthur's body was so very worthy of her desire, nor because of the fairytale romance of their very public night out. But because Arthur was right. This *was* companionable. She'd never had that before. But here they were, naked and chatty. Arthur had even thought she was beautiful in beige undergarments meant to hold everything in and push everything up. When he'd said it a few moments ago, she'd thought it was flattery, but now she realized it was true.

Amelia wondered how long it had been since anyone had touched him like this. If she so chose, no one else could ever touch him like this again. It was a heady thought that threatened to overwhelm her.

She heard the soft rustle of sheets as Arthur stretched out next to her. Amelia rolled to face him.

"What are you thinking?" he asked softly. He traced circles on her hip with his fingers.

Confessions were on the tip of Amelia's tongue; there were declarations she had harbored from nearly the beginning of this that were wildly unwise. Would declarations of love cause the moment to crumble? *Companionable* was a life she could live and enjoy, that was clear. She swallowed her heart back down, like any good princess, and kissed him.

Amelia could feel his smile against her lips. And that was lovely, but he was letting her control the kiss and that wasn't what she wanted.

"I won't break," she muttered into his mouth.

The only indication that he'd heard her was when he hauled himself up to sit. He brought Amelia with him, his arms strong around her back, and maneuvered her until she was straddling his waist. Distantly Amelia thought that, with any other man, she would have felt horribly exposed and vulnerable. Positioned like this, there were no sheets to hide under or pillows to press her face into. There was only Arthur, the muscled lines of his torso pressed along her smaller, softer form. This wasn't nerve-wracking, even with all the lights on; it was delicious.

Riding horses had strengthened Amelia's legs, too, but her thighs still trembled when Arthur put a hand under the curve of her arse and helped her raise her hips. Her breath came out in stuttered gasps, from both the effort of holding herself up and from the unfamiliar sensation of Arthur's cock nudging at her folds.

Arthur kept her balanced; one hand on her waist, the other on his prick, as he guided himself into her. It was a strange feeling, having him inside, and Amelia bit her lip and pressed her face in Arthur's shoulder, shifting her hips to try to make it more comfortable.

"I know it feels weird —"

"How would you know?" Amelia half-snapped, half-laughed into Arthur's shoulder.

"Just breathe." Arthur chuckled softly, causing him to shift inside her.

She gasped. Everything felt strange. It didn't hurt, but it wasn't exactly comfortable either. Amelia was still waiting for the wow. She wanted Arthur to move, to win her body over. She was glad when his fingers slid down her stomach and then pressed against her, right where she ached most.

"Much better," she murmured, tensing her muscles around him in search of the angle that was going to make everything *just* right.

"Keep doing that for science and this is going to be over before it's begun," Arthur said as he started to thrust shallowly.

"You mean —" she gasped. Arthur's fingers were good. Adding movement was definitely better.

"It's been over a year." Arthur's voice sounded strangled.

She could barely find her voice herself. "Want to race?" she managed.

He tightened his grip on her waist to thrust harder. "Would prefer you win," he grit out, flicking his thumb against her clit, sharp and perfect.

She made a startled noise. "Right there," she said. "Right *there.*"

Arthur obliged.

Amelia closed her eyes to force herself to give into the pleasure which shot through her body and crept up into her brain. There would be a madness to it, once she surrendered. And letting go had never been something she was very good at. She shoved her hands into Arthur's hair.

"I can't," she said in despair. She was so close, but it was all too much, as if her body were too overwhelmed to relieve her of this want and burden her with its consequences.

"Yes you can," Arthur said against the skin of her neck. He lifted his mouth to her ear. "Do it for me."

That was all it took. Amelia was coming, pulsing around him, and laughing in delight and at the absurdity of her body obeying Arthur, as if she were kingdom to his not-so-meaningless crown.

Before she could even catch her breath Arthur tipped her backward, his hand cradling her head as she hit the mattress. She wrapped her legs around him and urged him on with the heel of her foot now that he could thrust into her in earnest.

All his earlier restraint was gone. Amelia felt powerful, like a witch having summoned the wind, to be the cause of it. There was a sheen of sweat across his forehead, and his hair was a wild wreck from where she had run her hands through it. She was counting the flecks of gold and green in his eyes, when he closed them and came with a shuddering groan.

❦

"What do you think the papers will say?" Amelia asked Arthur's shoulder. She was quite enjoying her blossoming relationship with that part of Arthur's anatomy. And, indeed, every other part of his anatomy. Even if there was an awkward wetness between her legs. It didn't feel bad, just new. And the rest of her felt *fantastic*. Even the pull of unfamiliar muscles was pleasant.

"You mean about the state dinner?" Arthur's voice rumbled through his chest. He stroked one broad hand down her back, a line of pleasant warmth as Amelia gradually became aware of the cool air around them.

"Mmm."

"Probably that we're disgusting young things that couldn't keep their hands off each other."

"Do you mind?" Amelia asked.

Arthur blinked at her. "Why on earth would I mind?"

"We were rather supposed to woo Canada. Not each other."

He smiled. "People love a good romance, and I love a media that isn't angry with me or fomenting unrest. Although, I was dancing with you simply because I wanted to be," Arthur said with a squeeze to her waist.

"You were definitely a better dance partner than most of the people I danced with. Especially the Prime Minister."

"He's a brilliant politician."

"Good thing too. He can't find the beat to save his life."

Arthur chuckled. "All of my partners were perfectly lovely."

Amelia lifted her head so Arthur could see her roll her eyes exaggeratedly. "Always the gentleman."

"Mmm, not *always.*" Arthur's hand wandered onto her arse and pinched.

"Can I ask about Helen?" Amelia ventured. "Not jealousy, mind. Just, curiosity. I'm still learning who you are and trying to understand the history — the personal history that is — that I've been dropped down in the middle of."

Arthur frowned, but in thoughtfulness not anger. "Helen and I have been friends for decades. Really, since we were children. We almost went to bed together once, after Imogene died. Never mind that she prefers women, it was just too absurd to go through with. We even talked of getting married. If we weren't in love, at least we both would have had companionship and security. But she met Margaret, and the marriage laws changed, and it hardly made sense anymore. But for a while, that was my plan. Our plan," he corrected himself. "So then I got a new one."

"Me," Amelia suggested.

"Not you, specifically, at first. But, yes, you."

She rolled onto her back. To her surprise, Arthur went with her, resting his head on her chest. She pushed her fingers into his hair and marveled at finally being allowed to touch; maybe she'd been wrong. Maybe she had never needed permission at all.

❀

Amelia woke because she was cold. She pulled the duvet up more snugly under her chin, rolled over in search of Arthur to curl up against, and encountered...nothing.

She squinted her eyes open. The room was dark, except for a beam of light filtering in from the sitting room. Arthur wasn't in bed with her — because Arthur was sitting on the sofa, fully dressed, one knee crossed over the other, looking at something on his tablet. The clock on the nightstand said six a.m. Their first event wasn't until nine.

"Arthur?" she said.

At first she thought he hadn't heard her; he certainly didn't look up from his tablet. She had just sat up to go out to him when he spoke.

"You're awake." There was no pleasure in his voice, only something like dread.

"Yes?"

"Please explain this to me." He held out the tablet.

"I can't see what you're talking about." Amelia's stomach squirmed unpleasantly. What had happened back in England? Was it the ravens? Had York done something terrible?

"Very well." Arthur's voice was hard and cold, the way it was when he browbeat particularly intransigent wedding committee members into doing things the way he wanted. For all their difficulties, he'd never turned that voice on her before. "It's a tweet, from the University of California at Santa Barbara. Congratulating you on your acceptance and welcoming you to the next matriculating class."

Amelia didn't understand. "You knew I was applying to graduate programs."

"Yes, before we got engaged. Our wedding date is *weeks* away."

"I wanted to have options," Amelia said slowly.

"Options." Arthur repeated.

"I got the acceptance almost a year ago!"

"And you said *yes?*" Arthur dropped the tablet in a clear fit of incredulity.

Amelia clutched the sheets to her. "I didn't say no!"

"After everything we agreed to! I proposed to you. I'm uniting the country for you. I created a new kind of queen for you!" Arthur was on his feet now. "I shouted at the Prime Minister, to keep that crown on your head!"

"Did you?" Amelia put her hand over her mouth. There could be no more inopportune moment to ask the question, but she hadn't known that particular detail.

"I have spent years' worth of political capital and have no fallback position. I'm flying without a net here, Amelia, *and you deferred your admission!*"

"It happened before any of queen pari passu, Arthur. I didn't know if our experiment would work out, I wanted some insurance and made the best choice I could. And then, when I should have been notifying them of a change in my plans, I was trapped in limbo!" Amelia shouted back. She got out of bed, went to her wardrobe, and began pulling on clothes. She could not have this argument naked, she was far too vulnerable.

"I saw the ministers coming," she said as she pulled on a sweater. "I know what they wanted you to do. You met with Helen, but you didn't tell me anything. All I had was the speculation of the papers to go on and the crumbs George would bring me! What was I supposed to do, sit and wait until the headsman came?"

"Helen!" Arthur exclaimed as she marched out into the living area. "Did you hear anything I said to you about her last night? I had to decide what to do with you, and she's one of the only people I trust. She spent two weeks convincing me not to pack you off back north to your family!"

"Maybe you should have!" Amelia spat back. Angry tears stung her eyes, but she willed herself not to cry.

"After this," Arthur snatched the tablet up again, "What reason do I have not to?"

Amelia's coat was in the hall closet. She grabbed it and then pulled the door to the hallway open. She did not slam it behind her — queens to be did not slam doors — but she came close.

"Ma'am, can I help you?"

Amelia jumped at the unfamiliar voice. They'd been given a Canadian security detail when they landed, and she didn't recognize the man standing outside the door.

She put on her very sunniest smile and hoped her eyes weren't too red. "No, thank you." She darted down the hall before he could say anything else or think to stop her.

By the time Amelia got to the lobby — she pulled her hood up to avoid the eyes of strangers and the snow swirling outside — she was completely alone. It was so cold outside her breath contracted in her chest, and she coughed involuntarily. The tears froze and stung on her face.

For a moment she considered going back inside. She certainly had no intention of freezing on a random street in Toronto. But going back inside would mean facing Arthur. There was no way their argument could end well, although at least if he did break their engagement off now, she could flee to the States for school. Amelia laughed at the absurdity, and realized, suddenly, that she was completely alone for the first time in months. No Priya, no Arthur, no Macsen, and no Edward — he didn't come on duty for at least another hour.

Amelia took a deep breath. This time she didn't cough. "Well, come on then," she muttered to herself, before choosing a direction at random and setting out. Who knew when she in her impending ignominy would ever return to Toronto. She might as well see it.

Toronto was not, she quickly realized, an early-rising city. The sky was a dark, heavy blue, just turning light with the coming day. The area around the hotel was mostly tall ugly skyscrapers, surely lively during the week, but empty and silent this early on a Sunday. They'd driven through many interesting-looking parts of the city over the last couple of days but this was not one of them. Increasingly, Amelia was sure she'd made a mistake: Not just in storming out, but in agreeing to this entire ridiculous experiment.

For the lack of any other particular destination — and because it was freezing out — she looked for coffee shops. It didn't take long to find one, and she breathed a sigh of relief when it was actually open.

The girl behind the counter had to be about Amelia's age. She looked up from a textbook and dog-eared notebook when the bell over the door rang.

"Hi, what can I — oh my God, you're the Princess," she said all in a rush and bolted to her feet.

Amelia meant to say "I'm not a princess," but what came out was a sob.

"Are you okay? Are you hurt? Lost?" the girl behind the counter asked frantically. "Do you need me to call someone?"

"Please don't do that," Amelia managed through her tears.

"Are you sure? You, um…." The girl pulled a few napkins out of a dispenser and held them out for Amelia. Amelia took them with a mumbled a *thank you*, blew her nose, and scrubbed at her eyes.

"I'm —" Amelia said. "I, um, wanted to get away. Arthur and I had a fight."

"Arthur — you mean like, King Arthur. Or Gregory. Whatever he is now."

Amelia nodded. "Gregory. King Arthur sounded stupid."

"Did he hurt you?"

"No." Amelia shook her head. "No. Nothing like that."

"Do you want some coffee? You could hide in our storeroom while I get it?" The girl pointed awkwardly. "Am I supposed to curtsey?"

"I'm not a princess," Amelia said again. The girl flipped up a segment of the counter and dragged Amelia behind it, before pushing open the promised storeroom door.

"Sorry, it's full of stuff."

Amelia shrugged helplessly. She was happy to sit down on a cardboard box and brush the worst of the snow off her coat while her rescuer bustled back to the counter and returned a moment later with a steaming paper cup of coffee and a carton of doughnut holes.

"Thank you." Amelia croaked as she took the coffee and shifted so the girl — Robin, her nametag said — could set the carton down next to her. Robin then turned an empty bucket over and sat across from her. Their knees knocked in the small space.

"'Course. Um. Is there anything else I can do for you?"

"I don't want to keep you from," Amelia waved the hand that wasn't holding a scalding cup of coffee at the door and, beyond it, the counter.

"Eh, I'll hear anybody come in, it's all good. You sure you're not hurt or anything?"

Amelia shook her head. The warmth and smell of the coffee was immensely comforting. Although if she thought too hard about the world outside of this absurd little closet, she would start crying all over again.

"Sorry," Robin said. "I don't mean to pry. You don't have to tell me anything."

"No, no, it's okay." Amelia took a fortifying sip of coffee. "I don't have anyone I can tell about it anyway. Everyone else works for him or has way too many opinions. What am I going to *do*?"

"Drink coffee until noon and then drink beer?"

Amelia cracked a watery smile. Robin grinned at her.

"Arthur and I had a fight," Amelia said again. "Because a school I applied to before we got engaged accepted me and then tweeted about it. And I stormed out. Because, for a king, he can be a stubborn arsehole."

Robin looked torn between horror and delight.

"And now it's seven in the morning, and it's snowing, and I don't even know if we're getting married anymore."

"I'm sure it's not that bad," Robin said, with a friendly pat to her knee.

"There was a lot of yelling. Like, really ugly. A normal man would consider calling it off. *I* should consider calling it off. But I've been engaged to him for almost a year now. There's nothing else I can do. And my fiancé threatened to set me aside because I am a political disaster. I've failed my people. I've failed my king. I've failed myself. And the only reason I'm not scared for my life is beheading's gone out of style."

She took a breath and stared into the coffee in her hands. Brown, like Arthur's eyes. "I'm in love with him, and I'm not supposed to be," she said. "He needed a bride, and I wanted a purpose. And what we had — it could have been enough. Except now we're furious with each other."

"Does he know how you feel?"

"Of course not. He thinks I was going to run away to school in America."

The bell over the door jangled.

Robin hesitated before standing up. "You," she said, pointing to Amelia and then the doughnut holes. "Eat sugar and carbs. I'll be right back."

She shut the supply closet door behind her, for which Amelia was grateful. Even if she still had no idea what she was going to do.

Her mobile buzzed in her pocket and she froze in the middle of taking another gulp of coffee. It was from the trip coordinator. *Morning session with BSCE cancelled*, it read. Oh God. If they had to cancel appearances because she'd disappeared to a coffee shop, she was utterly out of luck. But then she read the rest of the message: *Due to inclement weather.* Maybe that was just what they were calling vanished princesses these days?

There was a gentle knock on the door, before it opened a crack. Robin stuck her head in. "Hey," she said quietly. "There's two people out here. One says he's with your security detail? The, quote, 'proper one, not the damned Mounties who can't find their way out of a paper bag.'" The girl made a passable attempt at Edward's accent. "The other one just looks worried. And kinda hot?"

"Edward? And Macsen?"

"Yeah, maybe?"

Amelia stood up and brushed crumbs off her coat.

"I can tell him to fuck off if you want," Robin offered.

"No, it's okay." Amelia smiled weakly at her. "I'll talk to them."

Edward's entire being sagged in relief when Amelia walked out of the supply closet. "Oh, thank God, Lady Amelia."

Macsen just waved at her.

"See! 'Lady Amelia.' That's the stuff I'm talking about. Are you sure I'm not supposed to curtsey?"

"Quite sure. Thank you," Amelia smiled at Robin as she flipped the counter segment back up for Amelia to go through again.

"You gave us quite a scare," Edward said. He looked like he wanted to hug her; Amelia wouldn't have minded if he had. But she was almost royalty — at least for the moment — and in his charge. It wasn't allowed.

"I'm sorry," she said. "I didn't mean to let you down."

"You haven't," Macsen said. "You ran away to a location where we could get a snack in the middle of the crisis, for which I think we're both very appreciative."

Amelia smiled weakly.

"I guess you're here to drag me back to the hotel to await my fate?" Amelia asked. Out of the corner of her eye, she could see Robin retreat to a discreet distance and start wiping down machines.

"Not at all." Edward looked almost offended at the suggestion. "I am here to protect you, Lady Amelia. What that means is up to you."

Amelia had always appreciated the extent to which Edward was in her corner. She felt something in her lungs loosen.

"I suppose I should go back, then," she said, with a frown out the big plate glass windows. The snow was coming down harder than ever. Apparently the event really had been cancelled for weather after all. "That's only going to get worse."

She waved at the snow but meant all of it — the fight, Arthur, the necessity of deciding all over again whether she would submit herself to this ridiculous life.

"Amelia," Arthur breathed when Amelia walked into hotel suite, Edward at her side.

"Your Majesty," Amelia said. Arthur had been striding toward her, but he stopped in his tracks. Something in his face shuttered closed.

"I'm glad you're all right," he said.

"I must apologize for raising my voice at you," Amelia said. She looked at the painting on the wall over Arthur's shoulder, not Arthur himself.

"Of course. I must as well," he said just as stiffly.

"I was told our event this morning was cancelled, is that correct?"

"Yes. Inclement weather."

"Then I will be in my room until you need me elsewhere. Good morning, sir," she said, and then turned on her heel, walked into her room, and closed the door — gently — behind her.

Chapter 25

ALL EYES TURN TO LONDON AS THE NUPTIALS OF THE CENTURY APPROACH

1 March
Year 1 of the Reign of King Gregory I

George turned eighteen last week. Princess Violet has officially recused herself from the line of succession. A single breath and any child I bear are the only things standing between George and the throne.

The wedding is still on. Not because things are good between us, but because Arthur is too stubborn to give in now that we've won over everyone except, apparently, each other. It's definitely not out of loyalty to me or even a desire to fix what's between us. In his mind I betrayed him, not just as a royal bride-to-be, but personally. And deeply.

Maybe he's not even wrong; I don't know. I definitely don't know how to go about fixing any of it. And I'm definitely not sure if going through with the marriage is the right choice. Who wants to spend their life with someone who can endure all the worst wounds of public life but not navigate any of the personal wounds of private life? We can't be allies in a grand scheme if we're not even talking to each other.

I feel like one of George's ravens now too. Trapped and with no good options.

❁

Formality was Amelia's refuge. Each custom and tradition and protocol that had grated on her was now a source of profound gratitude. She was not cold to Arthur; she was proper; she was not distant from Priya, she was merely doing what was required of her. She was not shutting out her own family; she was simply becoming a queen.

The formula worked in the reverse as well. Arthur was not cruel to her; he was simply ruling the kingdom via the traditions that had allowed it to endure centuries of its own chaos and bad behavior.

But the refuge of propriety was not companionship. Amelia was lonely. No matter how many people she saw in a day — helping her with her clothes or her meals or her protocol — she was isolated. And so she would soon forever be. Because that's what a queen was. Whether Arthur loved her or not.

❁

The only good thing about the final dress fitting was, as far as Amelia was concerned, the word *final*. She'd gotten to this point once before and that had ended in grief and disaster. What would happen now? If the wedding was going to go on, best to keep her head down and get on with it. She arrived at the bridal salon in no particularly sunny frame of mind.

She'd once found her dress beautiful, back when it had been a compromise and a victory between herself and Arthur. Sleeves and a boat neckline flattered her figure *and* fulfilled all that modesty could require. What had once been Amelia's favorite part — the skirt and train made of dozens of yards of satin embroidered with roses red and white — now struck her as grotesque with Arthur not speaking to her and her own future so bleak.

The buttons that ran up the back were also decorated with tiny roses. Not that Amelia could see them as she watched in the mirror as she was tucked and fastened into the gown. She could, however, see the head seamstress's frown in the mirror as she did up the buttons — or tried to.

"It still fits," she said, yanking on the back of the dress as if to make Amelia's body more readily obey its confines. "Or mostly does. It won't need any adjustments before the wedding, thank goodness, but do try to refrain from stress eating quite so much."

It was on the tip of Amelia's tongue to protest. She *had* been hungrier than usual of late, and more tired, but stress was an absolute monster on any body. She'd tried to be healthy about it. But as she raked her eyes over her own reflection, top to bottom, she felt her heart skip a beat.

She made herself wait until she could check her mobile to freak out completely. When she was finally back in her own clothes looking at her calendar it only told her what she'd already known: She was late. Absolutely, definitely, devastatingly late.

This was not the sort of overachiever she wanted to be, especially considering that she and Arthur still weren't speaking beyond what was absolutely necessary.

"Maybe you're stress hallucinating too," she muttered to herself, while she tried to come up with a plan. She was due at Westminster in less than two hours for a walkthrough of the ceremony and more premarital counseling. Not to address any issues between *them*, of course, but because she and Arthur were to be godly role models for the nation. As usual, everything in her life would be absurdly funny if only it were happening to someone else.

Edward, when he fell in beside her outside the bridal salon, tried to make small talk. Technically, he wasn't supposed to, but he'd been her friend from the moment she'd demanded he introduce himself and walk beside her. But Amelia didn't know how to make small talk right now. The impulse to take silent refuge in formality, to demand he walk behind her without speaking struck fast and strong, but she could not afford to give into it.

"Do we have time to stop?" she blurted as he handed her into the car.

"Yes, I believe so. Is something the matter?" He gave her a worried look as he slid in after her.

She slammed the button to raise the partition between them and the driver. "We need to stop at a Boots, and I need you to do something for me," she said.

Edward regarded her blankly, his expression so neutral and trusting she knew it was trained into him by his work. Surely, he knew she was about to say something at least vaguely awful. "Of course," he said.

She dug in her handbag and came up with nothing but a couple of pound coins. Everything about her almost-royal life was aggravating and intolerable. Absolutely everything. She looked up at him. "I need you to get me a pregnancy test, and I don't have any money on me because I'm an incompetent fake princess and —"

"Breathe," Edward said. He reached a hand out to settle her.

She did as he said. "I need you to get me a pregnancy test."

"All right."

"All right?! Aren't you going to ask what I've done or if it's Arthur's or —" She stopped herself. He'd agreed; that was all she needed. "Thank you," she said and meant it more than she'd ever meant those two words before.

"Do you want me to ask, ma'am?"

Amelia burst into tears. Which was, on balance, better than hyperventilating. Except that Edward's look of careful neutrality melted quickly into kindness and that, somehow, made everything worse.

"We slept together. In Toronto. After the state dinner," she said in between shuddering breaths. She may not have had money in her handbag, but thank God, she did have tissues. "And then there was that *awful* tweet and we fought about it and about everything. And I ran out. That's why you and Macsen had to come find me, and we've barely even spoken to each other since. I spent a whole week thinking he was going to call everything off and now — now —" There was absolutely no way to make blowing one's nose dignified, she reflected hysterically.

"Of course we can stop," Edward repeated gently. "And after that," he took a deep breath, clearly steeling himself. "I will do whatever else it is you need me to do. Do you understand?"

Amelia had no doubt that Edward would help her flee the country if she asked him to, or — well. Assist her. In any other decision she made about the still-technically-unconfirmed-pregnancy. Regardless of the fact that it was, if it did exist, the heir to the throne of the Unified Kingdom. She started crying all over again.

There was a Boots practically across the street from Westminster Abbey. When Edward slid back into the car he held a bag containing not just a pregnancy test but a bottle of juice and a chocolate bar. Amelia burbled her watery thanks, stuffed it all in her purse, and spent the three minutes until they arrived at Westminster frantically trying to fix her makeup.

She was still a mess by the time they arrived, but everyone at the abbey was willing to look the other way at a bride-to-be who'd gotten too emotional before the big day. Edward walked closer than he normally did in such a formal setting and stood guard while she ducked into the ladies' room.

There had been many terrible and absurd things in her life since she had said yes to Arthur's scheme. Taking a pregnancy test in the toilet of Westminster Abbey two weeks before the most elaborate wedding and coronation in living memory was definitely at the top of the list.

When the second line — the important line — appeared on the test, she took a deep breath and lowered her head. Now she knew, and she had no idea what that meant. For her or for her relationship with Arthur. Would this make him love her or would he use it as an excuse to discard her? Was Amelia now more trapped than ever and with no options at all?

None of those questions could be solved in a toilet. And as much as she wanted to stay here where no one could see or judge her, she couldn't. She was going to be queen. She had obligations. If she didn't appear, someone would come looking for her. She trusted Edward to protect her, but she also didn't need him dismissed from the royal service for starting a fight to keep her safe and hidden.

She hastily bundled the test back into its box and shoved the whole thing into her purse. She washed her hands, splashed water on her face, and marched back outside to meet her future.

The Archbishop of Canterbury stood from behind his desk to greet Amelia when she was shown into his office. Arthur hadn't arrived yet. Relief at a few more moments not in his presence quickly turned into dreadful anticipation of his arrival. Waiting was terrible. She had no idea what to tell him. Or when, assuming she was going to tell him at all. Either way, the Archbishop's office was the absolute worst location for it.

By the time Arthur finally arrived her nerves and her nausea had escalated. She felt like she was going to throw up. She assumed it wasn't morning sickness, but stress. In truth, she didn't even know if morning sickness could start this early and had to bite her lip not to succumb to hysterical giggles.

At first, the only notice Arthur took of Amelia was to nod at her; ironic, given that a large point of being here was to be lectured on how to be appropriate role models for all of England. If the Archbishop noted they were not quite as cordial as might be hoped of a soon-to-be-married couple, he gave no comment.

Halfway through an interminable spiel on their divine obligation to do God's work on earth, Amelia instinctively flicked her gaze toward Arthur to share a look of commiseration before she remembered that they weren't on those sorts of terms anymore.

Except Arthur was already looking at her, and when their eyes met, he gave a tiny but very distinct sigh. The Archbishop, unaware, droned on.

Amelia stifled the smile she would have ordinarily responded to that with and instead lifted her shoulder a fraction of an inch.

Arthur didn't roll his eyes. But he managed to convey through a tilt to his eyebrows the exact degree of his annoyance at the whole proceeding.

And so it went on for the rest of the session, Arthur and Amelia exchanging glances whenever the focus on the Archbishop wasn't on them. Amelia was fairly certain the point of premarital counseling was not to bond the objects of said counseling through mutual irritation at the endeavor, but her relief that they could still have some kind of connection was nearly overwhelming.

"Arthur," Amelia hissed at him once they were able to make their escape back out into the hallway. "I need to talk to you." They had five minutes before they had to be in place for the walkthrough.

For a moment Arthur looked stricken, but then he schooled his face into an expression of bland neutrality. "What is it?"

Amelia grabbed him by the hand and dragged him into an alcove off the main hallway. In the instant that she'd hissed his name, she had meant to tell him about the pregnancy. But as she looked Arthur in the face and opened her mouth to tell him, she found she just couldn't. It was too much for the here and now.

"Well?" he asked, his voice verging on the edge of impatience.

That settled it. There was no response Arthur could have that wasn't going to be a disaster for her ability to cope. For her own sanity, she would pretend she got pregnant on their wedding night.

"I just wanted to thank you. In there. It was nice, being on the same page."

❀

The night of the vigil for King Henry, Westminster Abbey had been dark and silent. Now, the sunlight spilled in dramatic stripes across stone pillars and the grave markers set into the floor.

The rest of the wedding party wasn't here; they would have their own rehearsal later. For now their places were taken by stand-ins from the palace staff. The little crowd of mute, unfamiliar faces turned toward Arthur and Amelia as they entered the nave.

Amelia felt a chill that had nothing to do with the coolness of the abbey on a damp spring day. Standing in a pool of sunshine, the stand-ins looked like spirits, waiting to welcome her to the next world.

She barely listened as the wedding coordinator talked them through the sequence of events, returning to the moment only when she heard her name.

"Lady Amelia, after you exit the carriage and come into the church, you and the Lord Kirkham will proceed down the aisle."

When the wedding coordinator looked at her expectantly, she nodded to show she understood.

"Good. Your Majesty, you will be at the altar, facing forward. When Lady Amelia and her father enter, please do remember not to turn around to look."

"Or what, I'll turn to a pillar of salt?" Arthur interrupted. He looked impatient. Why wouldn't he? He'd done this before.

"Quite," the coordinator said blandly. "Then, the Archbishop will perform the ceremony. Once you are married, you will proceed up the dais to sit for the coronation. Lady Amelia, your attendants can take care of themselves; you don't have to fuss over anything, just go where people put you."

Amelia made a face and tried to catch Arthur's eye, but he was staring up at the dais where St. Edward's chair already sat. Beside it was another smaller chair. Amelia's.

It was, she supposed, the natural order of things. They were each going to meet their destinies, and while Arthur was hers, she was just a tool on the way to his. The Archbishop had been plainer and more relevant than she'd realized.

At the coordinator's sign, Arthur ascended the steps to the dais alone.

"It's peculiar, isn't it?" a voice said benignly from Amelia's side as she watched.

Amelia startled. It was George. She hadn't heard her approach or had any idea that she would be here today. Certainly, she was not actively participating in this rehearsal. George, like the rest of the attendants, had a stand-in.

"What are you doing here?" Amelia asked.

"I came in case Arthur needed me."

"To be his court witch?"

George smiled faintly. "Something like that. I came in case you needed me, too." She gave Amelia a piercing look.

Amelia felt her gaze as if it were a physical thing, penetrating bone and soft tissue. She gave a little gasp. Did George know that she was pregnant? There was a smugness to George that suggested that she did. Like so many things in Amelia's royal life, it was impossible and yet true.

"I'm sorry," George said.

Amelia stared at her. Could George really read her mind?

"Why?" she asked.

"You have this life because of me. I begged Arthur to marry again."

Begged was such an un-George-like word. But if it were true — that would make several things make more sense. Or any sense at all.

"I didn't know that."

"I doubt anyone does. Except him and I. And now you. It's a strange, small world you're becoming part of," George said solemnly. "I wanted to welcome you to it. After all, you're a witch, too."

"I'm not," Amelia protested.

"You are. I saw what you did in York."

"That was inexperience. An accident. Or even coincidence."

George shook her head. "Yes, you see. Everyone has great power. Everyone. Only witches know it."

"I don't know if you're joking."

George lifted one elegant shoulder. "They locked up all the ravens because of what they thought you could do."

Up on the dais, Arthur turned around to look out at the abbey. His eyes scanned the rows of empty pews, the great windows, the ancient pillars.

"Is Arthur a witch too?" Amelia asked.

"Of a sort. You should know. You've felt it — his power."

"I suspected. But I wasn't sure…. This isn't. None of this is the sort of thing I've ever allowed myself to believe in. I was a scientist," Amelia said. She wasn't anymore.

"Science was once considered witchcraft," George reminded her.

Amelia nodded, absently, at the wisdom there. The bulk of her attention remained fixed on Arthur. He was the king and master of everything here. Yet the expression on his face was one of helplessness.

He turned his head, and caught Amelia's eye. He held her gaze, and Amelia found herself unable to look away.

"See?" George said quietly. "He needs you. No matter how angry or hurt he is. He needs what you can do. And it's terrible, to be needed by a king."

Chapter 26

ROYAL WEDDING BELLS...FINALLY!

6 April
Year 1 of the Reign of King Gregory I

Welcome to the end of the line.

I'm getting married tomorrow. Starting the day after, I have to write — daily — in an official diary given to me by the palace. For posterity and all that. I'm not sure if I get a day off for giving birth.

Arthur still doesn't know, and I have no idea how to tell him. He'll probably be angry that I waited so long to share the news, but there's nothing for it now. Life continues on — for me, for him, for the monarchy, and for this country. My body proves that, whether I like it or not.

The reality of queen pari passu actually happening tomorrow has brought an unease to the kingdom again even with all the strides we've made. But the wedding is only a beginning, and the gulf between our peoples is still wide. Some days bridging that gap seems all but impossible, but I will find a way — if not in my home, then in my land.

Amelia woke before dawn on the day of the wedding to a pounding on her bedroom door.

"Hello?" she asked blearily. How had someone got into her rooms? If a servant needed to wake her they would have done so much more quietly. A faint corner of her mind wondered if she was about to be dragged off to the Tower in ignominy and shame.

The latch clicked, the door flew open, and in rushed Priya.

"Priya!" Amelia threw back the covers and met her friend in the middle of the room.

Priya hugged her tightly and Amelia clung to her, grateful beyond words for her presence.

"How did you get in here?" she demanded when she found her voice again. Priya wasn't meant to be here until later in the morning when the rest of her attendants arrived.

"Your cute Welsh assistant thought you could use some company this morning. He worked everything out."

Amelia smiled. Macsen. Of course.

Priya eyed her up and down. "Don't tell me you were still asleep."

"It's six in the morning."

"Of your *wedding* day. Come on, you have to come see what's outside."

Priya grabbed Amelia's hand and dragged her to the window. It was a strange replay of the morning after Amelia's first date with Arthur at the observatory, when Priya had woken her and shown her the crowd of photographers outside their flat. It seemed a lifetime ago.

The roofs of London were just dark shapes under a sky slowly growing light. Rain from the night before glistened on the leaves of the trees just beginning to bud.

Indistinct shapes milled under the trees in the park. Slowly, as the sky continued to lighten, Amelia realized they were people. Huge crowds of people, gathering to watch her make her way from the palace to the abbey. Some had small flags, others, signs and banners; some bore red roses, some wore white, but a few — a very few — displayed roses with petals of both white *and* red.

She pressed her hand to her chest, hardly able to believe her eyes. It wasn't a victory or a guarantee, but it was *something*. Maybe, someday, the country would accept, not just her, but all the other people and history that were a part of it.

Maybe. Someday.

"Told you," Priya said softly.

❁

Priya, George, and Hyacinth breakfasted with Amelia in her rooms, or, rather, Hyacinth and Priya chattered happily together while George bullied Amelia into eating. She was too nauseated to want food. She had no idea if it was nerves or morning sickness.

They were breaking with all sorts of tradition by having both Arthur and Amelia get dressed at Buckingham Palace. But it was hardly traditional for a royal bride and groom both to be living in the palace already, and it made any number of logistical nightmares less nightmarish. Amelia caught no sign or glimpse of Arthur, though, and indeed wasn't even allowed to leave her rooms. Everyone came to her.

After breakfast Jo arrived, her arm wrapped around the shoulders of her sleepy-looking daughter Meg. Freddy would be with Charlie. All five of them — George, Hyacinth, Priya,

Jo and Meg — looked at Amelia, and she realized they were waiting for her signal. Or command, really, even if she remained for now lower ranked than most of them.

"Well," she said and hoped her smile wasn't as nervous as she felt. "Let's do this."

At a sign from her to an assistant, a flood of people entered the rooms. The phalanx of makeup artists started on her attendants while Amelia was shooed into the bathroom to shower. Once she emerged, a flock of makeup artists descended on her, too.

Amelia had never exactly fantasized about a wedding. With Gary, she'd been more focused on the victory of a proposal than anything else. With Arthur, logistics and politics had drowned out any fairytale focus on the day itself.

But here she was, getting her hair and makeup done with her best friend, her sister-in-law and soon to be nieces-in-law. She felt as she had never expected to feel: Like a perfectly normal girl before a perfectly normal wedding.

But her nerves increased as she was helped into the complicated undergarments her wedding gown required. The last time she'd worn anything close to this, she'd gotten it on herself, and Arthur had been the one to take it off of her.

An assistant did up the delicate buttons at the back of the dress. The head seamstress watched from the front, a faint crease growing between her eyebrows.

"Stand up straight," she said.

"I am."

"Straighter."

Amelia sighed and pulled her shoulders back more dramatically than necessary to show that she was, in fact, as upright as possible.

"Oh that is the opposite of helping," the woman muttered under her breath.

"What? What's the problem?" Amelia asked. The dress had been fine two weeks ago, and it was fastened now; her body was essentially the same.

"Boobs everywhere," Priya said as loudly and unhelpfully as possible. With hand gestures.

"What?" Amelia asked blankly. She leaned over to get a look of her reflection in the floor-length mirror. "Oh my God."

Priya made the hand gesture again, obviously pleased with herself.

Amelia's breasts were, for lack of a better word, *everywhere*. The so-modest neckline of her dress, instead of hiding them, had pushed them up so that Amelia resembled nothing so much as an extra from *Dangerous Liaisons*.

"I am getting married — and crowned! — in front of millions of people all over the world in a matter of hours," Amelia blurted, unable to contain her feelings. "And this dress is absolutely not going to work." She didn't even need the head seamstress's face to tell her that. Then Amelia did what she was fairly certain anyone, monarch-to-be or not, would do in her situation: she burst into tears.

There was a flurry of activity around her: The head seamstress snapped instructions at her assistant, one of the makeup people pleaded with Amelia not to ruin her face, and someone asked if they should fetch a doctor.

In all, they were perfectly competent people attempting to rectify the situation at hand. Except the situation was that Amelia didn't fit into her wedding dress because she was pregnant with a baby her king and soon-to-be husband didn't know existed. The tabloids were going to say she looked like a whore. The country would never see or accept her as queen. The riots would resume! And Beatrice was probably going to try to make her apologize again.

In the midst of the hubbub she heard George declare, "Please call my uncle and tell him to come down here."

"Ma'am —" the seamstress started.

Amelia moaned. Arthur was the last person she wanted to see right now. Even if she was about to marry him.

"I don't give a damn about tradition," George snapped. "Do it, or I'll go get him myself."

When the seamstress hesitated, George — already in her own bridesmaid's gown, her honey-colored hair half-finished being styled — bunched up her skirts, strode to the door and yanked it open.

On the other side was Arthur, his hand already raised as if to knock. Edward was at his side, on guard as always outside her door. Briefly, their eyes met. Amelia didn't know what he had heard through the door, but he knew enough to suspect what Amelia's problems today might be.

Her eyes flicked back to Arthur. He was fully dressed in his uniform with all his orders and medals. A sword hung at his side. Amelia looked a mess, but Arthur looked like the king he was. No one would ever question his right to rule. Not even York.

"What's going on?" he asked softly. His gaze broke from Amelia's to sweep around the room before locking back onto hers. "Amelia, what is this?"

Amelia couldn't answer him. She could barely breathe. Someone helped her into a chair, but that did little to help beyond preventing her from falling down. Arthur's forehead creased into a worried frown. He stepped forward slowly, and when Amelia said nothing to stop him, strode into the center of the room.

"Everyone, thank you for your assistance. Now get out," Arthur said.

No one moved.

"Out!" he barked, glaring around at them.

Priya tried to go to Amelia's side, but she waved her off.

George moved for the door. "You heard my uncle," she said. "Everyone out."

"It's okay," Amelia said to a still-reluctant Priya.

Once she went, everyone else finally followed, the assistants stealing wondering, confused glances back into the room. Twenty people in all, some half-dressed, all of them confused, spilled out into the hallways of the palace. Amelia had a brief moment of mirth at the thought of Edward and Macsen trying to manage them all.

Arthur closed the door — it wasn't a slam, but only barely — behind the last person out. Amelia flinched. The sudden quiet, except for her own choked breath, was deafening. She hid her face in her hands so that the only sign she had of Arthur approaching was the soft scuff of his polished shoes on the carpet.

"What's going on?" he asked again. All sternness was gone from his voice.

Amelia tried to put words together and failed.

"Amelia…." He sounded genuinely worried.

Amelia sucked in a sharp lungful of air, making the tightness of the dress around her chest even more apparent, like a bird that couldn't stretch its wings. She could lie to him. Pass it all off as wedding nerves. But he knew her too well to believe that, even if he didn't trust her or even like her anymore. And besides, she was so *tired*. Tired of the politics, tired of the strain between her and Arthur, and tired the pressure of always living with one eye toward the public view.

"The dress doesn't fit," she said. Her voice was watery and she had to clear her throat to get the words out.

"All right." He knelt in front of her and tipped his head to catch her eyes.

It was the kneeling that loosened her voice. "The dress doesn't fit because I'm pregnant."

Arthur blinked at her, but didn't say anything. Amelia's heart, if it was possible, sank even further.

"It's yours. I promise it is. Canada...." she trailed off. "I know you're angry and don't trust me. But now you'll have an heir, and you won't have to talk to me ever again after today if you don't want to." Her voice nearly broke at the end, but she managed to get the words out.

"Why wouldn't I want to talk to you?" Arthur sounded baffled.

"Oh my God, I am pregnant!" Amelia burst out. How was he missing the salient point? "Would you please react to that?!"

"It's difficult to be overwhelmed with joy when you're sobbing on our wedding day."

Our wedding day. Like this was a day of joy they could still somehow share. Like Arthur even wanted to be with her.

"So sorry to ruin the moment," Amelia said bitterly.

Arthur shook his head. "Why didn't you tell me?"

"I couldn't," Amelia sniffed.

"Whyever not? Amelia." Arthur reached for her, but then stopped himself.

"Because," she said. "If you have an heir you have no reason to woo me or love me or even be my friend. For all the progress we've made, a good chunk of the country still hates me and another good bit probably still hates you, no matter how handsome you look in that uniform. I didn't know whether to tell you or to say I had an affair and the baby wasn't yours, so I could run away and you and the ministers and the ravens could never find me."

This time, Arthur did reach for her and wrapped his hands around hers. Her hands were cold, but his were comfortingly warm.

"Do you not want to do this?" he asked, unbearably grave. "Any of it. The baby, the wedding, the crown?"

"No is hardly an option at this point."

"I would let you go. I would have always let you go."

"No. I don't want to," Amelia said, more strongly than she felt. "I told you that before."

"That was about the crown, then. And York."

"No." Amelia took another deep breath. Even the confession that she was pregnant was not as difficult as this. "It was about you. I just never knew if you wanted it, too."

"Of *course* I did," Arthur said fiercely.

"Really?" Amelia asked. "You could have said something! I've been trying not to be in love with you forever."

"Really?" Arthur echoed her. He looked as stunned as she felt.

"*Yes.*" Annoyance was warring with the terror of confession. "But then I overheard Charlie shouting at you, that 'I don't love her' was a terrible reason to drag me into this life. So clearly you didn't love me. And why would you? I was just a solution to your problem."

"You shouldn't eavesdrop," Arthur murmured.

Amelia ignored him. "And *then* I went to princess camp with your mother, and she told me about her relationship with your father, and I let it go. I thought we could be happy together, that we would love each other in some way. Eventually. In time. But then your father died and George told us there would be no more kings after you!"

"I'd apologize for that, but —"

"And the south hated me! So we made that big humiliating show about the Tower Crown and somehow, *somehow* it worked! And then Canada and Santa Barbara and you were so angry and it was all much, much worse."

"I can't say that was an easy time for me either."

"Any chance we had at a happy partnership was gone. And then I found out I was pregnant. I'd been useful to you, as much as you would ever need me to be. My part was nearly done, and I was foolish to think I could fulfil any destiny at all beyond that — for your people or mine. I'd been too arrogant to think I could have any of this. The Crown. You."

"Yet here we are," Arthur said.

"What do you mean?"

His hands tightened around hers. "I'm not relieved an ordeal is over; I'm terrified our life together — ours, not the one made up of the public's claws in us — won't even get a chance to begin. We've never had enough time to deal with our own problems before another crisis appeared. But I do love you. I've loved you since you demanded I kneel to you in the stable yard at Gatcombe. And the more I've gotten to know you, the more impressed and awed and in love with you I've been. And the more easily hurt."

"In Canada. You said…." Amelia's voice trailed off. She couldn't make herself repeat the words. That he saw no reason not to send her back north where she'd come from.

"I know. I was frightened. I thought you might leave me and the work we were trying to do together. After everything we'd been through together, it was all going to fall apart. The drive for survival makes people do terrible things — kings and wars, the cruelty of language, and, I suppose, even university waiting lists." He cracked half a smile.

Amelia mirrored it sheepishly.

"A country fighting itself to survive is no country," he continued. "A marriage struggling similarly is no marriage. But we're on the same side, Amelia, not as chess pieces in the great endless wars that we have too long let define us, but as people. Today isn't the end of our story. It's the beginning. I love you, and the only thing that should and can and *will* be over today is misunderstanding — in our hearts and, in time, throughout our country."

"Arthur," Amelia said. A thought had just occurred to her.

"Yes?" His voice was tense. With nerves, she thought.

"Why did you come to my rooms? George wanted to go find you, when I started to cry, but she hadn't even left the room yet. You're not supposed to be here."

Arthur dipped his head to press a kiss to her hands. "I suppose I should say it was the irresistible whim of the moment. That would be more romantic, wouldn't it? But no. For days I've wanted to come to tell you all of that. To apologize and try to explain."

"But why now? You could have done this earlier!"

"Actually, I couldn't. These were only finished late last night." Arthur reached into his breast pocket and drew something out. His medals and orders clanked softly as he did.

He opened his hand; in his palm were nestled two rings, one quite a bit smaller than the other.

"What are those?" Amelia asked, hardly daring to hope.

"They're our wedding rings."

"You said the king wasn't allowed to wear a wedding band."

"I said it was tradition. And the traditions we uphold mean nothing unless we know when to break the ones that don't serve us. The realm doesn't come before you, Amelia. Nothing does."

Amelia stared at the rings in his hand. They were engraved with —

"Are those roses?" Amelia touched the larger of the two rings gently with a fingertip. Minute etching suggested two different colors. Arthur's fingers closed around her hand, the rings caught between their palms.

"I thought you might enjoy the detail," he said. "I wanted something that bound me to the Yorkish rose the way your engagement rings bound you to the Lancaster one."

"Your timing is absolute *shit.*"

"I'm certainly not going to argue with that."

"I haven't always been the best, either," Amelia admitted.

"I put you in an impossible situation and then handled the fallout poorly. There's no one I'd rather have by my side. As far as I'm concerned, you're already perfect."

Amelia ducked her head to hide her blush.

"Also, Canada's happy, you're pregnant, and you'll always be York's queen. I saw some signs outside...."

"The roses? The red *and* white ones?"

Arthur nodded. "There's light on the horizon. That we made possible."

"After making things worse."

"It was necessary. I couldn't have done any of it without you. If you're willing to continue this adventure together. I promise I will do my absolute best to be the husband and partner you deserve."

"I think most girls don't get a second proposal minutes before their wedding."

Arthur smiled, the fine lines around his eyes crinkling up. "Most girls aren't you."

Amelia's cheeks hurt from how wide she was smiling. "Yes, by the way."

"I love you," Arthur said breathlessly.

The prospect of the rest of their future together was still terrifying, but with Arthur at her side — really, truly, at her side — she had no doubt that she could get through it.

"I love you too," she said. Then she looked down at herself, the dress that didn't fit, the smears of makeup on her hands. "I'm a mess."

"I'm the King of England. I have to be able to find someone who can fix your dress."

"My makeup too."

Arthur reached up to wipe away the tears and mascara on her face. "All right. I am going to go holler for lots of people to make sure we look respectable. Then we are both going to go perform our parts in this awful play."

He helped her to her feet and wrapped an arm around her shoulder. He walked with her to the door. With one hand on the handle, he pressed a kiss to her forehead. "I really am incredibly happy."

"Me too."

"So are you ready?" he asked her as he always had.

Amelia nodded.

"Then I'll see you at the altar." Arthur smiled and opened the door.

Chapter 27

A UNITED ENGLAND CELEBRATES

8 April
Year 1 of the Reign of King Gregory I and Queen Amelia I

On the day of his wedding and coronation, Gregory I, by the Grace of God King, Head of the Commonwealth, and Defender of the Faith, felt like the world had stopped spinning at a terrifying speed only when he was flying at five hundred miles an hour over the vast expanse of the Atlantic Ocean. He was on the way to his honeymoon. In the bedroom of the private jet that had been chartered for the occasion, his wife and queen, Amelia, curled against his chest, asleep. With the arm that wasn't looped around her shoulders, he sorted through correspondence: Some on his tablet, some on actual paper, including a letter from George, his sister's child, his court witch, and his faithful friend.

She must have written it hastily somewhere between the day's first and second receptions, a twilight hour when the rest of the world had been sleeping.

My dearest uncle,

I know you hate when I call you by your given name, as if you were a real man and not a king. And as if I were advising you in this life and not the other way around.

That said, thank you. I think this business of my telling you to remarry has worked out rather well. You have saved myself. And Hyacinth. The kingdom too, although perhaps not as you suspect and not in ways we are yet given to understand.

I know you think otherwise, but I feel certain royalty only suits those who grow into it, not those who are born to it. We must all find our own destinies, as Amelia has. It is your job now to enable that for all the rest of us.

Enjoy your honeymoon. I will make sure the ravens wait.

Yours always,
George

Arthur smiled at the certainty he always felt in the face of George's odd pronouncements. Amelia would be a wonderful queen, precisely because she had willingly chosen the role's burdens. For his own part, he hoped merely to be a tolerable king.

The coronation had unsettled him, the one moment of privacy in it making him feel oddly naked before all the world. He did not know if he would ever find a destiny as king in the manner George's letter suggested.

But he knew that with Amelia nestled here in his arms, he had found his destiny as a man.

Look out for more Royal Roses books coming soon from Erin McRae and Racheline Maltese!

More by These Authors

Visit www.Avian30.com to join Erin and Racheline's mailing list and get information about new releases!

The Art of Three

Jamie Conway has a charmed life. At 24, he's relocated from Dublin to London to star in his first feature film. Unfortunately, he also has one very big problem: He has a huge crush on his happily married costar.

British heartthrob to middle-aged women everywhere, Callum Griffith-Davies should have more sense than to flirt with his new-to-the-business colleague, but good judgement isn't one of the qualities for which he's known.

Nerea Espinosa de Los Monteros Nessim has better things to do than fret about her husband's newest conquest. She's busy planning her daughter's wedding at the family's farmhouse in rural Spain. Besides, she and Callum have been married and polyamorous for almost 30 years; she's content to let him make his own bad choices.

But when Nerea flies to London after her artwork is selected for a high-profile museum show, she falls for Jamie too. Soon Callum, Jamie, and Nerea have bigger problems, and surprises, than international logistics. From ex-lovers and nosy neighbors to adult children with dramas of their own, The Art of Three is a contemporary romance that celebrates families, and farce, in all shapes and sizes.

The Love in Los Angeles Series

Starling, Book 1
Doves, Book 2
Phoenix, Book 3
More coming soon!

Love in Los Angeles is a queer romance series, with elements of magical realism, set in and around the TV and movie industry.

When J. Alex Cook, a production assistant on *The Fourth Estate* (one of network TV's hottest shows), is accidentally catapulted to stardom, he finds himself struggling to navigate both fame and a relationship with Paul, one of Fourth's key writers. *Love in Los Angeles* is the story of Paul and Alex — and of their friends and family — as they navigate love, and life, both in and beyond Los Angeles.

The Love's Labours Series

Midsummer, Book 1
Twelfth Night, Book 2
More coming soon!

42-year-old John Lyonel has never been attracted to men before, but falling for 25-year-old Michael Hilliard is actually the least screwed up thing that's happened to him in years. Even if sometimes he thinks Michael's a changeling.

CPSIA information can be obtained
at www.ICGtesting.com
Printed in the USA
LVHW031702090119
603302LV00008B/74/P

9 781946 192073

1/19

Outer stains noted RML 3/24